THE RIGHT BUS

A novel by

GLENN WARD

Copyright Information

THE RIGHT BUS

'It is a mistake to look too far ahead. Only one link in the chain of destiny can be handled at a time'

Winston Churchill

N

0   50   100
NAUTICAL MILES

ULLAPOOL
INVERNESS
SPEAN BRIDGE
FORT WILLIAM
OBAN
CRINAN
ARDRASAIG
GLASGOW   EDINBURGH
CAMPBELTOWN
BALLYCASTLE
LARNE
BANGOR
STRANGFORD LOUGH
CARLINGFORD LOUGH
DUBLIN
DUN LAOGHAIRE
ARKLOW
WEXFORD
MILFORD HAVEN
LONDON
LUNDY ISLAND
EXMOUTH   WEYMOUTH
NEWQUAY   PLYMOUTH   PORTLAND BILL
    DARTMOUTH
LAND'S END   ST. AUSTELL
PENZANCE   FALMOUTH

PROLOGUE

Having received the full effect of the blast, they were hurled back, torn apart by both the explosion and the jagged metal of their truck's ruptured body. The vehicle then ignited, the fuel tank exploded, and the remains of the men's bodies were spread out beyond the shattered gas pump installation, enmeshed with the debris of metal and concrete.

This would be the evidence available to the investigation team from which they would try to unravel the cause. Sabotage? Terrorism? Accident? In the immediate aftermath, the emergency cut-off valves had automatically diverted the flowing gas along a by-pass route, and the receiving plant on the coast had simultaneously been advised of a malfunction.

Like all explosions, just as with the delay between lightning and thunder, the sound follows the visible expression, the time lag interval depending on the nearness of the receiver to the source. In this case there was effectively no interval. Nothing would have been seen nor heard by the three men from the maintenance service vehicle that had stopped in front of the concrete housing of the Transflow gas pipeline pumping station.

Three men. The only people in this remote part of the hot desert. They had walked the short distance to the steel door and one of them, the engineer in charge, had inserted a key into the lock to open it. Then oblivion.

As the members of both the repair crew and investigation team were being alerted, the latter knew that speed was of the essence in reaching the site, for the relentless sun and drifting sands would soon begin to obliterate the evidence and the desert would return to its unyielding, timeless indifference.

ONE

It was a cold, grey, wet, miserable January morning in London.

For Carl Lindeger's family it was the start of a normal day. His children, Danny and Louisa, were beginning the new term and Amanda Heston, a close friend of his wife Connie, had just arrived to take them to school with her own two children. Danny, their elder child, was nine, outgoing and adventurous and had already developed a wry sense of humour. He was tall for his age, had dark-brown hair, smiling brown eyes and was destined to be a handsome adult. His sister Louisa was two years younger, had a cheerful but enquiring nature, never accepting an unconvincing answer to a question. She had her mother's engaging smile, blue eyes and similarly coloured auburn hair.

The school run was a week-on week-off routine that Amanda and Connie had developed during the eighteen months of their easy friendship. Amanda was from Canada and she and her husband Alex had been away from their Ontario home for nearly three years on a company posting that was due to end in a couple of years or so. The alternate weeks of school transport duty suited them both. Neither of them worked and often when the morning run was completed they would meet up and relax over a coffee and try to put the world to rights. Although Connie was from the United States, coming originally from Boston, Massachusetts, they both enjoyed sharing their common North American origins.

As the car drew away Connie looked at the rain falling so heavily on the water-covered street that it looked like it was being machine-gunned. The rain was bad enough but even the air between the rain seemed laden with moisture. It was all so wet. As she watched the rear lights of the car disappear around the corner she felt the damp coldness of the air beginning to affect her and retreated to the warmth of her home. Well, she thought, it was hardly what you would call home. A house certainly, but other than the children and the central heating, there was little warmth.

This was certainly not the life she had envisaged. An only child, she had been brought up by parents who seemed more interested in their own lives than hers. She had been sent away to a boarding school from an early age and before she had graduated from high school, they were encouraging her to go straight to university. She chose to go to Boston to study journalism and during her first semester her parents announced that they were moving to live in Louisiana. Although this sudden departure was a shock to her, she was a resourceful person and made her own life in the university city.

Connie had character. It may have been that the apparent lack of interest from her parents had made her develop an independence that in its way matched her appearance. She had striking good looks; medium height, elegant poise, slim, with copper-red hair that rested on the top of her shoulders and eyes of intense lapis lazuli blue. She had broken her nose in an accident with a swing when she was eight and it had been re-set slightly to the right. As she grew older, it had developed a gentle downward curve accentuating the bridge and giving her a profile that had a Hellenic persuasion. Her career had progressed well and she had become a freelance science writer in which her name, Connie Renton – which she had retained after marrying – was a by-word for informed, objective reporting. But to Connie, that all seemed a long time ago and she doubted if she'd ever return to it.

She now lived in the house that she and her husband had bought some two years before. It had been one of those rare opportunities – a four-bedroom family property at the rear of a terrace of elegant Georgian houses on a square in West London. Originally the home, with stables below, of a coachman to one of the fine houses, it had become one of those most desirable of residences: a small, characterful house close to central London, described by estate agents as a 'mews' or 'studio cottage'.

The house was on three levels with an attic area. The first, the ground floor facing the street, had a garage leading out to a small open yard at the rear. To the left of the garage was the front door, which allowed access to a small hall that led up some stairs to the second level. This was an open-plan living area with comfortable sitting chairs, a kitchen-diner and a small room off the main part which was a 'quiet room'. This level stretched from the front to the back of the house with large sash windows facing out on to the street and to the rear of the house which looked out on to the gardens of the large houses that once owned the coach houses. On the third level was a principal bedroom with en suite bathroom, two smaller bedrooms, and a communal bathroom. A further flight of stairs gave access to a small fourth bedroom that had been built into the attic space with a sky-light window in the roof. Too small to accommodate a bathroom, there was just enough space for a wash-basin and toilet. A very pleasing aspect of the house was its position – it was in a quiet cul-de-sac. But a winning feature for Connie was the equally quiet and charming old pub just across the street.

She had heard about the pending sale from a business associate of Amanda's husband before it was due to come on the market and, as they had sold well in the States, they were able to make the owner an offer without the need to raise a mortgage. It could not have been smoother and within four weeks they had moved in.

And within four days her husband had moved out.

His company had assigned him to a position in Saudi Arabia to run the maintenance programme on a network of gas pipelines, a posting of indefinite duration that was structured around a schedule of six weeks on and two weeks off. As far as the company was concerned his base was in Saudi Arabia and he could take his leave wherever he wished. And that's precisely what he did.

He rarely came back to London. They had married ten years earlier in the States following a whirlwind romance. Connie's father had taken up a post as a petroleum reservoir engineer with an oil and gas production company in southern Louisiana, based in the city of Lafayette. Her parents' social life revolved around the Lafayette Petroleum Club, an establishment that attracted all and sundry associated with the industry. Here, the socially active and the loners alike could lose themselves in a world that catered for all tastes. It was to the club premises that her parents took her whenever she came to stay with them. It was not her style at all. Bored with the loud boastful types that seemed to be drawn to the bars, Connie would wander about the club premises to find a quiet place to while away the time until she could get back to the East Coast. Much as she missed her parents, she had never taken to her father's world like her mother had, a world that was always one of work hard, play hard and be seen.

It was on one of her wanders that she met her future husband. Carl Lindeger was a junior pipeline engineer who had recently joined the same company as her father. Born in Pretoria in South Africa, he had graduated from the university in his hometown as an engineer and joined a water company near Cape Town. A year later, disenchanted with his job, he had looked for an opportunity that might take him overseas. The oil industry beckoned and within a month he had found himself in the US with a new role. He was, however, one of those quiet Afrikaners who just didn't care for the life-style enjoyed by so many in the industry. His retiring nature dedicated him to his work and when he had free time he tended to keep to himself.

It was on such an occasion that Connie encountered him quietly reading in one of the lounges. He stood up on her entering and she was struck by his tall stature and rugged, weathered looks. Dark-brown, straight hair fell to one side in a sweep over his forehead and he had that seemingly permanent golden-yellow tan that characterised so many white people who had lived on the High Veldt. Although he appeared relaxed, his eyes never quite made contact, seeming to look just to one side of her line of vision. However, when she spoke to him he smiled and that was that. He was so different from the other men she had met at the club that she found herself captivated by his singular nature and beguiled by his innocent charm. Her subsequent visits to Lafayette, ostensibly to see her parents, were taken up with Carl and when he proposed to her the response was a foregone conclusion.

Some months after she had accepted Carl's proposal, her mother died suddenly from a brain haemorrhage. Her father was severely affected by her death and seemed to lose purpose in life. She had been his partner in all that he did. His life was her life, to the exclusion – as Connie knew only too well – of all others. One day he called Connie in Boston to say that he had resigned from his company and was leaving Louisiana to go and live in Hawaii. His explanation for this was that he needed a new start and that following his wife's death there was nothing left for him but to do this. Connie, although upset at her mother's death, was hurt by her father's reference to the death of 'his wife' rather than 'her mother'.

She gave up her job in Boston, moved to the Gulf Coast and she and Carl were married quietly without her father's knowledge. Since his retirement, he had not been in touch with her so she had decided, sadly, to accept the fact that he no longer had need for her in his life. They bought a house on the outskirts of the city and within a year Danny was born followed two years later by Louisa. By now Carl was working on a major seabed to shore pipeline and earning a salary sufficiently large for them to move up the housing scale. They bought a run-down antebellum mansion and spent the next three years restoring it to its former splendour.

Then, out of the blue, he announced that he was leaving his current post to take up a new position with a company based in Saudi Arabia. It wasn't going to be practical for her and the children to go out with him, but the salary was extraordinarily good and the leave generous.

There was no discussion; he had unilaterally accepted the offer and merely told her when the contract had been signed.

Looking back on it now, Connie knew all the signs were there. She was the motivator in just about all the things they did and when it came to the buying of the old mansion he had shown no real interest at all, just leaving her to run the whole project herself. Even the beautiful home they had created failed to bring out the togetherness that a young family might have expected.

Neither were the children of much interest to him.

And so the very nature of the man that she had fallen for – aloof, retiring, introvert – was now coming home to roost and it was she who was the object of his disregard. He was a loner and Connie's attraction to him in the first place, that very individual personality, the one that set him apart from the crowd and that had originally brought them together, was driving a wedge between them. The irony was not lost on her. That personality wasn't going to change – nor had it. Whilst there was no doubting he was his own man, he had become less and less hers.

And so life had continued in this vein until he left to work in the Middle East. The house had been finished and was acclaimed in the region for its faithful restoration. To most observers they were the successful couple with two beautiful young children. But all was not what it seemed. When on leave at his home, Lindeger was restless and distant towards his family and on the occasion of one particular leave, when he had chosen to visit his family in South Africa without even asking Connie and the children to come with him, she began to question the value of the life she was leading.

In an endeavour to rescue the situation, she had proposed that they sell up their Louisiana home and move to London, her reasoning to him being that it would be central to his place of work in Saudi Arabia, his family in South Africa and her father in the Hawaii. To her it was an attempt to keep things together and although, to her surprise, he agreed to it, she was left to prepare the house for sale and handle the entire logistics of the move.

And here she was now; in the city she had chosen, in the house she had found, trying to live a life she had lost.

Back in the house she cleared away the breakfast table. She had three hours to get organised before Amanda called back at mid-day to have lunch with her. Having tidied up the children's' rooms she sat down to read the morning paper, a half-hour or so that always relaxed her after they had gone to school. She had just settled into an interesting article on the improbable progress science and reasoning has made in the face of the barriers imposed by religious dogmas, when the doorbell rang. So much for that moment of peace, she thought. Leaving the paper open at the page she was reading, she went to the front door and opened it. Two people, a man and a woman, stood in front of her under the shelter of a large umbrella. The man was almost covered from head to foot by a light-coloured trench coat that was held tight to his waist by a belt. The brimmed hat he wore obscured most of his face, and his eyes, caught in that shadow, were impersonalised by a pair of glasses. Next to him, he was partnered by a middle-aged woman with short, dark hair wearing an equally dark coat with a high upturned collar. She didn't recognise either of them and for a moment looked at the two callers with a vague unease, feeling that by their very presence they were signalling that she should brace herself for unwelcome news.

"Good morning. I hope we've come to the right house," the man observed, making a point of looking either side of the door as if to check that the number was consistent with the address he had. "We've come to see someone called Constance Renton. Are you by any chance her?"

"That's right," replied Connie, warily – no one ever called her by her full name.

"Ah, good. I took the liberty of ringing you last night but there was no reply so I left a message on your phone. I wonder if by any chance you had a moment to listen to it."

"No, I took an early night and didn't bother to check this morning."

"Well, what I was calling for was to introduce myself and see if it would be all right for us to call on you this morning," he explained, "but as it's important for us to see you, we made the decision to arrive unannounced. I hope you will forgive us."

He felt awkward; it was all a bit stilted. A brief moment passed as he regained his composure. The woman accompanying him motioned her head towards Connie.

"Just that we might confirm it, you are the wife of a man called Carl Lindeger, an engineer with the pipeline company Transflow?" she enquired in support.

"Yeah, sure," Connie answered cautiously. "But why are you asking? I mean, who *are* you guys?" And then, after a brief pause: "So what do you want to know for? What do you *want*?" she uttered with a puzzled expression.

In the short time while she waited for a reply, Connie saw behind them a person walk by in the rain with a dog on a lead and for no particular reason thought that neither the dog nor the owner seemed to be enjoying it.

Both of the visitors stood there uncertain of how to reply. They looked briefly at each other and then the man turned to Connie:

"I'm sorry – please let me introduce us. My name's Peter Thornton and this is my colleague Anne Travers. We have been asked to make contact with you by the Human Resources department of your husband's employers. They don't have a London office but our company acts in a consultancy role for any issues relating to them in the UK."

He handed her a letter from Transflow that introduced them formally. She read it thoughtfully. It seemed bland enough, just a letter introducing them and apologising for not having one of the company's personnel available to be there. The letter asked if she could accommodate them on the matter of their visit. Whilst she had no reason to doubt the authenticity of the letter nor indeed of the two people before her, she felt out-manoeuvred, almost wrong-footed, by their sudden appearance at her doorstep. The sense of unease began to build up.

"Huh, you're going to have to show something more. Like some form of identification," she said, rallying. "You might guess I'm not too happy about this."

"Of course," apologised Thornton. "Here, these are our business cards, and these are our company ID cards. We both carry our passports with us for additional verification."

She asked to see them and although she satisfied herself that there was sufficient evidence to identify them she still felt uneasy about dealing with these two strangers at her door. Although an outward-going person, Connie was still reticent about accepting them and in her need to clarify matters repeated her earlier unanswered question.

"So, c'mon, what is it you want?" she ventured, her mind beginning to spin with a thousand possibilities of what might have brought them here.

"Would it be all right for us to come in?" responded Thornton.

"Well, I guess so; it's pretty damned awful out there. Yeah, come on in."

The man took off his hat to reveal a completely bald head. He left the umbrella in a holder inside the front door as she ushered them in, closing the door and then walking on ahead and up the stairs. She felt awkward leading these two visitors into her house and absentmindedly rubbed the knuckles on her left hand with the fingertips of her right hand, something she used to do as a child in Massachusetts whenever she went into a room and found her parents entertaining someone she had never seen before.

"Let's go over to the kitchen and sit at the table. It's cosier there," invited Connie, as they passed just inside the living area at the top of the stairs.

Not having dealt with anything like this before and realising it was going to be difficult at the very least, Thornton gathered himself.

"Look, we are Peter and Anne. May we call you Constance, it seems easier that way?"

"I guess so," she replied and added with a light nervousness. "Better make it Connie. Yeah, Connie. That's how I'm known. So what's this all about?"

They all sat down at the table. Thornton braced himself and thought that this was one of the most awful moments of his life. He wanted to say how lovely the house was, how you would never know you were in London, anything but the gut-wrenching task he had to do. Anne sat on his left and he looked across the table at Connie.

"Connie," he started, "thanks for letting us be here with you, particularly as you don't know us. It must be rather unnerving to receive two complete strangers like this but we had no other way of dealing with this other than seeing you face to face."

"No, it's okay. Carry on. I'm listening." She leant towards them, her elbows on the table, her chin resting on her folded hands.

As he began, his words – carefully spoken – were portentous, foreboding:

"Connie, we had a call through from Saudi Arabia late last night. Two days ago there was an explosion at one of the pumping stations on the pipeline that your husband was working on. We're so sorry but we have to tell you that

Carl and two other engineers were caught in the blast and..."

Connie heard these words and yet she seemed not to. She gazed away over their heads and noticed the remains of an old spider's web in the corner of one of the kitchen windowpanes and decided she would clean it as soon as they were gone. And the paintwork didn't look too good; those little curled-up flakes, better see about that too, she thought. Why am I the one who always has to deal with all this sort of thing? Damn Carl and his bloody pipelines. Damn him and his life away from us, damn his lack of interest, damn him and his...

"...Carl was killed instantly along with the other two men."

She was back with them again, aware that they were telling her that a fatal accident had occurred and that Carl Lindeger had been one of the victims. She thought about the first time she had met Carl in Lafayette and how he had given her life meaning. Despite their gradual estrangement over the years, it was a terrible shock to imagine that this man – her husband and the father of her children – could quite simply cease to exist. It was just too difficult for her to comprehend the shocking brutality of what they were conveying.

"I...I don't get it. This is crazy! You...you're telling me that despite the safety precautions they took, the fact that everything was always so goddamned over-safe and they all knew what they were doing, you're telling me that...the impossible has happened? I cannot believe it. You must be wrong; it's gotta be wrong."

"No, Connie, it was one of those one-in-a-million chances when the unforeseen happened. The investigation team was called in immediately the operations base detected the shut-down of the pump installation. A full assessment of the incident has been carried out and it is clear there were no survivors. The explosion was devastating..."

She sat there, staring at the pattern on the table surface, stunned. Her mind wandered off course and examined some of the minutiae of things that had made up her life: growing up, a solitary childhood, always a secondary consideration to her parents; those early years seemed devalued. And although even as a young girl she felt that one day she would become a parent, she never thought it would be such a solo effort being one. Her envy of other children whose parents gave them attention and used their free time to take them on walks or go camping – these and so many other things registered with her.

They ran through all the details of the handling of the situation, and how that, now she was the last of the families to be notified, the incident would be announced publicly. The question of disposal of the remains of her husband and what to do with his possessions were matters that just didn't get through, passing straight over her head, lost in a maelstrom of emotional disarray. This is absurd, she thought as occasional words broke through.

"...and of course, we don't know what personal life cover your husband had...he was very well covered by the company's death in service insurance...you will have no financial worries...little consolation, I know..."

Connie's mind was consumed with dislocated, irregular thoughts – her response to the incredible news they had brought her. She seemed to float away. For some reason she remembered a towering thunder cloud she had seen when she was on a school trip to the Woods Hole Oceanographic Institution and how her teacher had told her that the drawn-out top was shaped like an anvil. Then she thought of a plough bringing up an old horseshoe and weren't horseshoes meant to bring you good luck, providing they were the right way up? Odd sentences surfaced through a mist of muffled talking but nothing really connected with her.

"...do you think you will be all right...? Should we call the children's school...? Can we contact your husband's family for you...? Have you a friend we could call...?"

And then Peter's voice cut through and jolted her back with a start.

"Connie, there's no right way to handle this sort of thing. Anne and I have never had to do this before and we are probably handling it all the wrong way but we are doing our best to take you through the awful news. It must be so difficult for you but we're trying to keep steady and provide you with all the support we can. Look, we'll do whatever we can to help you. All the formal stuff will come later and Anne will personally look after it for you, but right now we have to get you through the rest of the day. Is there anyone we can contact for you, a friend perhaps?"

She looked at Peter Thornton, her mind beginning to process the information that they had given her. She stared into his eyes, locking on to them and then, as if coming back out of a hypnotic trance, spoke with clarity and purpose.

"No. No, look, it's okay. I'm good," she asserted. "What's the time?" she asked, looking at her watch. "Look, I've got a friend I do the school-run with who's round for lunch at twelve. She's a real close pal. I'm gonna be okay. This has got to sink in. I kinda need time. You guys are going to get in touch with me again, right?"

"Yes. Anne will deal with everything and call you in a couple of days."

"Here's my number in case you need me in the meantime. Are you sure you'll be all right?" queried Anne as she handed over her business card and a formal letter on behalf of the company notifying her of the accident and her husband's death.

"Yeah, yeah, I'll be okay. You'd better just leave me now to sort this one through."

And half an hour later, after what had seemed to Connie an eternity since they had knocked on her door, they quietly took their leave and saw themselves out.

The front door clicked shut. She just stood there at the top of the stairs, the image of their descending backs staying with her as some sort of surreal impression with the caption: 'did that really happen?' And in the hanging silence that followed their departure, the thing that struck Connie, more than Carl's death, was that she had not cried. Yes, it had been an awful shock. And she had genuinely felt disbelief that what they were telling her had happened. And yes, she didn't want to believe that it had happened.

But it had. And although this man was the father of her children as well as being her husband it was not as if they were expecting him home that night – or any other night come to that. The grief that she might have felt had not surfaced. Because it was not there. No, she had not cried.

She looked at her watch. She had about an hour and a half before her friend was due to arrive. The idea had been to have lunch in the house and relax through the afternoon until the children were back from school. But she realised that today it just wasn't going to work like that.

TWO

A late afternoon breeze whipped up the surface of the river. Forty-four days on from the shortest day, it was still brisk but no longer cold. Although he had pulled up the collar of his navy blue reefer jacket against the wind, winter was beginning to give way to spring and there was a general air of things beginning to happen. David Gregson, a tall, athletically built, single man in his mid-thirties, stood on the quayside flanking the south side of the River Wey and, through his greenish-hazel coloured eyes, gazed thoughtfully, eastwards out to the sea and the distant cliffs of the Dorset coast that had formed the backcloth to his time living in Weymouth. He faced the wind that blew the dark-brown, longish, slightly wavy hair away from his face exposing a handsome profile with a trimmed beard that seemed to complement the weathered hue of his skin – that of a man who enjoyed time in the open air. He had spent almost ten years in Dorset and for most of his stay he had lived in the small original old town of Weymouth which lay on the south side of the river. The larger, more modern part, developed from the time of Georgian popularity, was correctly called Melcombe Regis but nowadays most people called the whole built-up area Weymouth.

This moment of contemplation heralded an important change of direction in his life: his time in Dorset was coming to an end. Having graduated in Marine Biology from Trinity College, Dublin, some thirteen years before, he had stayed on at his university to carry out post-graduate research work for which he had been awarded his doctorate. He had been working at the Portland Marine Institute since then, specialising in the development and use of electronic tagging devices for the tracing of commercial fish shoals. As the research progressed, its successful outcome had evolved to produce smaller, more efficient and more durable tags.

In this context David had been awarded an additional grant by the Institute to test their efficiency on another long-distance traveller, the Arctic tern, whose annual migrations were known about from the well-established practice of ringing chicks at their breeding grounds. However, mortality rates over the tremendous distances travelled meant that few rings were recovered and then only by either netting the birds or by the chance discovery of a corpse. His system of hypodermically inserting a specially designed, battery-powered micro-processor, into the fatty tissue under the skin between the wings on the back of a chick, and linking to a global navigation positioning system, enabled regular monitoring of the birds. By ringing them as well, both systems could be tested. For his project, he had chosen a breeding ground location for this particular bird on a small islet off the island of Kerrera in the Inner Hebrides, near to the mainland coastal town of Oban. The work, besides being intellectually pleasing as well as technically challenging, was one that suited David personally, since, although it was a scientific venture in its own right, from his early childhood he had had a fascination with birds.

And so, as he looked out across the sheltered waters of the bay, he wondered what the next few months had in store for him. Close by him lay his yacht, *Cassiopeia*, moored up alongside a pontoon. She was a forty-foot sloop-rigged cruiser with a deck cabin and he had spent the last six months equipping her for a very special voyage. He had bought her the previous autumn from a man who had decided that old age and arthritic joints had got the better of him and the time had now come for a more leisurely life on land. David had kept her at the pontoon, which was close to his house in one of the narrow streets near the river, while he set about preparing her for the journey from Weymouth to the Scottish west-coast port of Oban.

The boat was to be his home, office and laboratory as well as his form of transport to Scotland. He had decided to do it this way when his four-year research project was entering its last year. The results of his work would be passed on to another group and so towards the end of the summer he would be hoping to secure new employment and accordingly he had been applying for various posts. His intention, therefore, was to take his time to enjoy the sail to Oban and he had planned a passage that would take him about a month, including a stop-off in Dublin where he would spend some time with his old course tutor and visit some of his old student day bars. On completion of his project, he would await the outcome of his work applications and then decide whether to bring his boat back to Weymouth or move it elsewhere. The idea of selling her was not an option he was inclined to consider.

As the port authorities would not permit him to live on the boat at the mooring pontoon, he had conveniently been able to carry out his preparative work from his house nearby. For two years he had lived there in a relationship with a girl called Camilla. They had met in Weymouth some four years earlier but about six months back it had all fallen apart and she had moved away from the area. So as he stood there, he took in his surroundings and dwelt on the prospect of the change to his world that was about to take place.

He had enjoyed a wonderful time in a beautiful part of England and his work at the Institute had been one of those rare and thoroughly pleasing times when a person was in fact being paid to carry out a hobby. The break-up of his affair with Camilla had hit him hard and, although he was fully occupied with his work, the time spent with her had left an indelible print on his emotions. The relationship had been special to him and he had convinced himself that the failure was his fault. But of course, that was a mechanism to cope with the loss. He had become hardened too, and swore that he would never let anything like this happen to him again. He was, however, never sure whether it was the losing of her or the loss of the companionship that he found in the relationship that had been the more painful. One thing he was sure about was that he enjoyed the warmth of intimate company and that his self-imposed exile would in the end be an unrealistic way to spend his life. But in the meantime, he had kept his guard up and had deliberately immersed himself in his work as a defence against emotional involvement with anyone.

Still, a new dawn lay before him and that sense of anticipation that the spring-like weather had brought made him impatient to be on his way.

But it was still February and he had work to complete, both on his boat and at the Institute, and he would not be able to move off until early April. Also, there was the question of his house. What should he do? It was, after all, his home and all his possessions were in it. There were any number of opportunities to let it, both long and short term, but he felt reluctant to enter into any fixed agreement. He was torn between maintaining this piece of established permanency in his life and shedding the trappings of his recent past and memories of the time spent there – both good and bad. The idea of selling it altogether seemed an attractive alternative too, a way of exorcising those ghosts and at the same time opening the door on a new life. Why did things have to be so problematic?

David shook himself back to reality. What was he thinking of? This was not him at all. The fact was, he told himself, he was simply ready to move on and the finishing of his project with the tracking sensors was a fitting moment to do just that. Spurred on by this clarity of realisation, he walked off along the pontoon on to the quayside and into his favourite pub to order a pint of beer and maybe chat with some of the early evening regulars.

The following morning, having spent rather longer with those regulars than he had expected, David Gregson entered his office and switched on his computer. He had some data to feed into a software programme but was not satisfied that he had designed the algorithm correctly. His somewhat delicate condition did not lend itself to imaginative thinking and as he sipped his first coffee of the morning he knew he needed a diversion from the task before him. It was not long in coming.

The alarm-call shrillness of his desk phone served to focus his mind. He picked up the hand piece.

"Hallo, David Gregson," he uttered, tonelessly.

"Good morning!" said a voice with a soft Scottish brogue that made David, on recognising it, instantly sit up.

"Dougal! Dougal Henderson!" he exclaimed. "Great to hear from you! I was going to give you a call to let you know of my plans for the summer. How are you?"

Dougal Henderson was a friend of David's from Oban. He was the senior partner of a firm of solicitors in the town and they had known each other for the last four years.

"Well, not so bad, I guess, but I'm calling you with some rather sad news."

"Oh," said David, rather uncertainly.

"Yes, well, you remember our old friend Helen McKechnie?"

"Yes, of course."

"Well, she passed away last night after a short illness. She had a fall in her flat in Oban about a fortnight ago and they took her into the infirmary to check her over. It seems that during the couple of weeks while she was there she developed a kidney infection and rapidly weakened."

Dougal's news fell heavily on David.

"That is so sad," sighed David. "She'd become such a special friend to me. I felt we were family."

He thought about his pending visit and how it would be his fourth year there. He had stayed at her house on the island since meeting her early on his first trip. He would not be staying with her now.

"Oh, I know what you mean. I'd looked after her affairs all her adult life and the firm had been advisors to the family for years before that. She had a damn good innings though. She was 87 and that can't be bad."

"You know, I wrote to her in December to let her know I'd be up again this summer but that I would be sailing there and would be living on the boat whilst I finished my work. She wrote back and said don't be daft, man! Sail up by all means but you're staying with me as usual. I'll miss that old dame."

"Aye, we all will. But David, look, we'll be holding her funeral a week tomorrow and although there'll be old friends there, she had no family left that I know of. She stayed on alone at the house on Kerrera for as long as she could but, as you know, she started to use the house in Oban some time ago to pass the winters in a little more comfort. She loved being at the island house in the summers and was looking forward to this one. Like you said, you felt like family to her and I'm calling to ask you up to the funeral in that capacity as well as a friend. Can you make it, man?"

"Of course I can," said David without hesitation. "I couldn't let her go without being there."

"In which case," proposed Dougal, "I'll fix you up with a hotel for the night before. Would you like to stay for a couple of nights, I'm sure there will be a bit of a shindig afterwards?"

"I will," replied David. "I'll come the day before the funeral but I wouldn't expect to be there until the evening. I'll check the flights and arrange a hire car from this end. I'll stay the following night too and drive back to Glasgow the next day. I'll let you know my schedule."

"That's great," concluded Dougal. "I'll book the hotel for you and send you the details."

"Okay. Bye then and thanks for calling."

"Bye, just now."

Well, that was a diversion he wasn't expecting. It was quite a shock really, the end of an era and curiously co-incident with his thoughts of the previous day. It concentrated his mind and got him thinking once more about his pending voyage and the things he had to complete before he set off. The data processing could wait until tomorrow and a clearer mind. Right now he needed to sort out his travel arrangements for next week and then get back to Dougal. After that he would write out a list of essential things that he needed to do before he left on his journey north. Although the planned departure date for his sail to Oban was not for another six weeks or so, events had a habit of catching up on the unwary and he needed to keep a tight rein on things.

THREE

Amanda Heston arrived, as arranged, at 12 o'clock.

A short walk down the street from Connie's house was a pub called The Guardsman. Formerly a regimental officers' mess, the bar had retained a warm character with a number of quiet alcoves where discreet meetings could take place. Connie had decided that when Amanda arrived they would have to leave the claustrophobic atmosphere of the house and she would suggest that they went to the pub. There she would tell her what had happened.

"Hi, Amanda," said Connie as she opened the door. "Come in from the weather for a moment while I get a coat and then let's get out of here and go get ourselves a drink."

Amanda had visited Connie on numerous occasions for lunch and it had become a routine that she knew and enjoyed anticipating. On this occasion, her reaction to Connie's change to the routine was one of muted surprise. She knew clearly that something was different today. If she thought that this was going to be one of their usual lunches, it seemed Connie had other ideas.

"Look," declared Connie, "something's happened and I want to talk to you about it but let's go over to the pub, y'know, where it's a bit more cheerful."

She dragged on her coat, grabbed an umbrella, and they made a hurried walk to the pub. They entered to be greeted by a blazing fire in the grate. That made Connie feel better straight away and they ordered their drinks for the barman to bring them to a table in a corner. It struck

Amanda that maybe a glass of red wine at mid-day was not a bad idea.

They sat down, clinked their glasses, looked each other in the eye and, whilst Amanda sipped hers, Connie, quite out of character, downed hers in one and looked for the barman to call for another.

"Hey, hold on there, you lush!" chided Amanda. "You'll leave me behind."

She watched her friend attract the barman's attention. The front of Amanda's long, straight, black hair fell over the side of her face making it look as if she were watching Connie surreptitiously. She self-consciously pushed the hair back over her ear and smiled as Connie turned to her.

"Sorry," said Connie, "but boy, I really needed that one. I've ordered you another. I need a partner for this."

The next round arrived. They had been there two minutes.

"Okay, Con," demanded Amanda as she twirled the stem of her second glass. "What the heck's this all about?"

Connie looked at her friend. How the hell do you even start to explain this one? Should I be doing this to her, is it fair to unload such a personal mess on to someone she had known only a short time? Damn it, she thought, she is not just my friend – she's my only friend. Here goes.

A deep breath…

"Amanda, Carl has been killed in an accident at work. A routine service check was being done on a pumping station, the whole bloody thing blew up and the entire team was ripped apart. No survivors."

Silence. Then:

"What? Jeez, Con! C'mon...Oh, no! You can't be..." The only words Amanda could utter. She felt utterly inadequate.

"I know," replied Connie, softly. "Just about my reaction too. Two people representing his company showed up a couple of hours ago and gave me the full story. It happened two days ago but they only heard about it last night."

Amanda stood up, nervously straightened her dress and sat down again.

"I can't believe it, Connie. I mean, hell, what are you going to do? What can I do? The children – how are you going to tell them?"

Connie looked up nervously towards the bar.

"Hi, barman, can we have the same again?"

"Certainly, madam, but I've only just brought you another round and you have yet to finish them."

"Hey, I'm sorry, so you have!"

She realised that she was losing control of herself. The situation needed calmness; she needed to focus on practicalities. She leant towards Amanda, her hands clasped as if in appeal.

"Look, Amanda," said Connie, "this is a pretty damned unreal situation. I've got to keep a hold on things. My immediate concern is for the kids. They'll be back from school, when, 4.30ish? I sure as hell need to collect my thoughts before then."

"Me too, remember I'm off to the school to get them!"

"Yeah, of course. Thanks. Look, look – I'm so sorry, I can't involve you with my problem; y'know, Amanda, this whole situation is like something out of a film…"

"Hang on!" interrupted Amanda, "I am here to be involved. And because I *am* your friend, I *am* involved. You got no problem there. We get you through this, whatever it takes. Right?"

"You sure?"

"You bet your sweet butt, I am!"

"I…"

"You hear me?"

"Thanks," acknowledged Connie with gratitude.

She looked imploringly at Amanda. She had to tell her about the situation that had existed with Carl. She had to tell her if only so she could hear herself say the words, hear words spoken that told the truth about her life. She took a sip of her wine, put the glass on the table and turned to her friend.

"Look, Amanda, well, I've got to tell you about this. You know Carl worked away from us for ages. Our lives were not like yours and Alex's. You've had a real family life, with the kids, together and all that. Carl and I had become like strangers. He was hardly ever here. The kids never missed him and I swear if I never told them what had happened to their father, they would never even wonder."

"Well," admitted Amanda, "Alex and I often wondered what the hell life was like between you two, I mean, how many times had we been out together, you, me, Alex and the four kids but never a Carl with us?"

"Yeah, I know, you see, my feeling of shock about this is all to do with the fact that an accident has happened and *not* that it happened to Carl. When the people came to tell me, I was like shocked to the core and just couldn't believe what they were telling me. And you know what, Amanda? I went through all the reactions that hit you immediately I told you about it. They were fully supportive in as professional a kind of manner as they could be. They would do everything to help me from the administrative point of view, y'know – the whole caboodle – funeral, personal effects, and the children and so on but I kept saying just leave me alone to come to terms with this, to sort it out in my own mind. When they'd gone I just looked out of the window and was just plain numb. I'd no feelings. I didn't shed a tear, Amanda – not a single bloody tear. And I just thought, what had my life been all about? Was this the sum total of all my experiences: laughter, happiness, hard times, work, hopes – like, you name it. And here I am in rainy, cold England with not a damned thing to show for it. Well, of course I've got the children and they have always been the centre of my life, even at the beginning. When I look back, Carl was a guy who always had a way of being a hand's distance away from me, y'know, like if he had any feelings he couldn't show them. So, the kids became more and more the objects of my affections, and again, when looking back, when I see how we grew apart, I realise just how ill-suited we were to be a family. That's the thing, isn't it? You can work out to run a marathon or climb Mount Everest but there's no training for marriage. You have to do it as you go along and who knows how anyone will cope with that? My folks seemed to be okay – they did things together and, though Mom may not necessarily have liked what Dad's work was and where it took them, she was always with him. You know, I hardly knew a thing about Carl's life. Maybe he had a crap family life and it just spilled over into ours?"

The wine was having its effect and Connie was speaking her mind freely.

"Well, you've got me thinking now!" said Amanda. "I've got a good relationship with Alex but why does it work? It's certainly a two-way process, loads of give and take and I imagine we both put as much in as we get out. But I could never quantify that. Just to say that it works. Hell, I don't think any marriage is a bed of roses – some thorns catch you from time to time – but it has to be like a math equation in which the balance has to be for the benefit of both parties. If it's fifty: fifty, that's good but you've got to work on keeping the balance. Less than that and you've got an increasing problem on your hands. I'm not a philosopher, a mathematician or a marriage guidance counsellor, but from what you've just told me, the odds were heavily stacked against you."

"And look at me now," said Connie, "I don't even have the other half with me to try and sort it out. And that, I guess is the whole point. He never really was there. And that's why when they told me what had happened, my initial reaction of shock turned to an emotional emptiness."

Amanda sat and stared at the fire. She had to guide this conversation into a more positive direction without appearing insensitive. But she felt her friend had given her the lead.

"Connie," Amanda started, "we've got to be practical about this. You're a smart lady, you've got a real situation on your hands and I want you to start telling me how you feel you can handle it."

"It's amazing, Amanda. My head's been in turmoil thinking about different options. Even while I've been telling you everything and listening to you, I've been thinking about what I'm going to do."

"Good! Tell me what you have in mind. I'm your sounding board so just throw everything at me and see what comes back."

"Well, right now I have to keep cool about it with the children. It'd be good if you dropped them off as usual after school but I'd like it if you all came in for a half an hour or so and mine can play with your two."

"Fine, makes good sense."

"The children have got until the end of June before the school year finishes and it doesn't fire me up the idea of remaining here in London after what has happened. My immediate thoughts are to go back to the States. I could put the house with a real estate agent and whether or not it was sold by the end of the summer term we could go back and I could get them into a school in time for the fall term."

Connie was thinking: how can I be so cool about all this? Has this been deeply hidden away in my sub-conscious for years and this accident to Carl has triggered off a course of action that I have wanted to take but lacked the courage to do? Whatever the case, here I am doing it and I feel extraordinarily invigorated by it.

"Wow!" said Amanda, "that certainly is taking the bull by the horns."

"Yeah, but the more I think about it, it is the logical thing to do. I must maintain some kind of continuity in their lives so a move during their school holidays would soften the blow of uprooting them from England."

"What part do you reckon you'd go to?" asked Amanda.

"Well, let me say the last place I want to go to is back to the South and with my father in Hawaii and effectively out of my life, my thoughts are to go back home to Massachusetts and try and pick up things there. Maybe Boston again, I don't really know."

"Did you tell your father about Carl?"

"Yeah. I called him but he just said the usual things about how sad it was but I really think his mind was elsewhere. Since Mom died he's rarely contacted me."

"Right. Now look," said Amanda, encouraging her. "You'll certainly need to keep yourself busy. You could get up and running in your old journalistic world again. That could be good and you'll need to keep the show on the road. By the way are you going to be okay financially?"

"Oh, yeah, I'd forgotten to mention that. They told me that Carl was well insured by the company for death in service. I've no idea what that means in financial terms – they're going to let me know about that – but we owned the house outright and I should get a pretty good price for it. I seem to recall that Carl also had some private life insurance. I suppose I'll have to see if he had a will or not.

But jeez, Amanda, y'know, I've absolutely no idea if he made one? I seem to recall that we had some basic one drawn up back in Lafayette that, in the event of one pre-deceasing the other, the survivor inherited everything. I guess the company administrators will let me know."

"Do you have an attorney, a solicitor or whatever they call them over here?"

"Well, I guess so, but I'll have to go through the papers and check out who it is."

"Always some damn detail or the other to complicate matters," said Amanda.

"Look, all this is making me feel hungry. Fancy a bite, a sandwich, maybe?" proposed Connie.

"Okay! And how about a last glass?"

"Oh, why not!" said Connie.

They called the barman over and put in their orders.

Connie thought about the relief she was feeling for having talked this through. What would she have done without Amanda to say all these things to? It was the catharsis she needed. Not only had Amanda let her speak freely but she had also had a sympathetic ear. She wasn't a shoulder to cry on – Connie had not needed that – she was there to let her release the truth that had been refusing to stand up and be challenged. What she had anticipated would be a dreadful, heart-rending time had turned out to be her liberation. And she had this friend to thank for letting her say what she needed to say and, above all, letting her hear herself say what she so desperately needed to hear.

Their sandwiches and drinks arrived. The barman put some more logs on the fire and as the two of them chinked their glasses together, they instinctively knew that today had been something remarkable.

"Amanda," Connie said, "you've been so good helping me through this, y'know, getting it out of my system, to see so clearly how things were, to see the mess I was in. How fortunate that I didn't love that man anymore; how lucky I was that he had drifted out of my life. I don't want to sound too melodramatic, but it's as if he barely existed for any of us."

"Connie, I'm just glad I was able to be here. You've actually done this yourself. It can't have been easy all these years being loyal to a relationship that only half existed. Think about it, Con, this accident's released you. Good times are ahead, honey, and if you go back to the States and us to Canada, we will always be able to look back and have a drink on this one!"

They paid up and parted, with Amanda promising to be back about 4.30pm to bring Danny and Louisa home and stop for a short while.

Connie didn't go straight back home. She strolled off, oblivious to the cold and the rain, fixed in a daze as all of it began to sink in. Can I believe this? she thought. Has this incredible thing actually happened? I have been living life for some eight years like an automaton. My life a routine of children caring, waiting for and wondering when my husband will return, house moving, home making. And now, although I will always care for my children, I am now free to start a new life on my terms. I will find my home where I want to live.

I will determine my future.

FOUR

David set about the arrangements needed to get up to Scotland for Helen McKechnie's funeral. The simplest route was to take a train up to London and then the underground out to Heathrow. There were scheduled flights up to Glasgow each day and it was straightforward to hire a car at the airport and drive straight up to Oban. He did all this on-line and then e-mailed Dougal with his itinerary. With this out of the way he put his mind to preparing a list of things he had to do between now and his departure for the summer. The software problem could wait; it needed an uncluttered mind to resolve the issue.

The boat was fully equipped for living on and he had made numerous internal modifications to the forward and main cabin to accommodate his work equipment and basic 'laboratory' as he liked to call his work area. He was effectively transferring his office at the Institute to his boat and he was surprised at how conveniently everything fitted in. There is no doubt that we collect and store things in houses, garages and offices simply because we have the space to do so. A boat requires a discipline that is dictated by its obvious limited space and the dual need to have on board absolute essentials and so placed that they are readily and quickly accessible. His living quarters at the rear of the boat were dominated by a large cabin made available by the central cockpit of the boat. Here he could stand up fully and besides having a couple of comfortable chairs fixed into the furniture structure that housed a wide double bed, he had cupboards and wardrobe space for all his personal effects. However, besides a spacious bathroom and a well-stocked drinks cabinet, luxuries were not high on his list.

Outside, David had fixed a couple of large photo-voltaic solar panels and a wind generator to charge the battery bank. To augment this power supply, he had fitted a diesel generator that, in the event of neither wind nor sun, he would always have electricity. In addition, the alternator charged the batteries when the engine was running and, of course, when in a marina, he could connect directly to the mains.

So, with a galley and refrigerator, the radar and navigation system up and running, all he had to do was stock up with food, fresh water and fuel and he would be ready to go.

All the final equipment he would put on board shortly before his sailing from Weymouth.

Dougal called later that afternoon with the hotel details, and so with things having been organised so quickly, David now had some five days before he was due in Oban for the funeral. His mind was sufficiently cleared now to deal with his software re-writing and so he set about it with a restored zeal. This recent turn of events had spurred him on and his mind was even more set on the sea journey ahead of him.

He decided that, as the funeral was not until the following Tuesday, he would take *Cassiopeia* out the next day or so for a final refresher sail along the coast. This would give him an opportunity to review his 'to do' list, check the boat at sea and ensure that she was ready for the long haul to Scotland. He also felt restless and, though these last weeks of his time in Portland would be consumed writing up his work to date, he felt unable at this moment to apply himself to this particular task. The funeral was on his mind and he felt he was in a bit of a vacuum, so a short sail seemed a sensible course of action to take.

Although David had made a number of trips along the coast between Poole and Exmouth both for the pleasure of sailing and also to test his mettle to face a full month at sea, he felt he needed this one more outing. So, on the Saturday he decided to sail eastwards for some 15 miles or so and then turn back to Weymouth. He was more than happy with the boat – she handled well both up and down wind – though on this occasion a southerly breeze gave him a relaxing beam reach which enabled him to sail close to the cliffs from Durdle Door towards Kimmeridge. The weather was fine, but in view of the voyage ahead, David was glad of the cover given by the upper cabin which would be essential when beating, more so if it rained. But the sliding door and windows – particularly in the cabin roof – opened to give the boat a true yacht feel, all the more so when the sun shone.

Monday came after his sea trial and he set off to take the early train to London. Although he had made this same journey many times before, this was probably going to be the last time. And that made him feel sad. David never ceased to be amazed at his capacity for feeling a sense of loss. It never seemed to be so the other way around. When something good happened to him he took it in his stride. Usually such things occurred suddenly and unexpectedly, and the surprise was part of the fun.

But this would be different because when he left Weymouth for good it was something that he would have planned, something he was going to make happen. How would he feel when he cast off in April?

And so he sat back in his seat and watched the countryside go by. The sound and rhythmic movement of the train recalled that poem by Stevenson, 'From a Railway Carriage', all so long ago when he had first been introduced to poetry at his school. He recalled some of the words: *'.... ever again in the wink of an eye, painted stations whistle by......each a glimpse and gone forever'*. Yes! That was it. Life was about moving on and in so doing leaving things behind. David wondered if this unexpected funeral was in some way a pre-cursor to his pending move, encouraging him forward. The journey passed on with him immersed in his thoughts and then, as the train shuddered slightly and began to slow down, the spell was broken and he realised that he was approaching Waterloo station.

The underground journey was about fifty minutes to Heathrow Airport so that would get him to the airport with an hour to spare before his flight up to Glasgow. So rare to have spare time, he thought.

At the airport terminal he browsed through the magazine stalls and bought a copy of a yachting magazine before sitting down at a coffee shop to await his call. He thought about his timetable. The flight would arrive about 3.30pm and after the usual delays in sorting out the hire car he would be on the road by about 4.30pm. The journey to Oban would take a comfortable three hours – he had no intention of rushing – so he would be there by about 7.30pm. Dougal had said he would meet him in the hotel bar at 8.00pm and they would have dinner during which he would let David know the procedure for the funeral.

The flight was just over an hour. Leaving Glasgow Airport, he turned westwards along the M8. He always liked that moment when he had passed over the centre of Erskine Bridge, looking down on to the estuary of the Clyde. He liked it because it was a defining line that told him he was on his way. This was not a place that he daily thought about but was a place which, though far away, he was pleasingly familiar with. Odd, he thought, I'm going to a funeral and I'm looking forward to it.

One of the enjoyable things about driving west from Glasgow is the suddenness with which the dreary suburbia along the north side of the Clyde gives way to the countryside. In no time at all, having passed the turning to Helensburgh, the greenery commences and the approaches to Loch Lomond are upon you. As he drove along the lochside road, David looked up at Ben Lomond to the east side of the loch and as ever, marvelled at the fact that it lay only 40 minutes from Glasgow city centre.

But he always had a thrill when he turned off the Crianlarich road and headed eventually up the steep incline to the crest of the Rest and be Thankful pass. Here he was brushing with the Highlands before descending towards the softer coastland of Argyll. This was a landscape that he never grew tired of.

The weather stayed good for his journey. Light rain had been forecast but had held off and, as the sky darkened towards 7 o'clock, David drove the rest of the way with his headlights picking out occasional white cottages, the eyes of roadside animals and those strange shapes of isolated trees bent by the prevailing winds.

The distant orange glow of Oban began to show ahead as he felt the excitement of nearing his destination. He also felt thirsty and hungry and, having made good progress, realised that he would be arriving at the hotel ten or fifteen minutes earlier than anticipated. He would be able to check in at leisure in readiness for Dougal's arrival.

Dougal had chosen him a well-appointed, comfortable hotel across the harbour from the town. With the extra time he decided to take an unhurried shower and a change of clothes before installing himself at the bar to await his friend's arrival. With legal punctuality, Dougal arrived at precisely 8.00pm. David stood up and greeted his friend with affection.

"Dougal!"

"Hallo, David," said Dougal, warmly, "so good to see you again even on such a sad occasion as this."

Dougal, in spite of knowing David well enough, was ever the formal man on their initial encounters.

"Yes, Dougal, it is sad. But I'm glad to be here. I haven't attended many funerals in my time – usually a distant aunt or what have you, and, to be honest, they never really registered with me because they were never really part of my life. As you know, my father died when I was very young and it's ten years past since my mother died. But enough of this! Let's have a drink."

The barman appeared on cue and David ordered.

"What'll it be, Dougal," he asked, knowingly, "the usual?"

"Aye, man, the usual."

"A large one?" suggested David.

"It wouldnae be the usual unless it was a large one," chirped the barman who had known Dougal for years.

"Well, make it two," said David, approvingly.

They sat at the bar and talked the usual niceties about David's journey.

"Yes, very easy – seemed to take no time at all. Mind you, I was wrapped up in a whole load of thoughts most of the way. I must say that the drive here from Glasgow was the perfect antidote to London and the underground. I don't think I will ever get used to that way of transport or the idea of living in that city," confessed David.

"Oh, I agree, man. It's a place I avoid unless I absolutely have to go there."

"But," declared David, "let's forget all that. I'm here now and before we know it, tomorrow will be on us."

David called to the waiter and asked for the menus. They ordered a couple more whiskies and looked at what the chef was offering.

"You know," said David, "I'm simply not going to mess about. I'm in the land of the finest steaks and so I will have one. And to precede it, it has to be a plate of smoked salmon."

"Well, now," said Dougal, "I'm with you on the salmon but I'm going for a grilled sole myself. I imagine you'll want a red wine with that steak – which suits me. A lot of people shun a red with fish but I must tell you I think it is the only wine to accompany it."

"Red it is then, from the start," said David, and they called the waiter over. A final round of aperitifs and they left the bar for the table that awaited them.

"Well, now, David," said Dougal, "the funeral service will be held at a chapel near where she lived in Oban. She was not a religious person in any way at all but was an old friend of the vicar who was quite happy to permit a short secular service and for her to be buried in the grounds. They'd forged a curious but genuine friendship over the years and used to enjoy deep discussions about religious beliefs and her complete rejection of them. I'm sure it isn't what she would have wanted but there was no one else to make a decision to accept his kind offer, so I went along with him. He'll carry it out at eleven a.m."

"That was good of him to help out," admitted David. "I suppose that, with her having no relations left, you have no idea how many or who will turn up?"

"No, but what I think would be best under the circumstances would be for us to meet the vicar beforehand and, David, would you like to say a few words to the gathering, no matter how small, as I think your relationship with her was very special?"

"Of course," promised David. "I would be honoured."

"Good man. Now look, here comes our wine and accompanied by the salmon too."

As they ate, the two discussed David's plans for the summer. He told Dougal how his tenure of the research programme was nearly at its end and that he would be coming up here by sailing boat during April, how it was his intention to complete the work by the time the birds had flown and then hope that one of his job applications would turn out to be successful.

"But surely, man," said Dougal, "you'll miss what you were doing and I know how much you loved being up here?"

"I know, but what else can I do? I'll live on the boat while I am here and await any responses."

"What sorts of job are you looking for? Where are they likely to be based?

"They vary. Some are for lecture posts, others are for research positions but not in the field that I've been in up to now. I have even applied to an oil company that wants to develop an environmental study group. That one's in Indonesia and is probably politically motivated to assist in gaining exploration licences. I've applied for it but it doesn't really excite me."

"Where are the other posts likely to be?" asked Dougal.

"Here in the UK, but, can you believe it, they are all in London!"

"You're out of your head, man."

"I know, but I can't let the grass grow under my feet and, with academic terms starting in October, I have to be on the ball," responded David.

"Maybe you think it's none of this old fool's business, but I wouldn't be in any rush if I were you. Stay on here, man, and have a break from the big wild world. You'll have your boat to live on and with all the fish round here you'll never starve."

"It's a lovely idea, Dougal," agreed David, "but I just feel that if I let it slip I'll be out of the loop in no time at all."

"All right!" he laughed, "but just don't forget that when you wake up one morning and realise the mistake you made, remember that I wasn't such an old fool after all."

"I won't. Look, here comes the main course. Let's get those glasses topped up."

The food was delicious. Dougal was such excellent company and a wise old boy too. He was now in his late-sixties, maybe early seventies, and headed up the family firm: 'Henderson – Notaries and Commissioners for Oaths'. Both his son and daughter had studied law and were away working in Edinburgh and Aberdeen respectively. One day, he hoped, one or other would come back to take over and he could then dedicate himself to some serious fly-fishing.

They parted company around 11o'clock and agreed to meet the following day in his office prior to going to the chapel. It had been a long day and once David was comfortably settled in his bed, he drifted off to sleep musing over the words he was going to dedicate to Helen McKechnie the following day.

The service and burial went smoothly. David said his words to a small gathering of friends and they all departed to a private room in a bar in the town to drink her farewell toast. The shindig that Dougal had intimated never materialised – there weren't enough people – so David said his farewell to Dougal and took the opportunity to use the afternoon to check out where he might moor *Cassiopeia* when he arrived there in May.

The following morning, as he was walking out of the hotel to his car, he passed a woman on the footpath in front of the hotel. He scarcely noticed her but she saw David, hesitated for moment and then turned back to him.

"It's David Gregson isn't it?" she said with a slight awkwardness. "My name's Olivia Lindsay, I was there yesterday at the funeral. I'd known Helen for many years, particularly since she moved from the island. She'd told me about you. And, you know, it was odd the way you spoke of her, I felt that you were one of us – that... that you belonged here."

FIVE

In the weekend following her meeting with Amanda at The Guardsman, Connie broke the news of their father to the children. They had gone for a Sunday afternoon walk in Hyde Park and were feeding the ducks on the Serpentine when she quite simply told them that their father had had an accident with his work and that he had sadly died. Maybe their pre-occupation with the ducks softened the effect; maybe the way Connie said it gave the news a gentleness, but there was initially no reaction. A minute or so later Danny spoke:

"What work did Daddy do, Mum?"

He said this in a slightly distant way as he was watching a duck trying to break up a crust that was far too large for its mouth.

"He worked for some engineering company in Saudi Arabia," Connie replied.

"Is that a long way away from here, Mum?" asked Louisa.

"Sure is, darling," Connie said, "a long, long way away."

"I suppose that's why we never saw him," stated Louisa.

"I guess so," she surmised.

"Well, he could have got a plane back to see us, couldn't he?" claimed Danny.

"Yeah, he could have," agreed Connie, "but he had to come a long way from the middle of the desert to get to the airport and he was always kinda busy with his work."

More duck feeding.

Then Louisa pointed across the lake, shouting.

"Is that a goose, Mum?"

"Of course it is, stupid," taunted Danny. "It's far too big to be a duck. It could get a whole loaf down its throat without having to break it up!"

Connie just marvelled at this interchange of conversation. She had just told them of the death of their father, listened to their briefest of comments about him then real life kicked in and suddenly they were more interested in the type, size and gastronomic capabilities of waterfowl. Well, if that was how they reacted to it she would leave it be and answer any other questions as they came along. For now, she needed to plan the smooth transition between selling the house and returning to the States.

During the week following the accident, the Transflow representative, Anne Travers, had called Connie and explained that there could be no formal funeral for her husband as the destruction wrought by the explosion had reduced the bodies of her husband and his colleagues to fragments and that, because of the climate out there, they had had to deal with the corporeal remains very quickly. As a result, under the laws of the country, they had been cremated and assigned to a grave in a civic graveyard. All the immediate families had been notified of this and supplied with official details. It appeared that her husband's family in South Africa had also been informed of this and, as far as Connie was concerned, any arrangements to follow it up were entirely up to them.

Connie had only ever met Carl's parents once and their reaction towards her was very obvious from the start. It seemed that, for no obvious reason she could fathom, they had refused to accept her as the daughter-in-law that they had hoped for. Maybe they had wanted him to settle down back home with a local Afrikaner girl, preferably the daughter of a family they knew well. Perhaps a foreigner, and an American at that, was something they just could not accept. This reaction had manifested itself by their not only ignoring her, but by behaving as if she did not exist. They had never made contact and they only ever sent letters or greetings cards to Carl. Like him, they seemed to have no interest in her or the children. In spite of all her efforts to win them over, their rejection of her deeply hurt Connie. For her, there was also the past spectre of the unfulfilled relationship she had endured with her own parents. A difficult burden to bear for it was not in her nature to dislike someone just because they didn't like her.

Nevertheless, she considered it the decent thing to contact them and go through the usual commiserations. Whether or not she ever heard from them again, time alone would tell.

Anne Travers had also dealt directly with Connie regarding the company's life insurance cover and revealed a staggering figure that left her breathless. Quite simply the amount was like a telephone number. And Anne told her, whilst she was reeling at this information, that she would never have to work again if she invested enough of the lump sum to provide an income. In addition, Connie knew that the sale of the house would provide her with sufficient capital to set up a new home in America.

Connie had told the children of her plans to go to live back in Massachusetts and, knowing that a new school would not be part of their lives for at least another seven months, they just accepted it as a matter of course.

So she decided to begin the process of selling the house and considered the best way was to find an agent in whose hands she could leave the property and for them to find a purchaser. It was a type of house in demand and she imagined an easy sale should follow.

Her life settled down and the routine re-established itself. It was just a question of waiting. She hadn't yet decided quite where she wanted to settle in the States but was trawling the internet just to get a feel for things. She liked the cooler climate of the north-east and, because of her previous association, Massachusetts or perhaps coastal New England seemed her most likely destinations.

And then one day, about eight weeks after Carl's death, she had another unexpected visitor to her house.

Just after 10 o'clock one Monday morning the doorbell rang and Connie went to answer it. She opened the door to see a man of about forty, of medium height and dressed in a rather well-worn greenish tweed suit. His brown hair was slightly askew in spite of the still air outside, giving him a slightly boyish, rumpled appearance. He had a thin briefcase under his left arm, held in place by having his hand tucked into his jacket pocket. The overall impression was one of a shy awkwardness which somehow put her at ease in the presence of this stranger.

"Hallo?" said Connie, with a sound of mild curiosity in her voice.

"Er, hallo," replied the man. "Please excuse me for calling on you unannounced but it was quite important that I catch you at home and I thought that maybe if I telephoned out of the blue you might refuse to see me. Sorry if that sounds a bit of a circuitous way of explaining why I am here at your door. Please let me introduce myself. My name is Charles Denholm," he said, offering his hand which she gingerly accepted. An odd sense of *déjà vu* swept through her.

"How do you do?" enquired Connie, a little smile on her face at this bashful fellow's attempt at clarity.

"Very well, very well indeed," he assured her.

"Good," she said, firmly, "in which case, Mr Denholm, perhaps you'd be kind enough to let me into the reason for your visit?"

"Tricky," he murmured, *sotto voce*, "tricky to know quite how to put this." And then, as if by some sort of revelation: "You see, I work for a company that has a name that I cannot reveal unless I am absolutely sure of who I am talking to. All very discreet and that sort of thing. Here, let me show you my business card."

He handed Connie a plain white card with his name on it and two telephone numbers. There was no company title or logo on it. She turned it over to reveal a blank reverse side.

"The company carries out a consultancy service, normally on behalf of legal departments for companies or lawyers, you know, people who want to get things confirmed beyond doubt."

"No, I don't. In fact, right now I haven't a clue what you're talking about, so if you can't explain yourself more clearly, I shall have to ask you to leave," she said quite firmly.

"I'm sorry, I don't seem to be doing this very well. Perhaps I should be quite direct. Are you one Constance Renton?"

The sense of *déjà vu* reasserted itself.

"Yes, I am," she replied smiling, amused at hearing her full name once again. "I'm very rarely called Constance; normally it is just Connie Renton."

"Ah, excellent. So I am talking to the right person, because if I had not I would have apologised and been on my way," he said.

"Right," observed Connie, "so we both know who I am but it's kinda puzzling why you are being so secretive."

"Normally, when I carry out this sort of visit, I ask the person in question to call the first of the two numbers on my card and ask the person who answers to explain my presence," he responded. "To provide authenticity, you understand."

"Okay," agreed Connie, "wait there a moment and I'll make the call."

Connie took her mobile phone from her pocket. Although he remained outside on the doorstep she looked at him with a little concern. Whilst he seemed a pleasant enough person he did seem a bit of an oddball but she had to admit that her curiosity had the better of her. She called the number. It was answered almost immediately by a female voice.

"Hallo, may I be of assistance to you?"

"Well, that all depends," ventured Connie, "I should like you to tell me who you are and the name of your company."

"Certainly. Ruth Haldane and the company is called 'Search'. We are a London based firm of private investigators."

The reply created sufficient surprise for Connie to reel slightly.

"Can you tell me who is calling, please?" the 'Search' person requested.

"Yes," she said slowly, "my name is Connie Renton."

"Then you are probably in the presence of one of my colleagues, a Mr Charles Denholm."

"Well," Connie replied, "there's certainly a guy by that name right next to me. Can you describe him?"

After she had done so, Connie replied: "Well, that's a pretty accurate description, but why's he here?"

"Well, let me tell you," said Ruth Haldane. "A client of ours has asked that we locate a person of your name. Mr Denholm's presence at your house today is the result of nearly two months of diligent searching. Our client had very little to go on and before we can reveal to you his identity, it is absolutely vital that we confirm beyond all doubt that you are the Constance Renton that he is trying to locate."

"Well, you've certainly got me hooked there," she admitted. "So what do I do now?"

"Well, if you are happy to continue with this interview with Mr Denholm, and we can satisfy our client that you are the right person, we would ask you to come to our offices for a formal meeting. Normally, we would then both sign an appropriate document of recognised identification and we could then reveal the identity of our client. Our work will then be finished and we can leave you both to proceed accordingly."

"Well, I guess that seems okay to me," replied Connie. "So what then, I just listen to his questions and answer them if I feel all right about it?"

"That would be great. Thanks for understanding our need for discretion. Poor old Charles always hates these seemingly roundabout introductions, but unfortunately that's the way of our business. If he can leave today satisfied that he has found the right person, we'll get back to you straight away when he has reported back."

"Right, but, before I do anything else I want you to e-mail me with all your company details and confirm that Charles is your representative, okay? I want you to do that right now while he is here with me."

"Will do; give me a few minutes. And ask for his passport as identification," she added.

Connie gave Ruth Haldane her e-mail address and turned to Charles Denholm.

"Well, you got that. How about a coffee while we wait for her?"

She invited him in and he sat down at her kitchen table while she made the coffee. True to her word, within five minutes an e-mail arrived from Ruth Haldane. As they sat there with their coffees, Connie read the e-mail. Satisfied that this was enough to confirm the legitimacy of his presence in her house she awaited his questions.

"Firstly," he said, "can I ask you to show me your passport? I know it seems a pretty basic first thing but I do need to see it and its details."

"Just a moment, I'll go get it. And hey, while I'm about it," countered Connie, "get your passport out for me, then we can start on an equal footing – right?"

She returned with it and Denholm handed his over in exchange. He wrote the details down and she likewise. With this formality over he began:

"Please understand that the questions I am about to ask you are designed to confirm that you are the person our client is searching for. You don't have to answer any of them if you don't want to, or maybe only some of them. In fact, if it becomes obvious to me that you are irrefutably the genuine person being sought, I will cease any further questioning and tell you so immediately. Are you happy with that?"

"Fire away," encouraged Connie.

"Good. When I have satisfied myself beyond doubt that you are who we believe you to be, that will be the point where we can hand you over to our client for him to fill you in with all his details. I would add that we have no idea why our client wishes to find you. So, here we go:

"Firstly, am I right in understanding that you are the widow of Carl Lindeger, a South African national who was killed in an explosion in Saudi Arabia in January of this year? I have noted various earlier press releases which announced the accident and his company, Transflow, confirmed them and gave me publicly available details of the accident. Also, again only using information available to the public, the company's insurers confirmed that the accident had happened. I would be grateful if you could confirm these various points."

And so it went on. Question after question – about her life in America, how she came to meet her future husband, her mother's sudden death, everything that led up to her coming to live in London. After about an hour, he closed his folder and put it back in his briefcase, leaned back in his chair and looked at her.

"That's it then," he said with a note of finality and satisfaction. "I have no further need to ask you any more questions."

"Meaning?" enquired Connie.

"Meaning that as far as I am concerned, you have corroborated all the information I have gathered, and I am absolutely sure you are Constance – sorry, Connie Renton."

"I guess you can imagine," Connie remarked, "that I'm pretty damn well exhausted after this and totally mystified over what it's all about. You're telling me that you have confirmed beyond doubt, on behalf of a client, that I am who I am but you will not – cannot – tell me anything more until you have formally notified this client that you have now located and identified me. This is kinda unhinging. Tell me, Mr Denholm, how the hell am I supposed to get to sleep tonight?"

"Sorry, I can't answer that one," he said, with an understanding expression. "I'm so pleased that our endeavours have been fruitful that I've rather overlooked how you might be feeling. I'll be returning to my office immediately I leave you and will write up my report on our meeting and will e-mail it to our client today. Ruth will contact you tomorrow and tell you of the reaction to my report. You see, our task will be finished at that point and, in the full knowledge of your successful identification, our client will explain everything to you."

"When…where...?" she stuttered.

"Possibly tomorrow, certainly the next day, here in London. I know our client is anxious to meet you. It has been quite a challenge to find you."

And at that point, a somewhat more relaxed Charles Denholm than the one who had arrived earlier, stood up, offered his hand, thanked Connie for being so helpful and bade her farewell.

"So you'll let me know about this mysterious meeting, then?" she asked him as he passed through the front door.

"Absolutely. Ruth will call you as soon as she has spoken with our client."

Of all the things to happen! What the hell could this all be about? Connie's mind raced through all the possibilities. It can't be anything to do with Carl, she thought. All of that has been dealt with by the company's representatives and the file closed. The house? Could it be something to do with the house? But what, how could the house involve private investigators? Her life back in America? It just didn't make sense. Well, she would try and contain herself. When the children got back from school she'd get them through their homework and then take them out to the cinema and for a bite to eat. The next twenty-four hours were going to need filling to keep her from going out of her mind.

The next morning, after she had done the school run, she came back to the house with a sense of trepidation. She checked the call register on her house line – no calls. Her computer – no e-mails. Her mobile – nothing.

And then at 10.30am on the dot, a call from Ruth Haldane.

"Hi, it's Ruth here from 'Search'. You'll be delighted to know that you really are who you say you are! I have just had confirmation from our client that he wants to meet you. Could we meet at our Palace Street office tomorrow so that we can sign the document I referred to? It's in Victoria, not too far from where you live."

"Yeah," Connie said, hesitantly, "how long might this meeting go on for?"

"Oh, it will be very short, maybe half an hour in total. You see, we have to sign the document in the office. It's the formal procedure, and it needs to be witnessed by a lawyer. When it has been done, we will call our client who will then contact you directly and meet you anywhere, your home, for instance."

"Yeah, that'd be cool, at my home. And when's that meeting likely to be?"

"The next day. As soon as I confirm the signature he will come to London. Let's see, today's Monday, we sign tomorrow. Are you okay for Wednesday? Can you keep the day free?"

"I have a school run at 8.30am and another at 4.00pm."

"I think it could be a long one. If you could make arrangements for someone to help you out it might be a good move."

Amanda – she'd give her a call.

"Sure, Wednesday's good. But for chrissake, Ruth," pleaded Connie, "tell me before I go out of my head – who am I going to meet?"

"It's a man from Scotland," confided Ruth.

"Scotland?" said Connie incredulously. "Scotland?"

"Yes, a solicitor. He'll be flying down to meet you."

"What's his name?" asked Connie.

"He's called Henderson," replied Ruth. "Dougal Henderson."

SIX

The following morning, Connie took a taxi to the 'Search' office in Palace Street. Her friend Amanda had agreed to do the school run for her the next day to free her up for the meeting with the solicitor from Scotland. She arrived just before 11o'clock and was met at the reception by Charles Denholm.

"Hallo, Connie – you don't mind if I call you that do you?"

"So long as it's not Constance, it's okay with me," she responded.

"Good, then welcome to our humble abode," he said with theatrical grace.

Their 'humble abode' was small but anything but humble. It comprised the basement, ground and two upper floors of a fine old Georgian terraced house and was elegantly furnished and lit. There were three offices, a reception area, a meeting room, a dining room and the usual facilities. One of the office doors opened and Ruth Haldane walked out to greet Connie.

"Hallo, Connie," she beamed, "I'm Ruth."

Ruth was one of those people whose face was radiant. She was in her mid-thirties, well above average height, with long brown hair with a gentle wave. She wore a well-tailored black trouser suit that elegantly concealed her love of good food and drink. But she could have been wearing an old potato sack for all it mattered because all you were aware of was her extraordinary radiance; it was like sunlight.

"So you are the other face behind 'Search'," observed Connie.

"Well, not quite," she confessed, "Alice, our receptionist and general office administrator, is on her way back to the office with the lawyer who will witness our signatures. Alexandra, our senior partner who founded the company, is away on business and, well, of course you've met Charles."

"Sure, yeah. Nice to see the place being run by a female majority, though," she said with an approving twinkle in her eye.

"Glad to hear you say so," replied Ruth, "but in fact we have a great number of independent associates, many of whom are men. We maintain a fairly light operation, keeping staff to a minimum and draw on the talents of a whole range of people as each case unfolds. Charles, Alexandra or I run each case individually and call on our associates as necessary. It's like a big network, really. It also enables us to cover a great amount of ground and therefore achieve results relatively quickly, although I may say in your case we were stretched to the limit."

"Why was that?" asked Connie.

"I'll leave that for Mr Henderson to explain," she replied.

The sound of footsteps and muffled voices from the stairs brought their conversation to an end.

"That sounds like them now," suggested Ruth, as Alice entered the reception area with a rotund, red-faced gentleman following her.

"Hallo, James," greeted Ruth, offering him her hand. "Let me introduce you to Connie Renton; Connie, this is James Winterton."

"Delighted to meet you," he responded, bowing slightly as he took Connie's hand.

"Thanks so much for coming around at such short notice, James," said Ruth, "but you know how these things are. Alice will have shown you a draft copy of the document to be witnessed so shall we waste no further time and proceed?"

They went into Ruth's office where the formal documents lay on an elegant leather-bound folder. She simply explained that the purpose of the document was to provide written confirmation that the evidence gathered had proved beyond doubt that Constance Renton was present before the lawyer, James Winterton, and that she had, in turn, read this evidence and confirmed that it was correct. Connie and Charles would then sign the document and the signing would be witnessed by the lawyer. The matter would then be concluded.

The document was duly read aloud by Ruth and when everyone nodded in affirmation it was put forward between the relevant parties for signing.

Pens were provided, signatures were made and hands were shaken. Alice collected the papers and went off to produce copies for all parties. Ruth was clearly pleased with the outcome of this drawn-out investigation. It was one of the most involved and complex ones they had ever dealt with, involving cross-referencing and extensive travel on both sides of the Atlantic. It was, however, an exercise that had produced the required results for the client and she was particularly pleased to have met Connie, for whom she felt a warmth and regard. In anticipation of the day's success, she had decided that they would 'professionally' celebrate by having a drink in the offices before going to a restaurant for lunch.

"May I suggest that we have a drink?" said Ruth. "After all, we've completed a complicated task successfully and can now let Mr Henderson know that his client is available to proceed."

"Well, let me tell you, I feel like a drink in any case," said Connie.

"I'm sure the sun's below the yardarm somewhere in the world," suggested the lawyer in agreement, "and even if it isn't, I certainly concur with Connie on this one."

The tinkle of glasses preceded a pop of suitable calibre which was followed by a collective clink and satisfactorily taken draughts.

"Well," chortled the legal gentleman, "better be off before this gets out of hand. Damned good bubbly, that." And with a perfunctory bow, James Winterton was gone.

"Have we actually got time to let this get out of hand or is the mysterious Mr Henderson not to be kept waiting?" said Connie, looking at her empty glass which was promptly topped up by Charles – as were the other three.

"Well," said Ruth, "I'm going to contact him by phone straight away and let him know that everything is complete. He wasn't planning to come down until the documentation was completed and scanned and e-mailed to him. Alice will do that while I'm talking to him. So hang on a moment while I do that."

Two minutes later the documents had been scanned, read, and the conversation completed.

"Well, this guy's not messing about," stated Ruth. "He's taking the evening flight down to Heathrow and will be stopping overnight in London. He's got your address and will be at your house by 10 o'clock tomorrow morning. I hope that's okay with you? I told him it would be since you said you could rearrange the school-run with your friend."

Ruth had booked a table at a place nearby. As they walked off to the restaurant, she took Connie's arm and said to her:

"Look, I've absolutely no idea what this thing with Henderson is all about. We just followed his instructions and we seem to have indeed come up with the goods. Often our clients give us a great deal of background information because, as you can imagine, every bit helps. But it seems he had so little to go on that he deliberately left it to us, presuming, I suppose, we were more likely to follow leads and pursue them through our professionally based system than he was. Anyway, all you've got to do now is hang on a bit longer. Let's go and enjoy this lunch."

That afternoon, slightly worse for wear, Connie Renton arrived home just in time to call her friend Amanda to ask her if she could collect the children and keep them at her house for a couple of hours longer. She explained as best she could how she'd had an unexpected lunch and that if she could hang on to them until six or so she would come round and get them. Ever the friend, Amanda came up trumps with the suggestion that Connie just went to bed and she would feed them, make them get on with their homework and then she would bring them back about 8 o'clock.

"I owe you one," she murmured, as she switched off the phone and went straight to sleep.

Connie awoke, fully dressed and with a mouth that felt like it was full of blotting paper. Wow! It was some time since she had enjoyed a lunch like that. A complete set of strangers had entered her life with what seemed like a crazy story about a Scottish lawyer coming to see her and she had no idea what it was about. They were lovely people, the sort she would have been happy to have made friends with, but after they had said their good byes, they had moved on to other things and she was left with a void that had to be filled with her children returning, getting them off to bed and then trying to get a decent sleep herself to be ready for the enigmatic Mr Henderson at 10 o'clock the following morning.

The doorbell rang and was simultaneously opened. In rushed Amanda's children with Danny and Louisa who both leaped at Connie with gleeful comments of what a good time they had had, how Amanda could really cook pizzas at home and that they had done their homework. They then went into the lounge and put on the television, leaving her friend looking at her with her head angled interrogatively, as if to say: all right, out with it, tell all.

Connie opened a cupboard and got out a glass. Before Amanda could say that perhaps she had had enough for one day, she filled it with water from the tap and drank it down in one.

"Dehydrated," she said. "I started at midday and I don't think I drank any water at all."

"Come on, Con, what was it all about? I've been thinking of nothing else all day. I've hardly been able to concentrate on anything – and by the way, your kids have not got educated taste-buds. Those were supermarket pizzas out of the freezer. I'm all ears."

"Well, the lunch really was incredible and I have no recollection of where the restaurant was or what it was called so I don't think I'll ever be able to find it to take you there but I'll try! The actual meeting was just to sign and have witnessed a declaration that I was Connie – sorry, Constance – Renton of this address so that this Scottish guy, a lawyer or solicitor or whatever they call them here, can come and meet me and tell me something. It seems that they are a firm of private investigators who were assigned to check me out for the lawyer guy who is called Henderson. I really don't get it at all. They just wouldn't tell me anything except that he is coming here at 10 o'clock tomorrow to give me the lowdown. Now what do you make of that?"

"If I didn't know you better," said Amanda, "I would say that you'd been out for a really good lunch. But then I do and you have. So clearly something is happening. You didn't even pick up a hint of what it was about?"

"Honey, nothing! They rang the guy up after scanning and e-mailing him the signed documents and they said he was coming on the evening flight down to London. That's all I know. He's stopping overnight in a hotel and will be here in the morning."

"Right. Well, I'd better get these two back home and into bed. Alex will be back about 10 o'clock and I don't suppose he'll want to face over-excited kids after a flight back from Stockholm. I'll pick yours up tomorrow as arranged," said Amanda, "and keep them until you call me later on. I'll bring them over and then you and I are going to have ourselves some time together while you divulge all."

"Okay," said Connie, "and thanks for helping me out. You're a real friend."

"Just hang on in there, kid! I'm as excited as you are."

The following morning, Amanda's car horn sounded outside Connie's house and Danny and Louisa rushed out with a plaster-loosening slam of the front door. It always went the same way when they left. A frenetic hour of washing, dressing, breakfasting and finding displaced school items that was concluded by the closing front door signalling a dust-settling peace. But today it seemed to pass by without being noticed as Connie cleared things away in readiness for her visitor. It was absolutely useless trying to think about what to wear. This was not a ceremony, a formal presentation or an honour being bestowed. A stranger was coming to her house to tell her about something about which she knew not. She would receive him as she found him and he would be as he was – the deliverer of…what?

In a world of falling social graces, it pleased Connie to see that she was not alone in believing that an appointment time should be kept, for when she saw that her watch was just about to reach 10 o'clock, on the exact second that it did so, her front doorbell rang.

SEVEN

Connie would always remember that morning when she opened her front door. Certainly she was expecting someone; a man, indeed a man from Scotland. But whilst she might well have expected him to have a Scottish accent everything else about him was not what she was prepared for. It's strange, she thought, how we compartmentalise people. Here was a man who she knew was a lawyer but for some reason she had built up an image of one that was so completely different. She expected a wizened, stooped little man rubbing his hands together deferentially, a briefcase at his feet as he introduced himself with practised self-importance.

Instead, the man standing before her was distinctly tall; he had a slightly gaunt face and an upright posture that made him seem taller still. He wore no hat and his grey hair, whilst thinning slightly, was straight and very conventionally parted on the left-hand side. He must have been in his mid-sixties and his face, although covered with a short grey beard, had a slight pallor to it suggesting he was a man who spent more time indoors than out. His nose was long and appeared to droop slightly, his blue eyes seeming to gaze along its slope as he looked down at Connie. Under his unbuttoned light-tan raincoat he wore a navy-blue suit, a white shirt and a tie that could well have been regimental in origin. Well-polished, quality black leather shoes completed his appearance of – what? A businessman? A banker? A doctor?

Certainly there was nothing about him that had a legal air. In fact, she could not categorise him professionally. What came across to Connie was the aura of a genial, warm person with a kind gentleness – someone who might have been that bachelor uncle that you always liked to see. She took to him immediately.

"Good morning," he said. "I am quite certain that you are Connie Renton and with this certainty, please allow me to introduce myself." Presenting his business card, he announced: "I am Dougal Henderson and you must be wondering what on earth I am doing here at your door?" He spoke with a soft accent that she assumed to be Scottish because she had been told that that was where he was from.

"Mr Henderson," confessed Connie, "in all my life I have never been addressed so directly and quite so charmingly. And you are right, I am totally at a loss. So please, please come in and tell me what it is that has brought you down from Scotland and has caused me such endless speculation. I can assure you that, from the day that Mr Denholm stood at the very place that you now stand, my life has been off-track to say the least."

Dougal Henderson stepped into Connie's hall. As she closed the door and climbed the stairs he continued his introduction.

"You will have been told by Mr Denholm and Ms Haldane that I am a lawyer. I am the owner of a small legal practice in Oban in Argyll on the west coast of Scotland. My company was founded by my great-grandfather and unless one of my two children take it over it will pass into obscurity. But that's by the by."

Connie ushered him into her lounge and directed him to a comfortable armchair. A low table stood in front of it and she took up the chair opposite him. Although she was desperate to get things underway, she allowed herself the formality of convention and offered him a coffee.

"Maybe later," he suggested, "it's not long since I had some with my breakfast. I'm sure we'll both want one in due course. But thank you nonetheless."

"Right, Mr Henderson," she said, taking a deep breath, "put me out of my misery. And by the way, please call me Connie."

"Indeed so. Well, I can only apologise for your discomfiture, but the procedure I was obliged to carry out was only delayed by legal niceties. Now that all that has been correctly concluded let me begin by asking you a straightforward question: have you ever been to Scotland?"

"No."

"Well, in that case do you have any connection with Scotland?"

"No."

"So Scotland is to you, as it were, an unknown quantity, neither a high road nor a low road that you have taken," he proffered with a chuckle.

"Mr Henderson," interjected Connie, "I am an American citizen who has lived in Britain for nearly two years. I can tell you during that time I've made one visit outside of London to visit the city of Oxford. Other than that I have signally ignored the rest of the country and certainly can tell you that I know little about Scotland other than that men are rumoured to wear kilts. But as you seem to be otherwise attired I guess even that rumour may be false."

"Fine, fine," he said, "in which case I am going to tell you a story that will reveal to you a Scottish family connection of which you are clearly unaware. Parts of this story I have known about for a long time but only regarding the early years. The remaining parts have come to light through the searches carried out, in the main, by Mr Denholm.

"I would ask you just to sit back and listen. If there any parts of this story that you are familiar with, please bear with me as I will bring it all to the present day. And the significance of it all will become evident to you. If you want to clarify anything just stop me.

"I shall begin by telling you of a family by the name of McKechnie whose ancestral home was along the Argyll coast on the west of Scotland. In modern times, the part we are really concerned with, the family lived in and around the town of Oban including on an island called Kerrera just off the coast from the town.

"Shortly after the end of the First World War, a couple called Hamish and Margaret McKechnie settled in the old McKechnie family home on the south-western end of the island. It had been empty for some years but when he came back from the war, Hamish and Margaret married and set up home there, running the farmland as a croft which is a fairly basic way of living, called subsistence farming – that is to say they produced all they needed from the land and sea and made money, if they could, by selling the excess. By the beginning of the 1920s Margaret had given birth to two daughters: Helen was born first and Lorraine followed some two years later. As two close sisters, they grew up together on the island – there were other children on the island and they all attended the local school. As the girls grew up they had to attend senior school in Oban and so each day they took the ferry across to the mainland.

"By the time they had finished school they had acquired a taste for town life and so when Helen turned twenty and Lorraine had reached eighteen they both found work in Oban and because it was quite a journey each day for them, they suggested to their parents that they should look for somewhere to live in Oban. This started a change in the McKechnie family. With no sons to carry on the hard work of life on the island, Hamish and Margaret were left alone. It was not as if the two girls had contributed greatly to the daily activity of the farm as they had little interest in the life of crofting subsistence. They were part of a new generation. No, it was the fact that they were now alone that made the major difference.

"And then the Second World War broke out. Only twenty years earlier Hamish had returned from the destruction of land and lives that had been the horror of the First World War. The then empty house on the island had given tranquillity and hope to him after four years in which he had seen friend and foe fight and die in what to him was an utterly pointless conflict. He always thought that in being one of the lucky ones to return he carried an intolerable guilt on his shoulders. But you know, he wasn't alone; this condition had altered the lives of thousands. He was now forty-four years of age and looked sixty-four. My father knew him well. The McKechnie family had been friends as well as clients of the firm from my grandfather's time.

"After the outbreak of war, the west coast became an important military zone. Not totally so, you understand, but certain areas more so than others. In the Argyll area, the Firth of Lorn became a major Atlantic convoy muster point. The Royal Navy had a strong presence, as did the Royal Air Force. The town of Oban was an important centre for the Services and was made a militarily secure town. Of course, I wasn't born then, but there are some old people who remember it well. There were army posts with barriers on all the roads into Oban and you could only get through with an official pass.

"The two McKechnie girls were employed as civilian staff attached to the military and of course, for these two young people this war business was all very exciting. Not so for poor Hamish. He was terribly affected by the military activity in the area and on the island in particular. The Navy had, amongst other things, a motor torpedo boat base there and the Air Force had a large fleet of seaplanes that carried out convoy protection. So you see, although he stayed put on the island he was constantly aware of the war, not just because of the presence of Service people, but also the constant sound and movement of shipping and the roar of the seaplane engines. Everything he had come to the island to escape from twenty years earlier was now following him. Can you just imagine, Connie, he felt hounded by the awful memories and here, here in remote Argyll of all places, another war was underway against the same opponents and, although he was not directly involved in it, he was under a sort of mental siege by those past ghosts.

"Hamish had a licence to net salmon and one day – a rare occasion this since Margaret didn't like going out in his small boat – she came with him because it was such a beautiful calm day. He would come alongside the net at one end and, using a glass-bottomed box and an old coat over his head to keep the light out, work his way along the supporting line and would gaze down into the water to see if any fish had been caught in the gill net. Neither of them noticed the corvette passing along the sound towards Oban, but some minutes after it had passed them, the bow wave caught his boat awkwardly and Hamish went over the side. He entangled a foot in the net and was held down sufficiently long for him to take a lot of water into his lungs. Had Margaret not been there he would in all probability have drowned. But she hauled him back on board and pumped the water out of his chest.

"He never got over this and within six months a depression overtook him and his doctor arranged for him to go to a sanatorium near Crieff in Perthshire, the town where his wife had originally come from. Poor old Hamish contracted pneumonia and died within a month. This was in 1941. Convoy activity was fairly intensive in the area and building up. Remember, Connie, we were relying on our links with your country to survive. Margaret went back to her home on the island but she was alone there and too many memories haunted her. She abandoned the house and went to live in Oban where she could be near her daughters.

"Well, Connie, are you with me so far?" he asked.

"Yep," she replied, "it sure is an interesting story, but I've no idea where it's leading. You carry on while I do us some coffee."

"That would be fine. Look, at this stage I'm going to shift the story slightly, so hold on to what I have been telling you so you don't lose the thread.

"In early 1943, the Allies were preparing for the Normandy landings. The logistics of this were far reaching. In the North West Highlands, north of Fort William, there was a training area for British Commandos. This was all very top secret at the time but such was the allied co-operation in these preparations, a number of US Rangers were also involved in training alongside their British counterparts. Two Rangers in particular, John L. Martin – I have no idea what the L stood for – and Harry Zielinski, both of them lieutenants, had been there for some months and were due to take a short period of leave. Because Oban was a militarily secured town they were allowed to go there. So they duly arrived one Friday to enjoy a weekend before re-joining their unit."

"Mr Henderson," said Connie, "I hope you won't consider it too early, but I was wondering would you like to have a little drink with your coffee?"

"A very good idea, if I may say so, and," he added, "it's never too early. What had you in mind?"

"Well, as this story has a distinctly Scottish flavour to it, I thought a glass of Scotch whisky would be very much the order of the day. What do you think?"

"Most appropriate," he acknowledged, with an appreciative smile.

As Connie carried in the tray of refreshments he continued.

"Arrangements had been made for the two Rangers to be billeted at the Marine Hotel on the sea front – the place, incidentally, has now been renamed the Regent Hotel – an interesting structure from the early thirties, very modern in its time but now a rare and valued art deco building. Sorry! I digress. This was one of the many hotels in Oban that had been requisitioned by the military. As it happened, this particular hotel was principally housing flight crews from the flying boat squadrons which were engaged in convoy protection. To assist them, they had been put in the hands of a Royal Australian Airforce squadron leader who was attached to an RAF group flying long-range Sunderland flying boats. To get their leave off to a good start, they were invited by him to be his guests at a dance that was being held that night in the hotel. He explained that it was really for Services personnel but as there were never enough girls to go around, if they should like to invite a couple along as their guests, they were more than welcome to do so."

She handed him his glass.

"Thank you, Connie," he said, and savoured the aroma before tasting. "Now that, I must say, is a very fine whisky and delivered at an ideal moment as our two Rangers are about to go out for a reconnaissance of the town and try a few of the hostelries.

"The two Americans could not have been more different. John L. Martin was tall, fair haired, and well-built. He had strong features, with what I believe is referred to as a lantern jaw – quite your American cowboy and a swagger to go with it – but a quiet man. He was what might be called 'old American', being fourth generation of an early nineteenth-century settler family from Wyoming.

Harry Zielinski on the other hand was of medium height, dark haired, of lean stature and constantly full of energy. He was the New York born son of Polish immigrants who, full of optimism, had come to America, like so many Europeans at the beginning of the twentieth century, simply to have the chance of a better life. Harry was streetwise and eager.

"They had joined up in early 1942, following the Japanese attack on Pearl Harbor when they were both twenty-two. Of course that brought the USA into the war and whilst John had joined up out of a sense of patriotic duty, Harry wanted to have a go at the Germans. The course of events transpired that they ended up in the same Ranger group and were both posted to Scotland."

"Some more coffee, Mr Henderson?" asked Connie.

"No, that's fine, thanks."

"What about a refill of your glass then?"

"Ah."

Connie leaned forward and poured a substantial, amber-coloured draught into his glass. He continued with his story:

"So, the two of them went out for an hour or so to try a few bars and have a look at Oban. Whilst they were walking by the harbour side, they met two girls who, when greeted good evening, smiled back at the two uniformed soldiers. Never one to miss a chance, it seems that Harry promptly invited them to join them for a drink in a bar close by. As they raised their glasses and drank health to each other, Harry told them of the dance at the Marine Hotel and asked them to be their guests. They introduced themselves: the girls were sisters, Helen and Lorraine McKechnie."

At this point, Dougal Henderson halted his story.

"You'll understand, Connie, that what I am relating is based on the work carried out by Charles Denholm. I have weaved into this the information I have from my own knowledge of the family and so, whilst I am not in any way altering the facts, I am doing my best to link those facts together in a way that provides a historical continuity as I imagined it would have happened."

"No, I quite understand, but carry on, please, I'm finding it quite enthralling."

"Well, they took them to the dance. Back in those days, the music would have been provided by a typical forties dance band and I would guess it was all very emotional, young people from all walks of life and from different parts of the world, caught up in a location that few, other than the likes of Helen and Lorraine, had ever seen before, all of them part of a grand effort to contribute to victory. They would have seen it in no other way.

"The net result of this night out was that John was totally smitten by Helen and, if I may lapse into music hall parlance, Lorraine was wild about Harry. The feelings it seems were mutual. This was a weekend leave for the two Americans and they had to be back with their units on the following Monday. So they spent the entire time with the two girls. They were two short days of laughter, happiness and promises. Because of their involvement with the assault preparations, they were unable to tell the girls about anything that they were doing or where they might be going and when. On that Monday morning, the girls met

John and Harry outside the hotel. Their kit was in the Jeep and they had to be on their way. But they had time to walk and say their farewells. How they felt we can only imagine. But what had happened was that four young people had met and fallen in love. Stoic John L. Martin dropped his guard and pledged that he would come back when this war was all over and marry Helen if she would wait for him, which of course she said she would. And impetuous Harry Zielinski told Lorraine that nothing would stop him coming back to claim her and he would then take her back to America with him if she would wait for him, which of course she, too, assured him she would.

"I imagine a lot of tears were shed as they said their farewells, and with their promises indelibly engraved on their hearts, none of them could have foreseen the way the years would unfold.

"Time passed and it seems that because of the war situation contacts were limited to initial rushed letters before they were dispersed and then nothing. The record tells us that the two Rangers were separated into different groups. On D Day, 6th June 1944, John was in the second wave of landing craft at Omaha Beach where he was torn apart by intense machine-gun fire within seconds of stepping on to the beach. Harry was part of a platoon of rangers that arrived at Utah Beach on the third day of the invasion. Their task was apparently to penetrate behind German lines and link up with the French Resistance to wreak as much havoc as possible on the enemy's support supply lines. In true Harry style, he managed to be at the liberation of Paris and then his group were seconded to Patton's 7th Army, advanced eastwards where they encountered some German groups still with a little fight left in them and then liberated some of those awful concentration camps and went right the way through to meet the Russians at the Elbe. By the end of the war in Europe, the Americans controlled the southern part of Germany and remained there as an occupation force.

"With the Pacific war still continuing, soldiers were being shipped back to the USA in order to re-group in regiments being prepared for the combined operations invasion of the Japanese mainland. Harry was in a detachment being sent back to Britain and was issued with orders to embark on a ship out of the Clyde. When they eventually reached Glasgow they were given a week's leave prior to the ship's departure.

"It's difficult to imagine how any soldier would be feeling after nearly three years of activity with scarcely a break. What would they be thinking? In Harry's case we can only surmise how he was handling the fact that he was only a three-hour train journey from the town where he had promised a young girl he would take her back to America when this war was over. And here he was, due to be shipped back to the States in a week's time and then sent across the Pacific Ocean to fight in another war. But what we know is that, however uncertain every next day was for all those soldiers at that time, Harry's next day was anything but uncertain. He said goodbye to his pals and took the first train up to Oban.

"On arriving there he went to the Marine Hotel – the only place he knew about to stay in Oban – to find that, although there were some military people still there, it was in the process of being returned to its pre-war use and he booked a room there. The reception people knew Lorraine and Helen and where they worked. Harry telephoned

Lorraine and didn't beat about the bush. They met up at her lunch break and he proposed to her there and then. And of course, she accepted. She called Helen and told her that Harry had come back and told her of her accepting his proposal. That night they met Helen and their mother Margaret to celebrate. Helen was wary about John's absence. Harry said that they had lost contact after they were re-assigned prior to the invasion but assured her everything would be okay and that he would check to establish his whereabouts. The next day, Harry set the wheels in motion to contact John."

"How on earth could he have expected to find him?" asked Connie, "I mean, there must have been thousands of guys who were transferred, de-mobbed, deserted even, lost in action and no witnesses. Even with the same name!"

"Well, find out he most certainly did. The Army's record was quite clear. John L. Martin had been killed in the first hours of the D Day landings. He learnt this the next day and suddenly realised that in the euphoria of his and Lorraine's happiness, they were going to have to tell Helen. When she was told she completely collapsed.

"You can imagine this put a great strain on the relationship of the two sisters as they found themselves at opposite ends of the emotional spectrum."

"What a dreadful situation," said Connie, "Oh, how I can really feel for them. But what happened then? I mean, Harry had to go back to the States and then go off fighting again."

"Yes, but fate or whatever you want to call it intervened for Harry and Lorraine. When he was half-way across the Atlantic the second atomic bomb was dropped on Japan and the war ended. He was discharged from military service within a month and came straight back to Scotland to claim his bride. They were married in Oban registry office and a week later had left for America."

"And poor Helen," sighed Connie, "whatever happened to her?"

"Well, she went into a state of deep despair. Her sister's leaving so enthusiastically for America compounded her sense of loss and, being the more introvert of the two – you know it was so sad; she and John were so well suited in character for each other – she left Oban and went back to the island and lived there alone until her mother decided to return as well."

"So they just lived there together, a widow and a widow of a lost love. Y'know," added Connie, "this is a really amazing story, but I just cannot see why you're telling me!"

"Bear with me, we're almost there. Harry and Lorraine moved away from New York and settled in Boston. She liked the coastal part of Massachusetts as it reminded her of her life on the west coast of Scotland. After two years of being blissfully married to Harry she gave birth to a girl who they called Helen after her aunt. When Helen was only two years old, her parents, the ever-buoyant Harry and the enthusiastic optimist Lorraine were killed in a head-on car crash on their way to collect their daughter from nursery school."

"You're kidding me!" said an astonished Connie.

"No," he replied back solemnly, "this story does seem to have its bleak moments, doesn't it?"

"I'll say," said Connie, "so what happened to the baby?"

"She was adopted by a kind, childless family who brought her up lovingly."

"Well, at least that was a move for the better. But why did that happen? I mean the adoption, did her family or Harry's family not want to look after the child?" asked Connie.

"Well," said Dougal Henderson, "it may seem strange to you, particularly in an age of the internet and more or less instant communication, but in the years during and following the war, such a great social upheaval had taken place all over the world that friend and family contacts were easily lost or neglected. Imagine, back on the island, both Margaret and her daughter were living in a state of reclusion. They had both suffered personal losses; they were not following the outside world. Our investigations showed that Harry's parents had divorced but we were unable to find any trace of them. So, at the time of the car accident, no one dealing with the aftermath had any contacts to follow, so baby Helen was placed with an orphanage and ultimately adopted."

"When did all this happen?" Connie asked.

"Harry and Lorraine married at the end of 1945 and their baby was born at the end of 1947 so the accident happened at the end of 1949. She was adopted sometime in 1950 when she was around two and a half.

"And now I have to tell you something, Connie," he said, leaning towards her. "The baby was adopted by a

Massachusetts couple, much the same ages as Harry and Lorraine, whose names were Albert and Lilian Chambers."

"What!" exclaimed Connie. "Albert and Lilian? They were called Albert and Lilian Chambers?"

"Yes," he said, eyeing her steadily. "And your…"

Connie cut him off abruptly and slowly spoke.

"My grandparents on my mother's side were called Albert and Lilian Chambers."

"The very same," he said, "and their adopted daughter, Helen Chambers, was…"

"My mother!" gasped Connie.

"Who married William Renton, with whom she had a daughter, Constance, who is sitting," he declared with a triumphant flourish, "right in front of me!"

EIGHT

No one in their right mind would attempt to sail or motor either east or west past Portland Bill without checking all weather, tide and current conditions. April was the month David had chosen to leave and although this time of the year offered the usual chance of showery weather, mainly from the west, it was nothing that would be that off-putting. No, the main thing about Portland Bill is The Race, and sailors often clear the Bill by as much as ten miles to the south to avoid the hazard. This is a powerful tidal current running in either direction which rips the water into a frenzied mass, at its worst when the wind is blowing against the tide. However, rather than pass to the south, there is another option. If the weather is reasonably stable, that is, either no wind at all or a gentle one that is with you, and the tide is on the turn towards the direction of the course chosen, the smart sailor will nip in between the tip of the Bill and a zone about a half a mile south which roughly marks the northern extremity of The Race. By taking this route in a timely manner it is a safe, quick and easy way of rounding this famous headland.

Although prone to the occasional tendency to reduce his mental alertness to an unacceptable level for sailing safely – due to being led astray in his local bar – on this morning David Gregson felt in remarkably vibrant form. His yacht, *Cassiopeia*, was ready for the journey. David had equipped her with everything he could think he would need and would only stop for water, some fresh provisions, possibly some fuel, or maybe just to break the journey if the weather dictated so.

He had planned his route to pass westwards along the south coast, northwards round Land's End, across the Bristol Channel to Wales and the South Pembroke coast and then across St George's Channel to County Wexford and up the Irish coast where he would make a deliberate stop at Dun Laoghaire, just south of Dublin. Here he would leave the boat at the marina for few days. David was planning a short break in Dublin, his old university city. He had spent seven wonderful years of his life at Trinity College where he did his degree in Marine Biology and then completing his time there doing his doctorate. He had made his arrangements to meet up with his old course tutor, Eddie McBride, and spend some time reminiscing, which was really an excuse for visiting all their old drinking haunts.

David had been watching the weather patterns over the last couple of days and it was clear that the time to go was perfect. A high-pressure system over the Baltic was sending a steady airflow from the east along the English Channel. With the tide due to turn westwards at about 10.30 the following morning, he would leave his mooring on the Wey a couple of hours before and slip past the headland at Portland Bill exactly as he had hoped he would be able to do. This would leave him clear to cross Lyme Bay for his first night's destination of Exmouth.

And so, having spent the day finalising everything and with his house nearby closed up, he settled in for an early night on his boat ready for the next morning's start.

The following day, 2nd April, he awoke to a clear blue sky with the promised easterly. David had chosen not to set his sails until he had passed the Bill to ensure that he reached it without having to risk any change in the wind.

He would use his engine for the short distance to be on the safe side. It was a strange mixture of elation and sadness that ran through him as he motored out of the short estuary of the River Wey and turned south to pass outside the long breakwaters of the Royal Naval base of Portland. Great warships no longer came here; that was of another age. So it also felt to David as he left Weymouth and the Institute behind that, it too, was of another age. He recognised this, but equally so – as when sailors over the years set out – new horizons awaited and that whilst there may eventually be coming back, there was no looking back. As he passed the Bill on the southern end of Portland, a group of guillemots flew off that angled block known as the Pulpit Rock and plunged into the water ahead of *Cassiopeia*. As he hoisted his sails, he thought it was a fitting farewell, a salute from his feathered friends.

The waters had behaved well and now that he was clear of any possible danger from the Race, he set his main sail and genoa on a starboard tack and set off across Lyme Bay on a comfortable broad reach towards Exmouth.

He had estimated the distance of the total journey to be about seven hundred nautical miles so that the stop off in Dublin would be about half-way. The idea was to take his time and enjoy the trip so he would not try to cover more than thirty or so miles a day and would stop each night at anchor or tied up in a harbour. Marinas he preferred to avoid except when conditions made it necessary. So with this daily target and allowing for some days when he would cover in excess of this and others when the weather dictated shelter, David considered Dun Laoghaire about eleven days away. With a further five days' stay in Dublin, that should give him the rest of the month to reach Oban. His estimated arrival date in Oban was 28th April.

The weather held well and the first night found him anchored off Exmouth. Thereafter, the easterly wind took him on via Dartmouth, Plymouth, St Austell and Falmouth.

By now the Baltic high had shifted eastwards and dissipated, allowing some more influence from the Atlantic. The wind began veering first southerly and then south-westerly by the time he reached Penzance. This held for him and he motored head-on into it to round Land's End and then sailed on north-eastwards towards the Bristol Channel. After six days of seeing the nights out at anchor he felt like a break so, after a pleasant sail with the wind blowing lightly from the south-west, he put into Newquay. Here his character defect set in and he found himself in a harbour-side pub amongst similarly minded people who seemed hell-bent on drinking Newquay dry.

The next day saw *Cassiopeia* sailing herself whilst the captain, greatly appreciative of the continuing gentle south-westerly, decided that a quiet anchorage on the south-east of Lundy Island would be a suitable palliative after the raucous behaviour of the people of Newquay.

He slept soundly, lulled by a persistent but gentle swell. Fully recovered, he set off early the next day and made a port beat from Lundy to Milford Haven for the night. A quiet night at anchor preceded a southerly change to the wind direction allowing a brisk crossing to Ireland for a stop-off in Wexford. Then, northwards up the Irish coast for a night in Arklow and the next day saw him calling up the marina in Dun Laoghaire as he passed Bray Head. By late afternoon, twelve days after leaving

Weymouth, he had reached the destination for his mid-voyage objective, a five-day break in Dublin.

David tied up his boat and, before going to the marina office to deal with the necessary paperwork, stood along the pontoon and looked at his beautiful *Cassiopeia*. She had performed well; he was well pleased with her. There was no doubt in his mind that this boat was going to serve him well. But of course, he would have to look after her.

Over the next five days this was probably what he was not going to do with himself.

As arranged, he rang Eddie McBride.

"Hallo?" answered a voice that had the wariness of someone trying to avoid a tax inspector.

"Ten years have gone by and you answer my call sounding like you're a man on the run."

"Just my little trick on the phone; keeps people at a respectful distance until I decide whether I want to speak to them or not. But Davey, Davey my boy, this is great, great; you're here, here at last! The gutters will be flowing tonight, man, and that's for sure. Where are you, where are you?"

"I'm in Dun Laoghaire," said David, "at the marina. I got here about an hour ago. I'm just tidying things up – should be about another hour, say by six thirty I'll be ready to leave."

"That's great," said Eddie. "Look, I'm just finishing a bit of marking so why don't you get the DART train up from Dun Laoghaire and get off at Pearse Street Station. It's about a fifteen-minute run and look, I'll meet you in the Windjammer – appropriately nautical. I know it's been ten years but I'll bet you haven't forgotten it."

"Not a chance, some of my greatest moments happened in that bar."

"Okay, give me a quick call when the train pulls out. I'll be in there waiting for you. I trust it will be the usual?"

"The usual."

"Oh, and bring a toothbrush," said Eddie. "You'll be staying with me."

As the train approached Pearse Street, David was charged with a boyish excitement. During the time that had elapsed since he had finished at Dublin he'd never been back again. This is amazing, he thought. All the fellow students he knew so well, all the non-university people he had met, none had the magic of Eddie, none had his special something. That's why I'm here, he thought. This guy is special to me.

He remembered it all so well. He turned right out of the station and there in front of him on the corner of the next block, as shabby as ever, stood the Windjammer. The 'early doors' bar it used to be called. It would open at seven in the morning for the dockers down at Ringsend. But he remembered the times when he had called in there with friends at half past seven for a couple of last pints on his way home from a party, the place would be a-buzz, just like another party.

In through the door, and there, at the bar, was the man himself. Two arms stretched out; one to greet and the other holding a freshly poured pint of stout.

"The drink first, man, the drink first!" said Eddie.

David drank, savouring the nostalgic taste of Guinness brewed in Dublin. They used to say you could tell Dublin Guinness from Guinness brewed anywhere else – something to do with the Liffey water. It was probably a myth, but a great one, nonetheless.

David put his glass down on the bar and turned to look at Eddie. For a moment, they just looked at each other and then, in enveloped arms, they patted each other's backs.

"I am tearful," said Eddie. "But I haven't had a happy cry for a long time. Where have you been in my life for these past years? I look back; you were not only my best student, you were my 'funnest' one, if there is such a word. How I have missed you, Davey."

David couldn't reply. He was, quite literally, speechless. He looked at this man who was almost twice his age. He was straight-backed; slightly built; white hair swept back; a neatly kempt short white beard and glasses. He wore dark-green cord trousers; brogues; a brown tweed jacket with leather elbow pads and, yes, with his hallmark braces for his trousers, the picture was completed. Tears rolled down David's cheeks unchecked, unashamedly.

"Here now, Davey, be careful and keep them away from the stout. There's enough water in it already."

And that fixed him. He couldn't speak but he just burst out laughing and hugged that old guy again.

"Sorry about this, Eddie, but it's just crazy being in this bar with you again. I mean, how many times have we been here?"

"Far more than was probably good for us. But we survived, although it was against the odds. Now let's get another one in and then we must go on to another bar. It's too dangerous to stay here."

"And you imagine it will be less dangerous in another bar?" suggested David.

"Not at all, the danger is that we might just stay here all night and there are other places we must visit. So after here where will it be?"

"Could we slip along to the Stag's Head?" said David.

"Great! Yes, an excellent choice, but before there we must do the Old Stand. You'll remember that was a favourite of mine. But let's drop by Kennedy's at the end of Westland Row on the way, a sort of oasis-stop before the walk along Nassau Street."

"How can I take five days of this?" pleaded David.

"And the nights," added Eddie, "don't forget the nights, Davey."

And so they continued, chatting, drinking, joking, and laughing. When they had done the next three bars, Eddie suggested that as they did indeed have five more days and nights of this he had taken the precaution of preparing a little food for them back at the college.

"I think it would be good judgement on our part if we were to pace ourselves. I have a good old Irish stew that's been in the oven for two days and some Spanish red to go with it. Are you on for that, Davey, as a way of completing your first night back in Dublin?"

"Sounds good to me," he said.

They walked back to his rooms in the grounds of Trinity. Emotional flashbacks were everywhere as they passed through what must be one of the most beautiful university campuses anywhere. It was his grandmother who had suggested Trinity to him when he was considering the possibility of a university education; break the mould, she had said, go to Ireland where they really know how to enjoy life. She was right on the money there.

Eddie had his rooms on the first floor of one of those beautiful Georgian buildings. A Professor's privilege and he had taken it without hesitation. As they entered, he handed David a bottle and a corkscrew.

"Would you open that now while I get the food on the table."

David pulled the cork to a sonorous pop and instinctively sniffed it. Wonderful! It was Eddie who had introduced him to the joy of Rioja wines during his period as an undergraduate and he had been eternally grateful. This is the real thing, he had said. Good as they were, most French wine producers were living on dubious reputations; can't see beyond the end of their own bouquets, he'd said. The memory of it was all so clear. He had been a mentor in so many ways.

After they had eaten, Eddie suggested that they relaxed in the armchairs with a bottle of Jameson's whiskey.

"This is the way to do it," said David. "So tell me, has Eleanor given you the night off for good behaviour?"

It wasn't an instant change that David noticed, more a sort of gradual slump into his armchair.

"You didn't know did you, Davey? Eleanor died a couple of years ago."

"What? Eddie – no, I didn't know, I'd no idea. I'm so sorry. We've been out of touch for some time; I never heard. She died? What…what happened? Why didn't you let me know?"

"For all my *bonhomie* with my friends, I was totally dedicated to my marriage. It was a wonderfully private business and I just didn't go around telling people about it and so when this happened, I had no need to tell the world. My grief was and always will be my own personal affair. And now I lose myself in my work.

"Eleanor died of pancreatic cancer just four months after it was diagnosed. They could do nothing. It's one of those violent cancers; they haven't got a treatment for it yet. And there are people who say there's a god. Maybe they'll crack it one day. I'm sure you remember her well. She was only a few years older than you are now when she died. When we married I had known her for only one year. She was thirty-two and I was nineteen years older than her – can you imagine it? I was fifty-one when we married. We had been married for ten years when she died."

He paused for a while, as if transfixed by his recollection and sipped a little of his drink. A still quietness descended on the room only broken by the sound of a branch from the creeper at the edge of the window intermittently touching against a pane in the night breeze.

David lay back in his chair, gazed vaguely into his glass and swirled the liquid round. The movement and amber colour of the whiskey helpfully distracted him. He just didn't know how to respond to his friend. After some moments he looked up at Eddie who caught his eye and carried on telling his tale.

"Did I ever tell you how I came to meet her?" he said, looking directly across to David.

"No," said David, "I remember the way you eased her into our lives. To us she didn't seem suddenly to appear on the scene. After a short while of first seeing her with you she somehow seemed as if she had always been there."

"That's it," said Eddie, patting the arm of his chair, "she was just so right. When I met her it was if I had been marking time waiting until then for her to be in my life.

"We met in a rather off-beat, or should I say, on-beat, manner. She hit me on the head with a fish."

This curious remark registered with David but he said nothing.

"I never learnt to drive a car, Davey. Being here at the university in the city centre obviated the need. Everything was, so to speak, on the doorstep. Some time before I ever met you I had taken to a rather curious activity. One Saturday morning I was taking a bus up to Howth to go and see someone and, probably due to a good night before, I wasn't paying attention and accidentally got on one going to Malahide. Well, I'd never been to the place before and thoroughly enjoyed the day out there. Thereafter, I decided that, every Saturday morning, whenever I could, I would simply go to a bus stop, not look at the timetable or the destination on the incoming bus and just ask the conductor for a ticket to the end of the line and get on and wait till I got there. Man, I saw dozens of places around Dublin, places you never dream of going to. Some were dreadful and I came straight back; others were wonderful and I would spend the whole day there. I used to love walking through the countryside. You see, deep down I must have felt that this was the antithesis to marine biology.

"Well, after a year or so of doing this, my mystery trips took me to Tallaght, which in those days was well out in the country – been engulfed by Dublin now. I remember stopping at a café in the village and having breakfast. I asked the waitress which direction I should go for a pleasant walk. I followed her directions and then just wandered aimlessly along lanes, pathways and across fields.

"It was while I was walking across a particular field that it happened. I recall a beautiful, breezy, sunny day with those white cumulus clouds being blown along when that trout landed on my head."

"A trout?"

"Yes."

"On your head?"

"That's it, on my head."

"Okay...ah yes, the fish!"

"My natural reaction, following that of surprise, was to look up; after all, I thought gravity should have had a part to play in this. Nothing was up there. I then noticed a movement in a thick, tall bank of vegetation, a little distance away on the edge of the field, and out of the foliage stepped a person clad in a dark-green coat and matching brimmed hat. The person was accompanied by a woman's voice apologising profusely for such an act of wanton carelessness but explaining that, as few people ever came along here, it was nothing short of – almost literally – a stunning co-incidence. I remember her saying that it would be a very good test for the Chaos Theory because, if we could work it back, we might have found out that, three weeks ago, somewhere, maybe in New Zealand, a cormorant had probably dived off a rock initiating a chain of events that resulted in this piscatorial percussion in Ireland.

"She then stood in front of me, took off her hat, and introduced herself as Eleanor Fitzgerald. As she swept her hat off her head a cluster of fine blond curls, parted on one side, fell across her blue-eyed, freckled face and I was done for. I couldn't have given a damn for any knock-on effect caused a bloody cormorant on the other side of the world. I was smitten, Davey, by this most extraordinary woman.

"She explained that she was using a method of fishing, taught to her by her father, which involved an old tank aerial – military green camouflaged it, rendering it branch-like to the fish – with a short length of thin line. A hook baited with a small flattened pellet made of bread paste completed the ensemble. She approached the little stream that meandered along the hedge-row, and, selecting a pool and passing the rod through the branches, she would flick the baited hook with her thumb into the water and watch it slowly sink in the peaty-brown water. As soon as it suddenly disappeared she knew it was in a fish's mouth. She then struck powerfully, pulling the fish, which, she informed me, was a brook trout, instantly out of the water, whereupon it would fly backwards over her head onto the grass, unless, of course it should hit an innocent passer-by.

"As a result of this introduction, she told me that her parents, who owned the farm and lived in the farmhouse which was through the next field, would be delighted to entertain this stranger to lunch based on the eight trout she had caught.

"So it was that I was fed freshly fried trout, introduced to her family and told her story. She was in fact a botanist. She was also an artist and was currently working on a commission for a firm of publishers in London, where she lived, who were awaiting her hand-painted flower illustrations. She had come home to Ireland to do the painting in peaceful surroundings. She had nearly finished the work and would be gone back to England within a couple of weeks.

"We fell in love: absolutely, immediately, totally in love. She came back from London to live and work in Dublin and within a year we were married. The rest is history, Davey, and sadly that woman who transformed my life so unexpectedly is no longer with me. You are the only person to whom I have ever told this story. Let me tell you, it is a measure of my feelings for you that my guard is down. Thank you for listening, it was quite cathartic for me. One last glass of that whiskey and then I am for my pit."

"Eddie," said David, "that was a remarkable story; I had no idea of this at all. So are you living permanently here now or do you still have that house, where was it...?"

"Rathmines; it's not far from here. No, after Ellie died the magic couldn't remain there. I had to take it somewhere else with me. So I came here and took up what I call my grace and favour residence. I seriously believe I've reverted to type but have the richness of those years to nourish me. I've a little while yet before they put me out to graze but I still enjoy seeing those freshmen arrive and watch them grow up or the odd one or two fall by the wayside. The latter I like to call natural de-selection."

"Eddie," said David, "I'm feeling a little emotional myself; I think I'll turn in too. On your invitation to stay I brought along a little more than a toothbrush, so I won't have to go back to the boat until I leave. What's the form for tomorrow?"

"I'm a little busy during the morning and things might become a bit involved as the day runs on. Look, have a lie-in, and amuse yourself in the town during the day or whatever. Do you remember Neary's Bar in Chatham Street?"

"Of course."

"Great, then let's meet there at, say, six o'clock and we'll put the world in order there. You're sleeping in the box room opposite the bathroom. It's a bit of a mess but the sheets are clean. 'Night, Davey, it's so good to see you again."

"Good night, Eddie, thanks for a great night and for your extraordinary story."

"Ah well, there could be a moral there somewhere; certainly was in my case. You spend your life going here, there and everywhere but to find what you don't even know you're looking for, you have to get on the right bus."

David got up to go to his bed, hesitated and turned to his host.

"But Eddie, surely you'd only know it was the right bus when it arrived at its destination and the events unfolded," he challenged.

"Yes, of course, but if you don't get on it, you'll never know."

"Well, I suppose that's true. Bit of a paradox, really," he mused.

"The point is, Davey, that while luck or chance comes into it, everyone has to be aware that such a thing as the 'right bus' does exist. It's really a bit of a metaphor for so many things in life – recognising and then trying not to miss the right bus. I was lucky; in my case I didn't recognise it but I didn't miss it."

"Serendipity, perhaps?" murmured David.

"Perhaps," conceded Eddie, "but the key is recognising it."

And with that, he disappeared to his bedroom.

The morning came and David's headache went. He was surprised that he was feeling so good. Eddie had already gone, so after he had showered and generally tidied himself up, he opened the front door of the building and stepped out into a spring Dublin morning. It was half past ten and he was going to see if an old favourite had stood the test of time. He turned left out of the college gates, walked along College Green, crossed over and walked up Grafton Street. About halfway along on the right he smelt that familiar aroma of freshly ground coffee. Yes, there it was, Bewleys, in all its understated glory. He walked in and took a seat at a table where a waitress asked for his order.

"A pot of fresh coffee, some soda bread toast, butter and some of your own marmalade," he managed to say coherently through a salivating mouth.

"Certainly, sir. Would you care for a copy of the morning newspaper?" she enquired.

"That would be most kind of you," said David.

He sat there looking around at the old wood-panelled coffee house. This was piece of Dublin history – an institution. As an undergraduate, when not conserving money for more frivolous activities, he used to treat himself occasionally to a breakfast here; it made him feel grown-up, even responsible. He could do this, every morning, during this visit to Dublin. That might show that he'd grown up, or at least that his financial position had improved.

After his late breakfast, he strolled up to St Stephen's Green and in a moment of inspiration he did something that he had never done anywhere before. He took a sight-seeing trip on one of those open-topped tourist buses. Eddie McBride would be impressed. It was a lovely morning and he wanted to see his old city. What better way? he thought.

The trip took an hour and a quarter and by the time he had disembarked he was feeling peckish enough to treat himself to a lunch time steak.

He let the afternoon drift slowly by. He ambled along familiar old streets noticing that many new shops and restaurants had opened up. This was change, certainly. After all, economies move on, tastes and styles change. That's what people are about. But looking up from street level, everything was the same. Those same old buildings that made Dublin what it was, they were standing the test of time. The Millennium Spire in O'Connell Street was new to him and didn't seem to fit in but he felt that way about millennium spires he'd seen in other cities. A stroll by the river, a quick snooze back at Eddie's rooms and he was out again for their six o'clock rendezvous at Neary's.

"There you are, man," said Eddie, "sure I never thought you were going to make it."

"But it's only two minutes past six," said David looking at his watch. "How long have you been here?"

"Three minutes, but I got here early and had a quick one."

"Well, let's get two more in," said David, rubbing his hands.

"I've already ordered them," said Eddie. "You know there are two types of drinker – the thirsty and the very thirsty. Right now I'm in the latter category."

"There is a third," said David, "the extremely thirsty and I'm in that category."

"Great, great! That's my boy, Davey."

And so it went on. They managed The Long Hall; Hogan's; Grogan's; Davy Byrne's; a repeat at the Old Stand.

"I think for completeness's sake we should go again and get one in at the Stags Head," said Eddie, "and then we're off up to the Shelbourne where I'm going to treat you to a char-grilled salmon and a bottle of wine with it. We'll carry on with the rest of them tomorrow night. In fact, tomorrow we'll take it easy. Sweetman's on Burgh Quay does a fine home-brewed stout on a hand pump that didn't exist in your day, and to miss The Palace on Fleet Street would be intolerable. Then we can dine at Nico's, a favourite little haunt of mine on Dame Street."

Oh well, thought David, only three more nights to go.

And he managed it. Eddie had Olympian qualities when it came to an extended session and this was a marathon. But by the time his five days were up, David was still there with him. As Eddie had said, he was his best student and he had taught him everything he knew. The master and the pupil were as one.

Nonetheless, by the time it came for David's departure there were certain parts of his body that were begging for a reprieve. His liver had done magnificently and he was truly grateful that nature had provided him with two kidneys. Luckily, his schedule had come to his rescue.

So the morning after his fifth night in Dublin, David took the train down to Dun Laoghaire. Eddie walked with him down to the station at Pearse Street.

"Let's see, now," said Eddie, "The Windjammer should be open now, it's half past eight."

"Absolutely and emphatically, no!" said David.

"Well, you're quite right, of course, you have a boat to sail and you need to keep your wits about you. I, on the other hand, have a group of first-year students to lecture to so when you've departed I might just go and ..."

"Eddie, you're incorrigible! Come on, give us a hug, I've got to be on my way."

"All right," he acquiesced. "Thanks for coming to see me. Don't make it so long before the next time. And Davey, you're having a rare old time and all that, but life can be a bit of a narrow corridor. It's good to share it, widens your perspective. You don't want to end up a lonely old sod like me. You know what I mean?"

"The right bus?" responded David.

"The right bus," said Eddie.

He settled with the marina and by eleven, having bought a few fresh provisions and topped up his water tanks, was on his way. A brisk westerly saw him around Howth Head and he then headed northwards where he planned to stop the night at Carlingford Lough. From there he continued a short distance to Strangford Lough where he had always intended spending two nights. This was a large, well-protected sea lough scattered with little islands and a famous tern location. He was on the lookout for that most beautiful of them all, the rare Roseate Tern, but it was a little early in the year and he wasn't hopeful. Strangford Lough, however, was one of its few breeding grounds and they would return from wintering in West Africa to breed. Mid-May was the usual time and in spite of conducting his vigil for a whole day from the deck of *Cassiopeia*, he saw none.

With winds generally blowing to the east from off the land, David continued his journey northwards. He anchored off Bangor in County Down and stopped at the ferry terminal port of Larne before putting into Ballycastle on the north Antrim coast. He had planned to leave there for Scotland and sail north-eastwards between Islay and the

Kintyre Peninsula to the little island of Gigha, but the weather forecast predicted a frontal system coming in from the west within twelve to eighteen hours. This was not a problem as such because it gave him the option of passing to the east of Kintyre and, being protected from the west by the peninsula, he could sail on up past Campbeltown and cross over by the Crinan Canal. As it turned out, he went into Campbeltown Loch and anchored while the system passed by. The cold front that followed the depression gave him an excellent sail all the way to Ardrasaig which is the small port at the eastern end of the canal. He stopped here and teamed up with two other boats that were taking the canal to Crinan on the other side. By doing the locks in a group it helped spread out the workload operating the lock gates. They stopped the night at the pool at the high mid-point of the canal and descended the following morning to Crinan Pool.

He had never been through the canal before and as it was such a beautiful sunny morning for the descent, he decided that he would stop at the little port of Crinan for the night. He passed a pleasant evening there, finding a small bar with some fellow sailors and they jawed away the time with the usual stories

The following morning the weather was very calm and David motored much of the way up to Oban only putting up his sails for the last 15 miles or so after passing west of the island of Luing. He arrived at Oban late on the afternoon of 28th April, as planned, twenty-seven days after leaving Weymouth. His priority was to moor up in the marina at the north-east end of the island opposite Oban, have a good rest and then work out a schedule for the next three months.

NINE

The impact of Dougal's conclusion left Connie's jaw hanging.

She had just been delivered a moving story that covered a significant time span about a family in two continents that meant absolutely nothing to her and yet, as the story progressed, she became more and more absorbed in it, empathising with the people involved and, as it unwound, she found herself as a character in the final part of the story with the revelation that the adopted child, Helen, was the same Helen as her mother. Her own mother! Dougal had put it together so well that, although she still did not know why he had come to tell her this story, she felt a warmth towards the people involved that drew her more and more into it. It was as if he had been gently teasing out her interest so that by the time of the *dénouement*, she had unwittingly become part of the drama.

"Mr Henderson!" she exclaimed. "What have you done here? An hour ago you came as a complete stranger to my house and just an hour later you've turned my life upside down. This is incredible. I hardly know which way to turn."

"I have to say it is a most pleasing outcome. It seems your life has many unexplored by-ways but maybe now you can bring it all together. Family histories are often quite involved but I must say this one is particularly interesting."

"Wow!" said Connie. "Interesting? This is downright staggering."

"Well, I'm glad that we have been able to make so many discoveries for you," continued Dougal.

"Y'know, Mr Henderson, I knew that Gramps and Grannie-Lil had adopted Mom but it was never something we ever talked about, like sort of once mentioned then forgotten because it just didn't seem to matter. They were a lovely old couple who died quite some time ago and all I had were lovely memories of them when I was a small child. I used to go and visit them back up in the north-east. They lived Vermont way. As far as I was concerned they were my grandparents and that was that.

"I guess with Dad's work we moved all over the place and saw less and less of them. It seems an age since they passed away. I never knew anything about my actual grandparents until you told me now. Killed in a car crash when my mother was two, you say? Isn't it weird how such a thing can pass into history? I guess as part of the adoption process you kinda become part of a new family, part of a new history. Just think I could have been a Zielinski – well, I was – with a Polish branch to the family. Did you pick up anything on that side?"

"No," said Dougal. "We were concentrating on finding you. Any follow-ups like that would have been an unnecessary distraction from the object of our exercise. What we did discover was your Scottish heritage. I have a very detailed dossier for you to keep and who knows, you may find something of interest to follow up. You just never can tell."

"Say, Mr Henderson," interjected Connie, "that kinda leads me to ask you something that's been in my mind since you began the story. You tell me you were looking for me, searching for me, kind of officially. Why? What on earth could have prompted you to do all this investigation just to find me and tell me this amazing story? Like I said, I'm at a loss here."

"Well, isn't that interesting? I was wondering how we were going to get around to it."

"Get around to it?" queried Connie.

"Yes," said Dougal. "You see, I was telling you about your grandmother's Scottish history and how her sister Helen had stayed put on the island after she had been told that John L. had been killed at the outset of the Normandy landings. Well, the simple fact is that she never met anyone else, never married, she never had any children and also various members of her family died of illness or old age until finally she was the only one of the McKechnies left. It does sound rather sad, her life just unused, but there are people like that and she was one of them.

"Sadly, back in February, old Helen, your great-aunt, died, and as executor of the family's affairs, it was left with me to attend to her last will and testament. She had deposited it with me about eighteen months ago when she was coming up to eighty-six. I suppose she was reaching a stage when she felt things needed to be tidied up. She had heard some years after about her sister's death, of how she and Harry had been killed in that car crash but didn't know what had happened to her sister's daughter. It may seem strange to you that she never followed this up but Helen was a very reserved and increasingly lost soul – she just never got over the death of John and then finally her own mother died. With her solitary life on the island, she just turned inwards and even when she finally gave up island life to come and live in Oban, she rarely went out and, although she had acquaintances from over the years, she wasn't involved in town life."

"It's so sad, Mr Henderson," said Connie. "I feel almost guilty about her being neglected by her family, me being one of them. But I guess I shouldn't feel that way. After all, I never even knew of her. But even so…"

"You mustn't let it get to you, Connie. Anyway, let's shift the emphasis back to where we were: why I am here. You see, I needed to tell you the story of your family to lead to a fundamentally practical – and indeed, legal – issue.

"The point is, Connie, that you are the inheritor of your great-aunt Helen's estate."

"The what?" gasped Connie.

"The inheritor," Dougal stated.

"I…I…but…how…?" she stammered.

"Indeed, yes, the inheritor. You are the inheritor." He said it slowly, so that it might sink in.

"Her will was very clear: she wanted to leave everything to her niece Helen, her sister Lorraine's daughter. She discussed this with me at length particularly as she had no idea where the girl was or even if she was alive. Helen gave me the very limited information that she possessed and asked that in the event of her death I should do all that I could to find either her niece or, if she had died, her offspring. If there were more than one, the estate should be divided equally according to how many children there were. She was also quite clear that if any or all of them were deceased, or we were unable to find any trace of her niece in the first place, my firm should set up and administer a trust with the proceeds of the sale of the estate for the benefit of local causes in the Oban area.

"Well," said Dougal, "now that we have found you, none of these alternatives is relevant."

Connie just sat there staring at Dougal Henderson but focussed beyond him. Out of the window, in the distance, large white clouds were billowing up against the blue sky. It looked a beautiful day out there, so clean and clear. Oh, how she would rather be out there, not having to take in all this confusion. Such a lot had happened to her this year. Carl's death had given her a clear opportunity to re-invent herself, a chance to find a life that had eluded her. She had spent restless nights until deciding that she would return to the States. She had mapped out a plan for her and the children and that had settled her: she knew what she was going to do. But now this. What can it all mean? She had to respond to this situation. She couldn't ignore the fact that she was inheriting something – she had to be positive. So what was this estate that her great-aunt had left her? She refocused on Dougal.

"I'm sorry; I was just, like, drifting away there with my thoughts. So, I'm to inherit part of Scotland then?" she said, smiling with a reassured confidence. "I think you'd better tell me about it. But hey, it's coming up to lunchtime and I haven't prepared anything so why don't we slide across to my local pub and we can have a sandwich and a drink?"

"I shall be taking an evening flight back to Edinburgh. My short visit to the Capital would be incomplete without visiting a London pub; so lead on, lead on to the watering hole!"

They walked the short distance across the cobbled street to The Guardsman. As they approached the pub, where a few people stood outside with their drinks, chatting and taking advantage of the weather, Dougal remarked at the unexpectedness of the pub's setting.

"I can hardly believe I'm in one of the largest, busiest cities in the world and yet, here we are in a sort of backwater, seemingly far away from the metropolis. It's so tranquil and the styles of the old buildings seem to make it feel from another world. I mean, look at every house, they're all different and you have mature trees growing in the street. What a wonderful place to have a house in."

House, yes, Connie thought, but not a home, no, never a home. Although she had loved the house and its location from the moment she saw it, living there had been an unshared time. But she was pleased that Dougal liked it enough to have given it his seal of approval.

"Yeah," she responded, "you couldn't ask for a better spot – and so close to a pub too. It was used for a time as the officers' mess for one of the Guards regiments and I guess the name stayed. It's my little bolthole; it's nice to come in here, even alone. I know the bar people now and some of the regulars. I just love that peacefulness you mentioned. The street is a dead-end, no cars come through, and the only way out other than turning back is through foot passages."

They went up the steps into the pub and Dougal continued to wax eloquent after they had entered. But Connie was curious to find out what he had to say about the inheritance and so she suggested they take a table in a more private part rather than stand at the bar. Of course all of this was preceded by ordering their drinks. He may have been in London but Dougal chose his allegiance with the malted barley. A glass of beer for Connie and rare beef sandwiches completed their order and they sat down.

"Okay, Mr Henderson," said Connie, "tell me."

"Well," he began, "I am going to give you the general picture. The details are a matter for documentation and of course you will have to see these at my offices where there will be papers to sign – though of course you may choose to be represented. It will all be dealt with under Scottish law which is of course different from that of the rest of the United Kingdom."

"Oh, c'mon, Mr Henderson, just give me the outline then..."

"Surely so, surely so," he accepted.

At that point their sandwiches arrived.

"Now those look excellent," said Dougal. "However, they may do well-filled sandwiches down here but I've never been impressed with their drink measures. I think a large one might be required."

"I see what you mean," laughed Connie. "Could we have the same again," she said to the person who brought the sandwiches, "but with my friend's measure improved upon?"

Their drinks arrived and Dougal continued.

"Well, your great-aunt owned over a thousand acres on the western end of the island of Kerrera, a house next to the shore that she lived in, and also a number of crofting cottages. Much of the land is used for grazing by sheep, the sheep being owned by different tenant crofters on the island who pay a rental. There is some very good fertile land alongside a group of streams that converge in the bay and that too is rented out to crofting farmers. I should tell you that a small part of her property was left in her will to a young Englishman she had befriended, a scientist who spent a number of summers doing research on the island. She left him an empty cottage in need of repair – she always referred to it as 'the ruin', but with a small stretch of land – on the north coastal part of her property. He had actually stayed at her house. She was very fond of him and he always found this spot a very beautiful place. Away from the island, she owned a house in Oban that had been in the family since the two sisters moved from the island to the town. This was the house she moved to when she finally left the island. Your great-aunt, besides being frugal, was also shrewd enough to invest the money she earned from renting her land and over the years acquired a considerable sum of money. At the moment, there is cash in her bank and an investment portfolio – the latter was managed for her by the bank – of a total value in the region of around one hundred thousand pounds. So other than the 'ruin' and the piece of land around it, that is what your great-aunt Helen has left to you."

"My god! That's some bankroll of money. Jeez! So what's the house on the island like?" asked Connie.

"Ah, Ardbeg. It's a solid stone building with three bedrooms, not at all like the typical crofter's single-storey cottage. It's also in a fine setting close to the sea with wonderful views. I wouldn't want to sound like I am trying to sell it to you but it really is a fine residence by any standards."

"How come she owned so much land? You told me that it was, what was the expression you used, subsistence farming, y'know, they made ends meet and sold off any surplus to make actual money?"

"Well," said Dougal, "this was all part of the guilt that burdened Hamish. You see, when the First World War broke out, many of the young men from the villages along the coast and on the islands joined the local regiments to go and fight in France. As you know, the carnage was sometimes on a horrific scale. Whole platoons, companies, were wiped out, often containing men all from the same locality back home. I should say that this was not confined to the west coast or Scotland as a whole; this happened right through the country, and communities in England, Wales and Ireland suffered enormous losses too, such that in many cases very few of the young men came back home to their villages.

"On the island, land that had been worked by the young sons often had no one return to it. Hamish was one of the lucky ones, but crofts that were worked by his friends fell into disuse, their owners either too old or too dispirited by their losses. He tried to help them out but working individual crofting lands as well as his own was a physical and administrative nightmare. So Hamish gradually bought up the contiguous properties and eventually made up a single crofting farm of over a thousand acres. But the poor man always felt that he had taken something away from these people. The reality was that they were probably grateful to him. But he could never see it that way."

"So," said Connie, "that is what has been left to me?"

"Except for the 'ruin'," he added.

"Sure, okay, except for the little 'ruin'," repeated Connie. "But what does it all mean, what do I do next? How do I deal with such an inheritance?"

"Well," said Dougal, "we need to undergo the process of probate. This is the legal acknowledgement of the inheritance and you then become the owner of what she left you. The land, the houses and the money become yours."

"I understand that but what I mean is what do I do with it? I don't know if you know, though I guess it must have turned up in your and Mr Denholm's searches, but my husband was killed in an accident in Saudi Arabia in January and as a result I have decided to go back to the States with the children. I'm putting the house in London on the market and we are due to go back in June. That's only about two and a half months away. I am advised by the real estate people that I should have no trouble with a quick sale but we'll probably not go back until the house is sold."

"Well, I suppose it's first things first," said Dougal. "Before anything can happen we must deal with the probate and I can get that underway tomorrow. But are you telling me that you basically have no interest in the inheritance?"

"Mr Henderson, you must understand that I have to rearrange my life right now. I do not know Scotland at all.

I don't even know where Argyll is let alone Oban. I must put my children first and right now I have to sort out a new home and school for them across the Atlantic. I don't wish to sound ungrateful or avaricious; the money is not a problem – but what can I possibly do with crofting farmlands and two houses in the west of Scotland?"

"Well, obviously you could choose to sell them, though it had passed my mind that you might like to see them first before making any hasty decision," Dougal suggested.

"That's very thoughtful of you, Mr Henderson, and under other circumstances I would have to agree with you. But I've explained my position. No, please go through the probate issue and I sure am happy for you to represent me. I'll then be in a position to sell the properties. My mind is quite clear. I cannot be sentimental over this. The family side of the matter does affect me. I have to admit that I will live forever with the extraordinary story you have brought to me, no matter where I am."

"In which case, Connie, let me settle our bill for lunch and we must go back to your house so I may collect my case. I have some documents there for your retention – details of the inheritance – and even a map or two so you can find out where Argyll and Oban are," he added dryly.

"I'm sorry, Mr Henderson, but I just hope you understand."

"Aye, sure enough, these things are never easy."

They made their way back to Connie's house and when he had explained all he could and handed over the papers, they made their farewells. As he was about to get into his taxi Connie gave him a light kiss on his cheek and took his hand.

"Thanks so much for all you've done and for coming down to see me. I'll wait to hear from you on the probate. That story of my great-aunt Helen has really gotten to me. Y'know, it may have had its sadness, but it's kinda filled a void in my life that I didn't know existed. Thank you, Mr Henderson," said Connie with sincerity.

He looked at her, sensing the depth of her feelings, detecting in himself a closeness to her that surprised him.

"For one moment, I thought you were going to call me Dougal," he confided with a gentle smile.

As the taxi drew away she waved. When it had disappeared out of view she remained standing there, detached from the reality of what had happened, looking at the empty street.

TEN

There is something uniquely special about the end of a day's sailing: the boat safely tied up; the silence that follows the wash of the water around the hull; the quietness after the wind in the rigging and, most especially, the peace of that moment when the engine is switched off. And then the well-earned drink with your friends on board. But, after completing a month-long solo navigation, the sense of achievement verges on that of triumph. And why not? The whole thing has been planned and seen through by you and carried out with a clear objective. So why not open a bottle and drink to your success?

And that's exactly what David did. On this occasion, though, he opened his fridge and took out a cold, cold beer, and drank to himself. That was what he needed and he decided that before going and checking in at the marina, he would have another one straightaway: the first one was vital – the second delicious. He had known the people who ran the marina from previous years and, having decided to keep *Cassiopeia* there, had been in contact with them before he left. He had radioed in on approach and they were expecting him. The paperwork done, he had a quick snack and then by six in the evening he had crashed out on his bed and in no time at all was fast asleep. Fresh air, physical activity and the plain emotional success of his journey ensured that he slept like a log until he awoke at seven the following morning, spending the first few waking moments wondering where the hell he was.

As he lay there, taking in the task that lay ahead of him, he decided that today, 29th April, he would probably just potter about his boat getting everything tidied up prior to going into Oban. However, before that, he needed to hire a small motor launch and he had asked the people at the marina if they could check with their clients to see if one would be available for a three-month hire. David needed the launch to travel locally and, in particular, to the tern islet. He wanted to keep *Cassiopeia* as his base, safely in the marina, and to use the much faster launch for getting about. He had two days to arrange and take charge of the launch, as he needed to be at the islet by 1st May. This was of importance to him for a very particular reason. Some four years ago, after David had chosen this location to tag the terns, he had spoken on his first visit to the owner of the house close to the islet – the person who would become his good friend, Helen McKechnie – and she had told him that this colony of terns was remarkable for the fact that the first ones returned on 2nd May every year and that within four days the complete colony was in place. He wanted to be there on the first of the month to see that none had yet arrived and then be there before daylight on the second to see the first ones arrive. He had followed this ritual for the previous three years and it had been repeated like clockwork. It never quite ceased to amaze him.

He got up and made himself some breakfast. The morning was welcomingly sunny and he sat out on the deck with some toast and a cup of coffee. Bewleys took some beating, he thought, but this place is in a class of its own. Billy Kilpatrick, who ran the marina, had promised to check first thing that morning about the launch. When David arrived at the office, Billy, blue eyes sparkling, was waiting for him with a confident look on his face.

"Well," he beamed, pushing his sweep of blond hair back from his forehead, "this must be your lucky day, David. Not only have I located the very thing for you, but the owner's over in Oban now. He's thinking of taking the boat out of the water for its annual anti-fouling and service and was planning on leaving it out until he's up here at the end of August. Here, I've got his mobile number for you. You'll need to catch him this morning, because I think he's off back down to Glasgow later today."

"Thanks, Billy," said David, "that was quick; what's he like?"

"Och, he's a fine man, George Coulter. We always call him Doddie. He's been coming here for years. We've looked after this boat and his previous ones. I told him about you and he seemed quite happy to consider a rental. Come on, his number's in the office."

"Thanks, Billy."

"No problem."

He returned to his boat and called the owner. Since he was coming back to the marina in his boat later that morning they agreed to meet there around mid-day. That gave David time to get on with restoring some order to his boat. The most immediate thing was a general tidy-up after his journey and then the rearranging of the forward cabin as his work area. Although it would be his main living area, he would use the saloon as his office and table as his desk. Whilst doing this he kept an eye out for the incoming launch of George Coulter. Sure enough, around twelve o'clock he saw a boat pull out from the harbour and turn in the direction of the marina. He walked around to the reception pontoon and awaited its arrival. It was only a ten-minute run from the harbour and when the launch arrived, David took the mooring lines and tied her up. It wasn't particularly new but he could tell straight away that it was just what he needed. The bright yellow hull and red and blue deck brought a smile to his face but, importantly, the launch was protected by a slightly scratched but serviceable windscreen. It had a small cabin with a door and an aft section with open sides and bench seats.

"Hi there, so you must be David Gregson," observed the owner, as he jumped off his boat onto the pontoon. "George Coulter," he said, offering his hand, "make it Doddie, though. Look, I have to be away fairly soon so shall we go and talk about this over a coffee?"

"Good idea," agreed David.

They walked over to the marina office to find Billy.

"Okay," he said, after giving them their coffees, "I'll leave you guys to it. If you need anything else just give me a shout. I'll be in the workshop."

They went through the niceties of introduction. It didn't take long. Doddie was perfectly happy about what David wanted to use the boat for and was comfortable that it would be in safe hands.

"Actually, it's quite neat this arrangement. I was going to lift her out until late-August when I come back up for a wee holiday with the family but if you're going to be using her it'll save me the cost of the in and out lifts and using her will help keep the hull clean. So what shall we settle on then? I know Billy well and he's recommended you, so that's good enough for me. I won't need any contract or anything like that."

They agreed a mutually acceptable rental for three and a half months and David agreed to pay him up front.

"We'll have to go across to Oban to the bank," said David.

"That's fine," said Doddie Coulter. "You can give me a lift back and I'll explain the basics of the boat to you on the way over. I was going to have to get Billy to give me lift over in any case."

It was all settled quickly. Doddie sat in his car and wrote out a receipt for the rental money.

"Oh, by the way," said Doddie, "I meant to tell you: there's an inflatable dinghy and foot-pump in the rear locker. Oars only, though you can use the back-up auxiliary to the main outboard motor on the launch if you need to. Oh aye, and there's a small twelve-volt fridge in the cabin. "

Better and better, thought David.

As Doddie Coulter drove away, David suddenly felt hungry. He decided to stroll over to a pub at the town end of the quay to get something to eat and as he was doing so his mobile phone rang. It was Dougal.

"David, it's Dougal Henderson here. Tell me, man, where are you? On the high seas? Are you getting near to us?"

"Dougal!" exclaimed David. "I'm here, right here in Oban. I got here yesterday evening and I've been settling in at the marina. Right now I'm on my way to that little bar at the beginning of the quay for a quick bite. How are you set to join me?"

"I can't see why I shouldn't stop what I'm doing. A first-rate idea. Just give me five minutes and I'll be there."

David was settled at the bar with a beer when Dougal joined him. He got up and hugged his old friend.

"I seldom make public displays of affection but in your case, I'm prepared to make one of my exceptions," Dougal said with his usual dry delivery. "So good to see you again. Happier circumstances than on the previous occasion."

"And somewhat sunnier. If I remember the day of Helen's funeral it was appropriately damp and sad. This is much more like it. On a day like today there's no place on earth that compares," said David, in elated mood. "What'll you have, Dougal?"

"In order that I might welcome you back to Oban I think a wee dram of the large variety would be fitting."

The barman, hearing this and also knowing Dougal well, proceeded to deal with matters.

"David," confessed Dougal, "I was going to ring you to ask you to come and see me when you'd arrived in Oban. It's quite fortuitous that you're here now. We can have our meeting sooner than I'd been expecting. But look, this is no place to be talking about what I need to see you about and I have a rather pressing matter this afternoon. How about meeting over dinner this evening, are you free at all?"

"Fine," replied David. "Shall we eat at the restaurant in the hotel I stayed at for Helen's funeral?"

"Excellent," agreed Dougal. "I'll pick you up here outside the bar, say seven thirty. That all right for you?"

"Perfect. I'll be here."

"Good, I'll book the table."

Following Dougal's departure, David had a light snack in view of the pending dinner arrangement and then returned to the marina. He soon put the evening's occasion out of his mind as he tested Doddie Coulter's boat and put it through its paces. It was a good boat. Five metres in length, fenders for both sides and a twenty-five horsepower outboard engine with a four horsepower spare in case of problems with the main one. He took the boat up to twenty knots. It was ideal.

Later that evening, equipped with his launch, David set off to meet Dougal. He moored up alongside the quay near the Oban lifeboat. This seemed a secure place and was about a ten-minute walk back to the bar where they had arranged to meet. He would see about a more suitable location to keep the launch in due course.

David arrived at their meeting point about five minutes before the appointed time in order to be ready. Dougal was a punctual man, and at exactly half-past seven his car drew up. David opened the door, got in, and they pulled away immediately.

Inside the hotel they relaxed at the bar with aperitifs and on being questioned about his journey David ran through the salient points of his month on *Cassiopeia*.

"You'd never get me on a boat in a month of Sundays," said Dougal. "I took the ferry to Mull many years ago and although it was only a short trip, I was introduced to sea-sickness for the first time. I had never known such illness before; all I wanted to do was just die, there and then. I swore that I would never set foot on a boat again. D'you not ever get sick yourself?"

"All sailors suffer from it from time to time. I certainly have but very rarely these days. It's absolutely true that you get sea-legs eventually. There are numerous brands of tablets that you can take to prevent it happening but so far none that I've found to rid you of it once you've got it. For me, just to lie down for a while usually works."

"Well, I'm a confirmed landlubber myself. I like flying, though."

The waiter came up to them with their menus and they spent a short while deciding their choices. For their wine, Dougal chose a red Burgundy – a Volnay.

"You'll forgive me, David, for choosing an old favourite, but I can't resist the wines from that part of France. When my wife Fiona was alive we once spent a long weekend in the Burgundian town of Beaune. We stayed at a rather unusual *chambres d'hôte* that was actually owned by and on the premises of a wine producer, Fatien Père et Fils. I remember it so well. Wonderful wines! I was a dedicated follower from that moment on."

"Not a problem for me, Dougal," he said, remembering Eddie McBride and his very clear views on the matter. He'd make his move later, he thought, as their starting course arrived.

David was by now becoming curious to know what it was that Dougal wanted to tell him but he knew his friend well enough to let him bring the subject up in his own good time. Dougal was a solicitor after all and didn't all legal people enjoy the drama of timing and delivery?

Before their next course, David suggested to Dougal that he might like to try a second wine with their meal.

"By all means, David, please choose away."

He signalled to the waiter who opened the wine list for him to inspect. He immediately selected a Rioja and in so doing noticed Dougal raise his eyebrows.

They were well into their second course and bottle when Dougal began.

"No doubt you'll be wondering why I have asked you to join me tonight, David. I can assure you it wasn't so that I could be introduced to a wine that I would never have dreamt of trying, though may I say that this Spanish red you have chosen is a most pleasantly different style to my usual choice, and well-priced, too," he added pragmatically.

Eddie, thought David, I'm passing on the good word.

"Well, now," continued Dougal, "what I have to tell you is that you have become the inheritor of a wee property here in Argyll."

David put his glass gently down and tilted his head quizzically to one side, then placed his elbows on the table, rested his chin on his hands and looked directly into Dougal's eyes and listened.

"It's quite straight-forward, really. Sometime before our old friend Helen McKechnie died, she came to see me to execute her final will and testament. As you know she'd been living in her house in Oban for some years, only going back to the island during the best summer months and always when you came up here. She loved those days because you always made the house there seem alive again.

Now you remember that old croft on the north side of the island that was actually on the most eastern part of her property, Banmellach?"

"Yes of course," said David.

"Well, she left it to you and the walled-off land surrounding it. The parcel of land goes down towards the little beach. She was absolutely adamant that you should have it. She told me of the times you would walk over there and sit and look across the sea to Mull and the mainland further north. She told me that you considered it the most peaceful place on earth. Well, it seems that she thought no one else deserved to own such a place unless they felt about it like you did. She had altered her will to make this proviso for you. So now, David, you are a landowner. How about that then?"

He continued to sit there, transfixed, as Dougal's face broke into a warm smile. Leaning back and taking a sip of his wine, David said the only words that would come into his head:

"Not possible," he managed to utter. "You're telling me that Helen has left me Banmellach? That's just incredible. I…well…It can't possibly be true!"

"Oh it's true, right enough," said Dougal; "she's given it to you, the whole lot – it's all yours. The probate's been cleared and all we now have to do is deal with the land registry, then it'll be legally yours."

David took a long drink of his wine and then topped up their glasses.

"Dougal, what does this mean? I can't come and live in the place. I'll just be an absentee landlord. What do I do with it? I don't even know how large the land is or what condition the house is in."

"Well, David, according to the registered deeds the official area is just over twenty hectares, which in old language approximates to about fifty acres, a typical croft land with a house. The house is not an original croft house but is a well-built two-storey stone house. The roof has lost a few slates though. It'll certainly need a little money spending on it."

"It was so kind of her to do this but I can't even begin to think of the ramifications of owning it."

"Well, you could live there, why not?" said Dougal. "It's a wonderful place and I know you love it up here."

"But it would be so impractical. I have to work, you know. And I don't have the money to do it up. I'll be finishing my project here by the end of August. I've already made a number of job applications."

"Don't worry about it now, man, just look upon your good fortune that someone thought enough of you to give you a piece of the most beautiful land that exists. Let's continue enjoying the evening. We still have wine left and another course to come and afterwards, I think that a dram in front of the fire will be beckoning us."

They sat in front of the smouldering, glowing logs and sipped their whiskies, a sensation of repleteness enhancing their gravitational collapse into the comfortable armchairs. Dougal swirled his glass and contemplated its contents. After some moments he turned to his companion and spoke slowly, calmly, clearly content in the equanimity of their surroundings:

"Y'know, David, every man has his favourite whisky. Me? Well, I'm an Oban man and this Oban malt is the man for me. But had I come from Tain, for example, up past Inverness, I'd have probably been a Glenmorangie man. Whiskies become special, you see, become part of us."

He paused to savour a sip.

"A rather nice little story for you," he offered. "The whisky world, you see, is a close-bound lot, almost a sort of family, friends but rivals. Well, following the passing away of an old distillery owner, two of the more eminent members of that fraternity, a Mr Teacher and a Mr Dewar, decide to travel to the funeral together. On the way they decide to stop at a hostelry for a dram before the service. Dewar asks the barman for two Dewars. When they have finished, Teacher suggests they should have one more before leaving and asks the barman for two more Dewars. When they are walking back to the car, Dewar says to Teacher: 'That was very decent of you, old man. When it was my round I ordered my whisky and when it was your round you ordered mine too. I would have expected you to have ordered yours.' 'Och, no,' says Teacher, 'as it's a rather solemn occasion we are going to, I didnae think it would be a good idea for us to go there reeking o' whisky'."

Dougal closed his eyes and laughed quietly with satisfaction, enjoying the moment, well pleased with his amusing joke.

David chuckled out loud in appreciation of a good story well told. Dougal was such a wonderful character. I'm so fortunate, he thought, to be here enjoying myself with such an extraordinary person. But that's the point, isn't it? It's not just the place, it's the people too. It doesn't matter really where you live if the people are right. But get the combination together, well…

ELEVEN

The real estate company – she could still not get used to the way the British called them estate agents – that Connie had selected was a small boutique-type outfit that specialised in properties within that particular area of London where Connie lived. She had bought the house privately through a personal contact so she had no idea what to expect when she walked in through the front door and presented herself.

She explained her situation to the young man behind one of the desks and when he realised that the house in question was one of those rare opportunities, he asked if she would wait for a moment while he asked one of the senior partners to join them. A tall, slim, bespectacled woman in her thirties came through and introduced herself. Her dark hair was piled up in a French pleat and Connie thought she looked like someone who was actually modelling the heavy, black-rimmed, ridiculously large glasses she was wearing. She was of course delighted that Connie had chosen them and assured her of a first class and discreetly efficient service which Connie thought made her sound like they were a private clinic dealing with embarrassing disorders of the uro-genital system.

They explained to Connie that the property in question was client specific and that whilst it was eminently saleable, they would recommend that the type of client they had in mind would be one who would enable Connie to maximise the return on the sale of her house – in other words, thought Connie, you'll get the highest commission that way. But no matter, it suited her to wait as she wasn't going to rush back to the States but she did emphasise that, as she wanted to leave London in July, they had only about two months to complete the business. She didn't tell them that she was not intending to leave until the house was sold, though she thought the two-month deadline should keep them on their toes.

Connie agreed the terms with the senior partner and settled on a day later in the week for their technical surveyor and valuer to come and visit the house to prepare everything for the sales brochure.

With that matter in order, Connie returned home and did a bit of tidying-up. She was off to Amanda's house later on for an early supper with her and the children but needed to start on preparing the house for the agents' people who would be there in two days' time. As Amanda's husband was away on business for a couple of nights Connie knew that they would be late getting back and so, in anticipation of this, she took not only a taxi but also a bottle of wine. Connie's children, who had been collected from school by Amanda, were already upstairs playing with her friend's two when she arrived at six o'clock.

They opened Connie's bottle and the evening was underway.

They chatted for a while as they finished preparing dinner before calling the children down to eat. After a typically chaotic, fun meal, the children disappeared to finish their homework with the promise of a video film if they had completed it to their mothers' satisfaction.

They remained at the table and relaxed back into conversation.

"How's it going, Con?" said Amanda. "We haven't had a heart to heart for a while."

"No," sighed Connie. "Sorry if I seem to have been ignoring you but since the matter of this inheritance hit me and the approach of the end of the kids' school term is getting closer, my mind has been focussing on what I've got to do."

Amanda filled their glasses up again.

"Yes, I was going to ask you about that," said Amanda. "What are your plans for your Scottish empire?"

"Well, the solicitor guy, Dougal Henderson, has informed me that all the probate matters and ownership registrations have been completed and I'm now the legal owner of the crofting lands and properties and the two houses. I've not had to sign anything in person as I gave him my Power of Attorney – it seemed an awfully long way to go just to sign a document or two and my heart just wasn't in it. But I do have to decide about disposing of them, y'know. I mean what the hell am I going to do with them when I'm living Stateside?"

"Sure," said Amanda, "so what will you do?"

"Well, I'm going to have to sell them, that's for certain. I could appoint Dougal – he's such a lovely guy, so traditional and gentlemanly, you'd love him – to be my agent. Quite honestly, I don't really know how to go about it. Should I sell the land and croft cottages as individual plots or with the house? What about the house in the town? I don't know what anything is worth. I would just prefer the whole lot to be taken off my hands and get off back to the States. Got any suggestions? I mean, what would you do?"

"Me?" said Amanda. "Well, I'd certainly like to know what it was all worth, you know, get it all valued and that. Of course, if I didn't have any immediate plans to re-settle my life in America, I guess curiosity would get the better of me and I would want to go and have a look at it all, take some time off and look around. I know Alex would want to do that – any excuse for a bit of a holiday."

"You know, you've got a point there," Connie admitted thoughtfully. "Dougal left me with a whole file about the inheritance: historical information on previous ownerships, maps, plans, photographs, addresses. When I told him I didn't know anything about Scotland he told me there was even a map in the file showing where Argyll was. I guess he was a little put out by my ignorance."

"I should think so, too," said Amanda.

Connie poured more wine.

"I've hardly looked at the file he prepared for me. He also left me the report by those Search people, y'know, the ones he hired to track me down? I've read that and was fascinated to dwell on it all, but the properties never really fired me up. But, Amanda, you're dead right; I should do something about it, and soon. I've just done nothing! I haven't even told my Dad about the inheritance, I mean, how dreadful is that? I've told him about the incredible story of the family connection that Dougal's Search people came up with, but y'know, although Dad showed some interest in it, I didn't get the feeling he was particularly connected. In fact, he seemed pretty unmoved. I wonder if the adoption scene, Mom dying and the mental distance from it all, closed him down a bit. Maybe I over-reacted to his response and tried to put it out of my mind. But you are so right, I've got to get some action going here."

Connie took a sip of her wine.

"Y'know, Amanda, it's just occurred to me that I could get the kids out of school a month early and take them up to Scotland with me. I can't see that it would do them any harm and after all, they're about to enter an entirely new education system back home."

"Why not?" said Amanda. "It won't make a lot of difference their leaving school before the end of term and what an experience for them! They could possibly never ever go to Scotland, certainly while they are at school in the States, so yeah, I think you should take the opportunity with both hands."

"This is a good idea," said Connie, "and it would also help to kill the time before we go. I think I'll go ahead and arrange it and not bother trying to explain anything to Danny and Louisa. We'll just go. The head teacher can't really stop me and I'm sure she'd understand."

Connie was charged with this unexpected enthusiasm, and Amanda, realising it was not as late as she had thought it was, opened another bottle of wine and the two of them chatted about Connie's Scottish project before calling the children to get ready to go when the taxi arrived.

The next day, after Amanda had called to collect the children for the school run, Connie telephoned to arrange a meeting with the head teacher who, most conveniently, was able to see her that very morning at 12 o'clock.

Kathleen Brooks was one of those women who made you feel at ease just by the very sight of her. She was tall, in her early forties, simply but elegantly dressed. She had long, jet-black hair parted down the middle and held in place by a thin floral headband. As she got up from her desk and walked across the room to greet her guest, her hair swayed in unison with her flared skirt which Connie noticed matched the headband. Undoubtedly competent, it wasn't just dress sense along with the high-heeled shoes that made her seem so different from the other teachers. She was simply a natural leader and fitted the part admirably. With her welcoming smile she beckoned Connie to an easy chair and then sat opposite her. Although they often saw each other at the school, particularly when it was Connie's turn to do the school run, they rarely had time to stop and talk. However, they had got on well together from the day that they first met and were sufficiently at ease to be on first-name terms.

"Thanks for the prompt appointment," said Connie.

"Not at all," she replied, "as you only need half an hour, it suited me as well. So, what can I do for you, Connie?"

"I've a rather unusual request to put to you: I want to take the children away from the school at the end of the month."

"Oh, I hope there's nothing wrong. You can take them out of the school whenever you wish, of course, but I must point out, from a purely contractual point of view, that you will have to pay the fees for the completion of this term."

"There's absolutely nothing wrong, Kathleen," insisted Connie. "In fact your school has been the most perfect place for my two children; it's the only time in their lives that they have actually woken up in the morning looking forward to school."

"So what's the reason then?"

Connie reminded her of the situation that had prevailed when they had first come to live in England. She of course knew about Carl's death but was unaware of their marital state of affairs – but then, why should she be? Connie then summarised what must have seemed such an improbable story and that, as she had made the decision to visit Scotland before they left for America, the children would be finishing school at the end of May.

"That's more or less in four weeks' time," said Connie. "I was thinking that the last Friday of the month would be the day to finish."

"Yes," she replied, "start of half-term, round off their time here nicely."

"So you don't think it'll be too much of a disruption to their schooling then?" asked Connie.

"On the contrary," she emphasised. "I think it's a splendid idea. Not only will it be an education in itself but who knows what other horizons it will open for them?"

As she stood up to leave, Kathleen Brooks said:

"And you as well, Connie."

TWELVE

Having finished off the evening with the promised after-dinner fireside glass of whisky, they reluctantly gathered themselves and prepared to leave. Dougal had been enjoying himself enormously and had perhaps taken a little more than he should have. He would have to leave his car. A taxi was called and before taking him to his house, the driver dropped David off near the harbour and he walked back to his launch which was moored against the quayside between the ferry terminal and the lifeboat station. It was a quiet place and although the lights from the harbour and the ferry terminal created an orange glow, when David was in the launch he was below the level of the quayside and hidden from the direct light. He looked up from the seat on the aft deck to the night sky. It was a vast blue-black space studded with stars. He instinctively located the constellation of Cassiopeia.

He had never doubted that he would call his yacht by this name. It went back a long way; to his childhood, just after his eleventh birthday when he was on holiday in Devon. He had been staying with a school friend near Ilfracombe where his friend's parents had rented a cottage for the summer. He had been asked to join them for a fortnight during the school holidays and while he was there his friend's older brother had taken them out on the river in a canoe one calm night. They had stopped paddling for a moment and when David looked up at the night sky and asked what it all was and how had it formed, his friend's brother told him that no one really knew but many theories existed. Most of these stars, he told him, had been given names by Arab, Greek and Roman astronomers. During the course of history new names had been added and groups of stars, the constellations, which had been seen to represent shapes in the sky, had been given names. There was the Great Bear – Ursa Major – which was useful for finding Polaris, the North Star. You could see Orion, the Hunter, which lay between the Seven Sisters and the bright star, Sirius. All of these, he told him, were in the vast galaxy that contained our own sun, and was called the Milky Way. But his favourite constellation, which lay on the opposite side of the North Star to that part of the Great Bear known as the Big Dipper – because it looked like a soup ladle – was a W shaped group of stars called Cassiopeia. David had instantly associated himself with Cassiopeia: it was the first constellation that he had been able to identify by himself.

Thereafter, he had become hooked on astronomy. He would look up in wonder at Shakespeare's 'brave o'erhanging firmament', his 'majestical roof fretted with golden fire', and this had opened the door to him for all things of nature. And as he sat there in the launch looking at the beauty above him and wondering what good fortune had brought him to this place, he fell into a deep sleep to be awoken some hours later by the morning sunlight dazzling everything with bright intensity.

He looked at his watch; it was 7.30am. He had been asleep for about seven hours and felt very stiff. A hard bench seat, the cool dew-laden morning air and a suggestion of a hangover brought him back to his senses and he decided to head to his yacht and sort himself out. It was now 30th April and he had just one more day before he was due to check that the birds did not return to the islet until 2nd May. He would motor over to there on the afternoon of the 1st, stay the night on the launch and wait. So far, he had not done any provisioning for his stay but now that he had the launch it would be half a day shopping about in Oban and then he would be set for a couple of weeks.

As he was motoring back to *Cassiopeia*, his mind being cleared by the fresh air, his thoughts were on what had transpired the night before and Helen's gift. He was going to have to visit Dougal's office in due course to complete the necessary paperwork and register the property in his name but then he thought: why not go and see him today and get a copy of the land details and then go over and have a good look at his inheritance? He could do his provisioning tomorrow morning and then go over to the islet at the end of the day.

So David returned to his yacht, showered, changed clothes and then rang Dougal. He wasn't available but the person he spoke to in the office knew him well enough to assure him there would be no problem and that if he called in by about 11o'clock a copy of the map showing the land in question would be ready for him.

David was genuinely excited by the prospect of owning this stretch of land and the house at Banmellach. Gone was the negativity, the doubt that overtook him the previous night when Dougal had told him. He had always loved the place and Helen had remembered this when making out her will. He would take the place on and relish the challenge of making it into a home. He realised, of course, that there was no possibility of him ever being able to live there permanently, but what a privilege it would be to be able to visit it and stay there whenever he could.

Motivated by this renewed enthusiasm, he quickly motored the short distance across to Oban, moored up and went ashore. He walked directly to Dougal's office to collect the papers. They were waiting for him as promised, and so, unexpectedly, was Dougal.

"Come in and have a quick coffee, man," he said, "I've just got back in and have to go out again shortly but I've ten minutes before I have to leave. I understand you called for a copy of the Banmellach map. When they told me, I knew I had to stop and see you. So tell me. What's happened? A good night's sleep brought you to your senses then?"

"I think it must have done," said David. "I'm sure it was an emotional response to the whole thing. Usually when you get a bit of news like that, particularly with the blood charged up a little, the reaction is to go completely overboard, but mine was almost a rejection. Probably saw it as an obstruction to my carefully planned life! Can you believe it? I really must try and loosen up a bit. But let me tell you, in the cold light of day I saw it quite differently. It was only when I realised the fact that Helen had quite deliberately thought of me, the fact that she had kept in her mind how much Banmellach had touched me, that she had decided to separate this part of her property and leave it to me...well, Dougal, that got to my heart's core. So I'm off there today to have a good look at it."

"Doubtless you'll appreciate how pleased I am to hear this. But look now, I have to be on my way, so keep in touch because, amongst other things, there is the little matter of the paperwork that needs to be dealt with. And I should let you know that Helen left instruction that the costs associated with it would be covered by her estate through funds she put aside for this purpose."

"An amazing woman," said David, "quite amazing. I shall for ever be in her debt."

"Not debt, man. She loved you. I think you were to her the son she never had. No, she truly wanted you to have the place and in this respect I'm sure she would have claimed to be indebted to you for accepting it. Now be off and away and enjoy your day on the island."

As David walked back to the launch he called into a shop to buy a couple of sandwiches for his lunch and then set off. Once in the launch, it took him only about twenty minutes to reach the jetty at the small passenger ferry terminal on the south side of the island. The ferry was moored up to the concrete decline that allowed vehicles to manoeuvre on and off, so David edged his boat gently to the side of the jetty and jumped off. As he was tying up he heard a voice over his shoulder.

"Well, I'd heard you were come back and was wondering how long it would be before you graced us with your presence."

David turned around with a smile. He knew that voice well: it was Duncan Robertson, the man who held the franchise for the ferry between the mainland and the island. Walking down the slope from the ferryman's house was a tousle-haired man in his forties, robust in figure and ruddy faced. An outdoor man who doubled up as ferryman alongside his croft. His face, too, smiled a greeting and the two men embraced in friendship.

"Forgive me, Duncan, you knew I'd be around to see you both as soon as I had got myself organised. How are you keeping? How's Annie?"

"We're both well, man. You'll have to call in and see her. Did you know she had started a tea-room on the road not far from the old castle?"

"I'd no idea."

"Aye, we had enough people over visiting the island last year asking if there was anywhere they could get refreshment of some sort that she decided to give it a go. She's done up an old croft house and barn and a few people come over every day. I've put a notice on the ferry to advertise the place and off they go. I do a little poll when they come back and it seems to be getting the thumbs up. The numbers visiting grow through the summer so we hope the business will build up accordingly. We've done up a wee bothy as a bunk house, too."

"It's a really good idea," said David, "I'll call in and see her tomorrow."

"So you're back for the birds, are you?" said Duncan. "I've not been down that end of the island for a while but I guess they should be arriving any day now. May second, isn't it, when they're due?"

"That's right," said David.

He loved the fact that they all knew of this – it was like a time reference point in the year and presumably had been since the terns had first been noticed, centuries, probably millennia ago.

"That's the day after tomorrow so I'm going to be there on the first to make sure they're on track and haven't arrived early. I'll then wait on through the night till daylight to watch the first ones arrive. I hope they stick to their schedule."

"Well, if they don't, it'll be the first time that I've ever heard of it happening."

David walked back up the slope with Duncan towards his house hoping that he wouldn't be asked why he was over on the island today. He would of course have to tell them eventually about Banmellach but needed the right moment – and just now he didn't want to have to say anything. But it didn't happen because, just as they approached the house, Duncan turned and looked back across to the other side of the water and saw that a vehicle had pulled up at the embarkation point.

"Bugger, I was hoping for a quiet day today but I'll have to go and collect that guy. He's from the marina and has a delivery of mooring chains in his truck. I was expecting him a little later. I'll not hold you up. Let me know if they arrive on time," he called as he walked off down to the ferry.

David climbed a little further up the hill past Duncan's house and stopped to watch the ferry ply its way across the sound to the mainland. The little ferry was capable of taking a couple of vehicles at a time plus foot-passengers. Visitors on foot came across in considerable numbers during the summer and he thought of Annie's tearoom and that he would call in there tomorrow. He wondered if she and Duncan had come any nearer to tying the knot. Private vehicles were not allowed on the island other than those of people who lived or worked there and he wondered if owning Banmellach might qualify him. He smiled at the idea.

He turned and walked on along the track across the island that led to his inheritance. The gravel cart-track went all the way to the small beach and passed directly in front of the gate to the house, which lay about half an hour's walk away. The bright morning had held and the sun cast a welcoming light for the new owner and although David knew this route well and always enjoyed it for what it was – a fine walk across the island – today he had a bounce to his stride.

The house of Banmellach stood back from the track which ran on down to the beach. When David had been there before he had not really paid much attention to the condition of the building since his time was spent either sitting down at the beach or just generally absorbing himself in the tranquillity of the place. Also the house was not part of his agenda. Helen had merely told him that he should visit the area and had never even mentioned that it belonged to her. Dougal had given him a plan of the house layout. It was strictly speaking not a croft. It was no more than 150 years old and had a slate roof – albeit in need of a little attention. Upstairs, there were a couple of bedrooms, a small utility room and a bathroom. Downstairs there were two rooms either side of the staircase, a lean-to extension which was the kitchen, and some outhouses. The house faced the sea with windows commanding a view across to the Isle of Mull. The front door faced seawards and opened out onto a garden. All in all, it presented a most pleasing aspect and David was surprised at the thrill it gave him. What really impressed him about the house was its solidity. Thick, mortared stone walls had been whitewashed and in spite of the years it stood defiantly, on call to the challenge of the elements.

But such defiance was not needed today. The sun shone down on Banmellach which lay calmly in the lee of the hill that protected it from the south-west and the white forms of sheep and lambs, grazing or resting on the green grass within the dry-stone walled area that defined the property boundary, lent a pastoral air to the island that he had never appreciated before.

Unfortunately, Dougal had been unable to find the key, so he walked around the house and peered in through the back windows. He had no idea how long it had been empty but his first impression was that it looked dry and the wooden floorboards seemed in good condition. There was no furniture to be seen and the emptiness provided a dimension to the eye that gave the rooms a sense of spaciousness. David liked simplicity and this place had it. How glad he was that the original stone fireplace had not been replaced with a modern one.

There was a sheltered kitchen garden at the rear on the south side of the house, overgrown and untended through neglected years. Within the walled area there were smaller stone enclosures, probably for keeping animals or for growing crops and at the far end a group of rowan trees had been planted to provide shelter from the wind. The seaward side of the property did not have a wall. The grassed area continued down to the pebbles and shingle of the upper part of the stony, rocky beach. It was not a large beach. At the top lay the old, rusted, hand-operated winch which had once been used to haul a boat up over the beach beyond the level of the storm line, and on the western end of the beach, lay the remains of an old stone pier.

The house had the appearance of having been abandoned but was not in any way derelict. He decided that what had actually happened was that the place had been vacated and was waiting patiently, unhurriedly, for someone to come along and care for it. That was it.

He began his walk back to the jetty by Duncan's ferry and to his launch. As he approached the water he was thinking about the fact that the land and house had been given to him by Helen McKechnie, not to someone else. Would this cause resentment amongst the islanders? How would he deal with it if confronted with such a reaction? Should he try and mitigate such a possibility by telling them about it before they heard about it from others? He concluded that it would be best if he told Duncan first. He was a sort of pivot on the island. After all, everyone coming to or leaving the island did so on his ferry. Yes, he would go and see Duncan in the near future and tell him all about it.

As he began undoing the launch's mooring lines he realised his imagination was fired. He now had a project to work on, a totally new project. Banmellach! He slowly opened the boat's throttle and turned its bow toward Oban.

He thought of how he would gradually make it his own special place. But of course it would be years ahead.

He still had to finish his work here and then there was the next stage of his life after Portland. The thought of those job applications and the probability of having to work in London provided an unwelcome dampener and he knew he would have to temper his enthusiasm. There were moments when David did not like reality. Just now was one of them.

THIRTEEN

The prospect of their visit to see the land and properties left to her by her great-aunt Helen had galvanized Connie into action in a way that she had not felt for ages. From total lack of interest to organisational frenzy she had become a new person and in the course of twenty-four hours she had changed from reluctant observer to active participant. During a light lunch at The Guardsman, she had thought the whole thing through: she wanted to sort out the disposal of the properties; have a look at the area; enjoy a holiday with her children and, above all, tell them about this part of the history of their family where it had actually happened. The following day, after Connie had had her meeting with the Head Teacher, she casually told the children during their evening meal that they would be going on holiday to Scotland.

"That's great!" said Danny. "Can we go and see the monster at Loch Ness?"

"Well," answered Connie, "we might get a chance to go to the loch but I don't think I can guarantee seeing the monster."

"Pity," he said, "I suppose I'll just have to put up with Lou instead."

As a ruse, Connie suggested that if they were to behave themselves for the rest of the month she would allow them off school four weeks early. Promises were made and sworn to and, leaving the children goggle-eyed, the matter lay there.

When they were at school the next day she set about arranging the trip. Having looked at the map of Britain and found out the nearest airport to Argyll, she looked up on the internet the best way to get there. It seemed simple enough: go to Heathrow airport, take a flight up to Glasgow, hire a car and drive up to Oban all in the space of a day. If the kids finished school at half-term they could be gone the following Monday which, according to her diary, was 1st June. They could have a sort of farewell party with Amanda and her family and then be off. They would of course be back again later to pack up and prepare everything for America but she wasn't quite sure when that would be.

Connie booked everything on-line except for the taxi to the airport. She would use her local guy for that and call him nearer the time. She had decided that they would probably be away for a couple of weeks – maybe a little longer, so she had kept open tickets for the return flight. In a moment of pure romanticism, she had booked the Regent Hotel in Oban for them. After all, she thought, in many ways this is where it all began.

The remaining weeks seemed to drag on and on. How curious, thought Connie, if this idea for a visit to Scotland had never materialised, she would have just continued on, with the summer gradually reaching the point where they would be due to take the flight for the States and leave England for ever. But because she had a point of focus so soon to come into view, it made the waiting seem interminable. She was itching to go.

They had their party on the Sunday afternoon, the day before their departure. Amanda and her family arrived for lunch which turned out to be much more extended than expected, the culprit, as ever, being bottles of red wine. This suited the four children who had the hours after lunch to themselves whilst the three adults relaxed and talked about all the things that mattered and many more that didn't.

Connie had taken the precaution of packing most of their things the day before because her instinctive early warning system had told her that there would be no way that it could be achieved after their Sunday lunch. And she was proven right. When their friends said their farewells and departed with promises of more fun to come on their return, Connie put all the washing-up into the machine and they were in bed by 9 o'clock.

Early the next day they packed their final things with Connie declaring that, if they had forgotten anything, they would buy it when they got there. The taxi arrived at 8 o'clock and the unusually light morning traffic made sure that they were at the airport terminal in plenty of time for their check-in.

It was a grey, damp day. The plane took off through the base of a low cloud layer which, as they climbed, seemed to go on and on until they eventually broke through into bright sunshine. Way below them, the top of the cloud layer reflected the sunlight and, as they were travelling northwards with the sun behind them, the clarity was spectacularly sharp. Although the flight was just about one hour, three-quarters of the time they just saw white clouds. And then, as the captain announced that they had just crossed the border into Scotland, as if by royal command, the cloud disappeared to reveal the mountains of the Southern Uplands. To the two children it was breath-taking; to Connie it was astonishing.

They looked down on a vast stretch of unoccupied land. Except for a few roads and occasional groups of houses or villages the land was empty of human activity. Where is crowded Britain, Connie thought? There are meant to be about 70 million people here. Where are they all? And as the plane began its descent towards Glasgow the emptiness continued until they commenced their approach from the west across the Firth of Clyde towards Greenock. And finally, with the River Clyde on their left, they dropped over the lowlands of Renfrewshire, west of the city, to touch down at Glasgow airport.

"Okay, guys," said Connie. "Here we are. Bonnie Scotland!"

And Danny and Louisa just sat there with their faces glued to the window looking out across the fields towards the Kilpatrick Hills to the north as the plane taxied to its stopping point.

"Come on, you two!" urged Connie. "We've got to go and collect our bags. If we don't get off soon, the plane'll go back to London with us still on."

"But, Mum," said Danny, "look at all those mountains. We saw them when we looked down on them from the plane and now we are on the ground and are looking up at them! They're amazing!"

"And, Mum," said Louisa, "when we came in across the sea I saw loads of beaches. Can we go and see them?"

This was going wonderfully well. The children were clearly enjoying the trip they were making, and even before they had got off the plane, they had shown their spirit of occasion that made the ordinary seem like an adventure. And even Connie realised that this was no ordinary thing and that, she too, had been caught up in and was being swept along on this strange odyssey.

"Sure, darling," she replied. "And I guess we'll see plenty more where we are going."

"And the mountains," said Danny, "will there be lots more like them?"

"You bet," said Connie. "More of them and ones that will be bigger and taller. And another thing; we'll see the sea as well, the Atlantic Ocean. It runs all along the coast and when we look out to the west, we'll know that 3,000 miles of sea lie between us and America."

"You mean where we are going to go and live?" asked Louisa.

"That's right, honey," said Connie.

"Seems an awful long way to have to go," mumbled Danny.

The doors opened and the passengers began to file out.

"Come on!"

They went down to the carousel to collect their bags and then Connie led them out to the main concourse to find the car rental office.

She checked her print-outs and located the right rental company. A very charming assistant, wearing a tartan suit that no clan could ever admit to being theirs, dealt with them quickly and efficiently. She agreed to let Connie have an open end to the hire up to one month due to the uncertainty of the date of their return.

"Thanks," said Connie, smiling, "but we certainly won't be that long. We've got to get back to the States."

"That's fine. Just call the office when you know you'll be back," she said as she handed over the keys and told her where the car was parked.

Connie checked the road map and they set off west along the M8 and after fifteen minutes or so they rose up over the Erskine Bridge that spans the River Clyde.

"Hey, Mum," said Danny. "We saw this bridge when we were coming in on the plane. It's not at all like those ones in London: it's a real whopper!"

On the other side of the bridge the road split eastwards towards Glasgow and west towards Dumbarton and Loch Lomond. Connie went west. As they passed the turn off to Helensburgh, they were back in countryside again and when the road turned towards the loch they caught their first sight of the Highlands.

Ten minutes later they were passing the shoreline of Loch Lomond with the magnificent rise of Ben Lomond across the water to the east. They reached a small parking place close to the water's edge and Connie stopped the car so they could get out, stretch their legs and have a good look at everything. The children ran down to the little beach and, with the inevitability of all children, started throwing stones into the water.

"Hey, Mum!" shouted Danny. "Come and throw some with us. This place is terrific. Look over there, there are islands and that mountain is…well, it's *big*!"

She came over to be with them and threw some token stones. Danny was right, she thought: this place is terrific.

Even more: it's beautiful. It's breathtakingly so. She found herself looking for the words of that song, something about the 'bonny, bonny banks of Loch Lomond'. There was something else; what was it? Something was in her mind and she couldn't work out what it was. And then it came back to her and she remembered Dougal Henderson saying something to her about Scotland being… what was it? Yes, 'neither a high road nor a low road that you have taken'. That's what he had said to her but his light amusement had never registered and of course, it was from that song! How did it go…? 'You take the high road and I'll take the low road and I'll be in Scotland afore ye'. Something like that! Well, they were certainly in Scotland and by the look of the mountains ahead they were heading for the high road. Oh, Dougal, you dear, dear man.

She called the children and they made their way back to the car and continued on their journey. According to the road map they were heading towards Crianlarich but had to take a left-hand turn at Tarbet and around the head of Loch Long towards Inverary. The road wound around the western shore of Loch Lomond until the signpost told them to go left. They rounded the top end of Loch Long and then began the long climb up to the summit of the road which, so the map said, was called Rest and be Thankful.

"What a funny name," announced Louisa, but Danny was there with his explanation.

"It's about horses, you see. If you had to pull a cart up such a long hill, by the time you'd reached the top you'd be very thankful for a rest. But that was a long time ago and now they have cars and lorries so it doesn't apply anymore."

"Not bad!" quipped Connie. "Good to see your brain is still working even though you're not at school."

"Didn't know he had a brain," murmured Louisa.

They passed the parking area at the summit and began their descent towards Inverary which lay some twenty minutes further on. It was now nearing one o'clock and Connie told them that they would stop there for some lunch. They continued downwards until they reached the eastern end of Loch Fyne which, like Loch Long, was a narrow, deeply indented arm of the sea. As they approached Inverary the loch widened and, with the tide low, they had their first scent of sea air.

The town of Inverary had been designed by the Duke of Argyll in the nineteenth century in an endeavour to improve the lives of the local people and to stem the emigration that was impoverishing the region. The town, built on a grid pattern, straddled the main street which was the only road to the west coast. This wide street gave the town a sense of purpose and presence. The houses of white-washed stone with grey slate roofs unified the development which was surely the successful intention and ambition of the Duke. Shops, restaurants and hotels completed the contemporary evolution of the town and visitors arriving from the east were welcomed by the view to the north of the impressive entrance to the grounds of Argyll Castle.

As Connie drove into the town she decided to park the car near to the quayside. Here, where a variety of colourful boats were moored, they got out and took in the picturesque setting. Strolling along by the boats, with the mountains and sea flanking the town, Connie felt a wonderful sense of freedom. She was so involved in the simple act of enjoying herself that she hardly gave a thought to why they were there.

The sea air invigorated them and as they walked along the high street their senses were assailed by the mouth-watering aroma of fish and chips being fried.

"Oh, Mum!" pleaded Danny. "I'm so hungry."

"So am I," said Louisa.

"Me too," said Connie.

They walked straight into the fish and chip shop and ordered three portions. With the food bagged up and some soft drinks to wash it all down with, they walked back to the sea front, sat on a bench, and tucked into their bags of food.

Connie mused: am I really doing this? Am I actually sitting here in the sunshine with my children in the west of Scotland, eating this delicious food?

And the children wondered what had happened to them too. Only this morning they were in their house in London; and in London they would never be allowed to eat fish and chips from a bag sitting outside. In fact, they couldn't even think where there was a fish and chip shop in London.

After lunch, they motored on along the coast to Lochgilphead and then northwards, past the turning to Crinan, on the road towards Oban. All the time Connie was enchanted by the scenery. It was quite unlike anything she had ever encountered before and more to the point anything she had expected. Green fields gave way to deciduous woodlands; sloping hills rose up to mountains with jagged rock outcrops. And only occasionally did they encounter houses. The first village they came to was a small cluster of houses called Kilmartin. It was situated looking over a plain of fields dotted with copses of trees. A small hotel faced over the plain. Connie pulled in and parked opposite the hotel and took in the view.

"Hey, guys, how about a walk?" she suggested. "It's so beautiful and with the sun shining we can't let a moment like this slip by."

"Great!" they responded.

Near to the car was a small graveyard with carved stone slabs with figures of medieval noblemen or warriors dating back to between the fourteenth and sixteenth centuries and while the children were looking at them, Connie went to the hotel to ask about a good place to take a walk.

Armed with information, they walked down a lane off the road towards what looked like a pile of stones but which, when they reached them, turned out to be the mound of an old burial chamber. The children climbed over the stones and disappeared inside the covered tomb. Connie watched Danny and Louisa. She had never seen them so excited and carefree; this was truly what childhood was all about.

At the hotel they had told Connie of the great concentration of pre-historic sites in the area and of the ones close to Kilmartin. When they had left the burial chamber they found stone circles in a nearby wood and saw other individual stones standing in the fields. They must have walked around, captivated by everything they saw, for at least two hours. When they eventually returned to the car, they went into the hotel to thank them for their help. By now it had passed 6 o'clock, and although the day was still light and the sun was still up, the air was turning a little cooler and she was anxious to carry on to Oban where they were booked into their hotel for the night. But when they entered the hotel a fire was blazing in the grate and it seemed so welcoming that Connie asked about room availability for the night. Certainly they could have a family room for the night and the owner would call the Regent Hotel – they knew the manager well – and tell them that their clients would be arriving a day late.

A perfect room with a view across the fields and woods where they had walked was lit up by the sun setting towards the west. They had a wonderful dinner and went to bed with the sun still above the horizon. As she settled down for the night, Connie, like her children, could hardly believe that just over twelve hours earlier they had been in London – as Dougal had remarked, one of the world's largest cities – and now they were in a sparsely populated land of endless surprises. It had taken her unawares, this strangely different landscape. She had come here on a straightforward mission to settle matters over her great-aunt's inheritance, yet already she was beginning to sense a feeling of being, a feeling of intimacy with somewhere that had previously been beyond the furthest imaginings of her consciousness.

It was, she felt, an awakening.

FOURTEEN

There are often adjectives that seem to apply most appropriately to a particular noun. The combination is usually specific, relevant and wholly appropriate. On this occasion, at a table in the dining room of a hotel in Kilmartin, the noun was breakfast and the adjective was hearty. However, even this well-used description fell way short of doing justice to their start to the day. For a family normally used to a rushed cup of coffee or a glass of milk and a slice of toast they were treated to the equivalent of a banquet.

Cereals, fruit juices, toasted home-made bread, fresh croissants, butter, jams, fruit; eggs, either boiled, scrambled, poached or fried; bacon, sausages, tomatoes, mushrooms, haggis – yes, even haggis! – black pudding, fried bread and potatoes. Everything was offered to them, accompanied by a never-ending supply of tea, coffee and juices.

They felt they would never need, or be able, to eat again.

Afterwards, when they felt they could manage it, they took a short stroll outside at the start of another beautiful, clear day. They then packed their bags into the car before setting off for Oban. The road took them partly near the coast but mainly through the green rolling countryside that was backed to the east by lofty mountains. As they approached Oban the rural landscape gave way to increasing numbers of houses and then, suddenly, the town lay before them.

It nestled along the coast at the foot of rising land to the east and was flanked on the west by the sea where colourful boats and a large black and white ferry were moored in the harbour. Trees covered the land, sometimes as pine plantations towards the mountains but also as groups of oak, rowan and birch growing amongst the houses, some exotic and tall, others bent and gnarled by the prevailing winds. To the north, into the distance, islands rose out of the sea, some rounded or flat, others high and jagged. A solitary, long island lay close by. The central part of the town was dominated by the sea front and harbour where fine Victorian buildings of brown and grey stone gave a sense of grandeur and importance.

Above the town a curious circular structure that seemed to be made up of tiers of arches reminded Connie of a Greek or Roman monument. Whatever it was, strangely she didn't think it was out of place. Its dominant position over the town made it seem like a sentinel on the lookout to warn the town of unwelcome visitors. Well, she thought, I hope they don't see us like that.

As they entered the town and drove along the waterfront she told the children to look out for the hotel. Everything looked so different to them. Firstly, they had never lived by nor spent any time by the sea before and secondly, the architecture of the buildings gave the town a totally foreign feel.

"Look! There it is, Mum," shouted Louisa.

And there it was: the Regent Hotel, set just back from the road and looking so 1930s that it brought a smile to Connie's face. She felt good about that. So this was the place that had once been the Marine Hotel; the place where those two American soldiers had been billeted for a long weekend in 1943; the place where they had danced with her great-aunt Helen and her true maternal grandmother, Lorraine McKechnie. A little shiver ran up her spine. She was transfixed by the sensation, caught between the present and a happening from more than half a century ago, a beginning frozen in a moment of history. Connie had not expected this reaction.

Her children were calling to her to park the car and get out but she couldn't move. She just stared at the hotel, images of that fleeting wartime encounter flashing through her mind. As the sound of their voices penetrated her far-away thoughts she knew that it would be here that she would tell them the story. This was, indeed, the place where it had all begun.

She pulled into a parking space on the street not far from the hotel in view of the steps leading up to the hotel entrance. They all got out and Connie told Danny and Louisa to wait by the car whilst she checked if their room was ready. She went inside and shortly reappeared calling to them to get the bags out.

The receptionist welcomed them saying that as the hotel was fairly empty at this time of the year she had given them a family suite with a bathroom, two bedrooms, one with twin beds, the other a double. While Connie was doing the paperwork, the children went looking about. They came back to her, Danny pulling at her arm.

"Mum," he said, "you've really got to come and see this. There's a big cabinet in a room around the corner with loads of photos of old ships and planes and things."

"And soldiers and people in uniform," said Louisa.

"Okay, kids," she said, "I'll be with you in a second when I've just sorted this out."

"It's a really interesting display, actually," added the receptionist. "The hotel was used during World War 2 as a flying boat personnel base, you know, pilots, navigators, crews and their back-up staff. The Royal Air Force had flying boats based here on Atlantic convoy protection. Many were operated by Commonwealth crews. This hotel had a Royal Australian Air Force squadron crew based here along with Canadian and…"

Connie's mind drifted away as the receptionist carried on talking. Australian? Didn't Dougal Henderson say that the two Americans were looked after by a guy from the Australian Air Force?

"…and there's a photo of one of their squadron leaders in the display cabinet."

"I beg your pardon?" said Connie.

"No matter," said the receptionist, smiling. "If you're interested, there's a very nice little museum to the right outside the hotel that has a very detailed section on the town's wartime history."

"I'm sorry…thank you," said Connie, a little embarrassed for not paying attention. "I'm really most grateful to you, er…?"

"Moira," said the receptionist. "If there's anything I can help you with don't hesitate to ask."

"Thanks again," said a more relaxed Connie, "I'd better go and see what the children have to show me."

"Fine," said Moira. "Off you go and I'll have your bags sent up to your rooms."

Connie found the children. They were engrossed in the display cabinet. Sure enough, it was filled with memorabilia of the hotel's part played during the war but the object that took her attention was the photo of the Squadron Leader from the Royal Australian Air Force. Could this have been the man who welcomed her grandfather and his colleague on their stay at the hotel? If not, from what Dougal had said, it must have been one of his men.

She had started to become quite enthralled by all this, to such an extent that in the last half-hour she had let slip from her mind the fact that she was here on a specific mission that needed her fullest attention, starting with a visit to the offices of – taking the business card out of her hand-bag: *Henderson – Notaries and Commissioners for Oaths.*

She had deliberately not informed Dougal of her plan to visit Oban. She wasn't quite sure of the reason. Perhaps because before they had started their journey, somehow, deep down, she really just felt detached from the whole business and simply wanted to get it all over with and, that by announcing her plan to make the visit, it would have made it all too formal. Whatever the reason, she was here now and must go as soon as possible to see him. Normally, she would telephone and make an appointment, but Dougal's relaxed character coupled with the unexpectedly comfortable sensation she felt in Oban, meant that she ignored such a protocol. So she told the children that, after they'd been up to see their rooms, they were going to visit a man she knew and would then go on a walk around the town and get their bearings.

Dougal Henderson's office was in one of the town's fine old buildings in a street that ran off the main seafront road and she had no difficulty in finding it. It was 12 o'clock as she walked through the front door to the reception area and asked if, although she didn't have an appointment, she might see Mr Henderson. She gave her name and a call was put through to his office. Within seconds an impressive oak door opened and through it, with face smiling and arms outstretched in greeting, walked the tall figure of Dougal Henderson.

"Forgive me if I don't show an expression of astonished surprise," he said, "but I just knew you'd come – not when – but I knew eventually! And now that you're here, confirming my anticipation, you'll come through and introduce me properly to your two fine children whom I already know to be Louisa and Danny."

"Mr Henderson, no, Dougal, I remember you did imply I call you by your first name and, after all, you are my only friend in Oban. So: Danny, Louisa, I would like to introduce you to my dear friend Mr Dougal Henderson. Dougal is the beginning of a long story that I will tell you about when we are back at the hotel tonight.

"Let me tell you why we are here, Dougal. I think I told you quite clearly when we first met that I was going to return to the States when I'd sold the house in London. I wanted to get back in time for the children to start their new school in the fall and that is still my intention. I also told you that I wanted you to dispose of the properties here in Scotland that I had inherited and that, too, is still my intention."

"Connie," said Dougal interrupting her. "I was wondering if perhaps Danny and Louisa would prefer to do something on the computer with Morag out in reception. I'm sure what we're going to talk about will be rather boring for them and you'll be telling them everything tonight in any case."

"Sure thing, good idea," agreed Connie, and one look at the two of them confirmed Dougal's perception.

He called Morag and they gratefully left the office with her.

"So," continued Dougal, "bearing in mind that I left everything on hold while awaiting your instructions, what do you want me to do?"

"Well, Dougal," began Connie, "after giving the matter very little attention it suddenly dawned on me that before doing anything, the very least I could do was come and see the properties and land that great-aunt Helen left me. I kinda disguised it to the children as a sort of holiday and they were only too happy to leave school a month early. I've told them absolutely nothing of your visit to London and of the extraordinary revelations you brought to me.

"You see, I've no real idea, y'know, what it actually is that I now own or indeed how much it's all worth or how easy it might be to sell. So I've come here for a couple of weeks or so to sort things out and give the kids a holiday before we go back to London and then the States."

"I see," said Dougal, pensively. "So what do you want to do first?"

"I thought, well, a sort of whistle stop look at everything would give me a feel and then we could get down to business. I would like you to act for me in any transactions."

"We need to slow down a little here, Connie. For one thing, I'm not very available for a couple of days to be free to take you around – and there's a lot to see, you know. You cannot do justice to the appreciation of everything by rushing. Also, as we will have to cross over to the island, we'll need some better weather than has been forecast."

"But it's beautiful out there!" exclaimed Connie.

"Sure enough," sighed Dougal, "but it's all going to change tomorrow and we'll be having rain for a couple of days at least."

"In which case," suggested Connie, "why don't you let me have a map showing the properties on the island and the children and I can take the ferry over and have a look this afternoon?"

"I can certainly do that if you like, but you'll have to go back again when the weather's better."

"Okay," agreed Connie, "it's a deal."

"In which case," added Dougal, "we can meet up here tomorrow around 12.30 and I'll have a couple of hours free to show you the house in Oban."

"The house in Oban?" queried Connie.

"Yes, the one that Helen lived in before she died."

"Of course," Connie replied, feeling rather foolish. "I had forgotten all about that."

"Well, I'm glad I've reminded you. It's a fine three-storey residence. Helen's parents bought it during the war at a knock-down price. The two girls lived in it for a while until Helen finally returned to the island. After the war it was divided into two apartments and rented out for years. Helen moved back into the lower one until the end. When the upper one became empty about five years ago she never re-let it. As a single property it has five bedrooms."

"Okay then, we'll be here at 12.30 tomorrow. Will you let me treat you to a little lunch afterwards?"

"I think that would be a grand idea."

He gave Connie a map of the island properties, instructions on the island ferry service and departed for his meeting as she left with the children.

FIFTEEN

David had been in Oban for nearly five weeks. The first terns had arrived on 2nd May, consistent with their time-honoured annual schedule and by the 5th they were all there.

He had arrived at the islet about 10pm on the night of 1st May still believing that some of them would get it wrong and arrive a day or two early, unlike the previous three seasons when they had been absolutely on the day. It was a clear calm night and he had anchored the launch in the narrow bay close to the rocky islet. His intention was to stay overnight and right through the following day and night until 3rd May. His vigil would only end when he saw the arrival of the first tern. Since arriving in Argyll, the weather had held steady and pleasant. The Azores high pressure zone was making its influence felt by keeping the Atlantic low systems well to the north of Scotland. This had not only helped the terns on their northerly passage but also kept the anchorage calm.

David recalled the time four years ago when he had waited and watched for them on the first visit he had made to the island. Then, he had camped in a tent behind some rocks on the south side of the inlet so he would have a clear view of the islet without disturbing the birds. When he had been told that they always arrived on 2nd May, he simply refused to believe it. He remembered how he had conversed with the elderly lady who lived in the house at the head of the inlet and she had been most amused by his scepticism. She had told him:

"Sure, you'll find out for yourself soon enough. They arrive that regularly, well, if you couldn't set your watch by it you could certainly fix your calendar."

She had told him that, as the rock on which they nested was part of her croft land, they were her terns and that she was the custodian of their nesting ground. He had appreciated her proprietary interest in the birds and told her so.

"It must be a wonderful feeling," he had said to her, "to know that they'll come back again each year and it's such a safe place for them too. I would imagine that with you being here, no one would risk going on to the islet?"

"No, no, they are totally safe with me," she had told him, "and in any case it's a protected site and you need permission from the authorities to go on to it. They are my wee bairns anyway so I always tell the people who come to count them that *they* need *my* permission to go there. But they don't come very often, it must be four or five years since they were last here to ring them. So what brings you here then?" she had asked.

And so David had told her who he was, where he was from and why he was there.

"Well," she had said, "you may have permission from the people in Edinburgh but you'll still need mine, as I said, they're my wee bairns. What's this electronic tagging thing about then anyway?"

So David explained to her that the traditional system of ringing was only fully helpful if a bird was recovered, usually dead, but told little about the route they took, how long they stayed anywhere and how long they lived. There were many other questions that the monitoring of these birds could answer but in some ways, because the Arctic tern was known to be a prodigious traveller, the research work he was doing was testing the system as much as anything.

"So, by sending out a pulse only once every forty-eight hours," he had explained to her, "the battery maintains a very long life. I'm hoping that it will have many other applications, not least in following commercial fish shoals, something on which a great deal of work needs to done."

"Well, it sounds good enough to me, but you'd better promise not to mistreat any of them."

"I shall handle them with kid-gloves," David had said smiling.

"Then it's all right with me and I'd be very interested to see how it all goes. I suggest you put your tent up by those rocks: it's dry and grassy there, and the sheep keep it good and short. How do you think you'll get over there?"

"I'll be bringing an inflatable dinghy."

"Very sensible; and by the way, David,' she had told him, "my name's Helen, Helen McKechnie."

And so had begun a lasting and deep friendship. When David told her that the birds had indeed arrived bang on time she merely shrugged her shoulders and with a little smile told him they were models of reliability. She often would ask him in for a bite at lunchtime and they spent many hours talking about each other, her life on the island, his time living in the south of England. And then one day she simply had said to him:

"David, it's such a journey for you when you have to keep going to Oban and back and sure it's fine for a couple of nights in the tent, but look, why don't you come and stay here in the house. I've got a spare bedroom and your equipment and things would be far better off under a roof. What do you say?"

He had been unable to refuse.

He had spent the remaining months of the summer with her. They would travel together to Oban to buy provisions, and he had always enjoyed her company wherever they went. She had been a cross between a grandmother and an aunt to David and he loved her company. Although she spent most of the year in her Oban house – and when there, rarely ventured out – she always came back to the island for the summer, always for the duration of David's stay.

And now she was gone. How sad that the house was empty and closed. He had felt after her funeral in February that it would be different this year, his last summer on the island. Just as well that he had brought his yacht, he thought.

Everything was ready for the implanting of the electronic tags. The birds had laid their eggs and hatching was due any day now. He had been to the town for the morning to arrange some final things before concentrating his time on the islet. All he had to do was wait. And so, on this warm, sunny day, before returning to the marina, David lay back on his hired launch, moored up at the quayside and reading, of all things, a modern interpretation of classical philosophy.

Having left Dougal's office, Connie decided that they would walk to the mainland ferry point to the island and use the opportunity to familiarise themselves with the area. The route she chose took them by the harbour and past the ferry terminal of Caledonian MacBrayne, that perennial life-line to the Hebridean islands. As they walked along the quayside they encountered a colourful motor launch tied up to a couple of mooring posts with a man on the rear deck lying on a navy blue reefer jacket, a book open on his chest. Connie wasn't sure whether he was just enjoying the sun and had put the book down or had fallen asleep. Either way, their passing shadows crossed his face and he stirred and looked up. Slightly conscious of having disturbed him, Connie tried to make light of it with a passing comment.

"Well, you're not going to catch many fish lying around like that in the sun," she said with nervous humour in her voice.

The man looked up, dazzled by the sun, and could only just make out the three part-silhouettes standing on the quay above him.

"The fish are perfectly safe with me around," he said. "I'm far too idle to bother with them, particularly on a day like this."

"So you're not a fisherman then?" asked Connie.

The man sat up and put a peaked cap on his head to shield out the bright sun. He could see them more clearly now: a woman and two young children – a boy and a girl. The woman had startlingly coloured hair, a sort of coppery auburn that scintillated with the sun immediately behind her.

"No, not at all, I'm very happy for other people to do it for me. Enough plundering of the sea takes place without me adding to it."

Well, thought Connie, this is an unexpected line of conversation and she decided to continue it.

"What quite do you mean by 'plundering' it? Are you talking about piracy on the high seas?"

"No," he chuckled, "it's just a thing of mine. I think we're guilty of indiscriminate, unmanaged fishing and although fish farms are a step in the right direction we take far more out of the sea than we put back. But look, you don't want to spoil a lovely day talking about fish-stock conservation with a guy who's got a bit of a bee in his bonnet about it."

"Not at all, I happen to agree completely with you. I'd hate to think of the day when I couldn't eat my favourite fish because some thoughtless individual had caught the last one."

He stood up.

"I'm sorry," he said with an apologetic smile. "That was very unsociable of me to start voicing my opinions to complete strangers. My name's David Gregson. Would you like to come on to the boat and maybe have a glass of something? You could dehydrate in this weather!"

Connie looked quickly at the children. The anticipation of being on a boat for the first time in their lives was evident on their faces. She answered for them all.

"That would be lovely, but we can't be too long. We have a planned walk ahead of us."

"Great," said David. "Let me help you aboard."

They sat down in the cockpit around the table and introductions were duly commenced.

Right," said Connie, "these are my two children, Danny who is nine and his sister Louisa who is...well perhaps it's indiscreet to give away a lady's age..."

"Oh come on, Mum! David, I'm seven."

"Good," stated David positively. "No secrets between us then, eh? Okay, what's it to be – I've got a selection of still or fizzy soft drinks – usual things: orange juice, coke..."

"I'd like an orange juice, please," answered Louisa.

"A coke for me would be great, thanks," chimed in Danny.

"Coming up," said David as he slipped down into the small cabin.

As he handed them up to the children he looked at Connie with a quizzical look that conveyed 'and for you?' and as he waited for her response he saw her eyes, lingered on them for perhaps longer than he should have, and thought they were the bluest that he had ever seen.

"Well, what're *you* going to have?" she asked him.

"Me? I think a beer," he said, looking at his watch to confirm it wasn't too early. "Would you like one?"

"Well, yeah, okay. Sounds good."

"I can offer you a boat temperature one or a cold one – I have a small fridge on board."

"Cold – that's perfect!"

He disappeared once more to the cabin and reappeared with two bottles with caps removed. Handing one to Connie he raised his bottle and the four of them clinked together.

"Cheers, everyone," announced David, and they replied likewise. "Sorry about the bottle, I have glasses on board if you'd prefer," offered David.

"Not a problem. Best way to drink it when you're thirsty. Keeps it cooler, too," said Connie.

"Absolutely," agreed David.

Sipping from his bottle, he smiled and said to her:

"I'm sorry, in all the haste of introductions and getting drinks, I missed your name," admitted David.

Turning to her daughter he said, "Louisa, will you do me the pleasure of introducing your mother to me?"

"David," she said, "this is my mum Constance Renton but you are only allowed to call her Connie."

This brought such a smile to Connie's face that for the briefest of moments his eyes could not leave her.

"Would anyone like anything else?" suggested David.

"It would be lovely, but we must make a move. We've to walk down to the ferry and then go across to the island."

"Let me take you over in the launch, it'll only take a few minutes," suggested David.

"No, no, thanks all the same but we are determined to do the walk and we want to take in a bit of the scenery en route," said Connie emphatically.

"Okay," said David, "but look, when you're coming back over, if you don't feel like the walk, call me and I'll collect you at the island ferry point. Here, let me give you my mobile number."

He helped them back up on to the quayside and watched as they worked their way from the waterside out to the road and away on their walk to the island ferry. Who are these people, he thought? She sounded American – on holiday probably. I'm lying there in the sun minding my own business and the next thing I am entertaining three total strangers and feeling totally at one with them. Two great kids and what a good-looking mother! He'd always been a complete pushover for that colour of hair – and those eyes! Why is it that it's the good ones who are married, he thought, particularly the ones who like a beer?

He picked up his book and turned to the section on Greek philosophers and started reading where he had left off. Maybe some of this ancient wisdom would give him the answer.

SIXTEEN

As Connie led the children along the road, each one was having different thoughts about their meeting with David Gregson. There was hardly any traffic to disturb them and they were sufficiently absorbed in their thoughts that much of the scenery went unnoticed. They passed a hotel and as Connie turned to look at it she realised that the road had risen and they were higher up over the sea. She looked back and saw the coloured launch.

That was a curious incident, she thought. What an interesting guy! Not a local by the sound of him and so affable. Wasn't it good to meet someone with something to say? And he was so nice to the kids. Not bad looking either and boy, didn't that beer go down well!

Louisa looked at her mother and seemed to be reading her thoughts. Yes, he was a really easy man, not one of the stuffy, boring people we so often have to put up with. And I liked it the way he asked me to introduce him to Mum.

Danny had very clear thoughts. He liked him. And on the way back he was going to tell his mum that he was too tired to walk back. He rather liked the idea of that boat trip.

As they descended towards the point where the ferry docked, Connie let the children run on ahead. The sun shone over the sound to the island and caught it with a hue that was greener than she could have imagined. Parts of the island had expanses of rock outcrop, others had trees and now and again a white house reflected back the brilliant sunlight. All her senses were enhanced by being here; this was beauty unsurpassed. She hadn't felt so alive in years. What was it about this place?

Her thoughts were interrupted by Danny calling.

"Mum, we couldn't have timed it better. Look, the ferry's coming over and we're the only people going to go across on it. There's no one else here."

Connie quickened her pace and joined them to watch the ferry slow down as the reversed thrusting propellers churned up the water. A man jumped off and picked up two mooring lines he had thrown on to the slipway to secure the craft.

"Hallo there!" he called above the sound of the engine. "As it's just the three of you, hop on and we'll be away."

Connie paid for their tickets and they climbed on to the bridge and looked down on to the empty car space. As they sped through the water Connie looked back across the sea towards Oban and the backdrop of mountains beyond. She could see the tall topside of the big ferry at the terminal and just to the right, faintly, she could make out the brightly coloured launch moored to the quayside.

"Are you on holiday?" asked the ferryman.

"Yes," replied Connie. "We're up here for a week or so and as it's such a lovely day we decided to walk from Oban and take the ferry to the island."

"Well, you'll have it all to yourselves. You're the only people I've taken over today. You chose a good afternoon. The forecast's giving us a clear night but rain and a bit of wind for the next couple of days."

"We don't mind," said Connie. "I bet it looks just as beautiful whatever the weather."

"Aye," he replied, "good to hear a positive mind. You're not from Britain, are you? I can detect something transatlantic there."

"You're right," said Connie with a little laugh. "We're from the US but we've been living in London for the last couple of years. We're moving back to the States in a few weeks so this was a last chance to have a look at some of the country before we go."

There was no way Connie was going to reveal anything to this man as to the real reason for their visit so she put on a very convincing act as a tourist.

"Well, one thing's for certain," he beamed proudly, "you couldn't have chosen a finer place to come to. Welcome to the island. I'm Duncan Robertson."

"Thank you, Duncan, what a great reception. I'm Connie and these are my children Danny and Louisa."

"Hi, guys," said Duncan, cheerily. "Pleased to meet you. Are you enjoying yourselves?"

"You bet!" said Danny. "It's terrific here!"

"Are you looking forward to going back to the States?"

"No way!" replied Danny emphatically. "This has got to be the best place I've ever been to."

"And what about you?" he said to Louisa.

"I want to go to school, there," she said, pointing to Oban.

Connie looked at her daughter in astonishment. What could possibly have put that thought into her mind?

"I don't blame you," said Duncan. "I'm from Glasgow originally but I worked as a sailor and travelled often to the eastern side of the US. But when I came back and stopped sailing I found this place and nothing would ever take me away from here. If I had children of my own I'd want them to go to school here too."

The ferry slowed as it approached the slipway and Duncan threw out the lines and jumped off to secure them. He looked back across at the far side.

"What time are you thinking of going back?" he asked. "I don't expect there will be anyone else coming over this afternoon."

"Well," Connie said, "we were going to walk to the end of the island past the old castle and according to the map there's a little beach at the end of the road and then we were going to walk back."

"Okay," said Duncan. "That's going to take you about an hour to get there and another to get back. Look, I'm taking a tractor with some things in the trailer down to the bunkhouse which is over halfway. How'd you like a lift down that far and then you can carry on by foot. It'll save you a little time getting there and you can have a good look at everything from the tractor on the way."

Connie looked at the children and there was no doubt what they wanted to do.

"Okay, Duncan, you're on!"

"Give me a moment then," he said. "Wait here and I'll go and get the tractor. It's all loaded up so I'll only be few minutes."

When he had gone, Connie put her arm around Louisa's shoulder and spoke to her.

"Darling, what did you mean about going to school in Oban? You know we're off back to the States in a month."

"Mum, I just like it so much here. It's nothing like London and I really can't remember back home, I mean, why do we have to go there?"

"Yes, I agree with Lou, Mum. It's great here and there are boats and mountains and you don't get them in London and it's wild and…"

Their conversation was cut short by Duncan returning with the tractor.

"Okay, everyone at the front end of the trailer and hold tight!"

It was impossible to talk on the journey. They held on to the bar at the front of the trailer as the tractor rolled from side to side and everyone was laughing and pointing things out. Connie looked at her children and saw that something special had overcome them, a transformation into lively, happy, buoyant individuals. Maybe there was something in what they were telling her.

They arrived at what Duncan had called the 'bunkhouse' and jumped to the ground. A woman, much the same age as Connie, walked over from the house to meet them.

"Hi, Annie," called Duncan. "I've got some people here from America. They're having a trip from Oban for the afternoon. I've given them a lift to here and they're walking on to the end of the island and back."

"Good to see you," greeted Annie. "Stop in on your way back and have a cup of tea. I run a little tea-room but it's closed today so the drinks are on me."

"Well, we sure will," responded Connie. "I don't suppose I could use your bathroom?"

"Certainly," said Annie, "come along and I'll show you where it is."

They said their farewells to Duncan and Annie and went on their way. The gravel-surfaced road wound its way inland, and then continued westwards past a path on the left leading to an old castle. They decided to take a quick look at it. The path led across a grass field for about ten minutes and twisted its way through boulders and gullies until it rose upwards to the castle which had been built on a raised promontory. It didn't look so large when they got into it, more of a fortified house than a real castle. But its position was perfectly located, overlooking the sea and protected from the landward side by a steep slope. Inside, a spiral staircase made of stone took them to the upper levels.

They ran hooting and shouting back down the hill to the path. Back on the roadway they walked on for another quarter of an hour until the sea was close by and finally the road reached the small beach with Helen McKechnie's old house standing above it. Connie looked at the map to confirm everything. There it was – Ardbeg. Ardbeg! This had been her great-aunt Helen's home for over eighty years. It stood now, as it had done for countless years in the McKechnie family, planted firmly amongst the rocks, facing the sea. And as the sun, still high in the afternoon sky, shone down on it across the sparkling sea, Connie was overwhelmed.

The children were playing on the beach, doing the things children do on beaches, throwing stones into the sea, finding shells. But Connie, Constance Renton, was silently crying. She was crying for a thousand reasons. She was crying for the heartache of her great-aunt Helen; for the loss of Hamish McKechnie's purpose in life after the Great War and for his guilt at having survived; for her grandmother Lorraine's enthusiastic optimism for life, finished abruptly in a car-crash; for her grandfather Harry who was her grandmother's soul-mate and who died with her. And she cried for herself because all of this made her feel so sad.

How, she thought, how on earth could she think of selling this place? This totem, this talisman, call it what you will, is the connecting factor between all those dashed hopes and the future that I want for those two children of mine. I never knew Helen McKechnie. I had never even heard of her before Dougal came into my life. But she has given me this house and because of her she has given me a new life. I will not let her down.

She turned and looked at Danny and Louisa; and gradually those tears of sadness became tears of joy. She wiped the dampness from her cheeks and went down to the beach to join them.

"Hey, Mum," said Danny, "this is such a great place; we've got to come here again. There's a small stream running through the stones on the beach and Lou and I are going to make a dam there to have a sort of swimming pool."

Louisa had a piece of sea-weed in her hand and she threw it at Danny and he chased after her, declaring that on catching her, he was going to kill her.

Again Connie could only wonder at the effect this place was having on them all. She wanted to look inside the house but, foolishly, she had forgotten to ask Dougal for a key. Well, no matter, they would certainly be coming back again. So while Louisa tried to avoid Danny on his homicide mission, Connie took a stroll around the land near the house. As with so much of the ground around the island, sheep had grazed the grass and it made walking easy, like being on a lawn. Economic lawnmowers, sheep, she thought. Trees had been planted around the garden walls and inside the garden. There were the remains of a once tended kitchen garden that had now gone wild – not even the sheep had been able to get in to enjoy controlling it. Lace curtains prevented her from being able to look in so she left the house and walked out towards the rocky shore.

From here the sea stretched towards the south-west. Islands, their names unknown to her, studded the sea, and she wondered if this was the place where those convoys had mustered all those years ago to make their perilous way across the Atlantic, to and from her homeland. Strange, she thought, yet another connection between here and America. As she turned to re-join the children, a cluster of small white sea birds arose from a small rocky islet nearby, calling raucously. And as she walked on towards the beach the dark-grey head of a seal broke the water and gazed at her with an inquisitive eye.

The children seemed to have settled their differences and Connie called them to get ready to walk back. As they regained the road, Connie looked back at the small bay beyond the beach. The children stopped and looked with her and as they did, the seal reappeared, now close to the shore.

"Mum," asked Louisa, "what's that in the water?"

"It's a seal. I saw him earlier when I was walking near the house."

"We saw him too, Mum. He came when Danny was about to strangle me with a piece of seaweed. We thought it was a man swimming and so Danny stopped. I like that seal; he saved my life!"

"I'm very grateful to him."

"I'm not," said Danny.

They began their walk back and Connie was able to take in the extent of the land she now owned from Dougal's map. Everything around her was hers! There were three or four cottages nearby which she assumed were tenanted by the crofters who rented the grazing land and whom she would have to meet. The whole of this end of the island was hers, even, she realised, the rock where the birds were. No, she thought, I cannot part with this. Even when we live back in the States, it shall always remain for my family.

They reached Annie's tea-room and knocked on the door to announce their arrival. As promised, they had their cups of tea and while the children went outside to look around, Connie and she talked of Annie's life on the island. She wasn't from the island. In fact, she was from the north of England but had come here on a holiday four years ago and fallen for the place to the extent that, when she went back home, she gave up her job and came straight back up here.

She was a teacher and had worked in Oban for a while before the idea of developing the tea-room occurred to her. She had decided to rent the empty house and gradually brought it up to a condition suitable for opening. It had been a great success with day-walkers and hikers.

"It was Duncan's idea to develop the bunkhouse. He has been such a great help to me," she said with a coy look. "I don't know what I would have done without him."

Connie told her they would try to come back before they left Oban, explaining that they were only there for a couple of weeks. She called the children and they set off on their way.

"Do your best to call back again," Annie reminded them as they left, "I cook some pretty good chocolate cakes and bake my own bread for the sandwiches!"

"We'll be back," said Connie, "won't we, guys?"

"You bet," they said together and waved goodbye.

The walk to the ferry point took about half an hour and when they arrived, there was no sign of Duncan. The ferry was tied up on the slipway so Connie walked up to his house. There was no sign of his tractor so she told them they would just have to sit and wait. Although the sun was still high it was now 6 o'clock and Connie was a little concerned that it could be some time before Duncan returned – if at all.

"Mum," said Danny, "why don't you call David? He said he'd come and get us if we were too tired to walk."

She looked across to Oban to see if his launch was still there. It had gone.

"I can't see his boat where we left him. He must have gone off somewhere."

"Well, call him anyway," suggested Danny.

"I don't like to take advantage of him," claimed Connie.

"Don't be silly, Mum, just ring him; he did ask you to."

"All right then," she agreed, and got out her mobile phone.

It rang and rang but there was no reply. She hung up and told the children they would just have to be patient and wait for Duncan to turn up.

Ten minutes later her phone rang.

"Hallo?" she answered.

"Connie? It's David Gregson here. How's it going? Did you have a good time?"

"Hi, David," she said. "Thanks for calling back. We've had an amazing time. It's such a beautiful place."

"It certainly is. Look, I'm sorry I missed your call earlier. I was in a place with very poor coverage, so I'm calling you back. Do you want a lift back in the launch or are you going to push on to the end by foot?"

"Actually, a difficult situation has developed. There is no sign of the ferryman and unless he comes soon we could be stuck on the island. So I was calling to see if your offer still held though I have to admit the real reason is that we're also whacked-out and would love to come back with you on your boat even if the guy does turn up."

"You just stay there at the slip-way and I'll be over for you in about a quarter of an hour. Okay?"

"Thanks so much, David, you're a life saver."

They sat down at the waterside and watched for his boat but saw nothing. The minutes ticked by. A stillness had settled over the island and the sun lit up everywhere with a golden richness. But there was still no sign of the boat.

They actually heard the launch before they saw it. And then it appeared along the shore of the island and they could see him lean and wave to them as the bow of the boat cut a white 'v' through the water.

He slowed down, came up behind the moored ferry, and threw two lines to Connie and asked her to pass them through two metal mooring rings and then hand the ends back to him. She thought he looked good. He was wearing the same dark-blue jacket he'd been lying on when they first saw him.

"I'll hold her steady while you all get on board," he told them, "then let the lines slip and we'll be off. Hold tight, now!"

They climbed aboard and with everyone settled they motored slowly away from the slipway and then he opened up the throttle a little and headed off in the direction where he had been moored in the morning.

"By the way," he mentioned, turning to Connie, "I saw Duncan just before I left the marina. He was loading some stuff on to his trailer to bring down to the ferry. I told him you'd called me and he sent his apologies for not being there but would have been at least another half-hour before he had finished. I told him I was going to bring you all back anyway."

"Thanks," said Connie.

"Where are you staying?" he asked her.

"We're at the Regent Hotel," she replied.

"Okay, I know it. Look, what we'll do is moor up by the quay in the harbour and then we'll be almost in the town centre and closer to your hotel."

While the boat was going at a gentle pace, David said to the children that they could have a few minutes at the wheel. Ladies first, he announced lifting Louisa into the seat behind the steering wheel, having first put a cushion there to lift her higher up so she could see out of the windscreen. Then he helped her down for Danny to have a go. As they approached the harbour, David took over.

"Normally the person at the wheel would wear the skipper's cap but unfortunately, when I leaned out to wave to you, the rush of air took it and my sunglasses as well. Stupid of me, I know, but I let my concentration go for just one moment and, disaster, two old favourites were in the drink. That's an important lesson about being on a boat, relax by all means, but never let your mind drift away from the importance of safety, for the boat, equipment and, most important of all, the people on board.

"Sorry, Mum," continued David to Connie. "No time for you today – we're almost in. You can take her next time."

He brought the boat into a space next to a set of steps leading up to the top of the quay. With fenders out to protect the side of the launch, he put a rear line around a mooring ring and jumped out to fix the bow line before jumping back on again.

"Okay, one at a time. Connie, if you could get out first I'll help them out to you then I'll follow you up. Everyone take care and hold on to the wall rail."

As they walked along the quay, Connie thanked him for everything, particularly the lift back but also for letting the children steer the boat.

"Glad to be of help, but it was my pleasure, and seriously, please come out again. It's definitely your turn at the wheel next," he said, with a winning smile.

"Sounds great, I mean, if you're quite certain, I'm sure we'd love to," she concurred, looking at the children who nodded in eager agreement.

Taking Louisa's hand and putting an arm on Danny's shoulder Connie positioned herself to leave.

"Well, David, thanks once again for helping us out. I'd better get these two back to the hotel and get some food and a well-earned rest," she said.

"Look," suggested David, "I've got a much better idea. To celebrate our having met today and you three having enjoyed your time on the island, let me take you all out for dinner. I've got a favourite restaurant I'd like to take you to. You're dressed perfectly for it and, as it's such a lovely evening, we can eat outside. Then you can go back to your hotel and have that rest. What do you say?"

"Well, er…" stuttered Connie, "I mean you've already been more than…"

"Well, then I'll ask Danny and Louisa what they think," interrupted David. "Okay, guys, would you like to come out to eat with me? Maybe if you accept your mum will be outvoted and she'll have to come along as well."

"Thank you, David, I'd really like that," said Louisa.

"I'm starving," said Danny. "I'm with Louisa."

"Well, Connie, I'm afraid that democracy wins the day. Heavily outvoted."

She looked at her two children in mock exasperation.

"But David," she protested, "shouldn't we go back and get changed, I mean..."

"Absolutely unnecessary," he insisted. "I know the owners well and I am sure we will be able to sit and enjoy a sea view. Right, follow me."

They walked across from the harbour to the main high street, crossed the road and walked a short distance along it until David stopped and said to them:

"Well, here we are."

And they turned and looked at the front window of 'Wally's Fish and Chip Restaurant'. A look of amazement came across the children's faces – they loved fish and chips – and one of astonishment on Connie's; they could not believe it. But the mouth-watering aroma emanating from Wally's establishment convinced them of the reality.

And they ate the very finest: crispy golden batter, white flaky fish and freshly fried succulent chips.

When they had finished, Connie was the first to speak.

"Restaurant; eating outside; sea view; David, you are incorrigible!"

"What does that mean, Mum?" asked Louisa.

"It means, darling, that we've been treated today in a way that no one could ever possibly repeat. What a day! I just don't think it could ever get better."

"No, I don't think it could, either," agreed Louisa.

"I know it couldn't," added Danny.

"Well, you're all wrong," declared David. "It's only just beginning and you've still got a couple of weeks to go! Come on, I'll escort you home."

David walked them back to their hotel and promised to be in contact the following day. Danny shook his hand in a gentlemanly manner; Louisa put her arms out and gave him a hug. And as they walked into the hotel reception, Connie turned and gave David the lightest kiss on his cheek.

"Thank you," she said, holding both of his hands at her side. "I cannot tell you what an effect today has had on us." And she turned and hurried off to her children.

That night they all slept well. Danny and Louisa simply drifted off. Connie lay in her bed going over and over in her mind the sudden impact on her life being here was having and how today in particular had taken her through such an emotional spin. And on top of which, her physical exhaustion finally opened a door through which she was just able to pass but with no energy left to dream.

And David? Well, he too fell into a sleep but he dreamt. He dreamt of a vast starry night sky in which every star in the Milky Way was visible and in which one group of stars, the constellation Cassiopeia, was made up of stars that were not white but of the bluest blue he had ever seen.

SEVENTEEN

The next day confirmed all forecasts. The rain arrived accompanied by a howling wind from the south-west that bent the trees and drove the rain with a disregard for everything in its path.

"We're enjoying the tail-end of an occluded warm front," David informed Connie when he called her, "so we're confined to quarters for the day. There's another front following right behind but it will all have blown through in thirty-six hours and then we're in for a grand spell of sunny weather – could last for a week or more."

"It's just as well," said Connie, "because I'm a little tied up today and maybe for some time tomorrow, so if things are looking good for the day after, maybe we could all get together then?"

"Fine," he said, trying to hide his disappointment. He had been hoping to meet up with her again but in fact knew he needed a couple of days to tidy his yacht and get ready to go to the islet to check on the progress of the hatching tern chicks. He had decided to ask Connie and the children to come along with him and show them what he was up to. It had now been well over a month since the birds had arrived so most of the chicks should have emerged by now.

"I'll call you tomorrow evening when I've got the latest weather forecast and if things go as anticipated, we should have the all clear. Would you like to come out for the day in the launch? There's something I'd like to show you that you might find interesting."

"Okay, we'd love that," she assured him. "Kinda sounds intriguing. Oh, again, David, thanks for yesterday. It was so cool. The children haven't stopped talking about it; a memorable way to conclude our visit to the island. Wonderful! Thank you so much."

Connie had kept her promise to tell the children about what Dougal Henderson had come down to London to tell her, although, due to the collective on-set of deep sleep the night before, she had waited until the morning and had told them after breakfast.

"So you see," she explained, "we've to go to his office at 12.30 today and then he is going to take us to see the house in Oban that your great-great-aunt Helen used to live in. It's just as well we're going to be inside today. It doesn't look too nice outside."

"Mum," said Danny, "Lou and I were looking out of the bedroom window and saying that we like it when the wind blows and the rain smashes against everything. We think it's part of what you have here. In London it just made everything seem miserable; here it's exciting. And anyway, it probably won't last long and the sun will come out again and that'll be great too. You know, the rain wets us and the sun dries us out."

"Well, I'm glad everything seems to suit you, fair weather or foul."

They went around to Dougal's office as arranged. While the children were with Morag she told him of their time on the island. She realised she was getting a little carried away eulogising about their visit, to such an extent, that when she had finished Dougal found himself admonishing her with a cautionary tone.

"Connie," he said, "it may well be outside my remit to rein you in, but I fear you may be in danger of over-indulging yourself in light of the fact that you are going to sell everything and shortly return to the United States. It's rather like me tasting a fine malt whisky in the knowledge that after one fabulous draught I not only have to give the bottle and its remaining contents back to the owner but also leave his house as well and never see the whisky again."

"Oh, Dougal," pleaded Connie, "what am I going to do? I came away from great-aunt Helen's house on the island and vowed that I would never – could never – sell the place or the land. Even when we go back to the States I must keep it for my family. I'm so sure that's what Helen would have wanted me to do. And what about this – the children have totally fallen for it: Oban, the island, the house, the sea, even the bloody awful weather, they love it!"

"Certainly it was very pleasant at the beginning of the week and I believe it will turn good again in a day or two."

"That's just the point, Dougal, they love it whatever the weather. And y'know what? So do I, and that's what makes it so difficult to be rational about it."

"Look," he said, "I think we'd better go and see the town house now. Then you will have seen everything and you'll be able to sleep on it and tomorrow perhaps see things in a more moderate light."

They left his office and, protected by umbrellas, made their way the short distance to the house. It lay in a street just off the main high street, nestling quietly away from the hustle and bustle of the harbour side but with a side view from the windows to the waterfront, the sea and part of the island beyond. It was one of a terrace of Victorian houses built from grey granite and pinkish-red sandstone. An imposing, panelled door was painted dark-green and decorated with a brass lion knocker above the letterbox. The house was not particularly wide but had a double frontage with a bay window either side of the front door. Connie looked up to the two sets of windows above and to the dark slate roof. Once again, she was taken aback by the feeling of surprise at what lay before her. How could she have paid so little attention to Dougal? He had given her a file with photographs of everything including this house and still he had to remind her that it was part of the inheritance.

Producing a bunch of keys and selecting one, he handed them to Connie.

"As the owner of a fine residence in the equally fine town of Oban perhaps you would care to open the front door and invite your guests inside from the rain."

"Of course," accepted Connie, as she nervously inserted the key into the lock and turned it. They stepped into the hall which revealed a floor covered with blue, white and green tiles all inset with imaginary seascapes.

"Those are the original tiles. It seems that, in spite of their puritanical ways, the Victorians enjoyed a brightly coloured tile or two," ventured Dougal.

"They're lovely," said Connie.

An elegantly banistered staircase ran up to a door which was closed.

"Where does that go to?" asked Danny.

"It's the door that opens into the apartment that takes up the next two floors. Your mother's great-aunt rented it out and kept the ground floor to herself. The house was far too big for her and she didn't want to be bothered with the stairs. When the tenants left about five years ago she never re-let it. It's been empty ever since. We can go and look at it when we've seen the ground floor."

They went into the two front rooms that opened from either side of the hall and then to the rear of the house where there was a large kitchen with a pine table and chairs that stood in front of a large cast-iron cooking range. Because the range had given out such warmth, Helen had never had to bother with central heating for the ground floor. Venturing beyond that, they discovered a door leading to a laundry room off which had been built a modern and stylish bathroom. With the bathroom downstairs, it had been a self-contained unit for her. Another door led out to an open area that would probably now be referred to as a patio but at one time was the back yard.

"You'll see that Helen had made one of the front rooms into her bedroom and the other into a sort of lounge, but she spent most of her time here in the kitchen where she could come and go as she pleased without having to use the stairs, but to tell the truth, in her last couple of years she seldom went out at all except for the odd errand."

"It's quite deceptive," remarked Connie. "Once you're inside it seems much larger than you'd expect."

"Well," said Dougal, "let's have a look at the upstairs; you may be even more surprised."

The door leading into the apartment opened out on to the first-floor landing but instead of duplicating the downstairs layout, a door to the left opened into a single room that occupied the entire floor area over the two downstairs front rooms and the entrance hall.

"This would have been the master bedroom," said Dougal with all the panache of an agent doing his best to sell the house, "with marvellous views down towards the sea."

Connie was once again speechless. Like the downstairs rooms, this room had beautiful plaster mouldings around the ceiling and wonderfully proportioned windows. All of this had been in the photograph dossier that Dougal had given her yet she had still managed to pass it over and not give it a second's thought. They moved along the landing to find two more bedrooms and a bathroom at the end of the corridor. A further staircase ran up to the top floor where there were two further bedrooms, a box room and yet another bathroom.

"This can be our floor up here," said Louisa to her mother, "and Danny can have the box room as his bedroom."

"You can go and live on the island, Lou, and we'll visit you once a week and bring you food," Danny informed his sister.

"It's an amazingly spacious house," continued Dougal. "So what do you think of it, Connie?"

"I hope you won't mind if I use the expression 'gobsmacked', because that's exactly what I am, gobsmacked. And even that fails to convey what I feel."

"All things taken into consideration, I think it's perfectly acceptable to bring such an expression into play. Though it's not a piece of vernacular I'm prone to utilise, I do believe that you've captured the essence of your reaction in it," said Dougal, with that masterly ability of his to slip lawyer-speak into everyday conversation.

On that point Connie declared that they should go off and have that lunch she had promised. At her request Dougal took them to a small bistro-style restaurant where he suggested they order a giant tureen of piping-hot soup that he told them was made with vegetables and lamb, pepped up with a little chilli and flavoured with what he called 'cooking' whisky.

"Perfectly all right for the children," he said. "Just the sort of day when all living creatures need a little shot in the arm to bolster them against the elements."

"I'm sure you ordered it just because you like whisky, Dougal," Connie observed.

"Aye, well, there could be something in that," he conceded, with an impassive look that failed to conceal that he had been caught out.

Accompanied by a freshly baked loaf of brown bread containing seeds, herbs and a topping of melted cheese, it was delicious. The meal passed pleasantly and with the children, Connie and Dougal well filled, they departed for his office to have what Dougal called a brief de-briefing, while Morag dutifully amused Danny and Louisa.

"Well, Connie," said Dougal, leaning back in his chair with his hands behind his head, "you've done what you came up here to do: you've seen the island properties and now the house in the town. You mentioned to me that you would want to have everything valued so you could get an idea of what you would get for selling it all." Leaning forward he added: "So we need to get a valuation agent…"

"Dougal," interrupted Connie, "stop right there! I can't do this, not right now. You told me to have a good night's sleep and think about it in what I think you called a 'more moderate light'. Well, the way things are racing around my brain at the moment I think it's highly unlikely I'll even get any sleep."

"Carry on then and tell me what's troubling you."

"Look, Dougal," she said. "I came here because I realised I couldn't just go back home without settling the problem – and it did feel such a problem to me – of my inheritance. I had almost buried my head in the sand over it. The thing dominating my every day was re-starting my life back in the States and, above all, bringing stability to the children's life. So you see, when the inheritance matter happened I was facing in a completely different direction and I couldn't get my head around it. It was my friend Amanda Heston who encouraged me to come up here and find out what I had inherited. She was so right to do so. She even told me that I should come here and treat it as a holiday and have a look at a part of Britain that I would probably never have reason to come to again. So I came.

"And you have no idea what has happened to me! From the moment we looked down from the plane and saw the mountains below us, we – not just me but the children as well – underwent a sort of transformation. As we drove up here from Glasgow airport we saw scenery and felt an ambience that had eluded us for years. My children started talking to me about where we were; they were giving opinions, making observations, something they never do; they were so happy. And it was infectious! I was feeling the same thing. But I kept telling myself this was a mission we were on; it had an objective: deal with the inheritance and get out, go back to London, finish up and get home to the States and make a new life.

"And then this, this happened," she said, rotating her hands around.

"What happened?" asked Dougal.

"The impossible happened! In the course of two days I have discovered a place where I know my children are content. I have discovered a place where I know I could be content, where I have a sense of being a part, but I have been trying to convince myself that it is an illusion and that the original plan must be continued, that I have to go back to the States. But each moment something new happens and I am challenged by a tug of war between what my head is telling me I ought to do and what my heart is telling me I want to do."

"Connie, I hear what you are telling me, but can you try to refocus and find the real thing that has got to you? There must be something. Everyone enjoys a change, a holiday or whatever, and it's very understandable to feel uplifted by something totally new, but did something tip you, direct you to see things so differently?"

She looked at him pensively, her mind searching for a connection. The seconds passed, slowly; and then, eyes wide open, she pointed at him:

"You've got it, Dougal, yes, that's it! Yes, now I think about it there was a moment. Do you remember when you came to London and told me the story of Harry and John L. and how I said it was such an extraordinary and moving story and how I really felt for all those guys even before you told me how it was directly linked to me? Well, yesterday, when I stood next to Ardbeg I cried openly for all these people, these people who were my recent ancestors. I realised that this place was the connection and that was when I swore I could never sell it. That was the point, Dougal, that was when it happened: it was at that moment that I felt I belonged here. I had found the place for this new life I kept thinking would be back in the States.

"And I think I'm going to do it, Dougal; I'm going to make my life here."

Was that a de-briefing, thought Connie as she walked back to the hotel with the children? More like a revelation. How could she ever thank Dougal? He had skilfully read the situation and drawn the explanation out of her; her explanation. She would go to bed tonight and would eventually sleep. But she knew that she would first of all have to think this one carefully through. There was no doubt in her mind about what she was going to do. She now just had to plan it.

When they arrived back at the hotel Moira greeted them.

"Hi there! Did you have a good day out, in spite of the weather?"

"Oh sure," said Connie. "Everything's fine for us, whatever the weather. That right, kids?"

They smiled and nodded affirmatively.

"Did you go to see the museum I told you about?" asked Moira.

"Jeez!" exclaimed Connie. "We completely forgot about it. Hey, guys, why don't we go now while it's still raining?"

"It's just across the way," Moira said. "It'll be open for a couple of hours more. See you later then."

They left the hotel and walked the short distance to the Oban War and Peace Museum. It was not what they were expecting at all. Far from being some sort of grand civic building, it was more like a large corner shop covering just one floor. They went in and found a gentleman at the reception counter who had a smiling, welcoming face. Although in his seventies, a sweep of brown hair that covered his forehead and the upper half of his black-rimmed glasses gave him a youthful air. An identification strip pinned to his jacket informed them that he was Michael Kendall – Curator. Connie asked him how much it would cost for the three of them.

"No charge," he said. "When you've finished you can make a donation, however small, to help us run the museum. It's entirely a voluntary set-up run by people like me who have an interest in the locality. We cover the history of just about everything from the first happenings to the present day, but a great deal features the Second

World War. It was quite a busy place then. Please have a look around. I hope you enjoy it. Any questions, don't hesitate to ask."

"Thank you so much," said Connie. "Come on, kids."

They had had a thoroughly good look around at the various exhibitions which showed the history of Oban from its early days to its fishing and marine industries and in particular its activities during the war. It seems it was originally established as a museum about the town's wartime experiences but was extended to include the town's more cordial history. Connie went back to the desk.

"It's a really fascinating insight to Oban. You're doing a fine thing running this place," she told him as she placed a generous donation in the box. "And we have at last found out all about the curious round building above the town."

"Ah, McCaig's Tower! Yes, it's really quite an extraordinary structure. They stopped building it when he died in 1902. It must have looked really out of place when they built it but now it's an essential part of Oban. And thank you very much for your contribution," he added. "I'm glad you enjoyed the exhibitions. Any questions?"

"Well, actually, yes," said Connie, "there is something I'd like to ask you about. I see that the area was pretty well dominated by the military during the last war and I was wondering if you would have any record of American forces being here at that time."

"Oh, I see. I can tell from your accent why you might have an interest."

"Yeah," she said. "I learnt that my grandfather was an American Ranger during the war and that he was with a group who were attached to a British Commando training unit up here in the Scottish Highlands and that he visited Oban once. I just kinda wondered if you might have any information about that sort of thing."

"Not really, no. You see all that sort of stuff was highly classified at the time and any such records of US personnel would probably be held back in your country. Also, everything was not only top secret but also happened very quickly as forces were trained-up and then sent off to their various destinations. No, I'm afraid we only have mentions of such things. I think you'd have to contact the US embassy in London to pursue such an enquiry."

"Well, it was just a chance. I guess I'll see what I can do when I'm in London next. Thanks anyway."

"There is one thing that you might find of interest. Do you have a car?" he asked.

"Sure," said Connie, "we've hired one for our stay."

"Good," he said. "If you have time – it's only about a couple of hours away and a lovely drive – you should go past Fort William and up to a place called Spean Bridge where they built a monument to the commandos who trained there during the war. There's a nice walk around the area and the monument, which is actually a bronze statue, is a very moving sight. If you are unable to find anything later about your grandfather, you might like the feeling of knowing he was there."

"Hey, thank you, that's a great idea. Look, I have to say we've really enjoyed our visit and all I can say is keep up the good work here. It's been greatly appreciated."

"Thanks," he said. "Have a good time."

It had stopped raining and they took a short walk along the seafront opposite the hotel.

"Okay, guys," said Connie. "Let's go back and freshen up, get some food a bit later on and have a good night's sleep. We're off to the Highlands tomorrow!"

That evening David made his promised call to Connie.

"Well," he told her, "the weather's going to continue blowing but it looks like the rain has passed. Seems that the day after tomorrow will be calm and sunny; looking good for our trip in the launch. Are you still okay with it?"

"You bet! We're really up for it," she replied and he told her that he would tie up the boat by the steps where they had done so the day before and meet them there at 10 o'clock.

She told him of their visit to the museum and the recommendation of the man there that they should have a look at the Commando Memorial monument and he told her that it was well worth the trip.

"Loads of scenery, Fort William is a pleasant town and Loch Ness isn't far off. When you leave the town you'll take the Inverness road," he explained. "After you've been to the monument, which is not very far on from Spean Bridge, the road carries on to Fort Augustus and then runs along the north-west shore of the loch and

I'm sure the children would love the chance of spotting Nessie. Be sure you set off early and make a good day of it."

They followed his advice, had a 7 o'clock breakfast and were away half an hour later.

The road northwards ran alongside the coast with the Firth of Lorn on their left and a fine view of the Isle of Mull. The low-lying, green island of Lismore marked the change from the firth to the deep indentation of Loch Linnhe which ran north-eastwards towards Fort William. They crossed over the bridge west of Ballachulish and by 9 o'clock they had reached Fort William which Connie suggested they look at on the way back if they had time.

In spite of her ignorance of the geography of the British Isles, she had heard of Ben Nevis. The signpost informed her of the direction to it, from which she deduced that the vast snow-topped mountain behind the town must be that mountain, the highest point in the country.

"Wow! Mum," said Danny, "they've got skiing up there. Look, you can see the ski lifts. Hey, we've got come here again and go up that mountain. I could learn to ski!"

"Great idea," agreed Connie. "Cannot believe there's still snow up there this time of year. I'm all for a shot at skiing. You too, Lou?"

"Sure thing, I'd love it."

The weather for their journey must have sensed their elevated mood. Gone were the driving wind and rain of yesterday, and in their place was a fresh breeze, and white clouds swapped places regularly with the sun. Half an hour after leaving Fort William they had reached Spean Bridge and found the road leading to the monument without any problem. There was a large, tidy parking area and as they pulled in they could already see the monument. The figures of three men stood high on a plinth built of stone on some raised ground. It was not what she had in mind at all. This was really something special: it was not in any way a typical military monument. The men were certainly in battle-dress but they weren't over-posing in a spectacularly fighting manner. They had a very ordinary human look about them, solidly gazing at the great mountains beyond. These weren't generals or field marshals; they were soldiers, plain and simple. But the way that they stood revealed something about the character of these men. They had been trained to defend freedom and if that meant that they had to do something out of the ordinary then that was something they had chosen to do. And here in this wild country they had come to be trained to be able to do such a thing. They may have been ordinary people but how good they looked, how courageous they must have been!

But, thought Connie, the statue of those three men is not just a monument to those special, ordinary men: it is a memorial to all those who died as well as those who made it through. This is a monument to my grandfather, Harry Zielinski, who did make it and to his buddy John L. who didn't. And why not? They were part of that piece of history and they had been here; they had trained with those commandos.

And that made the whole thing very special for her. The man at the museum had been right: whether or not she ever found out officially about her grandfather's presence here, she knew that he had been here and really, that was all that mattered.

She couldn't explain her inner feelings to Danny and Louisa because they had no reference point from which to recognise anything. Their day out was to enjoy themselves and they were certainly doing that. As Connie walked away from the monument to join them, they were laughing as they chased each other around the car park.

When they had completed their walk around the track they arrived back at the car and Connie told them they were going to go up to Fort Augustus and then on to have a look at Loch Ness.

"Yes!" said Danny, "it's monster time!" and he looked at his sister without saying anything, but she knew what he was thinking.

"Mum," said Louisa, changing the subject. "It's really weird places being called fort this and fort that. I mean we're not in the Wild West are we?"

"Well," said Danny, "we're in the west of Scotland and it looks pretty wild to me."

"You'll have to make it a project while we're up here to find out about the history of the place," encouraged Connie. "Y'know, I bet the guy at the museum would give you a hand."

"When do we have to go back, Mum?" asked Danny. "I mean to London and then to America."

"I don't know yet. I mean we're enjoying ourselves, aren't we? We could stay a bit longer if you like. The hotel's cool and we've got lots more to see and do, haven't we?" she said, keeping the turmoil of her thoughts to herself. "And we are going out with David tomorrow: he says he's got something to show us that we might find interesting."

"I want to stay here forever," stated Louisa.

"And don't forget I've got to go up Ben Nevis and learn to ski," reminded Danny.

"Right," said Connie, "we've all got to do that."

It didn't take long to reach Fort Augustus. They stopped briefly to buy some sandwiches and a drink. Connie liked the simplicity of the village with the now familiar whitewashed houses and cottages and their grey slate roofs. She thought she had seen a canal with locks on it as they approached and asked the lady in the shop about it.

"It's a great engineering feat," she said. "The Caledonian Canal started being built in the early 19th century by the Scottish engineer Thomas Telford, 1803 to be precise, to link the east and west coasts. Runs from Inverness where it enters the North Sea to near Fort William on the Atlantic. There are twenty-nine navigational locks and the sixty miles of canal pass through three freshwater lochs."

Clearly, thought Connie, she must have told this a million times to tourists like her passing through. Still, it was yet another fascinating thing about this land they were discovering. She thought they could spend a lifetime here and still only scratch the surface.

They drove for half an hour or so along the shore of Loch Ness which was staggeringly beautiful despite the total failure of Nessie to put in an appearance.

So they turned back and made their way to Fort William. They stopped there and walked around the town before going to the entrance of the canal at a place nearby called Corpach because Danny had said he wanted to see where the waters met

One of the things they were getting used to was the height of the sun towards what should have been the end of the day. They were beginning to feel tired as they approached Oban but in this high northern latitude the daylight made it seem it was like early afternoon. As Connie parked the car in front of the hotel she looked at her watch – it was 8 o'clock – and though the wind was stronger back here on the coast and the cloud cover was still present, the weather was undoubtedly on the change, in line with the forecast of an improvement for tomorrow.

Out to sea, the western sky was beginning to clear and there were still two more hours before sunset.

EIGHTEEN

They woke up the following morning to a pleasing and distinct shift in the weather. The wind had died down overnight and in total contrast to the day before, it was a cloudless sky. The previous day had been a thoroughly exhausting but wonderful one and it seemed that they had scarcely gone to bed before they were up again for yet another day out. David had told Connie not to bother with bringing any food along as he would prepare a picnic lunch for them to take on the boat. So, with no obvious need for waterproof clothing, they left the hotel and walked down to the harbour to meet their skipper for the day.

David's smiling face greeted them at the top of the quayside steps.

"Hi, there," he said. "Absolutely bang on time. That's what I call sailors! Let me help you all on board."

He climbed onto the boat and helped Connie on first. He then climbed off onto the bottom step and helped both the children into Connie's waiting arms.

"You'll soon get used to climbing on and off," he said to them. "It's just a question of getting your balance and timing right and being aware that the boat moves both up and down, back and forth and sideways. Once you've mastered that you'll then have the confidence and it all becomes second nature – piece of cake.

"Right, let's cast off. Connie, could you climb along the side deck and slip off the bow line. You'll see what to do – untie it from the cleat, let the untied end slip and then pull the return end so it runs through the ring on the quay then pull the line back on board. I'll do the stern line. Danny, as you're the strong one, perhaps you could give us a shove off from the side with the boat hook and we'll be clear. Louisa, you sit at the wheel and I'll come and help you steer away."

As they motored away from the harbour the three of them began to enjoy once again the thrill of being on a boat. The calm sea had just a remnant of the swell from the previous few days' wind and in spite of the disturbance of the water from the harbour's activities, it was incredibly clear. David now let Louisa take the wheel on her own.

"Give her a little turn to the left and then back again to the right; see how she responds to your touch," he said encouragingly to her. "When you get the hang of it you can let your mum have her patiently awaited turn," he said, putting his arm briefly around Connie's shoulder.

Louisa was so absorbed in steering that David had to exercise a captain's order.

"Okay, Louisa, Mum's turn now," he said.

"Sorry, Mum," she said. "It's a great feeling, I just love it; here you are."

Connie took over, feeling far more cautious than Louisa who had taken to it with the carefree way only a child can do. She quickly felt it respond a bit like a car and in no time at all was the queen of the sea.

"Hey, this is great! Where do you want me to head for?" she said.

"See the point on the far end of the island? That's where we're headed for."

As they passed the ferry point Connie was suddenly reminded of their visit to the island only a couple of days ago. They were heading towards the end of the island though Ardbeg was out of sight. Where was he taking us to she wondered?

"Isn't it a beautiful place?" said David. "I've been coming here for four years now and I love it more each time."

"You know the place well then – four years, you say? Forgive me, David, but I haven't appeared to show any interest in what you're doing here, but really I am. So what brings you here? Have you been here for four whole years?"

"No," he said, "I've been coming here every summer for four years. This will be my last visit."

"Oh," said Connie, restraining an unexpected sense of disappointment that took her by surprise. "Your last visit?"

"Yes, sadly so," he replied. "Unfortunately my work will be finished soon and I am expecting to take up a new job later in the autumn."

"So what do you do then?"

"Well, I'm a marine biologist but I've been specialising in developing an electronic tagging system involving a particular species of seabird that breeds on the end of the island. Actually, that's the surprise I was going to show you, so now I've let the cat out of the bag. Doesn't matter really, we'll be there in a moment. Why don't you open the throttle a bit and put her through her paces, we're doing about eight knots now but fully open she'll get about twenty-two. Go on!"

Connie pushed the accelerator lever forward and the boat immediately responded. The engine roared, the bow lifted up and threw a wave either side. Behind them a white wake trailed.

"Wow!" she said. "That really is a sense of power." She looked back at the children who were grinning from ear to ear. "Hang on, guys; this is where your mom shows what she's really made of."

As they passed the point, David told her to change direction towards the rocky islet.

"See the one with all the birds on it? That's where we're headed."

"Okay."

"Take her in gently and come around from the left keeping the islet on your right. We're going to drop the anchor between it and the main island. Are you okay with that?"

"Yes, I think so."

"I'll go forward and prepare the anchor."

"Aye, aye, Cap'n," she said.

Danny and Louisa looked in amazement at their mother. They had never seen her in a situation like this and were taken by how in control she was. And there was no doubt in their minds that she was enjoying herself, really enjoying herself.

As they approached David's planned anchoring point he called further instructions to Connie at the wheel.

"When I call 'now', you just pull the throttle lever back to its central position, which is neutral and then ease it back further into reverse. You'll find it will slow the boat to a halt. At that point push it back to neutral. I will then drop the anchor over the side and then come back aft."

"Aye, aye."

It all went smoothly.

"Thanks, Connie," he said. "It makes life a lot easier – and I'd even say safer – having someone to help with everything."

"Wow! That was such a good feeling," she admitted. "I can honestly say I've never handled a boat before in my life!"

"Did you enjoy it?"

"Totally, David. I'm in my element."

"You're a natural," he asserted.

David busied himself with one of the rear lockers.

"Danny," he called, "could you give me a hand pulling this rubber dinghy out, it's a bit awkward for one person."

"Sure thing," he replied.

"Okay," explained David, "I'm going to take about ten minutes to blow this up with the foot pump, so take in the view, folks."

As David started inflating the dinghy, Connie looked the short distance to her great-aunt's house – actually now her house – and realised that the little rock with the birds on it also belonged to her. This was really weird. David had actually brought them back to exactly where they were the other day. She had promised herself that she would come back soon but had never thought she would do it this way. She wondered whether or not to mention to David how she had come to own it but decided that, for the time being, she would say nothing. It would all happen in good time.

When he had finished with the dinghy, he tied a good length of rope to its bow and secured it to a cleat at the rear of the launch.

"Okay, guys, gather around and let me tell you what this is all about. I was telling your mum that I have been coming here for the last four years, at the start of the breeding season, to fix a special device to the chicks born on this little rocky islet. These pretty little seabirds are called Arctic terns and they have the honour of being one of the most highly travelled creatures on the planet. Quite extraordinarily, they breed in the northern hemisphere as far up to and beyond the Arctic Circle and then, when they have produced and reared their young, they all disperse and start off on a journey that takes them to the southern hemisphere, as far south as the Antarctic for the southern summer. No sooner have they arrived there than they turn round and start the journey back to breed once more up here the following year. This goes on, repeatedly, until they die, but each successive generation keeps the process going. And this has probably been going on for thousands of years.

"So why are we doing it? Why are we tagging each chick? Well, first of all we know of the great migrations of these birds because, over the years, people have organised the putting of rings on the legs of these chicks and when a bird had been found – either by being caught in a specialist trapping net or found dead – the reference number on the ring tells us where and when the bird was ringed and hence, since we know where it was found, we can put together a general picture of their travels.

"Well, I hope I'm not losing you! But what it all boils down to is that by fitting an electronic tag to each bird we can follow them on a daily basis for all their lives without ever having to see them. And whilst this in itself is valuable for understanding bird migration patterns, the project I'm working on is to do with the development of an electronic system for tracking any creatures on the move. So it has great development potential for so many applications."

"Well, did you get it, kids?" checked Connie.

"I guess sort of," said Danny, dubiously. "You're able to follow things moving about. But how do you do it, I mean, how do you track them?"

"Ah, that's the key to it, Danny. We use satellites and the Global Positioning System, also known as GPS. Have you ever heard of it?"

"No," admitted Danny.

"Well," offered David, "I take upon myself to teach you all about it during our time here together. Deal?"

"Deal," accepted Danny.

"And you, Louisa, what do you think of it all?" asked David.

"Well, I think it must be a really good thing, otherwise you wouldn't be doing it. And I want to have a look at the chicks and see what you do with them."

"Okay, then," agreed David. "Let's get ourselves over to the rock and I'll show you."

David then produced from one of the other lockers some brightly coloured lifejackets and helped to put them on the children.

"You too, Connie," he said, and helped her on with hers and then put on his own.

"We're pretty safe inside the launch but in the dinghy it's much more unstable, particularly when we climb out onto the rock."

David rowed the inflatable to a small inlet in the rock and held it steady while they scrambled ashore. As they did so all the birds arose in a white clamorous cloud protesting at the invasion of their domain. It was a marvellous sensation for them; Connie revelled in the intensity and vitality of the birds' environment. Danny couldn't believe he was involved in it and Louisa just stood there spellbound. None of them had experienced such closeness to raw nature before.

"David," said Connie incredulously, "it's the most incredible sight I've ever seen. There must be hundreds of them. We're so close! You can see them, hear them – wow, what a racket – and, boy, can you smell them!"

"We must all be careful not to tread on any of the chicks or the eggs that have not yet hatched," he cautioned. "I can see that there are some of them still to hatch. I'm not going to do any tagging today. I expect they'll all be out within a couple or so more days. What I wanted to do was let you see them all, a mixture of adults, chicks and eggs. We'd better quietly get back into the dinghy and move off so as not to disturb them anymore. I'll come back in two or three days and tag as many as I can and do the remainder later on in the week."

David made sure the dinghy was held fast while Connie got in first to help the children on board. When they were all safely in, he rowed slowly around the islet for ten minutes so they could see the colony from a little distance. The birds were still creating a commotion but began to settle down as they became used to their intruders.

"Look," said David, "we'll come back for lunch on board the boat but let's row ashore first and have a walk around. It's a lovely end of the island."

When they reached the small beach Danny and Louisa got out straight away and ran off to carry on playing as they had done when first were there.

"They really get on well together, don't they?" observed David.

"Yeah, they're a great pair. They like to have a go at each other but they have always been close and I guess I'm pretty lucky to have them."

"I'll say so," agreed David.

They strolled slowly away from the beach towards the grassy area in front of Helen McKechnie's old house, Ardbeg.

"Shall we walk on up towards those crofting cottages up the slope? We can see the children from there and if we call them they can run up and join us. I know all the farmers there and if they're about we'll go and say hallo. What do you say?"

"Fine by me."

"Also, I'd like to walk on further up to the top of the hill. There's something you can see from up there that I'd like to show you."

"Hey, more surprises!" said Connie. "You really are the mystery man."

"No, not quite," he said smiling at her, "I just want to share something with you, that's all."

They walked on a short distance and then David stopped; he stopped and looked at the house. Connie continued walking slowly on and when she realised David was not next to her she glanced back to see him staring at Ardbeg. She went back and stood beside him.

"What is it, David?" she asked.

"Oh, it's just a little moment of recalling something. You see this house? Well, I knew the old lady who used to live here, in fact I lived in this house with her for three consecutive summers, four months each year, so actually I lived in that house with her for a total of a year. It's just rather sad because she died earlier this year and I was due to stay with her this summer too. I came up to Oban for her funeral in February and I was asked to say a few words by the solicitor dealing with her matters. She had no family left, you see, and he thought I was as close to being her family as anyone. I loved her in a special way; she was sort of a cross between an aunt and a grandmother to me, certainly the kindest of people and a true friend. No, it was just a little moment of sweet reminiscence; I'm sorry. Come on, we have a walk to enjoy."

Connie just stood there looking at him. Speechless. She just didn't know what to say. It was then David's turn to say something.

"What is it, Connie, what's the matter?"

"David...I...I...can we sit down?"

"Of course, over there near the wall, there's a nice dry patch by that rock."

He took her arm and guided her to the place. The children were happily playing on the little beach, building a dam with stones to try and stop the stream.

"You looked like you'd seen a ghost!" he said, trying to calm her.

"Well, I might just as well have," she said. "David, what you have just told me is nothing short of the fantastic. In the brief time since we met, we have said very little about each other. We've just been having a great time with you. Today, for example, we found out a bit about you and why you are here and then, just now, you tell me you've been coming here for four years and that you knew the lady who lived here and, what's more, you actually lived with her. I want you just to listen to me and let me tell you why I'm here.

"It's too much to tell you the whole story now, but I want to, I really want you to know it all, tomorrow perhaps, when we have some time to ourselves I will. But just now, let me tell you what brought us here."

Connie began with the visit she had from Charles Denholm and then how Dougal Henderson had come to see her to tell her the extraordinary story of how it was that she had come to be the inheritor of her great-aunt's estate following her death at the beginning of the year. It was then David's turn to be lost for words.

"You? *You?* You are the...? I... Oh! I'm sorry Connie, I'm completely...this is incredible! I knew nothing of Helen having any living family, she never said a word. She once mentioned something about her mother having 'brought us up' but it was just a passing reference and she never mentioned it again. I completely let it go, never thought about it at all. So the 'us' must have meant Helen and her sister; and you're telling me that her sister was your grandmother."

"That's right," confirmed Connie. "Immediately after the war she married in Oban and left with my grandfather for America and although they had a child, my grandmother just lost contact with her family here in Scotland. A short time later my grandparents were killed in a car crash and with my mother's subsequent adoption, all trace of their history and whereabouts disappeared."

"And poor old Helen," said David, "she had lived all that time mourning the loss of her American soldier and the life that she might have had."

"It's so sad, isn't it, and she never told you about it?"

"No," recalled David. "She was a remarkably stoic woman but had such a warm heart. I just loved coming here and staying with her. She had real interest in what I was doing. You know, she owned the land all around here and in particular the islet with the terns. She even called them her 'wee bairns' and I was under strict orders to look after them during my work here."

"Strange, isn't it, how they must now be my 'wee bairns'," she said. "But don't worry, I have complete trust in you!"

"Did you come over here to see everything the other day I gave you a lift back in the boat?"

"Yes," said Connie, "but I couldn't say anything to you because..."

"No, I quite understand," said David. "Have you been inside the house?"

"You'll never believe this, but when we came over on our own I completely forgot to ask Mr Henderson for the key and as I had no idea we would be coming anywhere near here today, I didn't even think to go and see him for it."

"The children seem to be engrossed in their stream damming, come with me Connie and let's see if.... well, let's see."

He walked off through the garden gate and went to the wall at the side. He pushed aside some overgrown shrubs against the wall and exposed a stretch of stonework.

"Connie, see that white stone? Well, see if you can move the third stone to the left of it."

She took hold of the stone and it came away easily revealing a space behind it, and there, lying on the top of the underlying stone, was a rusty key.

"Ah!" said David. "Helen always kept that key there in case she ever lost the one she kept on her. She showed it to me once, though I never had any need to use it. Perhaps you'd like to get it and you can go inside and see your house?"

"That's amazing, David!" she gasped. "It's been there all this time?"

"I guess so. Maybe she and I were the only ones who knew it was there. Well, unless Dougal never knew or completely forgot about it, it must have been so. And there's another thing, Connie: I've known Dougal Henderson for the same four years I've been coming here. Helen introduced him to me and he's been a good friend ever since. Extraordinary, isn't it, that he actually came down to London to see you? And that he asked me to your great-aunt's funeral when you didn't even know that you had a great-aunt? Amazing. In fact, I've seen him a number of times this year already: I was with him about a week or so ago and in fact the reason I wanted to take you for a walk over the hill to show you something was a direct result of my last meeting with him."

"What do you mean?" asked Connie.

"Well, as I had no idea why you were here except for a holiday – and certainly had no idea of your connection with Helen McKechnie – I just thought that I'd like to show you and the children my good fortune at having just inherited a stretch of land and an old house on the north side of the island."

"So *you* are the 'young Englishman' Dougal told me had inherited the 'old ruin' from my great-aunt!"

"Is that what he said?" said David with a smile.

"Yes," said Connie, "he never elaborated on it, just mentioned it, and I never thought any more about it. I mean

I just couldn't even imagine what or who you might have been, though Dougal did say she was very fond of you."

"Well, it actually adjoins your property so we are now neighbours," said David.

"The whole thing's incredible," declared Connie.

She inserted the key into the lock, smiled at David apprehensively and turned it. Surprisingly, it opened easily. They went into the hallway. The house had that unlived-in feel about it, but although it seemed a little musty it was not damp. David pulled back the curtains to let in the light and opened some windows to let in some fresh air.

The two of them underwent different emotional reactions to being there.

Connie found herself in the heart of her ancestry. The feeling she had felt when she first saw the house had cut deep into the very fibre of her being; the sadness of her family's history had hurt her. This time she was calm. Serenity pervaded the house and having David with her somehow brought a comforting presence.

She did a rapid reconnaissance of the ground floor and then went upstairs. David followed her and opened the wide roof windows in the bedrooms. The view out across the sea was stunning.

"It's beautiful, David; I have such a feeling for it."

"Yes," David mused dreamily, "I never felt more at home than when I was here. You always hear people say how in certain places their worries evaporate: Well, it was here for me."

"Which was your room?" she asked.

"This one, the one we're in now," he said. "Helen's was the other, larger one: I kept my equipment in the small room between. For me this was ideal, I had a view of the islet. She used to say that I could just stand here at the window and keep an eye on the terns without having to move from the house. I actually did it quite often, watching them through my binoculars."

She gazed out of the window towards the islet trying to imagine how it must have been for him here, alone with the terns and her great-aunt Helen. Her thoughts were broken by a shout and laughter from outside.

"I've totally forgotten about the children: we'd better call them. They'll be wondering where we are."

"Look," David said, "why don't I nip back to the boat and get the lunch and we can have it here instead, sort of a housewarming."

"What a lovely idea, David. Could you tell them that and just leave me alone here for a few minutes, I'd like to absorb the atmosphere for a moment."

"Absolutely," he said and went out.

When David saw Danny and Louisa he told them what he was doing and asked them to wait for him to get back and they'd go to the house together.

Connie walked from room to room, conscious of the silence that seemed to descend after David closed the front door. She found herself absent-mindedly opening cupboards and drawers and rummaging through the contents. It was obvious to her that nothing had been disturbed or removed since her great-aunt's death and this gave her a greater sense of intimacy with the house. She opened a cupboard under the staircase and in the gloom noticed a shelf on which lay a large, dusty, brown envelope. Taking it out, she noticed it had the word 'Photos' written across the front.

Her curiosity raised, she opened it and took out a bunch of photographs bound by a length of ribbon. She undid it and began to flip through the contents. There were about twenty black and white photographs, most of them of poor quality and quite amateurish in photographic style. Two of them however were clearly taken professionally, in all probability in a studio. They were head and shoulder portrait shots looking straight at the camera, one of a young woman, and the other of two women in the same pose, side by side, one of whom, on the left, was the same woman as in the single picture. They looked to be in their late teens or early twenties. Their hairstyles and what she could see of their clothes were clearly from the 1940s. Who could they be, she wondered? Was the single photograph her great-aunt Helen and the double one Helen and her sister Lorraine – her grandmother? A paper-clip, slightly rusted and having stained the double photograph, held behind it two lesser-quality photographs. She separated the attachments and saw that each was a group of three men, one of three military personnel and the other of two soldiers and a civilian. Connie was just about to take a closer look at them when she heard David call her. She hesitated for a moment before returning the photographs and ribbon to the envelope and putting it into her shoulder bag. She would take them back to the hotel and look at them later.

As she walked into the kitchen, she stopped and gazed in astonishment at the spread of food that lay before her.

Plates were covered with cold delicacies: slices of rare beef, ham, chicken, cheeses, a mixed salad and a new crusty loaf that smelt as if it had just come straight from the bakers.

"How on earth did you manage this?" she asked as he passed her a glass of chilled white wine.

He laughed: "Well, you did give me the whole day off yesterday!"

They finished eating and, in a positive mood, David suggested that they set out on their walk.

"Come on, you lot!" he said. "We're off for a half-hour walk to the top of that hill and I'm going to show you my surprise."

They set off from the house, past the crofters' cottages leaving the grassy pasture area for the rougher higher ground. They reached the top and looked back to Ardbeg, the expanse of the sea and the launch looking so small, anchored in the inlet.

"Okay," explained David, "this is not the highest part of the island but we can get a pretty good all-round view from here. Now let's turn and look to the north-east. Follow the coast away from here and you can see a small house below us. That's Banmellach set back a little distance from the beach. The walled fields between us and the house belong to it. I was telling your mum that we are neighbours."

"What?" said Louisa and Danny, simultaneously.

"It's true," said Connie. "When great-aunt Helen died and left us the house in Oban and Ardbeg here on the island, she left Banmellach to David who was her great friend."

"Wow!" said Danny eagerly. "Can we go down and see it?"

"Of course, but let's go on another day. We can anchor off the beach and take the dinghy ashore. We can make a day of it."

"That sounds a great idea," added Connie.

"Right then," said David, "let's get on back to the beach. You two can carry on playing, Mum and I'll relax in the sun at Ardbeg and then we'll have to get on back to Oban a little later."

Danny and Louisa ran on ahead down the path and left David and Connie to walk slowly down at their own rate. As they descended they talked about the land and their two houses on the island but neither felt inclined to give away any thoughts about what they both might be going to do with them. For the time being, Connie only talked about their going back to the States as the planned scheme of things, the fact that she had decided to consider living in Oban was not something she felt she could tell David about yet.

David talked clearly about the next stage in his life and how he was awaiting responses to job applications. There was no doubt in his mind that his career lay before him elsewhere than Oban and yet something niggled at him about having to leave somewhere that was so special to him, particularly when he had no real need to set his intentions on an immediate move to a new place of employment. But he said nothing of this to her.

And there was something else; something they each recognised but did not actually speak about. They were enjoying each other. They were almost afraid to admit it to themselves but they were both experiencing an emotional awakening that neither of them had known in years – and it felt good.

"I think all your tenants are out at the moment," observed David. "There doesn't seem to be anyone about. What are you going to do about them, Connie, now that you are their landlord?"

"Oh, I'll let the status quo remain. I need to meet them all of course but perhaps I'll leave it in Dougal's hands to arrange something a little more formal than just dropping in."

"You'll like them," he said. "They're family people. Got kids, like you."

As they came closer to the beach, Connie, remembering the photographs, stopped and took out the envelope to show David.

"Hey! Look at this," she exclaimed. "I was noseying around when you went to get the lunch and found this on a shelf in the under-stair cupboard."

She selected the single portrait photograph and handed it to him.

"Do you think this was Helen?"

David looked at the image before him.

"Yes," he replied without hesitation. "Got a 1940s' look about it. I've never seen this before, in fact I've never seen a photograph of her before, but it's definitely her all right, no doubt whatsoever. I'd recognise those eyes anywhere."

"So this is what Helen looked like when she met John L. I must show Dougal. Having this photograph almost completes the story. But look," she said, showing him the double photo, "do you think this is her and Lorraine? Because if it is, I'm actually looking at my grandmother, and that really *does* complete it!"

"I guess it must be," agreed David, "but I'm sure Dougal will be able to tell you."

She didn't show him any of the other photographs so they carried on down to the house, packed everything up and rowed back to the launch.

As they moved off, the early evening sun bathed the sea and land in its special light that was so more golden than at mid-day. This was something that always made David feel special as well, and he wondered if it made anyone else feel quite this way.

NINETEEN

David reckoned he had two to three days before all the chicks would be hatched. He had estimated that there might be as many as three hundred or more to be tagged and he needed the next couple of days to prepare everything. He had ended the previous day by taking Connie and the children back to Wally's for a repeat feast and then told them he needed time to concentrate on his project. They had agreed to make contact again in a couple of days but David called Connie the next day to ask her and the children to join him for lunch in three days' time. It would be his birthday and he wanted to take them to a restaurant for a meal that would be a 'little bit special'.

Connie, too, was busy. She had decided that a meeting with Dougal was necessary in order to organise her responsibilities. She wanted to bounce a few ideas off him as well and make another visit to the town house. She also wanted to ask him about the photographs. So, with both her and David occupied for a day or two, the prospect of their lunch date was a pleasing proposition.

She met Dougal the following morning at his office.

"Do take a seat, Connie," he said. "It's good to see you again. I was wondering what your next move would be because when you left here after our last meeting, my, you were caught up in a bit of an emotional whirlpool."

"I sure was. And you told me to go away and sleep on it! Well, I never thought I would sleep, but I did. I slept *the* sleep. After our visit to the house, we went to the Museum:

it was fascinating about the Second World War in the area but the man there said there was no information about American soldiers. He did, however, suggest that we went to the Commando Memorial at Spean Bridge just to experience the feeling that, well, my grandfather had actually been in the area. And it was incredibly moving and set in such glorious scenery that it just added to my sensation of belonging here.

"So that night I slept! The following day we went to the island on a motor launch with this man we had got to know some days earlier, and what do you know, it's the English guy who you told me Helen had left an old house and a stretch of land next to mine? I mean, could you believe, we were on that boat and it wasn't until we went ashore and we were walking by Helen's old house that it all came out. His name's David Gregson, he told us about Helen and how well he knew her and he told us he knew you, that you were her solicitor. It was all such an incredible set of coincidences."

"Well, well, you met David. That's really very good. He's a fine fellow. I imagine I would have probably introduced you both one day but on the other hand, maybe not. You see your schedules were unlikely to have crossed with you only being here for a short while and him away by the end of the summer. But I'm delighted you've met him. He's one of the most decent people you'll ever come across. I tell you, he was like a son to your great-aunt Helen; a lovely man."

"He is, Dougal; we've all taken to him."

"I'm pleased," responded Dougal.

"After we left the island and came back to Oban the three of us were whacked out and again, I slept like the dead. I haven't had two consecutive night's deep sleep in years; amazing!"

"So you took my suggestion literally," said Dougal, "and slept on it."

"I did."

"And what was the outcome of all this?"

"Dougal, whatever went on in my sub-conscious overnight did not reveal itself to me in the morning. I didn't wake punching the air in realisation. No, I'm very relaxed about this. What I can tell you is that, for whatever reasons, I now have no doubt that I want to start my new life here. What I have to do is plan how I am going to go about it."

"Well, this certainly is very positive of you. And you're certain, Connie, absolutely certain that this is the right decision for you and your children. You don't think you should take a little longer to think about it?"

"No, Dougal," said Connie emphatically, "I'm quite clear about everything."

"So, what do you want to do next?"

"I need to appoint you formally as my attorney – sorry, solicitor – if you will take me on," she added.

"I am at your disposal, Connie. It would be a pleasure to act on your behalf, indeed an honour, particularly in the knowledge that your great-aunt would have been so pleased at the choice you have taken."

"I want the tenancies for the island crofters to remain the same. I can see no need to change anything and of course I'd like to meet them. David tells me they're good guys, some of their kids are the same age as mine."

"They most certainly are and will be well pleased to know that you want to maintain things as they are."

"I'm kinda sold on the idea of living in the house in the town but I'll need to plan the layout for us. Ardbeg will have to wait until we're settled in but I'm most certainly going to keep it. I love it. From the financial convenience aspect, I guess I'll need to open a bank account in my name for the money great-aunt Helen left me. As you know, my house in London is on the market and the proceeds from that I will transfer to my new account here. Also I want to transfer all my money in my London account to my new account here. How am I doing so far?"

"Break-neck speed, I'd say," replied Dougal. "Whatever happened to you during those two nights' sleep seems to have given you a most focussed clarity of purpose. Look, Connie, I've got the picture. What I'll do is detail everything that I think you'll need to cover in re-organising your life here and we can go through it together. Give me a few days and I'll let you know when I've compiled it."

"Fine. If I think of anything I want to include I'll call you. Can you let me have the keys to both houses? We'll continue to stay at the Regent Hotel for the foreseeable future; I'll see if I can do a deal for a couple of months."

As Connie arose and turned to leave his office she stopped for a moment, Dougal almost colliding with her.

"I'm sorry," she said, "I almost forgot but there's something else I wanted to ask you about, Dougal. Look," she said, taking the two portrait photographs out of her bag. "I found these two photographs at Ardbeg. They were in an old envelope in a cupboard under the stairs. They seem to me to be posed shots, y'know, maybe in a studio. You don't think they could be Helen and Lorraine, do you?"

Dougal took the two pictures, one in each hand, and stared at them.

"I never knew them when they were that age. As I told you, I hadn't been born then. But yes, it's them all right. Your great-aunt may have grown older over the years, but her eyes – yes, her eyes – I'd recognise them whatever her age."

"That's exactly what David said."

"And the two together," he added, "they're the two sisters, not a shadow of doubt. The woman on the right is your grandmother."

"Thanks, Dougal. At last I've seen her – this is very special."

She put the photographs back into her bag and they went out to the reception where Danny and Louisa were being looked after by Morag. As he followed Connie he couldn't help but feel pleased at her decision to make her new life in Oban. He was surprised at how quickly she had made such a positive step but was quietly happy that she had. He felt that her presence here would be well received by all who encountered her.

"Hi, Mum," said Louisa, "we've been thinking that as we're going for lunch with David on his birthday, we should buy him some kind of present."

"That's a great idea," agreed Connie.

"And we know exactly what it's going to be," declared Danny.

As she followed the children out of the office, Dougal placed his hand on her shoulder. When she turned around, he softly said to her:

"I hope you won't see it as presumptuous of me, Connie, but I just wondered if the presence in your lives of a certain Mr David Gregson might have been, as it were, instrumental in assisting you to arrive at this very satisfactory outcome."

Dear old Dougal, thought Connie. Had he read her sub-conscious thoughts that had been denied her in those two nights of sleep? Had that perceptive mind of his penetrated her inner thoughts, indeed, her inner feelings? Certainly David had made a great impression on them and she couldn't avoid the fact that he had made a very real impact on their enjoyment of their time in Oban. Yes, Dougal was probably right. A certain Mr Gregson's presence had made a profound influence on her, and the interesting thing was that, now that this realisation was upon her, she was happily prepared to acknowledge it.

But there was a problem associated with this and she told herself that it would be a folly to assume anything. David had been absolutely clear in explaining his future plans about his career. He was awaiting responses from job applications and was hopeful that something interesting would come from them. Above all, he was here in Argyll to finish his project field work and once completed he was trying to time things such that he would leave here to commence immediately with a new position at a university or research group. And although she now realised that she saw him in a new and warm light, she felt she had to contain her optimism otherwise she would risk a disappointment that would only result in pain, and she had suffered enough of that in her life.

Even so, the fact was she had decided that she was going to give her best efforts to living here in Oban, come what may. And what about David, she thought? How did he feel? In fact, *what* did he feel, if anything? Maybe back in England he had a girlfriend, a fiancée, even a wife. What was she thinking!

David sat at his desk on board *Cassiopeia* and found he couldn't concentrate. A strange sensation had entered his normally ordered and controlled life. He felt like a sailor of old who, having always understood the world to be flat, had just been informed that, not only was it round, but he was poised at that critical point between being in sight and out of sight of land. He knew it was safe to sail on into the unknown but was still hesitant.

Now, he had met this woman from over the seas and she excited him. These were, for him, tantalisingly uncharted waters.

It had been different in Weymouth. The years in his relationship with Camilla had defined that horizon and he never needed to go over it and when they had finished he wanted to stay safe within the realm of his former comfort zone and not risk the future. But the effect of meeting Connie had brought out in him strength to shed the shackles of his reticence. It was as if he was being tested and, surprisingly, was not found wanting. David was certainly not an impetuous man but in just a few days of knowing her, he had undergone a quiet uprooting of his past and allowed himself to feel emotions again.

Even so, there were problems. She had been quite candid with him and told him that she was going back to the States with her children as soon as she had settled things here and in London. And he was set on continuing his career in the autumn and had told her of this. Wasn't he expecting a communication any day now offering him a dream position that he would take with both hands? And anyway, what was he thinking, she was married, wasn't she!

Connie had decided that she needed to talk to David. This was potentially a difficult situation and she needed to keep it under control. The fact was that neither of them knew what the future held. She had told him the other day that she wanted to tell him her full story, not just about how Dougal had tracked her down and the link through from her grandparents during the war but she also realised it would be right to tell him her own story. She needed to tell him of her life, the failure of her marriage, Carl's death and what had been driving her to go back to America. And how and why she had now decided to make a go of things here in Oban instead. So rather than wait until sometime after their lunch date she decided to call him there and then to arrange to meet him that night.

"Hi, David," she said cheerily as he answered the phone.

"Connie! I was just thinking of you," he retorted, immediately surprised at himself for having admitted it so freely.

"Well, I was thinking about *you* and so I called to ask if we could meet tonight. I know we'll meet on your birthday but I wanted to have a chance before then to tell you about how we ever came to Oban – you remember when we were on the island I said I would when we had a quiet moment?"

"Yes," recalled David, "I'd love to. What had you in mind?"

"How about coming over to the hotel about 8 o'clock? The kids will have been fed and can watch the TV in their room and go to sleep when they're tired. Maybe you'd let me treat you to dinner for a change?"

"Great! I'll be there."

At 8 o'clock precisely, he walked into the cocktail bar of the Regent Hotel. She was standing at the bar in a black, close-fitting dress that ended just above her knees. Her hair was down and touched her shoulders; David thought she looked beautiful. He had managed to find a shirt and sweater and some trousers that were not jeans, relying on the fact that it was how you wore them and not what you wore that counted.

"I am totally disarmed," said David. "You look wonderful!"

"You look pretty damned good yourself," she said smiling at him.

They ordered drinks and Connie quickly got into her stride. She explained everything to him: beginning with her childhood in Massachusetts; her parents; her marriage to Carl; his death and what it meant to her and the children; her time in London. They sat at their table and over wine and dinner she told him the extraordinary story that Dougal had brought her and how she had planned to go back to the States and begin her new life.

"Connie," he said, "what amazing things have happened to you in your life! But I can't understand why you have chosen to tell me so much. I'm almost a stranger after all."

"Not really, David," she said, looking intently at him. "I feel comfortable with you. You've shown such kindness to me and above all, my children. I wanted you to know who I am. Oh, and there's one other thing I should tell you about."

She then took a deep breath, sat upright, looked directly into his eyes and told him of her decision to come and live in Oban.

"That is the most fantastic idea," he said, "I can hardly believe it. How do Danny and Louisa feel about it? I mean, weren't they looking forward to going back to America?"

"They will be as thrilled as I am, but without the trepidation. I haven't told them yet; but I know how they have fallen in love with the place and will take to it like ducks to water. America is just a name to them. They probably couldn't find it on a map!"

"I am so impressed with the decision you have made. How long have you been here, about a week? And in that short time you have seen so much, discovered so much, learnt so much."

"And felt so much," added Connie. "I have undergone so many emotional awakenings that the outcome was simply that I have to stay here."

"I think it's such a courageous move."

"No, David! It's not courageous. I am not that strong. I have for once in my life let my heart take over and rule my head. I don't care what anyone may say. I have followed my instincts. And you have in no small way contributed to my decision."

"Me? But, how could I?"

"By your love of this place! It exudes from your every pore. Your enthusiasm for it – not just your project – has overflowed on to us. Even if you are not actually saying so, I can see it in your eyes and actions. And your link through my great-aunt helped me hear you and feel how real this place is. You may go off to study birds on the other side of the world and never come back here again but I can assure you that my gratitude to you for helping to open my mind will forever stay with me.

"Oh, I'm sorry, David, that was a little over the top; but that was my heart in charge there."

"You really are something, Connie," said David, quite moved by her words.

"I think it must have been the wine," she replied without apology. "The wine and the occasion. But I meant everything I said."

"I know you did," said David. "You have such passion in you."

He reached across the table and took her hand. The soft light from the candle flame on the table danced shadows across them both and just for a brief moment, their eyes held, and unspoken questions, as old as time, passed between them.

TWENTY

Before their evening came to an end, David had told Connie of his life. It was not an immediate exchange of information. He started to tell her things but Connie needed to coax it out of him and, gradually, as he began to open up, he found himself in full flow. He told her everything and by the end of the evening they sat back, looked at each other and smiled.

"Well," concluded David, lightly, "after that, I don't think we'll have anything else to talk about!"

"That was so good to hear about you and your life. It's so rare to find someone who'll talk to you or listen to you. Over all the years, I've only ever had one ear who would listen to me, that was my friend Amanda in London, and I'd only known her a couple of years. Even then I have to say she never talked about herself, her real self, I mean."

David was quite astounded by his openness. He had never, never told anyone about himself – let alone how he felt – and he found the release exhilarating. He felt freed-up. He had even talked about how he was regretting having to leave Argyll to take up a post in London or wherever, but that he had to take this important step for his career's sake. And she had told him she completely understood. After all, wasn't she determined to make her new life here in Oban having only weeks before been totally committed to returning to the States? No, it was good to have a positive attitude and here was a person as equally determined as him to pursue their goal. He was, however, definitely in envious admiration of the choice she had made. Wouldn't he have chosen the same thing if he were in her position?

Connie watched David recede into the night before turning back into the hotel. It had been a successful night; she had said what she wanted to say. And it had been a lovely night too: David had been forthcoming about himself and they both now knew each other's status. She sauntered contentedly up the stairs back to her room.

David walked slowly back to where he had tied up the launch. That had been a great evening, he thought. He had recalled so much about his life that he hadn't thought about in years; and he had done it willingly, no, more than that, it was as if he needed to. And this was all because of someone who had come into his life so recently, so unexpectedly and so easily. Yes, it had been a great evening. And as he approached his launch and prepared to cast off the mooring lines and motor back to the island marina, he found himself looking up at the starry night and thinking that, whatever the future held for him, at this moment, he was as happy as he had been in a long time.

When they had parted company shortly after midnight, he had told her that the next day would have to be a working day for him. So they arranged to meet at 12.30 the day after, at the same place near the ferry terminal where they had met on that first day. He would moor-up alongside the quay as before.

Connie had told him that she would be spending the day at the town house, trying to work out how to re-shape the internal layout for her and the children.

"When we've decided a plan, you got to come around and see whether you approve or not," she had said.

"I'd like that," David had replied. "Maybe we could have a picnic lunch there to celebrate your new ideas?"

"Hey! No need for a picnic," she had countered with an enthusiastic smile. "All the services are up and running. And the place is fully equipped. Leave it to me, I'll do us a celebratory lunch at home!"

The following morning, Connie was passing the hotel reception desk when a man – whom she recognised but could not put a name to – walked into the hotel. Smiling, he made his way over to her and, to her surprise, introduced himself.

"Hallo there," he said. "That's a stroke of luck! I came over to find out how I might contact you – thought you might have left by now. I'm Mike Kendall from the War and Peace Museum, do you remember? You came in with your two children a short while ago."

"Why sure," remembered Connie. "You gave us such a good piece of advice to visit the Commando Memorial."

"You went then? That's great. Look, you remember I told you we had no information for our displays relating to American Rangers in Oban in the war?"

"Yeah."

"Well, a curious thing happened yesterday when we were sorting out some boxes in a storage cupboard. We found an envelope containing some photographs and two of them actually feature a couple of men in Rangers' uniforms. Look, I've got them here."

He took them out of an envelope along with a number of other ones and separated the two he had mentioned. Connie looked at them, momentarily transfixed. She then asked him to wait there for a moment while she went upstairs to collect something. She came back down with the old envelope from Ardbeg and took out the collection of photographs. She ran through them and took out the one of Helen and Lorraine. She removed the paper-clip and separated the two attached photographs.

"I thought so. Just look at this, Mr Kendall," she said, "the two shots of the soldiers you have are identical to the ones I have."

"Except," he pointed out, "that in this one of yours there is a man in a dark suit on the Ranger's left. In the photograph from the museum, he has been cut out."

"So he has," said Connie. "Now I wonder why that has happened. It's not in amongst the others in the envelope is it?"

"No," he replied, "but I'll just shake it out and run through the photographs just to make sure."

He did so and found nothing.

"So someone has cut the person off the picture," she observed. "Have you any idea how the photographs came into the museum's possession?"

"I've been here for the last four years so the person prior to me would have handled them. She'd been here some time before she went off to work at the Imperial War Museum in London. I'll see if I can contact her and find out how they got here. But anyway, we can't use them so please keep them. That's what I came over here for. If you hadn't been here I would have sent them on to you."

"That's so kind of you. Look, I'll be here for quite some time, in fact I'm in the process of setting up home here in Oban, so if you have any luck, you could contact me in the meantime through the hotel."

"You're coming to live here – that's wonderful!" he responded. "I retired here five years ago from the south-west of England and haven't regretted it for a moment. You'll love it here. Anyway, I'll hopefully be in touch soon about the photographs. I'll chase it up straight away. Well, bye for now then," he said, and strode out of the door.

Connie went back to her room and laid the four images on her bed. Since finding the photographs at Ardbeg she had been too busy to give time to studying them. She now looked attentively at the detail of the four photographs. Two of them showed the Rangers, one tall, the other noticeably shorter, with another man in military style clothing standing on their left. But his uniform was distinctly different from the others and he wore a cap slightly back from his face and at a rakish angle, more typical of the casual manner of an air-force officer. She wondered: could this be the Australian who had been assigned to look after Harry and John L? Why not? In which case, she was looking at her grandfather and the man her great-aunt had waited for. She turned over the picture from the museum to see if there was anything that might have been written there.

In very faded pencil were written, from left to right, presumably to equate with the positions of the figures:

Harry, John and Rod. So! It *was* her grandfather and his friend. Was Rod the Australian? He must have been! She looked at the identical Ardbeg photograph of the same group and turned it over. There was nothing written on it.

She then looked at the museum photograph with Harry and John L. from which the man in the dark suit had been cut out. Equally, in the same faint writing, were: Harry, John and D but because of the cut, the 'D' was at the very edge. She then looked at the back of the Ardbeg photograph which was complete with the man in the dark suit. There was nothing written there.

This was puzzling. It suggested to Connie that someone had written on the backs of the museum photographs to identify the subjects, but not on the Ardbeg ones. Why? Were they already known by Helen – or perhaps Lorraine? Yes, that was a possibility, too. Oh well, she thought, maybe Mike Kendall's contact might come up with something. She would have to wait.

Two days later, at precisely 12.30, Connie, Danny and Louisa stood by the quayside where they had first met David. But the launch was not there. Instead, they stood and watched as a beautiful yacht called *Cassiopeia* eased in next to the quayside and came alongside to a halt. David stood at the helm, smiled and raised his right hand in casual salute to his guests.

Connie, for a moment, fixated, looked unbelievingly at David on the yacht. Yet more surprises. She then glanced at the children and, nodding to them, the three turned to him and sang out their birthday greeting.

"Thank you so much," he said. "I definitely feel a year older, now!"

"What's happened to the launch?" queried Connie, wondering what David was doing on a yacht.

"Well," explained David, "as you'd never seen *Cassiopeia* before I thought I'd bring her over instead. This is my home for the summer; I live on her all the time I'm here and just use the launch for getting about. I sailed her up from the south of England last month. I don't own the launch; I just hired her for my time here."

"She looks wonderful!" exclaimed Connie. "And you're a sailor too! We never thought about where you actually lived. So this is where you go back to at the end of the day? You actually live permanently on your yacht? She's absolutely lovely!"

"Thank you," said David. "Yes, she's a good boat, sails very well and is great to live on. My office and laboratory as well. So come aboard and I'll show you around."

David threw the fore and aft mooring lines on to the quay side and asked Connie to fix the lines through the mooring rings and pass the ends back to him.

"Let the children watch you do it, Connie," advised David, "so they'll be able to do it when it's their turn."

When the boat was secured they were able to step straight off the quay and on board through a gate in the safety railing and take David's hand as he helped them aboard.

"This is incredible!" said Danny. "This is a real boat! The launch was pretty good but this is amazing!"

"Are you the captain?" asked Louisa.

"Captain and owner!" replied David, saluting her with authority. "And you are my guests, so welcome aboard; she's yours to enjoy."

When they were on the boat he invited them to come down below decks so he could give them a guided tour. They descended the companionway steps and before showing them around, he explained her layout:

"She's got this large deck cabin where we are now and, as you can see, bench sofas all around the table. This sort of doubles up as a dining and relaxing area with great views from the windows. One of the best things is that there's a wheel inside the cabin by the navigation table for steering when the weather's cold, wet, or both and a wheel at the rear to enjoy being outside when the weather's good. I've got this large double cabin – the captain's cabin – at the back and one smaller double at the front with two small single ones between the fore-cabin and the salon. I've made the front cabin into a sort of office and laboratory combined, though I tend to use the main salon for computer work as it's comfy and light. There's a galley – that's the kitchen, and two bathrooms – called heads on a boat – one at the front and one en suite with the rear cabin. And that's it! Let's go and have a look. Oh, and I named her after my favourite constellation in the night sky."

The inspection completed, they went outside and sat on the rear deck in the sun.

"Well," enquired David, "what did you think of that? You'd better say the right things. She's my pride and joy, after all!"

They sat there, spell-bound. No one seemed capable of speech, until:

"I think she is the most beautiful boat in the world," swooned Louisa, "and I think to call her after some stars is the best possible thing you could have done. I think it's so great that you can live on her, too."

"The coolest, coolest thing I've ever seen," purred Danny.

"Well, those remarks seem to have given her the thumbs up," granted David. "What about you, Connie?"

Connie sat on the seat by the rear steering wheel. She had heard, but only just, what her children had said and was only faintly aware of David speaking to her. There are moments, she was thinking, when you find yourself out of your emotional depth, when words simply fail to convey thoughts or feelings, simply because the brain is overwhelmed by its inability to respond in the way that it normally would. I can say words, thought Connie, but how could they possibly convey what I am feeling. It's a truly beautiful boat but I want to say so much more than that because it is only part of an extraordinary happening; but this is not the time.

"David, you are a man of continual surprises. How could you have kept this magnificent boat of yours a secret from us for so long? She is without doubt everything that anyone could ask for in a yacht. I love her; she is absolutely dream-like."

"Well, three out of three! You've got some new admirers here, *Cassy*, you'd better keep on your toes," he glowed, patting her.

The moment had arrived for David to clarify what his plans for the day were. Coughing slightly, as if to gain the attention of a distracted audience he spoke:

"This is a very special day for me," he said, suggesting a modest sense of occasion. "Due to their accepting my invitation, I have the great pleasure of celebrating my birthday with my recently acquired but very special friends. It is a double pleasure because, firstly, I seldom ever bother to do anything about it and secondly, on this birthday I am with three people whom I would wish, above any others, to celebrate it with. Connie, Danny, Louisa, are you ready to cast off the mooring lines so that we may take a short trip to our place of dining?"

There was hardly any wind so the task was very straightforward and Connie was able to show the children how to pull the lines through the mooring rings directly on to the boat. With the engine running, David called for them to coil the ropes loosely, leave them on the deck and come and join him at the wheel.

"I'll show you later how to deal with the ropes," he said, "but we only have a short distance to go before we will be using them again. One very useful gadget this boat has is a thing called a bow-thruster and it enables you to swing the front out from the quay without having to push it by hand."

They set off and David told them that the place where they were going to eat was only about a mile or two up the coast and that they could tie-up at a mooring stage close to the restaurant.

"We could have walked," said David said to Connie, "but I thought it would be more fun this way."

"It's brilliant," she beamed.

Ten minutes later they had tied-up at a small wooden jetty and walked up the short path to the restaurant. It was a curious single-storey stone structure with large windows looking across a wide lawn that swept down to the sea. The view across the sea to the island was panoramic. The road that passed the building passed behind it; they had arrived via the sea route.

"Now," David informed them, "we have a table for the four of us right by the window. No one will have their back to the view so we shall all be able to see the island, the sea and, of course, the boat. First, let's go to the bar and have a celebratory drink."

"Connie, Louisa, ladies first. What can I get you?"

"May I have a glass of orange juice like I had when we first met, David?" replied Louisa.

"Of course," said David. "And you, Connie?"

"I am feeling particularly thirsty, so I would like a cold beer, just like I had when we first met."

"I guess I'll have a coke," said Danny, "you know, like when we first met."

"Well now," considered David, "I don't want to feel left out of this, so I think I'll have a cold beer, just like…"

"…when we all first met!" they chorused in and had a good laugh while their drinks were served.

Connie looked around at where they were. He had chosen a very distinctive place, nothing like she was expecting. The internal set-up was of a long bar at the back of the room with a long mirror that enabled you to see the view out to sea without turning around. The kitchen was presumably at the far end and the tables were rectangular, their elongation enabling four people to sit two at one side and one at either end ensuring the view out to sea for everyone whilst still being intimate. The furniture was mellowed, natural wood, giving a warm ambience. There was no music playing, just the sound of the light breeze and the sea. Yes, he had chosen well; she was impressed.

"Cheers, everybody," announced David raising his glass and they all had a thirst-quenching draught.

"Now," said David, "let me tell you the form. I said this was going to be a little special and it is. Firstly, this is a seafood place, nothing but seafood. Secondly, you are not allowed to choose your main course because I have already done so for you. We are all going to have char-grilled lobster. They were ordered yesterday and brought here fresh, this morning from the sea just out there," he said, pointing towards the island. "So, to make this even more special, Danny and Louisa are having a medium-sized lobster each and you and I, Connie, are going to share a giant one between us. Have you all had lobster before?"

"Danny and Louisa haven't and it's so long ago since I had one that this almost might be my first time," said Connie.

"Well, if I may suggest, we don't spoil our appetites with starters, but get straight into the lobsters. If we still feel hungry afterwards we can fill up with a dessert. I have chosen my favourite for us: strawberries and fresh cream.

"But let me tell you how we are going to have the lobsters cooked. The chef cuts them straight down the middle, head to tail, and then grills them upside down on charcoal so that the shells act as a sort of lid and keep all the flavour in. When they're cooked – and they don't take long because they have to remain juicy – he cracks the claws and then it comes immediately from the grill to the table. A little accompanying salad, some home-made chips and off we go."

David called the waiter to start the food and bring the wine.

"No special meal would be complete without a special wine," he ventured. "Now I am no expert on wines, so we are going to have a wine that has been suggested to me by a friend of mine from Dublin, Eddie McBride, my old course tutor at university. I spoke with him the other day and he strongly recommended that we should enjoy a white wine from the southern part of the Spanish region of Galicia; it is a type known as Ribeiro. Everything has been arranged and the wine will be with us a few minutes before the lobster. I do hope that the mother of my two young guests will permit them a small glass each just so they can taste it."

"Well, I don't really think they sh—"

"Good, well, I'm glad that's agreed," said David. "After all, it's a special occasion," he said, smiling conspiratorially at Danny and Louisa.

"Am I mistaken or have I been outvoted again?" Connie said with a knowing smile.

The wine arrived in an ice bucket and David poured them all a glass.

"Happy birthday, David," they said.

And as Connie and he chinked their glasses together, they looked into each other's eyes.

"I must meet your friend Eddie one day, this wine is absolutely delicious," remarked Connie.

"What do you two think?" David asked the children.

"Lovely and fruity," said Louisa, almost precociously.

"Good-bye, coke!" hinted Danny.

The lobster was everything and more than he could have expected. Everyone loved it. Sweet and juicy, it had been cooked perfectly. When the plates were cleared away, Danny asked David if he and Louisa could go and have a look around outside.

"You go and enjoy yourselves. Make sure you keep away from the side of the jetty," cautioned David, "I don't want to have to leave your mum to dive in and save you."

"Promise!" and they were gone.

"I think this could have been a mistake introducing them to lobster," he observed. "It could turn out rather costly if they develop a taste for the high life."

"You're right," she agreed. "They fairly wolfed it down and I don't blame them, it was exquisite, the natural flavour, no spices or herbs. I think I could live off lobster, David. It was totally delicious! And that wine choice! Well, it was so perfect!"

David glanced towards the barman and within seconds another bottle had been placed in the ice bucket.

"Let's just enjoy this together while the children are out playing," he said.

He topped their glasses up and they raised them to each other.

"To the best birthday I have ever had, Connie, and I owe it to you. In fact, I owe a lot more to you. I feel as if I've known you and the children all my life. It seems impossible that we met only just over a week ago."

"It's the same for us, too," she maintained. "The way the children talk about you, well, it's like second nature."

"Connie," he said, gazing into his glass of wine, "I'll be here a couple of months more and although I have the work to complete with the birds, I want to spend as much of that time as possible with you. I want to take you out sailing in *Cassiopeia* and spend some time exploring around and showing you the things that I have discovered while I've been here. Maybe you'd let me give you a hand with the house, you know, sort of help you settle in."

"David, that would be so good," said Connie. "It'd be great to have you with us, y'know, to tell us what you think we might do to the house."

"You do understand that I'll be gone by mid-August because, whatever new job I take, I shall have to take time to arrange everything. This has been my objective, my goal, if you like, ever since my time at Portland was finishing."

"Yeah, of course – I know," she said suppressing a lump of realisation in her throat. "So we'd better make the most of it! We won't have you to ourselves for much longer, will we?"

"Connie," he said, taking her hand like he had done that night at dinner and looking deep into her blue eyes, "when we talked the other night and opened our lives to each other, you have no idea what it did to me. Afterwards I felt truly happy, for the first time in I don't know how long, I underwent a deep retrospective of my life and how I never really knew what I wanted and I realised that what I had been doing was what I thought other people wanted me to do. This had been a sort of driving force in me. Maybe I had been influenced at some time in my life to conform to some sort of expectation. Maybe it had been a desire to please my parents, to show that their dedication to me and the education they gave me was being rewarded, to be honourable. I just don't know. I remember a very special friend of my mother, Agnes Devereaux – she lives in Edinburgh now – telling me to beware of my father's adherence to convention. And you know, Connie, now that I think about it, she was right. Maybe it was genetic, maybe nurture; maybe some of it's still in me. But after the other night, talking with you and listening to what you told me, it was as if I had been held upside down and given a good shaking. All the loose change of my life fell out and I stepped away freed, no longer fettered and held down by that weight.

"And the extraordinary thing was that in its place was the emotional me. And I actually realised it. I told you of my relationship back in Weymouth and how it just couldn't work out. In the end all that was there was, conformity, the status quo, unfulfilled expectation and finally, nothing. In the end she went off to find what she wanted and I just continued being what I was."

"But David, you can't and mustn't change the real you," urged Connie. "If this really has happened to you, it's one of those moments in a lifetime, a moment that few people ever get, because we seldom find the chance to test ourselves against what life had done to us. I think that what you're telling me is that you've found yourself and you are, like, not unhappy about what you have found.

"The other night, after you'd gone, I felt a contentment that'd eluded me for years. In my own way, too, I guess I'd been conventional. My marriage was a mistake, quite simply a mistake. It wasn't his fault; it wasn't my fault. It was just something that convention made me do. I was afraid, uncertain – call it what you will, but y'know, I just carried on, drawn along by an indefinable momentum. When Carl was killed I remember the sense of relief. Relief! Can you imagine it? But even then, I'd decided that I would go back to the States and find my old life – and conventionally re-start it.

"But you and I talked; we sort of said things not just to each other but to ourselves. I heard myself and you listened to me. And you did the same! And we parted company that night, people who'd allowed emotion to come back into their lives."

"You're absolutely right, Connie," responded David, thoughtfully. "And I realise something else has contributed to this change. I have always loved this place. Four years ago I came here a stranger to the Argyll coast and it caught me in its spell: the people, the scenery, the ambience. But the thing that I am referring to, the thing that has made everything so different is, well, I'm going to say it, Connie, it's you – you and the children."

"David..."

"But it's true, Connie, you've given it a new dimension because for the first time I've seen it being enjoyed by other people who have independently fallen for it as I did. And just as it's changed your life, you've made it change mine."

"But David," said Connie, looking earnestly into his eyes, "it's a two-way process. Without you being here we'd have been lost. You lit it up! I came here to dispose of my inheritance. I'd told Dougal to have everything valued and sold off. But from the moment we met you, when you were lying in the sun on your boat, you were always in my mind; I'd never met anyone like you in my life. And y'know, just in the same way it got me, it had the children too. So, along with all my family history, coupled with your friendship and your involvement with the place, I was diverted totally away from my original intention and, well, just look at me now!"

"I am," said David longingly, "and what I see I am so..."

"Hey there, you two," called a voice from outside, "what about those strawberries and cream, we're starving!"

"We mustn't lose this moment, Connie, we'll come back to it," he whispered softly to her.

"All right then, you strawberry monsters," he said beckoning to them. "Sit ye down and we'll call for the feast to continue."

"What've you been up to?" asked Connie, as David turned to signal for the next course.

"Well," confided Danny, "we've been exploring and I'm certain we've been to places we shouldn't have. We've been down by the shore, had a look at the yacht place, you know, where all the little dinghies are and although we didn't actually go on *Cassiopeia* we sat on the jetty and just looked at her."

"And," added Louisa, "we have come to the agreement, David, that whatever might happen in your life, you simply can never, ever sell her. She's very beautiful and special and she's part of you. So that's what we've decided, isn't it, Danny?"

"Absolutely," he replied, looking straight at David.

"Well, in that case I won't," he yielded, looking with a smile at Connie. "To tell you the truth, I hadn't really thought about it," he said turning to the children, "but now that you've been so positive, it looks like I'm stuck with her. What do you think, Connie?"

"Well, I think it's very rude of them to tell you what you can or cannot do with your boat, but I must say I totally agree with them," she said smiling at them all.

"Right, everybody pay attention," ordered David. "Here comes our dessert."

And they watched in awe as a trolley was pushed towards them containing a plate stacked high with luscious red strawberries.

"But this is no ordinary plate of strawberries," pointed out David.

"It's a mountain of strawberries!" exclaimed Danny.

"Exactly!" agreed David. "But which mountain?"

The fruit had been stacked very carefully into an asymmetrical shape and the rounded top was covered with thick cream through which no fruit appeared. They looked at it. They pondered over it.

"Well, I'll give you a clue," he said. "The real mountain's made of rock and there's no cream on it. The real top of the mountain's covered in snow."

"Oh, I've got it!" shouted Connie.

"Don't say, Mum," begged Danny. "I'm still thinking."

"I'm not thinking now," said Louisa. "I know which one it is. Can I say, Mum?"

"Go on, darling, tell us."

"It's Ben Nevis, the highest mountain in Britain," she proudly informed them.

"Of course!" declared Danny. "It's where we're going to learn to ski! I should've noticed it straight away because this view of the mountain of strawberries is the same as the one from the Commando Memorial place."

"David," said Connie emotionally, "what an unbelievable thing you've made for us! And you planned it especially for today. That was so swell, so kind of you. However can we thank you?"

"Well, by helping to demolish it. I don't think we can take it home with us, so let's get on with it!"

"Well, before we do any demolishing," interrupted Danny, "we have a couple of presents for you, David."

"They're to go with *Cassiopeia* so you are not allowed to lose them," Louisa informed him.

Connie handed David two small wrapped parcels on both of which were labels saying simply: 'To David with love'.

He opened the first one to find a box which, when he opened it, contained a pair of stylish Polaroid sunglasses.

"These have got a bright yellow strap that goes around your neck," noted Louisa, "so you can never lose them and they can never fall off you and go into the water."

"They're wonderful!" said David. "Thank you all so much. I promise to be ultra-careful with these. They really are just what I needed."

He opened the second one. Inside the wrapper, laid neatly in tissue paper, was a felt, peaked sailor's cap, the same navy blue as his jacket. David held it in his hand, turned it and looked at it from every angle.

"Now this is a very superior piece of headgear. I've never owned anything as fine as this," he said, trying it on.

"Well, we thought of you as a true sea captain," asserted Danny, "and although we didn't really know what the one you lost was like, we didn't think it would have been as suitable for you as this one."

"How right you were," said David, "and thank you all, thank you all so very much for being with me today."

With the children oblivious to all but the task before them − that of single-mindedly commencing their assault on the north face of Ben Nevis − Connie turned to David and softly spoke to him:

"I have a present for you too, David; I couldn't buy it; it's not wrapped but it comes from deep inside me."

And she leant forward to him, looked into his eyes and softly kissed him, warmly and fully on his lips.

TWENTY-ONE

For the group of four, June's sunny days passed into sunnier July days, and that was how nearly two months crept by unnoticed as they enjoyed the contentment of a unifying time together. The odd cloudy day intervened, the occasional fall of rain, and life did have to carry on with its usual practicalities. But ask them what day it was, what date it was, and you would only have been given an approximation.

David completed his work with the terns, eventually tagging over 300 chicks, and the day he finished they had held a celebratory party at Ardbeg to acknowledge the occasion.

Connie had negotiated a deal with the hotel and they would stay there until the house in the town was ready to be occupied, which they anticipated would be sometime towards the end of August. Her agent in London had made contact to let her know that a potential purchaser had offered the asking price for her house which Connie had accepted and given instructions to proceed with the sale. The house would need clearing and the furniture would have to be delivered to the house in Oban. But these were mere details and Dougal, through his London connections, had liaised with the agent and set up a Power of Attorney for Connie so that she would not even have to go down there to complete the sale. And that suited her fine for that was a part of her life that she was more than happy to leave behind.

They spent time planning the alterations and decoration to the house and, true to his word, David had been there to lend a hand with his ideas and to act as a sounding board for Connie who was re-discovering an artistic expression for her design talents. It was all going smoothly. They found local building contractors who empathised with her proposals and, as the quotes for the work came in, a schedule for starting and finishing the work evolved. Inevitably Danny and Louisa met children of their own age who lived nearby and it was only a matter of time before Connie began to look at the schooling situation. She found a local school that was able to take them in September for the start of the autumn term and it was only a short walk from the house.

During the summer that had given the west coast more than its fair share of good weather, David had taken them out on his yacht not only to show them how to sail it but he had taken advantage of the good conditions to sail around the waters of the Firth of Lorn and beyond. They had taken one impromptu trip to the south coast of Mull and anchored for a couple of days in a quiet arm of the sea called Loch Spelve. This had happened after his promised trip to Banmellach where the sea had been so calm that they had anchored off the beach, lowered the inflatable dinghy from its davits over the stern, and, using the small outboard motor, gone ashore and visited the house.

"We must enjoy this," stated David. "To be able to anchor here is a rarity."

It was after they had finished their visit there that he had suddenly suggested the trip to Loch Spelve.

"It's a sea-loch. A lovely place and because it's almost enclosed the water might even be just about warm enough for us to get in a swim. Well, maybe!"

And by the afternoon a breeze had picked up for them to make the journey of about an hour and a half.

They stayed two nights at the loch, something that neither David nor Connie had even considered doing, but it just happened. The children slept in the forward bunks and she and David, in mutual contentment, happily slept together in the main rear bedroom.

It was one of those moments that occur so naturally. The children were fast asleep and they were sitting on the deck looking at the sunset glow when he turned to her, looked into her eyes, took her face in his hands and kissed her. It was a deep, long-held kiss in which exploration lead to discovery, discovery to realisation. He stood up, took her hand and led her down to his cabin. She would never forget his tenderness when he undressed her. How she had missed and longed so much to know this warmth of gentle, shared passion, as they both provided each other with the answers to those timeless, unspoken questions.

On their second day Danny asked David if they might try to catch a fish. He assembled his little-used fishing tackle and thought it best if they went out in the dinghy to be a bit closer to the shore. They all went and within an hour they had caught a variety of fish sufficient for their dinner.

"I've got an idea," suggested David. "If I drop you all off on the shore, you can gather some dry drift-wood, I'll go back to the boat, get some plates and forks and find something to light a fire and we'll cook them on hot stones around the fire. Okay?"

He returned quickly and organised them to collect the stones to make a base for the fire.

"Right, what we are going to do is use the stones to form a sort of oval shape open at both ends. We'll fill this with tinder and sticks and let it burn away until we've a bed of glowing charcoal. We'll then take these flat stones and place them on the side stones like a bridge across the hot embers and let them heat up. If we make the stones so that one end is open to the wind it'll blow through, really fire the charcoal, and quickly heat the flat stones. Then on with the cleaned fish and, hey presto, our meal will be ready in minutes!"

"This sounds great! Do you often cook this way?" asked Danny.

"No!" replied David with a smile. "I haven't done this since I was a teenager. I remember a friend's dad showing us how to do this when I was probably your age and thought what a great idea it was. I haven't had anyone to do this with for years so it's going to be a bit of a test to see if it still works."

It did. And when they had eaten all the fish, they sat back against some rocks, replete in the evening sun.

"That was amazing," sighed Connie, "and hardly any washing-up."

"I think Wally would be hard pressed to better that," observed David as they cleared up everything and took the dinghy back to *Cassiopeia*.

The following morning, they upped anchor and began their journey back to Oban. As they were passing the southeast point of Mull, David turned to them all and announced that the weather forecast was predicting a light, easterly wind that would mean that it would be more or less on the nose and so they would have to motor back.

"However," he proposed, "it would be a perfect wind to take us northwards and we could visit Tobermory at the top end of Mull. It's only about twenty-five miles and would be a lovely day's sail. What do you say?"

"You're the captain," acknowledged Connie, looking to the children for their guaranteed agreement.

And so *Cassiopeia* turned to the north and headed along the east coast of Mull with the wind pushing them along at about five knots all the way. They went ashore at the end of the day's sail to visit the port of Tobermory with its colourful seafront houses, bars and restaurants.

The next day promised the same weather conditions as the day before and prompted David to come up with another suggestion.

"Today I'm going to take you north-west for an hour or so to show you something that very few people ever get to see or possibly don't even know about. I want to sail back along the coast to find somewhere for the night, so we're going to motor to our destination because the wind isn't strong enough yet to get us there with enough time for our journey back south."

So they upped their anchor from their mooring in Tobermory harbour and headed off.

"I have to tell you, Connie," he admitted, "that I've never sailed to where we're going before."

"Have you actually been there then?" she asked.

"Oh, yes, but many years ago. I went by car."

"So it is accessible then?"

"Certainly, but you have to take a long, long, narrow road that seems to go on for ever."

"So sailing's the best way? Well, I'm fascinated, anyway."

Within a short time, a large, low headland lay before them and when the boat lay due south of it David called for their attention.

"Well, I hope you won't be disappointed," he said, "but lying before you is Ardnamurchan Point with its lighthouse, and its claim to fame is that it is the most westerly point of mainland Britain. Not a spectacular sight I'll grant you but something to know about. There is an old tradition that if you round the point you have to tie a bunch of wild heather to the bow of your ship. Well, we haven't got any heather with us so we'll have to do it another day."

"You realise that's two extremes of the country we've seen, Ben Nevis and now Ardnamurchan Point," said Connie.

"I wouldn't mind eating an Ardnamurchan made of strawberries and cream," said Danny.

And so the summer went on, with none of them really thinking much about the future. More than a month had passed since David's birthday lunch when he and Connie were so close to saying so much. Certainly neither of them had intended revealing how they felt about each other. The occasion had relaxed them and the wine had led them along an unexpected path and it was unquestionably a day of emotion for David – he'd planned it and wanted to spend the day with the three of them. But that half hour or so when the children were away had freed him up and he was on the cusp of telling Connie something that was absolute and from his heart when they came back and the moment was gone.

The opportunity never returned and though he thought about it again and again and wanted so much to say what he had just been about to say, the moment did not come again so naturally. And David was not a contrived man; he had to say it as it was or not at all. He had found a truly happy relationship and didn't feel that talking about it in a prepared way was going to help matters. In fact, although they had become lovers, he was afraid that such an approach might jeopardise the specialness. He just didn't know how Connie would react. No, the time would come, he was sure. He didn't know where or when and in the meantime they were all enjoying themselves. But it would come; it would have to come. Sometime soon they would have to talk about the future.

And it did come.

It came suddenly and unexpectedly.

The way that their time together had evolved was such that although David lived on his boat and Connie and the children lived in the hotel, they often spent days and nights on *Cassiopeia* or at the hotel. Very rarely did he spend the night alone on the yacht. Then one day the marina office telephoned him and told him a letter had arrived for him that morning.

As he motored over in the launch, his mind was pre-occupied by what the letter might contain; who might be writing to him. He walked over to the office where the letter was handed to him by Billy Kilpatrick, the manager of the marina.

"Morning, David," he said cheerfully. "We haven't seen much of you recently. Reckon you must prefer your American lady to us."

"Billy, I think you just might be right there. But don't worry. I'll always have time for a beer with you."

"Couldn't help noticing the university crest on the envelope, could be interesting news?"

"Maybe," he murmured, looking at the envelope. "Excuse me a moment, Billy, I must go back to the boat."

David walked slowly back to *Cassiopeia*. He was pensive; normally he would have torn open the letter in eagerness to read it, but he wanted to sit down, privately, and assess the contents carefully. The crest that Billy had referred to was from a university college in London. Now what can they be offering? he thought.

Gingerly, he slit open the envelope and took out a typed sheet of headed notepaper. Before giving it his close attention, he quickly scanned the letter. Words flashed at him: *...impressive...your career...specially qualified...*

David remembered that he had not responded to an advertised post in this case but had written to them to

276

enquire if there was any likelihood of an opportunity presenting itself in which his experience might be seen in a favourable light. The letter revealed nothing about a position but they were asking him to attend an interview to discuss something that might, in their 'esteemed' opinion, be 'mutually beneficial'. They advised him that they had followed up his references and that he was, indeed, more than adequately qualified for them to wish to pursue the matter further. Furthermore, they wanted him to attend the interview at 9 am exactly one week from today, that they would need his presence for the full day, and that they would, of course, reimburse him for all his travel costs and associated expenses. Perhaps he could be so kind as to contact the university department confirming that he would be attending.

They wanted him to come for an interview!

His heart pumped. To him this sounded very, very interesting. The timing was perfect; he would have completed his task here with the terns and could well commence his future in the forthcoming academic year.

He got up and walked back to the marina office where Billy was just about to have a cup of coffee.

"That coffee smells good, may I join you? Guess what, they've offered me an interview and I'm off down to London next week to attend it."

"London?" said Billy. "I wouldn't want to go and work there; not when there's a place like this."

"Needs must, Billy, you have to go where the work is."

"Even so," he protested, as if questioning David's sanity. "But London?"

David finished his coffee and was off. He went straight back to his boat where he phoned the university and confirmed that he would be with them a week today. He then went on line and booked his return flight from Glasgow and a hotel for two nights. He would be away for three days.

He then rang Connie.

"Hi, Connie, I'm just on my way back from the marina."

"Okay," said Connie. "Look, Danny and Louisa are off for the day with those children they met who live near the house. Their mother, Eileen, is taking them all down to the beach north of Oban. I'm free for the whole day."

"Great. Look, let's take a snack with us and go off in the launch."

"Yeah! Okay. I'll get something together and meet you at the usual place on the quay in, say, about fifteen minutes?"

"Fine; see you there."

He had only just finishing tying up when she arrived.

"Hey, you'll never believe this: the hotel made up a packed lunch and has even put in a bottle of white wine in a cooler. Let's put it in the fridge to keep it really cool. Oh boy! I'm looking forward to this. Where shall we go?"

"Why don't we go around to Ardbeg and have our lunch in the garden. It's been a couple of weeks since we were there. The terns have just about gone so we can just relax. What do you say?"

"Oh, David, that would be so lovely – let's go there!"

"Okay, but you're at the wheel."

"Fine by me!" she agreed.

They took the inflatable dinghy ashore and went up to the house. With a small table and two chairs from the kitchen they sat down in the garden under an apple tree and opened the wine.

"Cheers," said Connie. "You're looking a little preoccupied."

"Hmm. I've had a letter."

"The Inland Revenue tracked you down at last?" she joked.

"No," said David. "Nothing as sinister as that. In fact, it's a letter from a university college in London that I wrote to about six months ago asking if they had any opportunities for a fantastically qualified person like me. I had completely forgotten about them and then, out of the blue, they write to me asking me to go down to London next week for an interview."

"Oh," responded Connie warily, as she felt a rising sense of apprehension. "And what are they offering you?"

"Well, that's just the point," commented David. "They're not saying. They want me down there for a whole day to discuss something that they consider will be 'mutually beneficial'."

"What are you going to say to them?"

"Well, I rang them straight away and told them I'd attend the interview."

"Really?" said Connie.

"Of course. I then booked my flight and a hotel. I'm leaving on Monday. The interview is on Tuesday and I'll be back here on the Wednesday."

"What'll you do if they offer you a job?"

"Well," pondered David, "I'll have to see what it is first. The letter I sent was a shot in the dark, so although they are sufficiently interested in me to pay all my expenses, I don't really expect it'll be what I'm looking for."

"What if they'd something for you up here in Scotland?" asked Connie, angling for a clear response from him.

"Well, that would be perfect," he said.

"What if it was in Australia?"

"Australia, London, Scotland; I'll just have to wait and see what it's all about."

"So if it's a good offer, you'll take it?" she said.

"When I made all these applications and contacts beginning almost a year ago, I knew that I had to continue developing my career when the Portland research ended. This is really what it's about."

"I understand, David, it's just that I'm being a bit nosey and kinda don't like the idea of you being on the other side of the world."

"Well, I don't either," he replied, taking her hand, "but as I mentioned, I don't expect anything will come of this. I was just chancing my hand."

"Even so, David, if nothing comes of this one, there'll eventually be something, and you'll have to go then."

"I suppose so," he said, as he poured another draught of cool wine into their glasses. "Let's have some food, shall we?"

"Yes," she said softly, "just a little."

And though the dappled sunlight shone warmly on her face through the leaves, she shivered slightly. She felt that her appetite was not the only thing that she was losing.

TWENTY-TWO

The passing of the weeks and the time spent with David and the children on *Cassiopeia* had temporarily removed Connie from the worries and demands of reality. The builders had been left to finish the work on her house and as the kitchen would be the last thing to be completed, she had decided to remain on at the hotel until the decorating had been done and the units installed.

The announcement by David that he was going down to London for three days to attend an interview that could potentially change everything in her life was not something that she found comforting. She was in a bit of an emotional limbo, neither content nor despondent. But a change was happening and it put her out of kilter with the direction she felt she was taking.

Then something happened the day before David left for London that served to take her mind away from her worries. Returning from a visit to Ardbeg, she found she had received a note at the hotel from Mike Kendall from the museum, asking her to call in when she had time because he had some information that he felt would interest her.

She called in to see him later the following morning.

"Hi, Mr Kendall," she said, apologising for not having responded to his contacting her earlier.

"Not a problem," he replied, "and please, call me Mike!"

"Okay, sure thing. But you better call me Connie then."

"Right, Connie. Well, how about this: I finally tracked down the person who received the photographs that I showed you. She was still at the Imperial War Museum but had absolutely no problem remembering the circumstances that caused them to be brought to the museum.

"What had happened was that she had an old school friend whose mother had died and, whilst she and her father were sorting out all her mother's possessions, they found a box of old photographs that had actually belonged to her paternal grandparents. Obviously, most of the photographs had special significance in a family context but a few were not. They had separated these out and, as they were just mainly of local views, they had decided that they would throw them away. On looking at them one more time to check that they not overlooked any important ones, they'd suddenly realised that they were actually quite interesting since some of them appeared to have been taken during the War. So they decided to give all the non-family photographs to the museum in case they could find any use for them.

"The girl duly deposited them with my colleague who remembers putting them in a box in a storage cupboard with the intention of dealing with them in due course. And that's where I found them, including the two photographs with the Rangers."

"Did she say who it was who gave her the photos?" asked Connie.

"Yes. Her old school friend was called Catriona – Catriona Henderson."

So, Connie pondered, Dougal's daughter – who worked away from Oban in, was it Edinburgh or Aberdeen, she couldn't quite remember – had given the photographs to the museum, a collection of views of Oban and two of some soldiers, one of which had had a person in civilian clothes who had been cut out of the photograph. So why had the man in the dark suit been cut out of the museum photograph? Who *was* the man in the dark suit? She would have to ask Dougal.

Connie thanked Mike Kendall for finding out the source of the photographs and letting her keep them. After she left, she immediately rang Dougal's office where they told her he was at his home. They gave her his number and she called him.

"Connie," he said, "I'm just taking a day off to do nothing in particular, the proprietor's privilege, I feel. So what brings you to call me?"

"Dougal, would it be possible for me to see you for a few minutes? There are some things I'd like to check out with you."

"Of course," he replied, "always happy to see you. Let me give you my address. My house is only a few minutes' walk from the Regent."

She was with him in less than ten minutes.

"Dougal, you remember the other day I showed you some photographs of my great-aunt and grandmother?"

"Yes."

"Well, I didn't show you them at the same time, but there were some other ones with them too."

She handed him the two other photographs with the soldiers on them she had found at Ardbeg. Holding them both side by side, he looked at them pensively then laid them down, one each on the arms of his chair. He leant back and putting his fingertips together, looked up at the ceiling.

"You recognise them, don't you, Dougal?"

"Aye, Connie, I've seen both of them before, but not these actual copies."

"No," said Connie, "I found those ones at Ardbeg." Then, taking the museum ones out of her bag, she said: "But maybe these are the ones you mean?"

With a quizzical reticence he asked of her: "How did you come by these?"

And she told him the story of how Mike Kendall had discovered the photographs and of how they had come into the possession of the museum

"Yes," confessed Dougal, wearily. "I remember it well enough when we cleared out Fiona's belongings, the accumulation of both her and my memories."

"So in the picture with my grandfather and John L., was that the Australian Air Force officer with them?"

"Yes. The photograph of the three of them was taken by the man in the dark suit, and the other was taken by the Australian."

"So, c'mon, Dougal! Who *was* the man in the dark suit – the one who was cut out of the Museum photograph?"

"Just a moment, Connie," Dougal said as he arose from his chair, "while I get something."

He walked across his living room to a cabinet with shelves on the wall above it. A collection of family photographs in frames of various shapes and sizes were displayed there. He returned holding two of them. Both held black and white photographs. One was an elegant portrait picture of two people, side by side, in their forties. The other, set in a narrow frame, was a poorer quality photograph of a man in his twenties, a man in a dark suit.

"This one here is of my mother and father – somewhat formal – taken some twenty or so years after the War and the smaller one… well, let me show you this,"

He proceeded to dismantle the back of the frame and take out the photograph.

"Connie, just give me the photograph you have there, the one of your grandfather and John L."

Connie handed it to him and he put the two of them together. He turned to her holding the composite photograph. She saw before her eyes the same view of Harry, John L. and the man in the dark suit that she had found in the envelope at Ardbeg.

"You see," pointed out Dougal, "the cut-out part fits precisely with the other part. And look on the back."

He turned the two photographs around, holding them together. There, on the back of the photograph, was written: 'Harry, John L and Donald'. The cut had gone directly between the 'D' and 'o' of Donald, leaving 'onald' on the back of the photograph of the man in the dark suit.

"Yes," said Dougal, pausing for a moment in thought. "That was my father: Donald Henderson, aged twenty-three. He had known the Australian squadron leader, Rod Wallace, for some weeks and had met Harry and John L. with him on the night of the dance at the Marine Hotel."

"But why was he cut out of the photo?" asked Connie.

"Well," began Dougal, "you must remember again that all this began before I was born, but let me explain first of all why my father's photograph was put into the frame I just took down off the shelf. You see, when my daughter Catriona and I were going through my wife's belongings we found the photographs in an old box that had belonged to my mother and father. But with regard to the one that had included my father, he had *already been cut out* and the piece with him on was mixed in with the other photographs. These photographs had been collected by Catriona's grandparents and when she found the cut-out of her grandfather she said it was the only one she had ever seen of him when he was young and so she had a frame made, mounted the picture in it and it has been on that shelf ever since. It was as simple as that.

"But the question of *why* it had been cut out, well, that is another story altogether and one that I will tell you about."

"Hey, Dougal, this is beginning to sound a bit like when you came to see me in London!"

"Well, yes, I suppose it is in a way. In fact, it is closely related to the story I told you then and, who knows, maybe I should have told all of it to you. But in my own mind I felt it was best left out because this was very much to do with my family. I kept my original story to you to the events uncovered by Charles Denholm from the 'Search' company, albeit, embellished by me with things I knew about that were pertinent. Believe me, it's quite a story in its own right."

"Look, Dougal, you don't have to…"

"No, Connie!" he said, interrupting her forcefully. "I want to tell you. It has been with me for many years and I have never told anyone. It has weighed on me and I think I'd like to get it off my chest."

"Okay, Dougal, fire away! You know I'm a good listener."

This unfamiliar outburst by Dougal seemed to relax him. Turning his chair towards Connie and leaning forward earnestly, he began to tell her:

"I was well into my thirties before my father first told me. One evening when we had been away fishing on the river up near Ballachulish, we sat in the lounge of the hotel we were staying at and he told me of how his marriage to my mother, just before the end of the war, although adequately content, had never been a passionate one. He told me that although he had grown to love her over the years he had never been *in* love with her. His first and only real love had been none other than Helen McKechnie, your great-aunt. He was only two years older than her but when he was eighteen those two years might have been twenty. She never even noticed him and being a very shy man, he could never bring himself to tell her of his feelings.

"By the time he was twenty-three your great-aunt had met and fallen for John L. Martin. My father had been at the very dance – invited to come along by his Australian friend Rod Wallace – that Harry and John L. went to. And so the poor man watched mortified as the object of his love of nearly six years, fell for another man within a day of meeting him.

"The next day, before the two Americans were due to leave, Rod asked my father to take a photograph of him with the two Rangers in front of the hotel. He then told him to go and stand with them while he took a photograph of them too. Sometime after they had gone, Rod had the photographs developed. He had copies made for my father and copies made for Helen and Lorraine – hence the ones in my parents' collection and the ones that you found in Ardbeg. It was my mother, some years later, who wrote the names on the back of the photographs, you know how you sometimes do, having asked my father who the soldiers were. On the day the two American Rangers left Oban, knowing that Helen was waiting for John L. to return, my father decided to cease his fruitless quest for Helen. His pain was relived those few years later when my mother asked him the names of the soldiers on the photograph. And that was when – unbeknown to her – he cut the photograph. He made it clear to me that he was separating the two soldiers from him and not him from the soldiers! Semantic, maybe, but it gave him a sense of closure."

"Dougal," sighed Connie, "such sadness, such loss. Maybe the whole goddamned human race is blighted with the ability to make a mess of their lives."

"Yes, Connie, they may well be. In fact there is a continuation of this story in which I have to make an apology to you. An apology because I told you an un-truth or perhaps I might get away with calling it a mis-truth, if such a word exists."

"Jeez!" uttered Connie. "Whatever are you going to reveal next?"

"You may remember me telling you of how Harry, your grandfather, came back to claim Lorraine, and that he was unaware of where John L. was? Well, he promised he would try to find out where he was. He did go searching through all the channels he knew to find him but when he found out what had actually happened to him, he couldn't bring himself to tell Helen the truth."

"What do you mean 'the truth' for heaven's sake? Surely he was killed; it was official wasn't it?"

"No. He did leave the landing craft on that day but wasn't killed by machine-gun fire. He was caught by a mortar shell blast that wounded him terribly. His chest was ruptured and he lost one of his lungs but he didn't die. He, along with thousands of other casualties, was taken back to Britain and then to America on a hospital ship. Harry discovered that he had been taken to a hospital in California, San Diego to be precise, where he underwent convalescence in the warm, dry climate."

"So he recovered then?"

"Yes, but in the process a specialist nurse was assigned to him and during his recovery an affair began. They married as soon as he was discharged by which time she was pregnant with their son. Well, it seems that his new wife was a bit of a play-about and not long after their son was born she left him for another man and he had to bring up the child alone."

"And all of this," said Connie taken aback, "happened between June 1944 and the end of the war?"

"It would seem so," replied Dougal.

"So on finding this out, my grandfather decided to tell Helen a lie; why? To protect her from knowing that the guy had cheated on her?"

"Well, it was agreed between Lorraine, her mother and Harry that she would probably get over him never coming back for her because he was dead rather than because he had, as you say 'cheated' on her. Yes, rightly or wrongly, they took this decision."

"I guess I'm in no position to judge what they did," admitted Connie. "It was a long time ago and I suppose the whole world was still trying to recover after the War. But when you think about it, from your father's unrequited love for Helen to her hopes and expectations based on two days of wartime romance with an American soldier, and add on to it the story of Hamish and of Lorraine and Harry being killed, even John L. and his failed affair with the nurse, you just wonder where we all go wrong. I mean…Dougal, even my *own* life has been hampered with making wrong decisions. Or perhaps we just don't know how to recognise what should be the right decisions."

"Connie, don't dwell too hard on that because you could become even more depressed," recommended Dougal. "This story is not finished yet.

"John L. Martin's son grew up with his father who never married again. You may remember that I told you that I didn't know what the L stood for in my original story. Well I did later find out, because he switched his own names around when naming his son Lincoln J. Martin."

"How did you find that out?" asked Connie.

"How did I find out? Because he came here to see me."

"What?" cried Connie in astonishment, "John L. came to see you? How on earth…?"

"In his later years John L, became quite ill. His one lung wasn't doing well and he spent much of his day in a wheelchair being looked after by his caring son. About eight years ago Lincoln brought his father over to Europe to visit the landing grounds in Normandy where his father had been so badly wounded. It was a very moving time for him and it was while he sat in his wheelchair looking at a memorial to the fallen at Omaha Beach that he fell into conversation with another veteran. He, too, had survived but further along the coast. He had been a Ranger like John L. They swapped stories. The man told him that, although he had never trained with the British Commandos, after the War he had visited a site in Scotland where a monument had been erected in their memory, some place north of Fort William he had said.

"Well, that set him going. He got Lincoln to find out the details and they returned to England and flew up to Inverness. They hired a car and drove down to Spean Bridge. On seeing the monument and remembering his time there during the War, the emotion was almost more than he could take. And he then told his son of his wartime visit to Oban and of the woman with whom he had fallen in love.

"He asked Lincoln to take him there just to see the old place. When they arrived there he remembered the Marine Hotel which had for some reason now been re-named The

Regent Hotel. They stayed the night there and the following day they made enquiries about the existence or otherwise of my company. John L. had remembered my father's name after all these years. They called on me and explained their presence, John L. telling me everything I have just told you. He asked if Helen was still living here, indeed if she was still alive. Had she married? Did she have children? And so on.

"She was, of course, living in the town house and I told him so. I told him that, after he had left Oban, she had waited patiently for his return and that since the end of the War she had believed him to be dead. I did not tell him of the story that had been woven to protect her. He was quite stunned by the fact that, in waiting for him, she had never married. I asked him if he would like to meet her and I remember him looking at his son as if to seek his opinion. Lincoln said yes, it would be a great idea but wondered how the best way of going about it would be. I suggested that we call her but John L. said no, that he would like to see her first from a distance and then approach her.

"We decided to take the car to near her house and just wait for her to come out. We waited a couple of hours and then her front door opened and she stepped carefully out of the house. It really was quite an emotional moment. John L. just stared at her. Small tears formed in the corners of his eyes and rolled down his cheeks. His son said come on let's go and meet her and John L. just sat there slowly shaking his head from side to side. No, he had said, no, let's leave her alone. Let her think me dead because when I see her now and know of the pain I caused her to suffer, I wish I was dead myself.

"I received a letter from his son some three weeks later to say his father had died in his sleep and that he had forever been talking about Helen from the moment they left. I recall that Lincoln concluded his letter by saying how, in his remorse, his father had understood, far too late, that in failing to recognise the significance of meeting her, he had missed the most important opportunity in his life to determine his destiny. Because of his failure he had let such unhappiness pervade both his and Helen's lives."

"What a sad story," said Connie, as she reflected on how easy it was, as in her own marriage and John L's situation, and indeed countless others, for the unwary to fall into the wrong relationships.

TWENTY-THREE

He took a taxi to the airport. What the hell, thought David, if they want me there, they can damn well pay for it. Well, they had offered anyway. He had made up an overnight bag on the boat and then stayed at the hotel with them for the early arrival of the taxi. Although he had set himself an early alarm call he had slept lightly and woke before the ringing tone, switching it off before it disturbed the others.

Connie had hardly slept that night. In fact, since their outdoor lunch at Ardbeg a week ago she had been preoccupied with her thoughts day and night. Life, she kept telling herself, is a dynamic affair. Nothing is or should be set in stone and we should always be ready to take on new opportunities for ourselves and to accept that others, equally, may have an entirely different agenda of their own. In other words, we should be flexible, understanding, and reasonable...

David had been totally clear to her when they first met about his work and his plans. His personal life had been relatively ordinary; mundane even. A sheltered upbringing; educated to take on a scientific way of life; encouraged by parents to achieve; having to be dogged by their expectations. And then on top of this, an encounter with romance that ended leaving him determined never to risk anything like it again. But Connie was quite sure there was another side to his determination: a driving force. After all, he had been successful with the tagging project and another thing, you don't sail single handed from Weymouth to Oban without some special qualities.

And as for her, she couldn't have come at him from a more different direction.

Connie hadn't been as open with him as she might have been when they first met but then her background had been so much more complicated and encumbered. Her parents had put themselves first. She hadn't wanted for anything materially, but – and she had never understood this – they indulged themselves at the expense of her feeling part of a family. She was almost an irrelevance to them. That she went the way she did and married Carl Lindeger was somehow an inevitable outcome of this upbringing. But she had changed or if not changed at least a side to her had emerged that had never before shown itself. It had taken Carl's death to put her in the position to be able to allow this change to come about.

She and David had found each other in the most improbable of circumstances and whilst she had been able to allow her new persona to dictate a dramatic change to her plans, David was trapped in his conventionality. She was going to go ahead with her plan to settle in Oban with her children whatever David decided to do. But she was under no illusion that what she wanted was for him to be able to break away from his lingering sense of career expectation and to be with her. But not under her terms. No, that was something he had to do because he wanted to. And right now she had decided that she would let him do just that. Although deep down in her heart she felt she was going to lose him, being manipulative was not her style.

The taxi was outside the hotel; it was time for David to go. He opened the children's door and blew a kiss to their sleeping forms.

Connie got out of bed and came over to him. He held her close to his chest. She tucked her head under his chin and it felt good.

"You must go now. Take care of yourself," she said. "I'm sure it will all go well."

The taxi dropped him off at Glasgow airport and a short wait in the departure lounge allowed him time for a quick cup of coffee.

The flight touched down on time at Heathrow and with the minimum of fuss he took a taxi to his hotel near Russell Square. David was feeling slightly nervous since the interview had been set for Senate House, the administrative centre of the University of London and not the college itself. As a result, he had somewhat lost his appetite for lunch and decided to take a stroll around the area and perhaps stimulate it for dinner.

It was interesting for him to be back in London again, not just because it had been a long time since he had been there, but because having been on his boat and in the relative remoteness of the Argyll coast, he was reminded of the enclosed feeling of a big city. He had forgotten about how lonely one can feel in such a place and, eventually, when he sat down for his dinner, he felt quite foolish sitting alone at a restaurant table with no one to enjoy the food or the occasion. That night at his hotel he lay in bed thinking of Connie and the children; of *Cassiopeia*; of the last two months. Pull yourself together, man, he thought, you've come down here to do something important, this is your future career you're talking about. And anyway, you'll be back up there again in a couple of days.

The following morning at 8.55am, David entered the reception area at Senate House, told the security desk who he was and waited for someone to meet him to take him to his interview.

A rather matronly, bespectacled lady in her fifties approached him.

"You must be Dr Gregson," she boomed, peering over the rims of her glasses. The tone of her voice made it unclear as to whether she had asked a question, given an order or simply made an observation.

"Yes," he replied, covering all possibilities, "David Gregson."

"In which case, please follow me; I have a group of people who wish to meet you," she continued in her stentorian manner.

I don't think I like you, thought David, as he followed her waddle along the corridor.

They entered an oak-panelled room that had in its centre a large rectangular conference table.

"Dr David Gregson, gentlemen," she announced.

"Thank you Miss Small," replied a slight, bald man wearing an ill-fitting suit far too large for him.

Miss Small, thought David; how unfortunately inappropriate.

"Dr Gregson," he began, his thin, piping voice complementing his general appearance yet denying the gravitas implicit in his position, "my name is Sir Jocelyn Napier, and I am from the Research Board of the University. May I present on my right Professor Trevor

Royston, a marine biologist also from the University. To his left is Mr Alan Trenchard from the Foreign Office and next to him M Charles Emanuel from the French Embassy.

"You may well be wondering," he continued, "what on earth you are doing here in the company of this seemingly unconnected group of people. Well, let me tell you first of all that we requested your presence as a result of the recommendation of Professor Royston. He is, as I am sure you are aware, a fellow marine biologist, pre-eminent in his field – the mass movement of planktonic and nektonic organisms in the world's oceans – and as such has been following your progress at the Portland Marine Institute with more than just a cursory interest. Of particular importance to him has been not only your tailoring of a tracking system to a particular species of bird but your close liaison with the company who manufactured the device. Additionally, your activity and monitoring of the results means to us that you represent the full package. By this I mean that you encompass all the aspects that we are looking for in placing critical personnel in an international oceanographic team.

"I will be handing you over to Professor Royston after this meeting and we would like you to spend the rest of the day with him so that he may enlighten you further and brief you fully on what we are proposing, namely that you be chosen to be considered as the project Operations Leader representing the United Kingdom, in conjunction with a French counterpart, in a combined operation to monitor the movements of the various turtle species that breed in the western Indian Ocean.

"As you well know, this is not a new concept, but what our respective governments are preparing to carry out is the total monitoring of both sustained and endangered species. This emanates from a United Nations directive brought about by the need to prevent natural resources being depleted to the point of no return. We know for example that turtles are caught indiscriminately and end up on some epicurean menu in China. So what we are doing is putting a team together to monitor everything from the laying of their eggs on a beach to their unfortunate demise in a steamy oriental kitchen.

"Mr Trenchard from the Foreign Office will be the reporting line for the UK and M Emanuel will be in contact with Paris after this meeting when a corresponding representative – Mr Trenchard's opposite number – will be selected. It is our intention for this to be a three-year operation financed jointly by the two respective governments and the UN. The results will be reported to both government and UN committees by Professor Royston who has been appointed, by agreement of all parties, as the Project Manager.

"Well, that is all I have to say just now. I propose a short coffee break so that Dr Gregson can meet everyone in an informal manner and then we will leave him in Professor Royston's capable hands."

And bang on theatrical cue – she must surely have been listening at the door, thought David – the competent Miss Small swept into the room with a trolley laden with refreshments.

David spent a thoroughly enjoyable day with the Professor who was probably in his late fifties but with his professorial beard, unkempt thin hair, a rather gleeful expression and boyish enthusiasm, he could have got away with being seventy or forty.

"Call me Trevor, David; I really can't be doing with all this reverential crap. I've made the grade and they all think I'm a genius but the reality of it is that they need people who look and behave like me. It gives them a sense of propriety. I mean, can you imagine a chap holding this high scientific post in a Savile Row suit? Absolute poppycock if you know what I mean?

"Look, I know your work. You've a damn good brain on you and I'd love to have you on board. They're going to offer you a whacking good salary and all the extras plus living costs and you'll get exposed to all the brass both here and over the water. The UN love this sort of thing; sense of purpose and responsibility to the planet and all that sort of stuff.

"Right, let's have a look at a map and get a feel for what we're at."

He took out a large paper map of the eastern African coast that included Madagascar, the Comoros islands, Mauritius, Réunion, the Seychelles and numerous islet groups way out into the Indian Ocean.

"We're going to operate from Victoria in the Seychelles – well they used to be British – and the French, well, there are lots of old Froggy places around but I think they'll go for Mauritius or Réunion. We'll be involved with the appropriate authorities from Madagascar, some East African states like Tanzania and Kenya; India, Thailand, Malaysia, Indonesia, the Aussies and so forth, but we'll really be running the show. The French give the impression that they are keen to be seen involved but my view is that they're a little half-hearted about it; all this gastronomic stuff that Napier was going on about, well, let's face it, they probably like eating the bloody things.

"I may appear to be a bit flippant at times, but believe me, it's a very serious matter and I intend to have a very forthright and disciplined approach to it. Here, I've got a synopsis of the project and I've highlighted the responsibilities that would be yours. Browse through it when you have a moment. It's quite important that you do so because when I deliver you back to Napier he'll be asking you a load of pertinent questions. He may look like one but he's no fool. Any questions you want to throw at me?"

"Yes. Timetable; you say it's a three-year project but from a logistical point of view, when would you want me to start, I mean actually go out there?"

"As soon as you can. Give you a couple of weeks to tie up your affairs here and then off we go. I'm going out to Victoria two weeks tomorrow. We could travel together. We'll do all the organising and contacting when we're out there, so make sure you bring your address book with you."

They took a light lunch and then continued an extensive question and answer session. At the end of it David felt exhausted but exhilarated. It was an incredible opportunity, way beyond anything he had anticipated and the prospect of heading up an operation with international partners was heady stuff.

When the Professor had finished his presentation, he took David back to the conference room where the indomitable Miss Small took it upon herself to tell him to 'wait here' as Sir Jocelyn would be along 'shortly'. I must have upset this woman in another life, thought David.

Sir Jocelyn Napier entered the room some ten minutes later apologising profusely for keeping David waiting. He was holding a number of papers in his left hand and a pen in the other.

"Dr Gregson, how did it all go? We have a fascinating project on our hands here; very important and very prestigious. Did Professor Royston convince you of the importance of having you on board?"

"Well, absolutely," said David not wishing to risk being over enthusiastic. "It seems that the Professor is as committed as yourself and I do have to say that it is infectious. I see it as a wonderful opportunity to progress and develop my own ideas whilst being part of an impressive set-up. I also happen to believe strongly in what the project has been conceived for."

"In which case, subject to me presenting our offer formally, are you interested in taking up the post?"

"Most certainly," replied David. "Professor Royston asked me if I would be able to join you within the next two weeks and actually to fly out there with him."

"And?"

"Well, I have no commitments other than to deliver all my documentation and equipment back to Portland. I have a house to sell and a boat to put into storage but I should be able to sort that out in time."

"Excellent! In which case let me lay out the conditions associated with the post."

David read over the documents that Sir Jocelyn had put before him. This was not a university appointment. It was actually a UN appointment run under the auspices of the University of London. That would have impressed his father – the UN! And the salary was unreal.

"Well, if you are happy with what you see before you, I would ask you to sign this document which is by way of a Letter of Agreement containing the essential elements of your contract, the object being that, with your signature on the Agreement, I can draw up the official contract and have it ready for your signature when you come back and for us to be able to do all the necessary paperwork for visas, security, powers of attorney, et cetera, et cetera."

David took the pen offered to him and duly signed his name at the appointed place.

"I will now call Miss Small and ask her to take a photo copy for your retention. Perhaps on your way out you could be good enough to present your travel costs and expenses to her plus your bank details so we can make good what is due to you."

He stood up and extended his hand to David.

"Thank you, Dr Gregson, for coming to see us today. I must say I am delighted at the outcome and can assure you that not only will it be a most interesting project for you but will be a major stepping stone in your career."

He opened the door and David passed through to the antechamber where the ogre stood awaiting him.

"I understand from Sir Jocelyn," he addressed her, "that if I present an account of my travel costs and associated expenses regarding this visit you will be able to transfer the appropriate amount to my bank account, the details of which I have appended to this list of costs, not all of which, I would point out, have accompanying receipts."

"In which case, if there are no receipts I cannot possibly make a refund."

"I appreciate your point, Miss Small; however, as I will not be paying my hotel bill until tomorrow morning nor will I be paying for my remaining taxi fares until tomorrow, I have taken the liberty of presenting you with the rate per night for the hotel and with regard to the taxi fares, I am, not unreasonably, assuming they will be the same as yesterday. I will not be presenting a charge for my evening meal tonight as Professor Royston has kindly invited me to join him."

"This is all most irregular," she said as her employer walked towards her desk on his way out. "Sir Jocelyn, Dr Gregson is seeking to claim for expenditure on expenses that he has not yet incurred. I really must…"

"Just do it, Miss Small. If we were to be so pernickety over such minor details, we would still be living in the Stone Age."

And Sir Jocelyn Napier, man of letters, shining pate and indifference towards his attire, was gone. David placed his expense papers on her desk, patted them and said:

"I believe three working days is the normal period."

He had a thoroughly enjoyable evening with Trevor Royston during which they talked about all and everything and never once managed to mention the project.

The following morning David left London for the airport at Heathrow. By 6 o'clock he was back in Oban standing at the Regent Hotel bar with Connie, drinking a well-earned cold, cold beer.

TWENTY-FOUR

"You've no idea how much I needed that," said David, draining his beer in one go.

"Yes I have," countered Connie, as she put her empty glass down on the bar next to his.

"Ah! I think you do," he agreed. "Do you think you need the next one as badly as I do?"

"More so," she asserted as the barman poured them another two.

"Cheers," they toasted, looking straight at each other.

He gazed at Connie and thought how much he had missed those blue eyes.

She looked at David and thought how empty it had been without him these three days.

"How've you been, Connie?"

"Oh, just fine, y'know; busy as a bee. One thing happened while you were away. The kitchen people called the morning you left and told me that the units had arrived and they would come around and fit them in if everything was ready: plumbing, wiring, that sort of thing."

"When are they coming then?"

"Well, that's the problem, I'm not sure if it's ready for them yet. I'll have to get the builder around and make sure. Could you come around tomorrow and have a look? I'm sure you'd know if it was ready."

"Sure," said David, "we'll check it out tomorrow."

"And you, how did your London trip go? Did they…"

"Thought I might find you both here!" interrupted Danny, climbing up on to one of the bar stools. "Lou has just gone up to the room to drop off the bags; she'll be down in a mo."

"Hey, how did it go for you guys?" She turned to David: "They went to the school today; it was an open day for new pupils."

"Really cool! We both liked it. I hardly saw Lou except at lunchtime. There are about thirty new kids coming in September, apparently that's just about the same number who are leaving to go on to the senior school. Everyone was really friendly and some of them know Ronnie and Alison who live around the corner from us."

"Hi, Mum! Hi, David!" chimed in Louisa.

"Danny says it was good today," said David.

"It was really fun. I can't wait for the term to start."

"Wow, that's not what we usually hear, is it?" reminded Connie.

"You'd better enjoy the rest of the summer holidays," cautioned David, "you've only got a week or so to go."

"I'm really looking forward to going there," enthused Danny. "I want to be at the school; I just like it here."

"Me too," added Louisa.

"I love to hear them say that, David, y'know – that sense of belonging."

"Who's for a visit to Wally's?" asked David, anticipating that it might be awkward to start talking about belonging in Oban when he was just about to leave. He would have to find a way to tell the children as well as Connie but, for now, he thought he could deflect it with an offer he knew they wouldn't refuse.

"Yes!" they chorused.

"But we'll have one more drink here before we go. This beer tastes too good to leave alone," he said.

Two more were ordered. The children wandered off around to the hotel lounge to see what was on the TV, leaving David and Connie with their beers, just as they had been when the children came in.

"Right," said Connie, "C'mon, tell me about it. What happened?"

"Well, they want me to be part of a UN team tagging and tracking turtles."

"What, you mean like what you've been doing with the terns?"

"Yes, sort of, only this is much more geo-political."

"Geo-political?" she said incredulously.

"Yes, it's part of an international effort being run by the UN."

And he then proceeded to tell her everything. He knew he would have to tell her some time and this opportunity had been handed to him so he took it.

"The Seychelles! But have you actually accepted the job?" she asked, hoping against hope.

"No, not yet. I've signed a Letter of Agreement so that they can draw up the contract. Then when I go down to see them next, the contract will be ready for me to sign."

"Are you going to sign it?"

"Connie, this is beyond my wildest dreams to be offered this sort of opportunity. You know I have to do something now that the Portland research has come to an end and these people have headhunted me. It's not only a great honour but it's taking my career a quantum-leap further."

"I know, David, I should be rejoicing with you over this and drinking champagne, not beer. It's just that I shall miss you and so will the children. You have become such a part of our lives that we must have taken it for granted that you would always be in it. I know it's incredibly unfair of me to say so but that's me, I'm afraid."

"But, Connie," said David imploringly, "I'll come back to see you all. It's only a three-year contract and it'll be gone in no time at all."

"Of course, I know you will, but three years is actually quite a long time and the Indian Ocean is a long way away. The other day I jokingly mentioned Australia; well, David, for me it might as well be Australia, or Mars come to that."

"Oh, Connie," said David.

"No, David, you have always been honest with me. I've known that you had been seeking this kind of opportunity long before we met. We have only known each other for a couple of months and even after we had first met I didn't tell you the real reason we were here, and remember, whilst our friendship grew, I told you we were

310

back off to the States for the Fall. It's just that something very special happened and you were a vital part of it and I made the decision to stay here and make my life. I've no right to expect you to stay here."

"Connie, we'd better get the children and go and eat. Perhaps when they have gone to bed we can come back here and talk some more."

"Maybe, maybe not," she said wearily. "From what you've told me of the last couple days, you'll be off to London next week and then before you know it you'll be in the Seychelles. No, as I see it, I have a life to make; you have a career to make."

She went off to get the children and they all walked off to the restaurant. Wally's was a favourite of theirs and they were always made welcome there. This was very helpful because whilst the children were intent only on gorging themselves, David and Connie were finding it hard to be buoyant.

When they got back to the hotel, Connie told David that she was tired and wanted to crash out.

"You go back to *Cassy*, David. You've had a busy three days with all the travelling as well and you'll have a lot to sort out. Better that you spend your time arranging things and let us know when you are planning to leave."

"But Connie, the kitchen! I promised I'd come around tomorrow with you and check that everything was ready for the fitting."

"Don't worry about the kitchen, David. That's the least of your worries. I'll get Mr McColl around in a day or too; it'll be fine. Now I'm off to my pit before I fall asleep on my feet."

She gave him a light kiss on his cheek, turned, called the children from the lounge and walked to the lift.

David slumped away from the hotel, dejected with the outcome of events, emotionally drained.

But what had he really expected? It was obvious that they had started to develop a very happy relationship and they had both spoken intimately about their emotions, about how each of them had stirred something in each other. She had become special to him, of that he had no doubt. He had initially been bowled over by her blue, blue eyes and that, combined with the colour of her hair, was something he had never seen before and he was enchanted by her. And then her personality took over: she was fun and undaunted by a challenge and her two children, yes, her children, they had all combined to make him lose his way – or maybe to find his way. Yes, that was a possibility that he hadn't considered before – finding his way.

If this hadn't happened and he'd just come up here, finished his work and been offered this job, it would have been just as he'd planned. The best-laid plans and all that, so why not follow his instincts? But no, he'd made his decision. This UN project was such an opportunity that it would be unthinkable to turn it down. No, he was committed; he was determined to take it with both hands. That was the way he had to go.

He took the launch back to the marina and his boat. When he opened his e-mails he found a couple of letters from the University waiting for him. They had wasted no time! The first letter was from Napier confirming everything and letting him know that Professor Royston was to be his point of contact henceforth. He had also attached a scanned copy of the Letter of Agreement that David had signed, an official letter offering him the post and a copy of the Contract that he was to sign, for his perusal. This was efficient, thought David.

The second letter was from Trevor Royston expressing his thanks to David for coming and looking forward to seeing him next week when he came down to sign the Contract and plan their starting date and prepare the schedule of work.

He quickly sent acknowledgements to them both and told Trevor that he would call him as soon as he had tied up all his loose ends.

David looked at his watch. It was just after 8 pm, still early evening and, in spite of the shortening days, still light outside. He wandered over to the marina buildings to see if the bar was open. He could do with a nightcap and a little company. The marina launch was still there suggesting someone was still around. He went into the bar and there was Billy on his mobile. He quickly finished the call and greeted David.

"Hey! Good to see you again, twice in four days," he said, leaning back in his chair. "That was someone enquiring about Doddie Coulter's launch. He's decided to sell it; you interested?"

"No, Billy, sadly not. In fact, I need to speak to him in any case. I'm off away next week and need to return it to him."

"What? You're not going are you? Did that job offer in London come to something then?"

"Yes. But it's not going to be in London. Would you believe that I'm off to the Indian Ocean? The Seychelles to be precise."

"Man, that's incredible. Come on, let's go to the bar and celebrate."

"Open up then, Billy, the drinks are on me."

"Lucky for you the bar's not full then," he said and went around to the other side.

"What's it to be then, Champers?"

"No, Billy, I really came in for a quick one to help me sleep but let's put a dent in that Oban malt. I feel a large measure will do for starters."

"Right you are, then; anything with it?"

"No, let's keep the bottle on the bar. You've got more in stock I hope?"

"A box or two, enough to keep us going until breakfast, I should think."

"Good man! Cheers then."

"Cheers, David! Here's to your new job in the sun."

David and Billy then proceeded to finish off both the whisky and themselves. But before darkness descended on the day and oblivion on their senses, David arranged for Billy to take *Cassiopeia* out of the water and deal with her de-commissioning. He would also get the launch back for Doddie to sell.

Whist Billy was under the impression that they were celebrating, David was clearly drowning his sorrows. The fine malt whisky disappeared as renewed draughts depleted the contents of the bottle. Another bottle was placed on the bar and they made further inroads into the inebriating liquid.

As the evening drew on Billy listened to David trying, unconvincingly, to justify leaving both the most beautiful woman and the most beautiful place in the world, to spend three years of his life studying turtles in the tropics and, apparently in so doing, further the development of his career. David told Billy how Connie was the most wonderful thing that had ever happened to him and that he was leaving her and where he wanted to be because he just didn't really know why. He spoke with slurred passion as he heard himself say the words, for deep down inside him *in vino veritas* was playing out its time-honoured maxim: a drunken man's words are a sober man's thoughts.

But it was all to no avail because the next morning as they awoke, having slept in two of the bar's armchairs, neither of them could remember much of what they had said the night before.

David left Billy to nurse his hangover and returned to *Cassiopeia* where he tried to gather his thoughts. He called Connie but there was no reply from her phone. The hotel informed him that she had taken the car and they would be away until the weekend. The receptionist had no idea where they were going.

He had to sort himself out. He couldn't stay around in Oban waiting for her to return. He had to start gathering his things together, contact Portland, and make numerous other arrangements. He decided to call Dougal.

"David!" said Dougal with surprise in his voice. "I was wondering when I would hear from you. As ever I'm a busy man, but come around and we can talk about things over lunch together."

"That would be great, Dougal. Your office at 12.30?"

"Make it one o'clock."

"Okay, bye just now."

With three hours to get on with things, David tried to put his hangover to one side and make progress. It was slow but sure. Gradually, he watched the list of things he had to do grow longer, slow off and then stop. The problem of the house in Weymouth was something he had to resolve. It no longer held any emotional ties for him – he had moved on now – and he was certain that he had to either sell it or generate an income by letting it. In either case he would have to go down there to put something in motion. He decided that a day's visit next week would be the best thing and planned to pick up a hire a car after he arrived at Heathrow and drive straight down to Dorset. That would optimise his time as he could call in at the Institute and wrap up his business there as well.

He would have to go over the details he had discussed with Billy the night before about *Cassiopeia* but he decided it would be kinder to leave him alone until his system was restored. For now, he considered the best thing would be to take her out of the water – after all, he would have to do so for the winter anyway – and then worry about her later.

He made a few further calls and sent some e-mails and then went to see how Billy was. He found him in the marina office sitting at the desk. No words were necessary to enquire after his well-being because he wasn't being well. He raised his arm in David's direction with a limp halting gesture indicating that he was not up to receiving visitors. David nodded at the invalid understandingly and told him he was off to Oban, that he hoped he would be better soon and that he was sure he would make a full recovery.

David reached Dougal's office as arranged.

"Come on, David; let's get out of here before the phone rings again. Morag, I'm taking the afternoon off. I shall be attending to business matters with our friend here."

She smiled at him, knowingly.

"David," Dougal said, "why don't we go again to the restaurant at the hotel where you stayed for Helen's funeral? It's quiet and civilised there and I'm sure we could do with some tender, loving care. I've had a trying morning and if you don't mind my saying so, you're looking slightly under the weather yourself."

"As perceptive as ever, Dougal," said David, who always felt good in this wise man's company.

As they sipped their aperitifs, Dougal looked quizzically at David.

"I can tell you wanted this meeting, David. I can read you like a book."

"I got slightly out of order with Billy at the marina bar last night; the Oban malt – I'm sure you understand."

"What, that which the whisky caused or the cause that necessitated the whisky?"

"What?" he said, somewhat befuddled.

"No matter, but I can see that you are troubled, man, so shall we order the smoked salmon, steak and a bottle of wine and then you can tell me all about it?"

"Dougal, you should have been a psychologist."

So David began to tell him the whole story. He started with Connie and the summer months they had spent together; the warmth and closeness that had grown between them; how she had made the momentous decision to stay and make her life here in Oban; how he had loved every day they spent together and how her two children just seemed the most natural accompaniments.

"And all of this in just two months, Dougal. Two months packed with fun, laughter, revelations, and, above all, an awareness that I had never known before of how very special being here was and that she had made me feel this."

"Well, David, so far so good; now deliver the mortal punch."

"You knew that I was looking for a job to follow on with when I'd finished my work with the Portland people. More than a job, a career step-up?"

"Yes," recalled Dougal, "I remember it well. You told me of your ambitions."

"Well, after all the applications I'd made and received only acknowledgements in return, out of the blue I receive a letter inviting me to an interview in London and lo and behold the dream job is offered to me."

"That would appear to be just what you wanted."

The waiter arrived to open their wine and place their first course in front of them.

"By the way, David, as I'm buying you lunch I've selected a red Burgundy, not your wine from Spain as it appears they have no more in stock."

"I hope it doesn't become too popular," he said.

"Carry on with your story, David."

So David told him of the job and that he had accepted it subject to the contract being signed.

"Well," surmised Dougal, "if it's only now a matter of signing a contract it would seem that you are home and dry and on the path to greater glory."

"Yes," concurred David. "It would indeed seem that all that I am aspiring to is there before me..."

David hesitated, lost for a few moments, so Dougal picked the conversation up.

"But?"

"I fear that I have allowed Connie too far into my life for her own good."

"And what about you? Has she allowed you too far into her life for your good?"

"Maybe we have both let things run a little ahead of ourselves. What I feel is that this career opportunity has to be taken. This is what I've been directingmy life to achieve: I have planned to do it."

"Then, man, you must do it," Dougal said. "You must make that decision and act on it."

"But I…"

"It's easy to make decisions, David, but carrying them out, that's the testing bit."

"Testing bit…?

"Of course. If you know what you want to do, you say so and get on with it. It's easy. But if there is any doubt about your decision, or you are faced with real difficulty in making it or a seemingly insurmountable obstacle, then – for whatever reasons – that's when you're tested to carry out the decision. That's when you have to think hard and fast about the consequences and how you will handle them."

Their steaks arrived and for the rest of the meal they talked about the weather, politics and other inconsequential matters.

"Dougal, I have preyed upon your valuable time and imposed my troubles on your relaxed lunch. So enough of my problems. It's up to me. Your counsel, as ever, has been invaluable, but we make our own destiny. No one can do it for us."

"I'm sure that whatever you do, David, it will all turn out for the best – and for the very best of reasons."

TWENTY-FIVE

They followed the same route that they had taken to the Commando Memorial on their first trip. They stopped there but only for about half an hour, so that Danny and Louisa could have a run around and burn up a bit of energy. There were only two other cars in the carpark, nothing like as busy as on their first visit and she felt it was safe for them to enjoy a little freedom.

For Connie, the moment was sombre. She knew David would take this job and why not? It was being offered to him and was his for the taking. And he deserved it. Surely he deserved to follow his career and achieve the goals he set in his life? She knew she would have done the same thing if she were in that position. A free person, unencumbered with a family, no ties, no restrictions – independent.

For her part, she was not a schoolgirl caught up in some dreamy infatuation. She was a grown-up woman. She was encumbered with a family, she had ties, she was restricted – she was not a free agent. But she was hurt. She had found in David a soulmate, yes that was the expression, a soulmate. And he was going, after two unbelievable months. He was going away and leaving a soul without a mate. She was desolate. Here at the Commando Memorial, this place that celebrated the actions of brave, courageous men, she felt she was an empty, bereft woman.

And then her children came running back to her, laughing and playing some chasing game with each other and she realised that she wasn't alone in this world: these were her mates, they were part of her. That was something to celebrate!

She had decided to take them away for a long weekend, up to the north, towards a town on the coast called Ullapool. She wanted to distance herself from David's pending departure and although she wanted to see him before he went and even had been on the point of calling him several times, she couldn't face saying goodbye to him; never goodbye. So she called the children back to the car and they continued on their journey towards Fort Augustus but turned off before it to take the road towards Kyle of Lochalsh and Skye.

Connie had decided that they would take a route that took them along the coast to Ullapool and back via Inverness. She had decided to miss the Isle of Skye on this occasion and continue up towards Gairloch. There they found a hotel for the Friday night.

They had fun. They occupied themselves with regular stops and walks: sometimes it was on a white sandy beach, others on wild headlands, along loch sides or hilly tracks. The scenery was different from Argyll; it was wilder, sparser, and more rugged. The villages were different and they found Ullapool, where they spent the Saturday night, charming, a little like Oban only far smaller, and it, too, had a Caledonian MacBrayne ferry terminal, though to Stornoway on the Outer Hebrides.

On the Sunday, they left Ullapool and drove south-east through the mountains towards Inverness. As they travelled on, the mountains became smaller and the land fell away towards the east coast. As they approached Inverness over the Kessock suspension bridge they were surprised to see such a large town with grand buildings. The river Ness ran through the town giving it an open feeling. This was the first metropolis Connie had seen since leaving London and she delighted in it. A hotel by the riverside was their base to explore the town and by Monday morning, they were ready to travel alongside Loch Ness on their way back to Oban to have another good look out for Nessie.

"Let's go and have a look at Urquhart castle," Connie suggested. "The people at the hotel said it has a great view over the loch and if we're going to see anything the castle is as good as anywhere."

They parked at the visitor centre and crossed over the old dry moat on a stone bridge. It was a wonderful example of an old castle and its position by the loch gave it an almost magical air to Danny and Louisa. They explored all of the interior of the castle grounds running over the grassy slopes and searching through the part ruins of old buildings. They stood on the turrets of the Grant Tower on the northern end of the castle and, like every visitor over the years, gazed hopefully across the waters. Danny was running along from one end to the other, alert, on the look-out, whilst Louisa stood there holding Connie's hand.

"David said that no one was really sure if there was a monster here, Mum. He thought it was very unlikely but he liked the idea of it."

"I think he's probably right, darling, but I do agree with him: it's a nice idea."

"Where is David, Mum?" asked Louisa.

"Oh, I think he had to go down to London to see about a job," she replied, gazing distractedly out to the mountains beyond the loch.

"That's why he's not with us then?"

"Sorry, darling?" she said.

"I said that that's why he's not with us, because if he hadn't had to go away he would've been with us, wouldn't he?"

"I'm sure he would have," reassured Connie.

"Well, I should certainly hope so," said Louisa emphatically.

Danny came back to them declaring that there was no monster in Loch Ness and it was all a big trick to get people to come here as tourists and spend money.

"I shall have to talk to David about this. He'll know," he said confidently.

"Okay, guys," ordered Connie. "Let's get moving. There's still a lot to do and see before we get back."

They continued along the loch side, stopping here and there to walk along paths on the loch bank. At one small beach they threw stones into the water and skimmed flat ones.

"Do you remember when we first came up to Scotland? And we stopped at a beach by Loch Lomond," said Danny.

"Yeah, I sure do and we threw stones just like this," recalled Connie.

"I'm so glad we came to live here," said Louisa. "I just love it."

On their way back they had to have one more stop at the Commando Memorial and climb up to the statue of the soldiers. And as they drove away they saw the mass of Ben Nevis in front of them.

"Look, Mum!" exclaimed Danny. "That's exactly the view of the mountain that David had the strawberries and cream made for us."

"So it is," she said, holding back the emotion that was welling up inside her.

They arrived back at the hotel shortly after 8 o'clock that Sunday evening. The children went straight up to their rooms and Connie walked over speak to Moira at the reception desk.

"Well, aren't you the popular one!" she said smiling at Connie. "Almost as soon as you left on Friday morning, David Gregson rang and has been on the phone again and again trying to contact you. He's called round here as well and today he left something for you that we put in your room for you."

"Yeah. Well, I deliberately left my phone off and I haven't even checked to see who has called me," Connie said. "Did he say what he wanted at all?"

"He called to say he was going down to London again and when I asked him when he would be back he said not for a while."

Connie felt that hollow sensation again. 'Not for while' could mean anything but she knew what it really meant. She thanked Moira and then went up to her room.

The children were watching the television so she left them alone and went into her bedroom. There on the table in front of the window was a vase containing a dozen red roses. Next to it was a sealed envelope. She picked it up and held it close to her chest. She knew what red roses were meant to symbolise. As she gazed out towards the sea, she found herself slowly easing open the envelope. She looked at the card that was inside. It was in his handwriting and a simple message read: 'You changed my life.'

She remained still, looking out to the sea and the island. The sun was getting lower but still shone down and reflected off the sea as well, giving twice the amount of light and it dazzled her. Her tears had already started to fall when Louisa walked in.

"Are you crying, Mummy?" she asked with concern as she came up to Connie, wrapping her arms around her waist.

"Not really, darling, the sun was just a bit bright, that's all."

The following morning, she hardly needed to wake at all as she had hardly slept. She looked at herself in the mirror and thought how dreadful she looked. Dark shadows under her reddened eyes told their own story. It was hopeless, she said to herself. All night long she had been thinking about her situation and now knew, without doubt, that the future for her and her two children in Oban was not a possibility without him. It was a lovely place to live; it was an ideal spot to bring up her children. But what had happened was that David had enhanced the place with his very being and that having him in her life had made everything possible. She had said this to him and had he not said the same to her? Together they made things so much better: the ordinary became the extraordinary, the superlatives became superfluous. And now he had gone. She understood his need to fulfil his career aspirations. Maybe she was being over generous, she thought. Maybe she should have told him what he meant to her – but then she had, hadn't she? That night, here at the hotel, they had both expressed a sort of gratitude to each other for making each other see things differently. And now he was gone. How crazy!

No, she had to do something positive and regain control of her life. She rang Eileen, the mother of Ronnie and Alison, and asked her if she could possibly look after Danny and Louisa for the day as she had some important matters to sort out.

"Not a problem," said Eileen. "I'd be pleased to help you out and I know my two will be wild about it. Just bring them round when you're ready. It's another good day so we'll probably go to the beach again."

She thanked her, rang off and then immediately called Dougal.

"Connie, my dear, grand to hear your voice again. I was thinking about you only the other day. I'm almost ready with the list of things we need to talk about. But just now, how can I help you?"

"Dougal, I need to see you this morning about something else. This is pretty damn important. Is there any chance that you could give me a little of your time today, just for a short while?"

"Of course, come around right now if you like. I've no commitments this morning. It would be lovely to see you."

"Thanks so much, Dougal. 'Bout half an hour then?"

"What's it all about then?" he asked, though he had an inkling he already knew.

"Hang on in, I'll tell you all when I'm with you," she said.

"I'm agog with anticipation," he replied in his usual phlegmatic way.

She dropped the children off with Eileen and went straight round to Dougal's where Morag ushered her into his office.

"I'm all yours, Connie, fire away."

"Dougal, let me get straight to the point. I am not one to sensationalise but my whole world has been turned upside down."

"Well, such a happening is not an everyday occurrence. Tell me more."

"Dougal, I'm leaving and going back to America. I'm taking the children with me and I want you to take charge of selling everything. We are as when I arrived here – back to square one."

"Connie, might I say that in the light of how things have been appearing to evolve for you here, I would be inclined to disagree with you. This declaration of yours does bear the hallmark of sensation."

"Okay, okay. Let me explain."

"Please do."

"You know why I came here and what my objective was. But I met a man who had such an effect on me that not only did I fall in love with your beautiful Argyll, I fell in love with him as well."

"Aha!"

"Here's where I wanted to be; he's who I wanted to be here with. I gave no thought to the possibility of it not happening. I simply ignored the fact that he was only here for a short while this summer and was actively looking to move on with his career and that this would almost inevitably involve him not only leaving the area but the country as well."

"Hmm."

"And that is precisely what is happening. David Gregson has left and has gone to pursue his bloody career and my heart is broken. I know it is totally unreasonable of me to say so but it is a fact – I simply cannot stay here and settle down without him. The agony of what might have been would dog me daily and without him your beautiful Argyll would be, to me, just plain Argyll. I'm sorry, Dougal, but I am quite clear on this. I have to leave, so I'm off Stateside as soon as I can get things arranged."

"Connie, it would be remiss of me not to tell you that David came to see me last Thursday and told me a story that basically contains all the elements of your own explanation to me. He too, it would seem, had not so much ignored as overlooked, in his enjoyment of the time he spent with you and the children, the fact that he was looking to move on with his career and that a chance might present itself at any moment. The fact that it did and that the offer was an absolute gem concentrated his mind somewhat.

"Now, there's no way that I would tell anyone how to live their life. At best I might suggest how not to live it, but if someone asked me my advice I would try to give it my best consideration.

"There's no doubt in my mind that your and David's feelings are mutual; I have listened to you both. *You* have not asked for my advice; David *wanted* it. But all I could say to him was that when it came to decisions one had to weigh up the pros and cons very carefully before carrying them out and that whatever the decision, it had to be carried out for the very best purpose – and for the very best of reasons."

"And that was it?"

"That was it, Connie," concluded Dougal.

"Well, thanks for letting me know this but I've made my mind up, my decision, if you like. Dougal, I've known too much pain in my life to want to go through any more. I came, unexpectedly, so close to happiness but I'll go back to the States and start my life again back home."

"Well, Connie, this is a matter that only you can decide on. I will carry out your instruction regarding the disposal of the properties, albeit with a heavy heart, because you, too, have become special to me."

"I can't take any more of this, Dougal! Please forgive me, but I'm off now to set about our travel arrangements. I want to get away as soon as possible. I'll let you know when we're leaving. And when I get to the States, I'll write to you confirming everything and ask you to tie up matters for me here. Dougal, whenever you see him next, please tell David for me. Tell him as best you can how I had to react to the situation. Tell him I understood his decision and tell him how he, too, changed my life, and that I couldn't stay on here without him."

She almost ran out of Dougal's office. In her haste she only managed a weak wave to Morag. She knew she had to act immediately. To wait longer would be to prolong the agony she was already suffering. On arriving at the hotel she told Moira to prepare her final account ready for payment first thing the next morning.

It took Connie just the morning to finalise everything. Tomorrow, Tuesday morning, they would leave first thing and take a taxi to Glasgow airport, a flight to Gatwick and then onwards to Boston.

Connie was dreading telling the children. David meant so much to them. He was, in many ways, the father they had never really had. But when she explained everything to them she was surprised at their acceptance.

"Mum, we'll all miss David, he's such a great guy," said Danny, "but if he's going to be away almost for ever, well, being here without him just won't be the same, will it, Lou?"

"No," she said. "Everything came alive with him, but we understand, Mum."

"And we had such a great time with him and all the things he taught us," said Danny. "We'll always remember *Cassiopeia*. Hey, when we're in America maybe we can get a boat and give her the same name."

"Great idea!" said Louisa.

"You know it's good to meet people like David," said Danny. "You learn so much from them and you realise that grown-ups can be pretty cool guys."

Such wise heads on such young shoulders, Connie thought.

After that, she confirmed with Moira the time that they would be leaving the next morning and asked her to book the taxi for them. Connie contacted the various contractors regarding the house and asked them to put everything on hold, submit their bills to Dougal and await further instructions. It was quite daunting to think that within thirty-six hours they would be in Boston, Massachusetts, USA.

Although she was pretty impressed with her decision making and the speed with which she had single-mindedly carried everything out, she was cut up inside. She didn't want to go but knew that there must be another horizon for her to seek and she consoled herself as best she could by remembering that, other than the emotional side, two months earlier she had come up here to have a look at her inheritance, sell it and then go back to the States.

Yes, that was it, just a little two-month interruption to her plans; just two months. But what a two months it had been!

TWENTY-SIX

At about 5 o'clock on the Sunday afternoon when Connie was driving back from Inverness, David had made his last call to the hotel to leave the flowers for Connie. He had tried to phone her but without success and finally decided that it was not going be possible to speak to her before he left. Perhaps it was just as well because he was not feeling good about it. In fact, he felt that he had cruelly let her down just so that he could do what he wanted to do. When he had suggested to Dougal that he had let her too far into his life, he knew that he had. He should have kept her at arm's length, but in his own defence he could justly argue that she – for her own sake – should have done the same. But then why should she? She had told him that for the first the time in her life she was letting her heart rule her head. That's what led her to make that sudden decision to stay and make her life in Oban.

No, he thought, the course of events had been unexpected for both of them and now it was best for them both to get back on track and resume their respective plans.

Billy Kilpatrick was sitting in his car outside the hotel waiting for David. He was giving him a lift down to Glasgow, as he had to go near the city that evening on his way to Inverkip marina on the south side of the Clyde, where he had to collect some equipment for a client's yacht. David was going to visit his mother's old friend Agnes Devereaux in Edinburgh the next day. He would stop over Sunday night in Glasgow and take the train from

Queen Street station the following day and stay with her until he left for London on the Tuesday morning.

He found a hotel near George Square, not far from the station. A much needed and relaxed dinner followed by a deep night's sleep allowed him to wake early the following morning. He showered and dressed, decided to give breakfast a miss and went for a long walk around the old merchant part of Glasgow that had now been transformed into high quality town dwellings. He wandered down to the Clyde and walked over the Halfpenny Bridge and stopped midway to watch the water of the river passing underneath. Turning back to the quayside he thought what a fine city Glasgow had become. The second city of the Empire it had once been called. There may no longer be an Empire he mused, but Glasgow seems to have survived and prospered.

Feeling ravenous after his walk he went back for a good lunch at the hotel. He relaxed afterwards in the lounge and by mid-afternoon he was ready to go.

He took the 5pm train from Glasgow arriving half an hour later at Edinburgh's Waverley Street. He had last been to see Agnes Devereux almost a year ago and, in keeping with this frequency, had called her the previous day to let her know of his pending arrival. A life-long friend of David's mother, she had moved to live in Edinburgh following her husband Robert's death over twenty years ago. Although of mixed English and French parentage, she had been brought up in London and later had been an undergraduate in Edinburgh, some fifty years ago. Now in her seventies, she had returned to the city of her student days to live out her life amongst the places and with some of her friends from those past years.

It had been a total success. She had been happy from the moment she arrived there and the social life suited her sharp, alert and artistic mind. A woman with an intelligence and wide-ranging intellect to match, she had thrived in a world that, in many respects, had remained unchanged since her first days at the University. It was to this world of hers that David had made his annual pilgrimage for the past three years and was now about to make his fourth, and probably last, for some time.

The taxi dropped him off in the quiet, Victorian Belgrave Crescent near Dean Bridge and he rang her doorbell. It was just before 6 o'clock in the evening and David could guarantee that he had arrived just in time for her first dry martini.

The door opened and there she stood, looking fabulous. Her honey-coloured eyes sparkled as her long, straight, silver hair fell back over the shoulders of a multi-coloured silk kaftan. In her day, she would have been described as being a pre-Raphaelite beauty – and even now, after the passing of the years, she still had an undeniable allure. Amber beads hung around her neck, bracelets dangled from her wrists and as she leant forward to embrace him, her perfume, as exotically oriental as her dress, wafted around him. She stood in her bare feet with her back impossibly straight, almost as tall as David.

"My darling boy, you have arrived at the hour, indeed on the hour, for us to take refreshment."

He produced from behind his back a bottle of her preferred vermouth.

"So good of you; ever the thoughtful one. But did you really think that I would allow a situation to arise whereby we might run short?"

"No, of course not, Agnes," he replied, "but this one is a special one, only for you, to enjoy for yourself. However, I suppose if we should by any chance drink your dry martini supply dry, then we could view it as an emergency back-up."

"Thoroughly practical point of view. Now come on in, before we die of thirst discussing the issue."

Agnes had bought a house set in a terrace of light-coloured sandstone buildings, a couple of dozen or so houses opposite a well-manicured, mature garden that was the domain of the terrace owners. It had three storeys, a basement and four bedrooms; far more space than she ever needed, but it was a beautiful house and quintessentially her.

"Let us go to the lounge on the first floor overlooking the gardens. Everything is ready. We have enough ice to sink the Titanic!"

David mixed the cocktails as she had instructed him on his first visit. It was a little ritual that had commenced when she had shown him how she liked her martinis four years ago. He had never forgotten the procedure and loved doing it.

"Now before we get underway, David, just remind me of your schedule for tomorrow."

"Very simple, Agnes, I have a flight that leaves at 9.30 in the morning so I shall be leaving the house at about 7.15."

"What an unearthly hour! Still that's your misfortune. I shall be fast asleep and trust you will leave the house quietly. Now, tell me all about what is happening in your life."

They clinked glasses.

"Cheers, David."

"Here's to you, Agnes, forsaking all others."

"Silly boy!"

"Well, this has been my fourth and final session with the terns. All the work has been done and the process set up for others to interpret the results. I have to go down to Portland tomorrow to return all the equipment, debrief my colleagues and hand over all the data."

"So where do you go from here?"

"The Seychelles," he replied.

"How splendid!" she said. "A holiday?"

"No it's a job." And he proceeded to tell her what he was ready to sign up for. When he had finished she simply said:

"Turtles? Bloody turtles? What on earth can you find of interest in following those things for?"

"Well," he said, "it's not just turtles. It's also the system that I've been working on. They want me to apply it to the turtles."

"Well, it strikes me that you're going to be doing the same sort of thing with turtles as you have been doing with the terns except it's in the nasty tropics. Also terns are much nicer creatures."

"But Agnes, think of the opportunities it will open for me; the contacts I'll be making. This is career stuff, real career stuff. It's being promoted by the UN involving international government co-operation, for heaven's sake!"

"Sounds like a boring bunch of pompous civil servants to me, almost as boring as turtles. And can we stop saying the word turtle; it's beginning to sound like an odd word?"

"Okay," he laughed, "it does rather, doesn't it!"

"You've been doing this sort of thing for four or five years now, haven't you?" she said.

"Yes, if you include the development work first it's nearer six years."

"David, don't you think it's perhaps time for a change, you know, sit back for a while and contemplate your navel, see what else is going on in the world. I'm not much of a role model, but when I think of some of the crazy things I've done with my life, I look back with no regrets.

"You know, Robert and I had so much fun together. There was no one else like him. That was why I came up here after he died. It was a chance I took: thought there might be some like-minds. I hit it right on. It's been wonderful. People, you see, people of the right kind and mind; people you gel with, have a good laugh, a good drink. They keep the brain active!"

"You make me sound like a right old fossil and I'm only thirty-six!"

"No, David, you're anything but that. But tell me, what about women in your life? I remember you telling me about that disaster down in Weymouth. Need to avoid ones like that."

"Well, Agnes, I've just been through an incredible episode in my life. I'll tell you about it. In fact, I don't think I know anyone else I *could* tell this to."

She sat back and he told her about Connie. He told her everything, every last detail of her and of how this had all happened in just two of the happiest months of his life. When he had finished she just sat there with her mouth gaping.

"Agnes!" he said. "Say something. I've never known you lost for words."

"When do I get to meet her?"

"What?"

"When do I get to meet her? She sounds almost too good to be true but I love her already!"

"Well, you won't be able to."

Why not?" objected Agnes.

"Because I've left Oban now. Within ten days I'll be on a plane to the Seychelles."

"You're going to let her...but you can't! You can't let her go. Are you out of your mind or something? Quickly, David, mix me another drink, I am in need."

"I think I need another one too."

He arose and went to the drinks table.

"What is she going to do?" probed Agnes.

"I've no idea other than the fact that she has decided to stay in Oban with the children."

David came back with the drinks.

"So you will never see her again," said Agnes.

"Well, I told her it was only a three-year contract and that the time would pass quickly. That was really the last thing we said about it."

"I can't believe what you're telling me! Do you really think she will stay around waiting, hoping that you might come back to her after three years?"

"Well, the long and short of it is I decided that this job I had been offered was too good an opportunity to turn down. She never tried to interfere with my ambitions. She was sorry I was going but she was staunchly supportive of my career objectives."

"Objectives, my arse! David, no woman worth her salt would try to talk a man out of something that seemed that important to him. If she wanted you to stay, she would know that it would have to be you and only you who made the decision. You bloody fool! She sounds like the real article to me and you've let her go. Take my word for it, David; you're in love with her."

Agnes gazed momentarily into the treasury of her memory.

"Blue eyes! Robert had deep-blue eyes. They melted me the moment I saw him."

She knocked her drink back in one go.

"Another drink for me; what about you?"

"I guess so."

He got up and walked around once more to the drinks table. As he was mixing them he said:

"Agnes, I'm going to get completely pissed unless I have something to eat."

"Me too, David, isn't it great!"

"But seriously…"

"Fear not, dear boy, one of Auntie Ag's famous piquant beef casseroles has been in the oven all day. And just before you arrived the jacket potatoes were put in to start baking. It'll all be ready in half an hour."

"Well, how about a crisp then?"

"Crisps? Not good for you! But smoked salmon is! I'd completely forgotten about it whilst listening to your enchanting tale. It's on a plate in the kitchen. Be a darling and get it will you?

When he returned, her mood had changed slightly.

"David, we have much to talk about and reminisce about, but before we do I want to finish the story of Connie. Not because I'm no longer interested – on the contrary – but because I do believe you need to think twice about this. You didn't just tell me any old story. I could tell from the intensity of your words that she has made as deep an impression on you as you have on her. The right partner in life makes you twice the person, David. I know, I've been there. And, David…"

"Yes, Agnes?"

"Bloody turtles! How could you even think about them?"

They finished the smoked salmon and two more martini cocktails. Agnes had produced, quite magnificently, a bottle of a reserve Rioja that she asked David to uncork.

"Remembered you like this stuff. Some chap in Ireland wasn't it, thought the French reds were somewhat lacking by comparison?"

Over Agnes's delicious dinner she recalled the fun she and David's mother used to have. Agnes was as outrageous as a teenager as she was a seventy year old.

"Some of the things we did would undoubtedly now be on the nanny state's danger to health list. We got away with blue murder and lived to tell the tale. But I'll be honest with you, David, she married the wrong man. I don't mean that unkindly. Your dad was a good but stolid man. What she needed was a kindred spirit. He sort of knocked it out of her and she became ordinary. I was lucky with Robert. I didn't know what a kindred spirit was until I met him. Shortly after his death I often used to feel very angry that he went and died. But after some time I began to think that if he made me twice the woman I was, then perhaps I made him twice the man he was and that he therefore got twice the fun out of life than he otherwise would have done."

"Agnes, I would have loved to have been a fly on the wall of your life."

"More wine, David, I bought a case of that Rioja. Never underestimate a man's need, ha!"

"I think tomorrow will see my third hangover in as many days," said David.

"Seeing it doesn't worry me; it's feeling it I don't like."

"When I've got a hangover I usually can't see anything anyway," he said by way of a witty riposte.

"David, I do love it when you come to see me. When you're here I never ask anyone to join us because I don't want to share you. I know that's extremely selfish of me. But look, when you've woken up to reality and abandoned this turtle nonsense, bring Connie over with her kids and we'll have a big party and I'll show you all off to my friends."

When they had finished their cheese course, Agnes suggested to David that since they were doomed to hangovers tomorrow they might as well go out with a bang.

"I have long since ceased drinking brandy after a meal because I so much prefer a single malt whisky, so will you join me in a night-cap. The cupboard's over there. Select your choice and pour out two adequate measures. I'll go with whatever you choose."

David opened up a cupboard that was one bottle deep but stretched almost from floor to ceiling. It was full of bottles of Scotch whisky. He looked across the selection and the one that caught his eye and his fancy was an old favourite: Oban single malt.

Bringing the glasses back to the table, he handed one to Agnes and held his glass up to her.

"Agnes, to your indomitable spirit."

"And, David, to you getting your act together."

It was approaching midnight when David announced that he was off to bed. Agnes stood up and stated that the washing-up would get done some time tomorrow afternoon and then declared that she, too, was ready to retire.

It had been a delightful and enlightening night. She was a special person and he loved her dearly. He also took on board her words of wisdom, and just hoped that by tomorrow morning he would be able to remember some of them.

And as he went to his room he could hear Agnes down the corridor muttering to herself as she closed her bedroom door.

"Turtles! Bloody turtles!"

TWENTY-SEVEN

David woke at 6.45 in the morning, not feeling too good in spite of having had a couple of glasses of water before turning in to help him re-hydrate during the night. He was inclined to the belief that the painfully shrill noise of the alarm suggested that manufacturers of alarm clocks have really got it in for people who have to get up early and in particular for those who have had a boozy night as well. Still, on the bright side, he thought a few more hangovers like this and I'll probably start getting used to it.

A cold shower followed by a cup of coffee and he felt remarkably refreshed. Before leaving, he wrote a note to Agnes thanking her for everything and promising her that he would try not to let another year go by before he saw her again. He quietly slid the front door lock and closed the door to leave her in peace. He walked down the road and turned right onto Dean Bridge and then up to the main road that led to the airport.

He didn't know where there was a taxi rank so he stood on the main street and decided to give it ten minutes to see if one came along that was free. As he waited, a number of buses came along and then suddenly there was one with 'Airport' on the front. It was a single decker bus with only a few people on it and so he hopped on, paid his fare and sat down.

He took a seat that faced the front of the opposite one because he liked the extra legroom. There was the same layout on the other side of the aisle and an attractive girl in her early twenties sat there with a backpack on the seat in front of her. They smiled to each other an early-morning acknowledgement as the bus set off.

At the next stop a young man of similar age got on, also with a backpack, and walked along the aisle looking to choose his seat. He saw the girl's luggage on the seat and, in identifying a fellow sort of traveller, asked if he might put his pack next to hers and sit with her.

David watched this and thought of the common ground they found that had enabled them to sit comfortably in light conversation. He couldn't help but overhear what they were saying.

"You headed for the airport?" he asked her.

"Yes," she replied.

"Me too."

"Where are you going?" she asked.

"Down to London. I've been looking around Scotland for a few days and now I think I'll give England a check out. I've got some distant relations in Cornwall so guess I'll head down there first, but I've got no solid plans. And you?"

"London too," she said, "but I think after there, I'll head on across to France. I came over from Norway. I had some distant relations there too and I went to look them up."

"Where are you from, then?"

"Oh, New Zealand; and you?"

"I'm Canadian. Like you, I guess, a bit of a mixed bag really. My mother's family came from Normandy in

France and my dad's side originated in England, that's the Cornish link. Did you find your Norwegian family?"

"Yes. A cousin of my mother; he never married and that was the end of the line. Actually he was about seventy and although he spoke pretty good English, he was incredibly boring; no sense of humour."

And so it went on. More people got on and it began to fill up. He picked up little bits of their conversation but eventually lost them when he got up to give his seat to a grateful elderly lady and had to move along slightly and stand.

She got off a couple of stops further on and David sat down in his seat again.

"So what do you think then?" he heard the backpacker guy say. "After Cornwall and London we could go over together on the ferry to France. My mom was going to check out any family connections, addresses and so forth, so I'll have to call her later to find out. How'd you like to help me find them?"

"That would be brilliant," he heard her say. "Maybe after that we could do a bit of travelling around Europe together?"

"I'm all for that. Sounds a great idea! How much time do you have?"

"I only arrived a month ago, I've got almost a whole year," she told him.

"Hey, me too! We could have a brilliant time doing this."

"It'd be really cool to do it together. It can get a bit bleak on your own."

"Okay, you up for it then?" he said.

"Let's give it a go."

"Wow! Today's my day," he said, as they sealed the deal with a high five. "Looks like I got on the right bus."

To say that David felt like he had stuck his finger into an electrical mains socket whilst simultaneously being struck on the back of the head with a gong would be a severe understatement.

All of his senses were awakened. The hangover evaporated.

There was no doubt about it. Eddie McBride's prophecy was enacting itself before his very eyes and ears. Only it wasn't him, it was this backpacker Canadian next to him. And this wasn't metaphorical; it was actually happening on a real bus!

What was he listening to? Two people who had plans but were sufficiently flexible to change them. Two people who understood the advantages and fun of doing something together. Two people who had only just met but had taken an instant liking to each other. Two people.

David Gregson sat there riveted.

"Come along, sir, you're the last person on board."

"I'm sorry…What?"

"We're at the airport, sir. We've been here five minutes and the Edinburgh-bound passengers will be getting on in a moment."

"I'm so sorry," he said. "I must have fallen asleep or something."

David got up and collected his luggage from where he had stored it in the rack at the front of the bus. He collected a luggage trolley, loaded his bags and walked with it to the airport concourse. When he was inside he looked up at the screen displaying boarding and departure times.

There was his flight to London Heathrow. It was now just after 8 o'clock, checking in time was 08.45, departure at 09.30. So he had sufficient time to eat some breakfast before boarding.

It's amazing, he thought, the body. You treat it so badly and yet it turns up again the next day for more punishment. But he didn't care. He was going to eat a massive fried breakfast because that's what his body was telling him to do.

And afterwards he felt strong and revitalised. It must have been the right thing to do, he thought, because I feel so much better.

Having finished his breakfast, he went on upstairs to the departure lounge. It looked like it was going to be a fairly full flight and he was glad that he had booked himself a seat at the front of the aircraft as he never liked the crowded feeling towards the centre and back of the plane.

He sat down to await the call. He looked around at his fellow passengers but couldn't see his back-packers anywhere. A voice over the speaker announced boarding and most of the people got up to form a queue. As David sat there, watching the queue diminish to the last couple of passengers, content that his seat was safe, the back-packers came running in past him to the desk.

"We were lucky there," he said to the desk official. "We managed to get my seat changed so we could sit together."

The man smiled, gave them their boarding pass slips with the seat numbers, and ushered them through. David got up, the last passenger, on his own.

He walked down the descending covered footway and entered the aircraft. He accepted a newspaper that was offered to him and took his aisle seat in the front row. Reading was probably a good option, he thought. Keep his mind off other matters. Or maybe he'd try and sleep for the short journey.

The cabin crew went through the usual safety announcements and procedures. He gave the impression of both watching and listening but in fact his mind was far away, wondering what Connie was doing and, moreover, what she might now do. And above all, he was wondering why he had put her in a position where she might have to even think about having to change anything.

As the plane taxied down the runway he prepared himself for the take-off. In spite of it being one of the least safe moments in a flight he always got a bit of a kick as the engines opened up and the acceleration pushed him back in his seat as the plane lifted off. He looked out through the window across the other passengers next to him to see the countryside receding and in no time they were buried deep in a cloud mass. He leant back, aware of the bumpy movement as the aircraft flew through the cloud. And then, some minutes later, light burst into the cabin and the bumpiness disappeared as they flew upwards into the blue sky.

The blue sky; those blue eyes. What should he do?

In the last few hours he had been given some pointers, if only he had been prepared to see them. Well, in fact, he was now beginning to see them, and with the plane in level flight, he concentrated, and started to analyse things more closely.

Agnes Devereux had laid it on the line pretty bluntly to him. You're being a bloody fool she said; don't let her go; have a change in your life; bloody turtles she had said, bloody turtles; pompous civil servants; nasty tropics. She was right he said to himself, absolutely right. He hadn't even bothered to think it through. It was as obvious as that! All he could see was the career path, the contacts, the kudos. Really, what did it all matter? He had the chance to make a real life for himself and what was he doing?

Well, Agnes; dear, sharp-witted, perceptive, direct Agnes had taken half an hour to show him the way.

And if Eddie McBride had never told him the story of how he eventually met the love of his life, how would David have been alerted to the little drama that happened between the two backpackers?

That was it!

He would go straight back up to Glasgow when the plane arrived in Heathrow. He'd get the first flight available and go back to Oban and tell Connie that he was staying there with her and the children. Someone else could worry about the turtles; someone else could toady and suck up to the boring, pompous civil servants. The

351

house in Weymouth could wait a bit longer and he'd send all the Portland stuff by special delivery. Cancel the hire car! Call Sir Jocelyn Napier and tell him he wasn't going to sign his contract! Call Professor Trevor Royston and tell him thanks for the honour of the recognition but someone else would have to deal with his bloody turtles! I'm going off to make a life!

He sat back in his seat. An air of contentment, of liberation, came over him. If only this plane could get a move on.

It touched down about at about 11 o' clock. They had had a slightly late start and were stacked over London for longer than usual. But no matter, he was here now.

He collected his luggage and made his way to the exit into the main terminal area to look for the ticket-purchasing counter. There he bought a single ticket to Glasgow for the next flight which was due to depart at 3 o'clock that afternoon. So he had a couple of hours or so to pass before the flight would be called. He checked his luggage on to the flight and then went up to the shops and restaurants area to pass the time.

He thought of ringing Connie but somehow he felt it would be a much happier moment if he told her face to face. No, he'd wait till he got back to Oban. Instead he made all the necessary calls, to the University, the hire car company and the Portland Marine Institute. The latter two were straightforward but with the two calls to the University he had to tell a slightly tall story to save face, although it was perfectly correct to tell them he was unable to take the job for personal reasons. Sir Jocelyn Napier was unavailable so David had the great pleasure of informing

Miss Small that he would unfortunately not be seeing her later this week and in all probability, he thought to himself, never again. In his excitement, he quite forgot to ask her if she had made the expenses transfer to his bank account. Trevor Royston perfectly understood, though he was not quite sure about what, and wished David well for the future and held him to a promise to keep in touch.

So that was it. All he had to do was get to Oban.

The car wound its way through the green countryside that they had first encountered over two months ago. The children watched quietly as they passed places they didn't remember, but as they passed through Kilmartin, Danny called out:

"Hey, remember the hotel? What a great time we had there!"

"And those stones, too, and the tunnel. Can't we stop and have another look at them, Mum?" said Louisa.

"I'm sorry, guys, but we've a plane to catch and I don't want us to miss it."

The journey became more and more uncomfortable for Connie as the children kept remembering places. As they passed over the top of Rest and be Thankful, even she began to share the children's feeling. When they passed the little beach on the shore of Loch Lomond where they had really breathed their first pure Scottish air, even she wanted to stop the car and skim a few last stones.

As they approached the turning to the Erskine Bridge, Connie knew that this was really it. They were only about fifteen minutes from the airport and then just a couple of hours before take-off for London Gatwick. Their flight to Boston was overnight, but because of the time difference they would arrive at around midnight East Coast time in America.

And then she would have to start a totally new life. She found it all quite depressing. She had planned to go to a hotel in Boston that she knew of and carry on like she had done at the Regent Hotel in Oban. She would have to find a school for the children, a house to live in. And then what? What was she going to do with the rest of her life? Financially she need never work again, but she knew her brain would seize up if she had nothing to stimulate it. She might well meet someone, but she knew she had set herself a high standard since David. No, it was all going to be an unknown process. But then she knew that was exactly how it was going to have to be when she had made the decision those few months ago back in London that she was going to return to the States to make a new life. She just needed to keep focussed and it would all work out okay, wouldn't it? Well, it had to.

They dropped the car off and found a trolley for their luggage. Between the three of them they managed to find their way to the check-in desk. When they got there and Connie presented their booking-in details, she was stopped short in her tracks by a grovelingly apologetic person who had to advise them that, due to an overbooking for the Gatwick flight, they would have to take a later one.

"But look, we've to catch a flight to the States this evening," she protested. "Can't you upgrade our seats? Maybe someone's cancelled; surely you can check?"

"But, madam," answered the man at the check-in desk, "every seat is taken. We have been trying to contact you on the mobile phone number that you gave us for the last twenty-four hours. We have left voice-mail messages but with no response from you."

That was right thought Connie. She had switched off her phone because she didn't want the pain of having to talk to David and she had deliberately not listened to her voice-mail or read text messages for the same reason.

"Well, I can't think why," she said dodging the honest response. "So what can we do now? I don't want to risk missing that flight."

"What we have done is put you on the next flight to Heathrow, which leaves half an hour before the Gatwick one and then you can take the connection coach from Heathrow to Gatwick. It's a little inconvenient since you will have to collect your luggage at Heathrow and put it on the coach to Gatwick. I do think it is your best option because, according to your schedule on the screen here, you will arrive at Gatwick three hours before boarding time starts. You have sufficient time and so won't have to wait too long before the Heathrow flight leaves from here. We have given you priority boarding to help make things easier for you."

"Okay," she said, feeling calmer. "I guess we'll do that then. Sorry I was a bit sharp there but it's all a little stressful, y'know, with the children too."

"No problem, madam, I'm glad we were able to sort it all out."

As it was, they only had to wait an hour before their flight would be called so they would be at Heathrow by about 1 o'clock. They would have to move fairly quickly though as there was a connecting coach every hour on the hour, so they would be able to make the 2 o'clock coach. As their flight to Boston didn't leave Gatwick until 9 o'clock they would have plenty of time on their hands before the flight was called.

However, she wouldn't feel relaxed until they were on board their transatlantic flight.

They passed the time at Glasgow airport with the breakfast they had missed in Oban. The flight was duly called and they made their way with the rest of the passengers to the departure lounge. They had allocated them three seats in a row at the front of the plane and they were given extra special treatment by the in-flight crew because of the booking mess-up. And it always helps, she had thought, to have some well-behaved children with you.

They touched down almost on the stroke of 1 o'clock. They were first off the plane and Connie led them along the labyrinth of corridors to the luggage arrival section where they waited by the carousel to collect their bags.

Odd isn't, thought Connie as she stood there: you arrive first and your luggage is invariably the last to appear. In this case, not quite but it might just have well have been; another anxiety she could do without.

They took hold of their luggage and Connie led them out to the main terminal area to find the pick-up point for the Gatwick connection coach. They found it without any difficulty and they put their bags down to wait the fifteen minutes or so for the bus.

So that was it. All she had to do was get to Gatwick.

TWENTY-EIGHT

The coach stop was immediately outside a glass sliding door. The vehicle hadn't arrived yet and Connie assumed that it would pull up, discharge the Gatwick to Heathrow passengers, load up with the Heathrow to Gatwick passengers and be off. The turn round would be as long as it took the passenger movement and luggage handling on and off.

Only ten minutes to go now.

And then Louisa wanted to go to the loo.

"Mum, please, I'm bursting! Please."

"Oh, Louisa, why now? The coach will be here in a few minutes? I can't take you, the luggage trolley and Danny into the ladies' toilet."

"Mum, I'll wet myself!"

She looked around. There was only one solution. She ran to a security guard and explained her situation.

"…and if you could just keep an eye on the bags for us we'll be only a couple of minutes."

"I'm sorry, madam, it's absolutely forbidden. All luggage must be looked after by their owners otherwise they will be treated as suspect and dealt with accordingly."

"But it's only for a couple of minutes," she pleaded.

"Madam, security matters are very serious and I am unable to do as you request," he said with professional patience.

"Well, what if my son stays with them, that should be okay, shouldn't it?"

"He would appear to be a minor, madam, and as such cannot be deemed responsible."

"Oh, please, please," said Louisa," and then we will be able to catch our coach; otherwise we'll miss our plane to America."

The security guard looked at Connie and then Danny and then back to Connie again.

"Oh, all right then. But hurry up! It's more than my job's worth."

Connie thanked him profusely and she and Louisa ran off together to the ladies' toilet. He smiled at Danny who promised the man that they would be back in no time at all and that it was really kind of him to help them. The Security guard stood to one side and surveyed his area of responsibility.

David had a few minutes to go before he was expecting the call for boarding his flight. He had reserved a hire car at Glasgow airport for his journey to Oban but it had not occurred to him at the time of doing the booking that he would not need the car once he was in Oban. So he quickly made his way to the hire car counter to cancel it. After all, he wouldn't have any difficulty convincing a taxi driver to take him there. It would be a lucrative run.

Having cancelled the reservation, he turned to go towards the departure area and in so doing walked straight past a boy who was standing next to a piled-up luggage trolley and looking out through the glass sliding door. He hadn't noticed the boy and neither had the boy noticed him. David turned around a corner to go to the departure area when his flight was called. He looked at his watch. There was an hour to go before take-off so he decided he had time to buy himself a magazine to occupy him on the flight. He turned back to go to the newsagent store and as he walked up to the entrance he now saw the boy standing next to the luggage trolley, watching a coach pull in. On seeing the coach, the boy turned looking anxiously in the other direction. The boy ran towards a security guard and started talking to him, gesticulating with his arms and pointing to the coach.

David underwent a double-take. It looked like Danny but it couldn't be Danny because Danny wasn't here. Danny was in Oban. But it was Danny and he was here. The boy went back to the trolley and sat down on the floor next to it. The security guard walked slowly in the same direction. David ran towards him.

"Danny!" he gasped. "What on earth are you doing, here?"

"Hi, David! Wow! Have you come to say goodbye to us, I mean, all the way from Scotland?"

He knelt down on one knee next to Danny. The security guard came up to him them both.

"Is everything all right, sir? Do you know this man, son?"

"Yes," said Danny. "He's a friend of ours. A great friend and he's come to say goodbye."

"Good. So long as everything is okay. The luggage will be secure now you're here, sir."

Still kneeling, David turned to Danny and put his arm round his shoulder.

"But what do you mean about saying goodbye? Where are you going to? Where are Mum and Louisa?"

"We're going back to America and they're in the ladies because Lou wanted to go to the loo," he said, smiling. "That's quite funny isn't it?"

Although David found the whole situation perplexing, he couldn't help but smile.

"But why are you going back to America, Danny?"

"Well, Mum said that she couldn't live in Oban unless you were there as well and we both agreed with her. She said you were going away on some job and would be away and she had no idea if we would ever see you again. So we all agreed, 'cos Mum said it would be better in America 'cos Oban wouldn't be really any good without you."

"But what are you doing right here?" asked David.

"Well, if we're lucky and they get back in the next few seconds, we're going to Gatwick airport on that coach and then we're flying to America tonight."

"But you can't go," implored David.

A hand rested on David's shoulder. He turned back and looked up at Connie's blue eyes looking down at him.

"David's come to say goodbye to us all, Mum, he came down specially."

"Thank you for coming, David," Louisa said, smiling at David. "It would have been awful to have gone without us saying goodbye."

He stood up.

He looked straight into Connie's eyes.

"I haven't come to say goodbye. I could never say goodbye to you. And I never will, to any of you. You are my life, all of you."

Connie just stood there looking at him. Out of the corner of her eye she saw people climbing up into coach and the driver helping people load their luggage into the hold.

Still she looked at him; time seemed suspended.

"It's true, you know," he continued, "you changed my life. And I was so stupid, so reckless in not seeing what you meant to me."

She saw the coach pull away and the security guard looking at their luggage and then she saw him shrug, smile and then walk away.

"David," said Connie, "in one hour another coach will pull up outside and will then go on to Gatwick. Do you think that in that time you can convince me that we should stay?"

"In one hour," said David, "a flight leaves for Glasgow, if we are very quick I could buy three more tickets and we could all be back in Oban by the evening."

She looked deep into his eyes.

"Why three tickets?"

"Because I already have one."

"Please tell me why you have a ticket, David?"

"Connie, I had no idea you were going to leave. I have been such a mindless, self-centred fool and it took a kick in the seat of my pants from a seventy-year-old woman to make me realise that I was just about to make the biggest mistake of my life. On the flight down to London it all fell into place and I realised that nothing else mattered other than a life that included you. So I got off the plane, bought a single back to Glasgow, phoned my would-be employers and told them that I had something of far greater importance to dedicate myself to."

"You're getting there, David, but I've cried so many tears that I feel I've none left to cry. I've had enough pain in my heart that I can't bear any more. If I'm to entrust my heart to you I have to have yours in return, and only you can give me that."

"Connie, we are kindred spirits; we are soulmates."

"I believe that, too, David."

"Then we are inseparable. Trust in my love. It'll never leave you."

Hoots of laughter followed by a mighty crash indicated that the children were chasing each other around the luggage trolley. Connie called them over.

"Okay, guys, here's the situation," she said. "This man here has made a suggestion. It does, however, necessitate a quick decision followed by a turn of speed. The suggestion is: would you like to wait for the next coach to Gatwick and then fly to America or go back and live in Oban?"

"Is this man going to live in Oban as well?" asked Danny.

"Yes," replied the man.

"Is he going to live there with us?" asked Louisa.

"Yes," replied the man.

"So is his suggestion acceptable to you two?"

"Well, only the bit about living in Oban," said Danny, "we don't want to go on a coach and fly to America, do we, Lou?"

"No," she said, "we don't."

"In which case, sir," Connie said turning to him, "your suggestion has been unanimously endorsed and accepted."

She put her arms around his neck, held him tightly and kissed him sweetly on the lips. And leaning back slightly, she said, looking into his eyes:

"How long have we got to get those tickets?"

After they had taken off and the plane had levelled out, David turned to look at Connie. Her eyes held his. He took her hand and started to tell her of the story Eddie McBride had told him, of how he had owed his own happiness to getting on the right bus and that he had done so without even knowing he was doing so; how Eddie's parting words were not just the importance of getting on but, most crucially, of being alert and recognising that it was the right one in the first place and *then getting on*, otherwise it was so easy to miss that chance that life was offering you.

And then Connie told David of the story that had begun with her discovery of the photographs at Ardbeg, how Mike Kendall at the museum had led her to Catriona Henderson and Dougal's admission of how he had held back his side of the story from her.

"When I think of John L. and Helen," she said, as she leant into his shoulder, "it's another case of not recognising the right bus: certainly as far as he was concerned. But how do you explain *us*, David?"

"You know, Connie," said David, "life's really a jungle, isn't it? I look back at my own life and my own parents' relationship. I look at your life, your parents – them to each other, you to them. I look at the lives of Harry, John L., Helen, Lorraine, Hamish and Margaret; even Dougal's parents. My mother's friend Agnes; and Eddie – they've all been through dark times.

"And us! Look at us! Here we are and we've found each other. An awful lot of people have suffered before us and more will after us, I'm sure. But we two, we *have* to be the beneficiaries of all the past misfortunes of those others. It's up to us to take note of where they went wrong. They have inadvertently taught us to be alert in that jungle. We cannot fail them, because if we do, we'll fail ourselves.

"When Eddie McBride told me his story about getting on the right bus, his metaphor was extended to being alert enough to know, realise and recognise that it was the right one – and then get on it. A tall order for anyone! But that was his message. In his case he realised it sometime *after* he had got off it. But he did get on it! It's not a random thing; everything that they had done in their lives determined the course in which they would eventually meet. They were lucky; but as Eddie said, you've got to be alert.

"How close *we* came to being devoured in that unforgiving world. I was leaving, you were leaving. But awareness of the experiences of other people, who had failed or succeeded the hard way, alerted us, brought us back."

David sat back in his seat. He felt mentally exhilarated but physically exhausted.

"Sorry if I seem to have become a bit philosophical," he softly said to her, "but I just realised it all at once. I had finally recognised it; just in time!"

Connie looked at him, smiled and put her hand on his arm.

"We're going to be fine, my darling. We're going forward one step at a time and we'll deal with each problem as it arises. No planning too far ahead. We won't need luck, we're sharper than that and we've got each other – we got it right, David. We must never forget that."

TWENTY-NINE

David and Connie were quietly married in the Oban Registry Office the following year on the morning of 2nd May at 11 o'clock. Those present at the ceremony were Dougal Henderson, Eddie McBride, Agnes Devereux, and Connie's two children, Danny and Louisa.

It was a fitting gathering because they were the important people in their lives. It was because of them, that, in one way or another, they were together. It was a fitting date, too, because that was when the terns always began their arrival at the islet, and they, too, had played their part in Connie and David finding each other.

Eddie, David's old mentor from Trinity College, had flown over to Edinburgh from Dublin and they had arranged for a car to collect Agnes at her house and then to meet Eddie at the airport. They had then been driven, in style, to Oban, where they all met at the town house. Agnes and Eddie had hit it off instantly and had had a wonderful journey, chatting all the way and seeing absolutely nothing of the scenery. They had stopped briefly at a bar in a small village on the way to have what Eddie referred to a 'sharpener' and then again at another one twenty minutes later to have what Agnes referred to as 'another sharpener'.

By the time they arrived in Oban they were already in good form and before going to the Registry Office they convened at the town house where they preceded the ceremony in equal style by David popping a bottle of champagne. Although Connie and David had invited Agnes to Oban previously – an invitation she had eagerly accepted – it was Eddie's first time there. But here they were together and though he and Agnes were such recent acquaintances it seemed they had always known each other. Indeed, when Connie raised a glass to the gathered group with a toast 'to kindred spirits', they looked at each other in mutual appreciation. Like the champagne it went down very well. David took the opportunity to surprise everyone, by telling them that Eddie, after a little persuasion, was to be his best man.

After the ceremony, they all de-camped to the bar at the Regent Hotel where others were waiting to meet them: Duncan and Annie were there; Billy Kilpatrick; Wally and his wife Lottie; Eileen Elliot, their close neighbour, with her husband Joe and their children Ronnie and Alison. Moira was there as was Morag, along with Dougal's daughter, Catriona, who had returned to Oban to take over running the business thus enabling Dougal to get on with his fly-fishing. More champagne was opened and glasses were refilled.

Five minutes after they had arrived at the hotel a taxi drew up outside and discharged four passengers. They walked to the hotel entrance and straight into the bar. David walked over to greet them. He had never met them before but knew immediately who they were. After all, he had arranged for them to be there. To Connie's total and utter amazement, there stood Amanda and Alex Heston and their two children Tommy and Vivienne.

"I don't believe it! However did you get here? I mean…this is wonderful…Amanda, you're here, you're actually here!"

"Con, so good to be here; so happy for you! This lovely man, David, contacted us and told us everything and insisted that we be here. We're so sorry we missed the ceremony. David so wanted us to be there, but the flight was delayed. We came as quickly as we could but we're here now. Let's celebrate!" she said, as they took hold of their glasses.

Danny and Louisa got together with the other children and they ran off shouting happily.

"That's got all of them out of the way for the day!" joked Alex. "Now we can get on with the serious fun!"

The sun shone on this merry gang as they left the bar after an hour or so to be taken by a train of taxis to the ferry point to the island. Duncan had left the ferry there and when they arrived two couples were waiting to cross on it so they all got on together.

At the other side, Duncan had decked out the long trailer for his tractor with bunting and everyone climbed up a ladder leaning against the side and piled on board. He informed the four other passengers that the ferry would be going back later on but that he had absolutely no idea when and suggested that they have a good long day. The tractor set off with everyone hanging on to the sides and each other.

When they reached Annie's tearoom, the tractor pulled up.

"Fuel stop. Everyone off!" shouted Duncan and the whole lot trooped into the house where Annie had prepared a punch for them all to drink.

"Has to be finished before we leave," she informed them, as she filled up glass after glass from four large jugs.

With much difficulty and laughter, Duncan managed to get everyone back on the trailer and they set off along the road. A more unlikely group of revellers had never passed this way before.

They arrived at Ardbeg without any serious mishap and everyone got off to be greeted by all of Connie's tenants and their families. They were all standing outside the front door where a long table was covered with a white tablecloth which in turn was covered with glasses and bottles. For those who didn't know each other, hands were shaken, introductions were made and names were immediately forgotten.

It was a glorious day: a few fluffy clouds, a mild breeze and clear blue skies. Danny and Louisa knew the children who lived on the island and, and with the ones who had come to the wedding reception in Oban, they all ran about the place just being children having a marvellous time whilst their parents were busy drinking, talking and laughing. A great party was in progress.

David walked away from the group towards the beach. When he got there he looked out to the sea and islands beyond. It was such a beautiful place. He looked back at the people, some standing in groups chatting, others sitting on chairs, and the bulk clustered around the drinks table. It made such a pastoral picture and his thoughts drifted to dear Helen McKechnie. How happy she would have been to see this today: her great-niece having her wedding party at Ardbeg; all the people here and the children running about. It was so alive, alive like it had once been, all those years ago. And it pleased him to know how quietly thrilled she would have been that he was here too, that he was now the husband of this woman that she had never known, yet because of her, was now ensuring the continuity. Connie had inherited so much more than land and properties: she had inherited the future.

David saw Connie looking at him and he waved her to come over.

"What are you doing over here, alone?" she said, slipping her arm into his.

"I'm not alone, darling," he said. "How could I ever be alone when I have you and all this?"

She put her arms around him and looked up him. There was just a hint of moisture in her eyes.

"David, I've cried tears here. I've cried tears of sadness and joy. Right now I think I am about to burst into tears of happiness."

And she did, oh how she did! She sobbed on his chest and held him tight as tears poured down her cheeks onto his shirt. He held her as if he would never let her go.

And then he said something that stopped her.

"It's official now, you know?"

"Darling, I never needed a piece of paper to…"

"No," he said. "I mean we've been given official approval. Look!"

He turned her around and pointed out to the sea.

"They've come to celebrate with us, join in the party."

And there, over the little islet, were a few flashes of white and some high-pitched piping calls. It was 2nd May and the terns had started to come back.

They walked slowly back, arm in arm, to the party.

"Have a glass of this," offered Eddie, his hands extending two glasses of red wine. "You won't believe this," he said, "but there are two dozen, well, now only twenty-two, bottles of this superb Rioja. Agnes and I have moved the cases slightly out of general sight. We don't want people drinking it carelessly, do we, my dear?"

"Absolutely not, Eddie. This is a wine only to be appreciated by those who, well, appreciate it," she replied.

"That's us," he said putting his arm round her shoulder. "Come on, let's get another bottle opened and check that it's drinkable."

"They are amazing!" said Connie watching them walk off together towards the house as Dougal came out clutching an unopened bottle of Rioja.

"There you are," he called to them. "You wouldn't by any chance have seen a cork-screw, would you?" and then, conspiratorially: "Just between the three of us, there are a couple of cases of this inside the kitchen. They were slightly on view but I've hidden them under the table, we don't want *anyone* drinking them, do we now?"

The party was well under way when four strangers walked up to the gathering and picked out Duncan. They were the two couples who had come over on the ferry with them.

"Excuse us," one of the men said in a slight though distinct foreign accent, but impeccable English, "but you are the ferryman?"

Yes," said Duncan, "but don't you worry; we'll have you back on the mainland, nae problem at all."

"But when are you going?"

"Nae bloody idea; why don't you have a drink with us? When the party's over we'll give you a lift back on the trailer. Say, where are you folk from; don't quite recognise the accent?"

"Ah, we are from the Netherlands."

"Oh."

"Yes, but what is going on here, is it some kind of Scottish cultural thing?"

"Eh? Oh, yes, well, these two lovely people have just got married so we're raising a glass to them."

"Ah, yes, we do this in the Netherlands too!"

"Well then, we've got something in common with your country."

"What is that then?"

"Having a right good party!" replied Duncan. "Come on; let me get you all a drink then."

And so it was that four perfectly innocent Dutch holiday tourists got caught up in a wild celebration that didn't just end when the last bottle had been emptied. It wasn't a totally liquid occasion. Annie and the rest of the neighbours had put together a fabulous spread of food that kept everyone sustained for the duration. When the party was going strong, Dougal Henderson called for silence so that he could say a few words.

"Ladies and, if there are any present, gentlemen, could I call on your attention for a wee moment while I deliver a few spontaneous words that I prepared yesterday. Ahem," he said, steadying himself for his delivery. "On this solemn occasion…sorry! Wrong speech… On this happy occasion it gives me great pleasure to thank whoever it was for bringing those two cases of Rioja wine to the party. I don't know about anyone else but I'm sure Agnes and Eddie would like to express their appreciation too. Now, having got the serious bit of my speech over, to the real matter in hand.

"David and Connie, what can I say? Er… hang on, I've got some notes somewhere, Ah, yes! This is what I wanted to say…"

And Dougal's speech rambled hilariously on confusing not only the Dutch tourists but most of the guests as well.

"…and so before I finish I want to do something that, to me, is fundamental to this whole wonderful day happening. I want us all to raise a glass to the woman who would have so wanted to have been here today, whose sad death actually made it all happen. To you all, I give you the lovely, much missed, much lamented – Helen McKechnie."

"Helen!" echoed the gathering.

David then stood up to add his thanks to everyone for being there, for arranging so much and to reiterate Dougal's moving toast to Helen. He added that 'that was it', he was grateful to Eddie for being his best man, but would not be calling on him or anyone else to perform such a role again. He smiled at Connie as he said these words.

But these were not the last words of the party. Up stood Wally Angel and pronounced that when everyone finally managed to get back to Oban, they were all welcome to come back to his restaurant where it would his pleasure to provide a fish and chip supper to anyone who was still alive, and what's more it would be on him, the latter words ensuring the biggest cheer of the afternoon.

The party came to a halt as the last drinks were taken. Kind people helped to clear everything and put it inside the house. Washing it all up would be for another day.

There was even enough room for the four happily bewildered Dutch tourists as they were packed onto the departing trailer. Duncan stopped the trailer at Annie's where she went inside and brought out a tray with small glasses filled to the brim with whisky of an unknown pedigree.

"To give us strength for the next leg of the journey," she said as everyone drained their glasses in one.

On reaching the ferry, Duncan made a general announcement that due to a technical matter the ferry would not be leaving straight away. He excused himself and walked back up to the ferry house himself only to return a few minutes later with two plates covered with smoked salmon on brown bread and butter.

"I got this for you because I know how much Dougal likes it," he said passing the plates around.

He then went into the shed on the jetty and came out with a tray covered in empty whisky glasses and three bottles of whisky: Oban Malt, as it happened.

"I got this for you too, because I know how much Dougal likes it," he said dissolving into laughter.

It had been Annie's task to remember to call the taxis to let them know when they would all be on the other side. She played her part admirably, adding that they needed an extra taxi, preferably with a driver who understood some Dutch.

So the ferry made another inebriated journey across the sound and she was finally tied up to be left until the driver was considered capable once more. The taxis all arrived hooting their horns to show they appreciated the festive mood of their customers.

They all arrived at Wally's, including Wally. His staff, having been briefed as to what might be expected, had put reserved signs on just about all the tables. In addition, as his restaurant wasn't licensed to sell alcohol, he overcame the problem by giving it to his customers. He had made an assumption, based on the vast amount of wine and spirits that had been consumed, that they would all be thirsty for something quenching and so had stocked his soft drinks fridge with bottles of beer. It was a well-placed judgement for seldom in the course of human drinking had so many been so grateful for so much.

It had been a truly great day. David and Connie's honeymoon would wait for a little longer; they had to get over the wedding day first. The party gradually came to an end as people had to go due to exhaustion. Connie and David thanked Wally for his generosity who replied that he would expect them and the children back regularly so he could gradually make up the shortfall.

Dougal took a taxi home, poured himself a nightcap and promptly fell asleep in his armchair. He did, however, wake up two hours later, see the glass in his hand, pondered over it for moment, then knocked it back and went upstairs to bed.

Agnes and Eddie were staying at the Regent Hotel where they quietly retired to a corner of the cocktail bar to consider how best to organise each other's respective invitations to visit Dublin and Edinburgh.

Like Agnes and Eddie, they were all staying at the hotel for the night. Danny and Louisa declared that it had been the best day of their lives and that they were now going to sleep for a week.

And David and Connie? Well, Connie took David's arm and said:

"Let's go for a stroll along the seafront. The sun will be going down soon and I would love to sit on the seawall and watch the sunset with you."

He smiled at her, took her hand and guided her to the front door of the hotel. Outside it was still a lovely evening but the sun would descend behind the island soon. This was a special moment. Everyone had either gone home, gone to sleep or was occupied. Connie and David were alone.

"I know that at last we're truly heading together in the same direction," David whispered.

She stopped him, turned and looked deep into his eyes:

"Y'know," said Connie, "when we sat together that night in the hotel and had dinner and told each other all about ourselves, it was what they call a defining moment. That was the moment when we set the stage for our lives. As you said on the plane when we came back up, nothing about us has been random. It's as if we have followed the inevitability of the laws of nature and within those laws we made the chain of our own destiny, link by link."

"Yes," he agreed. "All the parts were there. We just had to allow them to come together. And we did."

"Yes."

They walked on, towards the setting sun, arms linked; kindred spirits – soulmates.

EPILOGUE

It was not long after their wedding that David received a call from the agents in Weymouth telling him that someone had put a good offer in for his house. He accepted it without hesitation and contacted Dougal's office for them to deal with it. Dougal's daughter was now a partner in the company, with Dougal effectively retired.

David had decided that he was going to invest the proceeds from the sale in restoring Banmellach and creating a laboratory so that the house could be used as a small scientific base for a business that he and Connie had been planning. By using the facilities at Banmellach and Ardbeg plus Cassiopeia, they were in the process of setting up a summer school in marine biology. The facility at Annie's bunkhouse would allow up to ten people at a time to stay on the island and already they had set up a website to promote the project.

This was the perfect solution for all of them. David remained working at what he liked most, where he wanted to be, and with the people he most wanted to be with. The opening of the Island Marine Biology Centre happened exactly a year after David and Connie had married, on 2nd May. It was also followed with the birth, later that summer, of their son whom they chose to call Hamish.

ACKNOWLEDGEMENTS

I would like to express my gratitude to the following people who have contributed, in many different ways, to the completion of this book:

Robin Burnage (whose technological skill was invaluable), Adrian Bracken, Vivienne Holliday, Billy Ward (who designed and painted the cover), Suzie Kendall, Ed Ward, Helen Norris (who copy edited the book), Michael Storey, Amanda Brear and, in particular, my wife Gwendoline, who has been my absolute critic, encouraging me when I flagged and my guiding hand when I have drifted off course.

I also want to thank my mother-in-law Lily Hartingdon, who urged me to finish the book before she died! I am happy to say I have not let her down.

Printed in Great Britain
by Amazon